THE GOODNIGHT KISS

THE UNSEELIE COURT BOOK 1

GWEN RIVERS

❀ Created with Vellum

THE GOODNIGHT KISS

An unremembered past. A deadly power. A destiny she never saw coming…

Nic Rutherford is tired of feigning a normal life. She'd rather embrace her strange ability to track local predators and kill them with a kiss. And when her best friend dies, she demands a secretive werewolf help her cross the veil to bring the dead girl back.

When her shifter partner reveals the truth behind Nic's forgotten history, she pushes further into the treacherous Fae realm. But when she trains with the Wild Hunt warriors, she may be signing a magical contract with deathly consequences…

Will Nic unlock the mystery of her former life, or will sinister forces swallow her soul forever?

The Goodnight Kiss is the first darkly violent book in the Unseelie Court urban fantasy series. If you like vigilante justice, relentless heroes, and graphic scenes, then you'll love Gwen Rivers' thrilling and explicit tale.

Buy The Goodnight Kiss and embrace the darkness today!

INTRODUCTION

"Nicneven with her nymphs, in number anew
With charms from Caitness and Chanrie of Ross
Whose cunning consists in casting a clew."
– Alexander Montgomerie in his Flyting Between Polwart
and Montgomerie, 1585

CHAPTER 1

CREATURES OF HABIT

Any hunter will tell you that understanding an animal's routines are essential to trapping it.

Hunting humans is no different.

Instincts are what most animals rely on to notify them of potential harm. Millennia of being the most dominant life force on earth have suppressed the biological early warning system in most *homo sapiens*. There's a level of arrogance that comes with being the pinnacle of the food chain. An air of *go ahead, let 'em try*. The signals are still in us though, if one knows how to interpret them.

That's how I know someone is following me.

Even before I hear the heavy footfalls, the hair rises on the back of my neck, almost as though the stranger's breaths land against the exposed skin. I stagger from the rave like a wounded antelope, through the rear door into the dark alley, leaving the thumping music and seizure-inducing lights in my wake. The trash that litters the cracked concrete beneath my boots and the scents of damp air from earlier rain mingling with decaying leaves are my only companions.

Until now.

Wind whips through my thin dress. I didn't bring a coat or purse, just what I need sewn into a pocket at the fold of my skirt. It is big enough for a tube of lip gloss, a few bills, and my cell. I consider hiding, but there isn't enough time. My pursuer is closing in and there's no real shelter to be found. I don't run—never run from a predator. Fleeing is a sign of weakness and invites chase from the wrong sort. I put one foot in front of the other and don't look back. Maybe I'll make it to the street, out into the open. Maybe he really isn't after me.

My heart races, blood pounds in my ears, every nerve ending aware of my situation. Distantly I hear the thumping club music and the sounds of tires on rain-slick pavement. And him. The footsteps quicken.

The mouth of the alley is feet away when he catches me around my waist and pushes me face-first against the cinder block wall.

"What's a hot little piece like you doing out here all alone?"

His voice is thick and accented by New Jersey. His body feels massive pressing into mine. He towers over me and is massively built with thick shoulders and arms.

"Please," I whisper. "Don't hurt me."

One hand traps both of mine behind my back as the other travels along my spine. I can't keep from shivering in revulsion at his touch.

I beg again, "Please, what do you want?"

In a sudden burst of movement, he spins me and pins both of my hands above my head in one of his. His face is cast in shadows but there's no mistaking the sinister intent gleaming in his dark eyes. "I want to fuck you," he rasps, that hand fumbling for the side zipper of my dress.

"I've never done that," I tell him honestly through my trembling lips. "I'm only sixteen. Please."

"You want it. Girls like you always want it." His gaze fastens on my mouth. My lips are slick and shiny with my recently applied gloss. I can see his intentions clear as day. He is going to force me in this filthy alley, use my body while he enjoys my screams of terror and pain.

He is a monster.

His hand snakes inside my dress, touching bare skin that crawls at the contact.

Heart racing, I look up at him and ask, "Would you at least kiss me first?"

I can tell my request throws him. He studies me for a minute as though wondering what game I'm playing.

"So, I can at least pretend," my voice trembles.

He appears to come to a decision. The free hand fists in my hair. He yanks hard. Even in this, he wants me to feel pain. My lips part and then his mouth is on mine, brutal, punishing, an invasion.

Monster, meet your match.

He attacks me on several fronts, pressing his body into mine as though promising the punishment to come while meting out the full-scale assault on my mouth.

I don't struggle or try to fight him off in any way, my heart thunders—with anticipation. Any second now.

He breaks away suddenly and shakes his head as though dizzy. I straighten my disheveled dress and watch dispassionately as he staggers back and then slumps down to the ground.

"What did you do?" His eyes grow wild even as his gaze glazes over. And then it happens, the moment I crave. The light of true understanding dawns an instant before it flicks out forever.

Our roles have been reversed. Now he's the hunted. The victim.

My victim.

"You have been found guilty." A small smile curves my bruised lips as I watch him die.

He twitches once, a final spasm as his central nervous system shuts down for good. The last of the spark leaves his eyes and then I am alone once more in the alley with only a corpse at my feet.

Stooping down, I check his pockets, removing his wallet from inside his jacket. It's a battered old thing, nylon with a cracked plastic sleeve holding a few credit cards as well as a driver's license. My victim's name is Paul Anderson. I study the photo and compare it to the dead man at my feet. He's porked up since the image was captured, extra adipose tissue gathering at his midsection. Probably an athlete gone soft. It's too dark in the alley to make out his eye or hair color but the license lists him as blond-haired and blue-eyed. Possibly of Norwegian descent. I'd been right about the accent. His address tells me his permanent residence was in Hackettstown, New Jersey. No explanation to why this middle-aged man had been at a rave in the Blue Ridge Mountains. Not that I need one.

Like me, he'd been out hunting.

I pocket the license and keep digging. Credit cards are too easy to trace. I keep the cash though. Waste not, want not as my Aunt Addy always says. A photo of a plain woman with a pretty smile and a blonde toddler is stuck behind a Starbucks card. Distantly I wonder if I've done her a favor or ruined her life. Personally, I wouldn't want to be tethered to cheating, raping scum, but I'm zany like that. Not that it matters. Paul's fate was sealed the second he tracked me into the alley.

"Speaking of Fate," I grumble as my phone lets out the obnoxious hamster dance ringtone. Aunt Chloe's idea of a joke. "What?"

"Status?" Addy asks in a tight tone.

The echo on the line tells me she's put the call on speaker, so I talk directly to Chloe. "One of these days that ringtone is going to scare one of them off."

"Don't be such a worrywart," Chloe calls from the background. "You sound just like Addy."

I toe my victim's bulky arm. "It's done. The package is big though. I'm debating leaving it here."

"No." Like everything else about her, Addy's tone brooks no nonsense. "Not in our own backyard. The three of us will manage."

"Something to look forward to," Chloe hollers. "Been too long since I got a hold of a big package."

"We'll be there in thirty," Addy informs me tersely.

And they would have the wood chipper ready to rock.

IF YOU'RE WONDERING why my kiss can fell a full-grown man like a rotting tree, well, join the club. It's been that way as long as I can remember, all the way back to before Addy and Chloe adopted me.

Giving a man the Goodnight Kiss is one of my earliest memories. I'd been six at the time and he too had been of the Uncle Bad-touch persuasion. I attract that type like flies to roadkill. Ten years of practice has taught me how to handle them.

I shut Paul's eyes and prop him up against the wall, knowing it'll be better to have him seated before full rigor mortis kicks in. Also, it's easier to pass my cover story with him slumped over rather than lying flat on his back.

"Come on, Dad." I speak loudly, putting on a show for the three millennials who exit the alley the same way we'd come. Out of the corner of my eye, I size them up and dismiss them as a minimal threat. Probably looking for a nice quiet spot to get lit. "Mom and Aunt Franny are on their way. If they see you like this again, there'll be hell to pay."

My theater is a little *Weekend at Bernie's*, but it works. The college students scurry on their way, not wanting to get caught up in our family drama. If they'd bothered to take a closer look, they would note that good ol' Paul and I look nothing alike. My hair is also blonde, but a much paler shade, almost white. I'm short, barely five feet four with pale blue eyes. Icy eyes, my best friend Sarah called them once. He wears ratty stained jeans and a flannel shirt and a grubby parka where I'm dolled up in what Chloe refers to as my best "bait" outfit. A stretchy purple dress and black over the knee stiletto boots.

Lucky for me, most people are more concerned with their own ends and tend to see what they want. If I talk to the dead man like he is my drunken lout of a father, then they have no reason to think otherwise. With any luck, they'll smoke away the memory of us in this alley long before the police start asking questions.

The forest green Subaru Outback parks at the mouth of the alley exactly twenty-nine minutes and fifty-nine seconds after I'd hung up the phone. The brake lights illuminate the corner of the cinder block building and I hear the engine idling. Addy's as punctual as a drill sergeant so I know she's behind the wheel.

"Oh, you weren't kidding," Chloe says as she joins me in the alley. Her red-gold hair is piled on top of her head a big twist of beautiful curly cues that frames her perfect features. So close I smell her strawberry aroma. Chloe always smells like food for some reason and her scent changes with her mood. "He's a bigg'un. Good catch, Nic."

Addy only shifts her waist-length brown braid over her shoulder and mutters, "Each of you, get a leg. I'll get him under the arms."

"This ain't our first rodeo," Chole grunts as she hefts a limb.

I also do as she instructs. Paul is, as advertised, deadweight but as Chloe pointed out, we've done this before.

"You coming with us, doll?" Chloe asks once Paul is secure in the backseat, hidden beneath the heavy blankets Addy keeps there.

I shake my head and toss the wallet in on top as another item for disposal. "Need to be seen inside. I'll be back later."

"Have fun!" Chloe waves cheerily and Addy gives me a reassuring nod before driving off.

Most people think Addy and Chloe are lovers. I can understand why. They bicker like an old married couple. They share a house as well as an adopted child. It's rare to catch sight of one without the other. They even run the veterinary clinic together. Addy's the straight-laced vet and Chloe's the bubbly receptionist. The odd couple vibe suits them perfectly. Neither is married or, to my knowledge, has ever been involved with anyone else. To the untrained eye, the underlying tension between them might be attributed to a sexual relationship. My aunts are completely content to let normals think whatever they please as long as the truth stays hidden.

Their truth, as well as mine.

After one final scan of the alley, I circle back around to the front of the building and let myself in through the unlocked glass doors.

The music assaults me first. Raves are not my usual scene. Too much chaos and light for me to relax. Too many people on different drugs letting go of their inhibitions. Bodies press too tightly together. Anyone can sneak up on you. Now that Paul is taken care of, I half hope the sheriff will come shut it down, so I can go home early.

"Nic!" My best friend, Sarah Larkin gyrates between two

mouth-breathers who occasionally double as football play-ers. She's tall and graceful. Her hair is dyed black as ink and streaked with crimson strands. Her pupils are so dilated her eyes look black instead of brown. "I've been looking for you for ages!"

"I was in line for the bathroom." A plausible lie. The building had originally been some sort of furniture ware-house, back when America still made furniture. Abandoned for at least a decade, it isn't exactly well facilitated and never meant to hold a few hundred drunken normals who need to pee.

Sarah isn't the brightest bulb in the strand and a steady diet of ecstasy chased with vodka doesn't help. It never occurs to her that any time we party together I spend an inordinate amount of time in the bathroom. Or maybe it does, and she just chalks it up to a nervous bladder. In fact, I'm pretty sure she's just glad she doesn't have to compete with me for male attention. I'm her perfect wingman—always sober, always willing to go out.

Now that I've been identified, I make my way to the corner where the bottles of water and cans of beer are stashed in a giant ice vat. I grab an Aquafina, check to make sure the cap is still sealed and then put my back to the wall, propping one stiletto boot against the painted cinder blocks for balance. From my position, I see Sarah swaying like a willow between two giant hardwoods. The comparison makes me snort.

Because of the whole deadly lip lock shtick, I've never had a boyfriend. It's too bad. Like having a BFF, a boyfriend would help sell my cover. Nic Rutherford, normal teenage girl. Sarah, who changes guys as often as she changes under-wear, once asked me point blank if I was gay. The question startled me, not because I was offended but more so because it had never really dawned on me that normals would view me as a sexual being. Predators, yes, but they seek power, not intimacy.

"If you munch rug, that's cool. Like your "Aunts"." Sarah had been stuffing tissues into her bra at the time but paused to do the air quote thing.

I don't think I'm gay. Or straight for that matter. I'm asexual. No relationship could possibly give me the satisfaction I derive from taking down the biggest game going. Of course, explaining that to a hormone-crazed teenage girl is like trying to get a cow to walk on its hind legs.

Oblivious to my struggle, Sarah did what she does best—fill the silence with her prattle. After giving me a slow up and down, she turned back to the mirror. "I'm only asking because if I ever like, want to experiment, I'd totally do it with you."

I offered a tight-lipped smile and no comment. Mercifully, she'd dropped the subject. How like Sarah to believe that every being who encountered her would want her. Sometimes late at night I wonder if I'm so arrogant. After all, I always assume any game I sight will pursue me. And so far, they always have. I have a perfect record when it comes to perverts. Batting 1000 for a decade and counting.

"You want to dance?" A tall, lanky guy wearing a host of glow in the dark bracelets swings his hips in what normals might consider an alluring rhythm.

I study him for a moment. Eager yes, but not one of mine. Even if he had been I won't hunt in the same spot twice. I move about to lessen the risk of exposure. With what passes for a regretful smile, I decline his offer. He shrugs as though I'm the one missing out and then wanders off in search of greener pastures.

The strobe light flickers annoyingly. I shut my eyes, tired of the whole scene. Partying bores me and I'm always fatigued after a takedown. Addy explained why to me once.

The chemical process that goes along with the hunt. Antici-pation combines with a spike of adrenaline to see me through the danger. When it's over, the spike crashes and depletes my reserves. I want to get in Sarah's rattletrap Camry and head back up to the farm, see how Chloe and Addy are getting on with Paul's remains and then stumble to my room and pass out cold.

But judging from her bump and grind, Sarah doesn't look at all ready to leave. One of the meatheads has left, but the other seems determined. I could hound her, feign sick, perhaps. I know she'll take me home if I ask. For all her many faults she is a decent friend. My only friend. I like it better that way.

I decide to give her a few more minutes to enjoy herself though. Sarah's home life is rough, and she lives for the nights when we escape. Though I desperately want to take her drunken lout of a stepfather out of the picture, Addy has forbidden it.

She'd been wearing her bifocals, studying one of her medical texts when I'd brought the subject up. She'd peered over the top of them at me all school-marmy and stern. "It's too close to home, Nic. Don't shit where you live."

"He's one of mine," I'd whined like a child denied a treat. The aunts had never said no to me before. "I'll take extra precautions. Lure him to a city."

It was Chloe, fun-loving, live-in-the-moment Chloe, who'd tipped the balance against me. "There are too many angles, sweets. If you give him the Goodnight Kiss too far from where we can properly dispose of him, he'll be on record. You know the FBI has a task force looking at your victims already."

It was true, though they had nothing concrete other than a stream of missing persons and unexplained deaths. On the rare occasions the aunts and I leave the body behind, the toxin in my kiss doesn't appear on an autopsy. Still, you can only gank so many convicted sex offenders before the red flags go up.

Sarah endures as best she can while I continue to seethe in impotence. With any luck, her stepfather's liver will implode before the thin thread of my patience snaps.

Self-denial isn't my designer handbag of choice.

The noise and the crush of bodies are getting to me. Decided, I wind through the writhing bodies until I can lay hands on Sarah's bare shoulder and shout into her ear. "Going to wait in the car."

She rolls her eyes but forks over the keys. "Take it. Cliff's giving me a ride."

Cliff, who I assume is the knuckle-dragger groping her ass, smirks at me. "There's always room for one more."

I taste bile even as I force my lips to tilt upwards. "I don't share." Except with Death herself.

The night air caresses my skin like a lover, lifting my hair off the base of my neck in a playful tease. I drink in the breeze and it restores me, as fresh air always seems to do. I could never exist in a city, where the wind is blocked by tall buildings and thick with the scent of humanity. Car keys in hand, I stride briskly toward Sarah's POS. It's a standard, but I've driven it before. Our farm is only twenty miles from the factory but still a world apart.

The engine catches and I roll down the driver's side window, glad for the breath of fresh mountain air that joins me for the ride. The dashboard clock reads 12:01. The spring equinox. No wonder I'm tired. Since I'm a nocturnal predator, longer nights mean more time to hunt. At least I live in North Carolina, not Norway or somewhere where the summer nights are practically nonexistent. If I ever visit the land of the midnight sun, I'll be sure to do so in winter. The cold doesn't bother me the way daylight does.

I turn off the factory road and onto the main highway that's more a series of switchbacks giving way to the higher elevation of the Blue Ridge Parkway. The high country is quiet this time of year. Too late for skiers, too early for hikers and after full dark, I have the road to myself.

I've just turned off onto the gravel drive that leads to our farm when the small hairs lift on my arms. The reaction has nothing to do with the plummeting temperature. Someone is watching me.

Not following. I don't have that same urge to escape as I had earlier with Paul. No headlights in the rearview either, not since I turned toward our land. My instincts, carefully honed over the years, give me no clue where to look for the source of my discomfort. It's a physiological response. A tightness in my stomach, an increase in heart rate. There *is* a predator out there. One who has me in its sights.

My foot taps the brakes lightly, halting all vehicular forward motion. The Camry's headlights form two clear trails through the darkness. I scan the shadowy shapes of the evergreens on either side of the road, trying to pick out whatever it is that doesn't belong. Naked branches stir in the wind and some of the heavier boughs creak with age, but otherwise nothing.

I sit longer than any normal would sit. My instincts have never steered me wrong when it comes to prey or predators. Of course, I'm tired. It's the first day of spring. And I did just hunt. Even a well-disciplined mind can play tricks if the reserves are too low.

I prepare to lift my foot and creep ahead when he appears in my headlights. A massive black shape on all fours. I suck in a breath, stunned by the sheer size of the wolf. We have bears and mountain lions in this area, but wolves are rare and never so large.

He turns and looks right at me. Something electric shoots

down my spine. His eyes are the color of new spring leaves and he stares, not half as nonplussed at spying me as I am at seeing him.

My heart stops as our gazes lock. He seems to take me in and not just my appearance. Me, he sees me, Nic. All my misdeeds, every secret I keep as though I've been laid out for him like a sumptuous feast.

Not a wolf! My instincts scream.

But before I can question them, he turns and vanishes into the trees.

CHAPTER 2

SERIAL VEGETARIAN

Mornings come early on a farm. Even earlier when a pissed off Fate slams your door open sans knock.

"Where is it?" Addy storms into my room, gold eyes ablaze.

I sit up and the blankets fall past my waist. "What?"

"Don't play games with me, Nic." Her braid lashes around like a whip as her head snaps from side to side. She heads to my dresser and starts opening drawers, rifling through socks and underwear, yoga pants and tanks. "It won't end well."

"I'm not playing games. I need to know what you're looking for." It's a lie, one of my habits coming back to bite me. I know *exactly* what she's so determined to find.

"The license," Addy snarls. "Did you think I wouldn't check the wallet?"

"Calm down, sis." Chloe drifts in and perches on the foot of my bed. Her scent de jour is vanilla. "It's not that big a deal."

It's the wrong thing to say. Addy rounds on Chloe, hands on hips, eyes ablaze. "Don't even start. She can't keep trophies. You know that. I know that. She knows it. Trophies means she's a serial killer."

Chloe winces and raises her hand in mock abashment. "Hate to point out the obvious, but she kind of already *is* a serial killer, trophies or no. I have the crud under my nails to prove it."

"It's a mindset." Addy retorts as if she hasn't been stating the same thing every single day since they brought me home. Sure enough, her work-roughened hand starts ticking off all the reasons she doesn't consider me a serial killer. "She's not a Caucasian male. She's not in her prime. She isn't compelled to kill. And she doesn't keep trophies as evidence for the fucking FBI to use against her!"

Chloe opens her mouth, some pithy retort at the ready, but closes it again at the sound of a heavy vehicle on the gravel drive.

"Are we expecting someone?" Chloe rises and moves to the window, pulling back the curtain to peer out.

I get out of bed and stand on my toes, so I can see, too. A big black truck skids to a stop in front of the farmhouse. "It's Sarah. I took her car last night. That's probably her date dropping her off."

Addy's nostrils flare but all she says is, "Get rid of it," before storming out of the room.

"What crawled up her ass and died?" Chloe rolls her eyes.

Her nonchalance doesn't fool me. My aunts have adapted a good cop, bad cop stance. Addy is the heavy hitter, the one who keeps her temper on a short leash, while Chloe is the gal pal, the confidant. The closer.

"She's wrong," I watch Sarah do the walk of shame from the truck to our front porch. Her hair is a wreck, her sparkly top is inside out beneath her ragged denim jacket and even though there's frost on the ground, her strappy heeled shoes are in her hand. She waves jauntily at the driver and then sashays out of view.

I let the curtain drop. "I don't know why she's in denial. I am a serial killer. I kill people I don't even know. What else could I be?" There is no self-pity or remorse in my words. I don't feel either, only frustration. I was born to kill, and I don't understand why.

Chloe puts her hand on my arm. "You have a purpose. Not knowing isn't the same as not possessing."

Of all the infuriating things she'd ever said to me, this might be the worst. "Do you know?"

She stills. "Don't, Nic. You know I can't say."

She's right, it isn't an appropriate time to press for answers. Not with Sarah in the house and Addy on the warpath. But what's the point of being adopted by the Fates if they can't at least drop a hint about my destiny? "I'm some sort of weapon, aren't I? A mystical assassin?"

Chloe's eyes land on my overflowing bookshelf. I am an avid reader, devouring history, mythology, religion, and fairytales by the gross. The stories come from somewhere and I've gleaned bits of truths in each one, reflections of the real world buried in someone's make-believe.

The aunts know about my research, but they're deliberately obscure when I question them. Some things are obvious, like that they don't age. Not a wrinkle or a gray hair has appeared in the decade I've been with them. Other times I've eavesdropped, hoping to hear something they'll never discuss openly with me. At one point, before they took me on, there was a third sister. Her name hasn't come up and there's no indication if she died or just moved on. The holes in my information gnaw at me.

I probably shouldn't complain. How many parents would literally hide bodies for their children?

Chloe won't—or can't—give me a direct answer. Instead,

she brushes some of my hair back over one shoulder. "Right now, the only thing you need to be is a teenage girl. One who'll be late for school if she doesn't get moving. Come on, breakfast is hitting the table in five."

Chloe shuts the door behind her. I listen as her footsteps fade down the hall, the murmur of voices, the sound of laughter. My aunts go out of their way to make Sarah feel at home. They aren't exactly social butterflies. Neither am I. It's hard to be the life of the party when you have the potential to kill someone by accident.

The Goodnight Kiss doesn't require lips on lips. That is, it doesn't have to be a conventionally accepted sort of kiss to do the deed. Through trial and error—some of it dicey—I've discovered that any contact my mouth has with a normal's bare skin will do the trick. The rest of my parts aren't toxic. I haven't killed anyone with a handshake or a sneeze to date. Sarah has even given me hugs with no ill effects. The first time she embraced me I knew the true meaning of terror. Not only did I worry that I'd "Nic her" by accident, but that I'd do so in front of half the school. There would be no coming back from that sort of scene. In the era when social media reigns supreme and everyone has a camera phone, denial isn't an option.

Dread coils in my gut at the thought of exposure. No wind lifting my hair, or fresh scents to mark the changing seasons. Locked away in a cage. Or worse, studied, vivisected so some mad scientist could figure out where my ability originates. The fear isn't enough to make me stop, though. The world is better off without the likes of Paul Anderson.

I dress in jeans and a flannel shirt over a tank top and hiking boots, standard high country all-season gear. In the winter add a parka and gloves. In the summer swap the jeans for cut-offs and the flannel goes around my waist instead of over my shoulders. But otherwise, my clothes are simple, comfortable and nondescript because I don't care how I look. Apart from the bait clothes but those aren't for school. I sported a capsule wardrobe long before anybody on Pinterest.

Once my hair is brushed and my boots are laced I pause and crack open the door. Chloe and Sarah are chatting away in the kitchen. Sarah at the table, her back to me, the wild red and black streaks illuminated by the sun streaming through the skylights. I don't hear Addy but she's most likely with them. She doesn't trust Chloe not to slip and say something she shouldn't in front of normals.

I shut the door again and stride over to my bookshelf and separate *Modern Paganism* from *The Iliad*. The book between the two tomes is a chintzy pink fluffy nightmare thing with a heart-shaped lock and a key the size of my pinky nail. A gift from Chloe the year I turned twelve, to write down *all my tender wittle feels*. I'd shaken my head, sure I'd never use it.

I'd been wrong. The diary is my most prized possession. I leave it hidden in plain sight, always in the same exact spot so the aunts won't know. Even in their wildest imaginings, they wouldn't guess that the cheesy faux fur covered diary has been repurposed.

Unable to resist, I flip to the latest entry, the one with Paul Anderson's driver's license taped to the page, and smile.

"And then he asked me to forgive his sorry lying ass," Sarah says. "Can you believe that shit?"

"Forgiveness is for quitters," I say the words at the same time as Chloe. She turns from the stove, a grin in place and casts me a wink.

"Morning, sunshine." Sarah sets down her glass of fresh-squeezed orange juice and smacks the table dramatically. "Gimme my keys afore I cut a bitch."

I roll my eyes at her. "You've been streaming too much *Orange is the New Black*."

She forks pancakes onto her plate. "Ain't shit else to do on the weekends. Besides, it's a good show. You should watch."

"Our internet speed isn't fast enough for streaming here." Chloe sets down a plate of bacon on the table. Bacon only Sarah will touch. The rest of us are vegetarians, something Sarah doesn't know. Another part of our look as normal as possible cover. In some areas of the country, eating vegetarian wouldn't be out of the norm, but on a Western North Carolina farm, it would raise a few eyebrows.

Ignoring the pancakes, I help myself to a bowl of steel-cut oats and chia pudding.

Sarah makes a face at my breakfast. "How can you eat that? It looks like fish eyeballs."

I shrug. It's the fuel my body performs best with, like a tank full of high test. But I murmur one word that's like a free pass. "Diet." It is the easiest explanation, one any teenage girl would swallow.

"You don't need to diet. Half the rave was eye humping your bod last night."

"Half the rave was drugged out of their minds."

"Do tell." Chloe sits down, hands wrapped around a mug of coffee. "Nic never mentions the eye humping."

"She's the Ice Bitch." Sarah chomps on a piece of bacon and I curl my lip at the nickname. "Plays it all cool. It drives the guys fuckin' crazy, pardon my French."

Addy nods, as though this is what she wants to hear, then rises from the table. "If you'll excuse me I have an early surgery."

"We need to get going, too." Sarah rolls up the remaining

bacon in a pancake and then slings her shoulder bag over her arm.

I raise a brow at her *been there done that* ensemble. "Um, do you want to borrow something to wear?"

She rolls her eyes. "Like I'd fit in any of your munchkin outfits. Nah, I have a change of clothes in the car. Let's motor already."

I slurp down what remains of my breakfast, say goodbye to Chloe and Addy and follow Sarah out to her car. She unlocks it, then, stuffing the makeshift sandwich into her gaping mouth, leans over to unlock my door.

"Why did you bother locking it?" she grumps. "It's not like there's anyone wandering around on the zillion acres you guys own."

I climb inside, tossing my backpack on the backseat. "It's only 140 acres. And Addy's practice is down at the other entrance. She leaves it open in case of an emergency." That isn't why I locked the door though. For some reason, I don't want to tell her about my eerie encounter with the wolf.

"' Scuse the shit outta me." Sarah backs up to the hundred-year-old oak that shades the farmhouse, then, just when I'm sure she is going to hit the tree, cuts the wheel hard to point the car back down the drive.

"So, tell me about that guy who was all over you." I really don't care. One big dumb goon is the same as the next. Asking people questions is another one of my pretending to be normal tricks with the added bene it keeps their focus on themselves instead of on me.

"Eh, he was okay. Oh, and just FYI, we spent the night here, working on our French paper. In case my mom asks. Which she won't, but you know."

"Sure." I'm only half-listening to her, my gaze roving over the landscape, looking for anything out of place. Did I imagine the wolf with the piercing green eyes?

"Nic?"

"French, got it."

Sarah rambles on. I have no idea how she can put so much garbage into her system—including whatever bodily fluids she exchanged with the bruiser of yore—and then bound through the day like everything's fine and dandy. I tried to tell her once that all the drinking and drugging would catch up with her eventually, but she'd laughed like I made the funniest joke she'd ever heard.

We are early to school, no other cars in the lot and I hit the sidewalk while Sarah changes in the car. To pass the time, I pull up my latest kindle purchase on my cell and read a few pages. Staring at a phone screen is a completely acceptable teenager pastime and I like apps because no one can tell what I am doing.

The tome is not especially interesting and my mind drifts back to the wolf. The way he'd looked at me...it felt familiar. My instincts had shouted that the wolf wasn't really a wolf. How could that be?

"Hey." A familiar voice startles me from my contemplation.

I glance up and paste on a smile for Sarah's devoted fanboy. "Hey, Glen."

Glen is what books often refer to as a "late bloomer." His body is pudgy from hours spent sitting in front of his computer, playing online games and scarfing Doritos and Mountain Dew. His pallor is milky and spotted with acne and his dark hair is always a mess. He has a decadent crop of freckles and an obvious overbite. He's Sarah's neighbor and is hopelessly in lust with her. She, in return, occasionally chooses to acknowledge his existence.

Glen shifts from foot to foot. "Were you guys, uh, out again last night?"

It's too soon for reports to come in about Paul Anderson's

disappearance and Glen isn't exactly looped in to the police bandwidth. Most likely he's on a fishing expedition about Sarah's love life. She'd indicated the lie about the French paper was meant for her mother, but I doubt she'd appreciate Glen knowing her business either. "Yeah, big project in French. We pulled an all-nighter." The wood chipper had, anyway.

"Okay, well. Good. I guess that's good. Better that she wasn't at home." Glen readjusts the backpack on his shoulder as though it's giving him discomfort.

"Joe crawl back into the bottle?" It's not a guess but a certainty. The piece of human trash is even worse when he's under the influence.

He nods. "And I think they got into a fight or something. The police were there." His puppy dog brown eyes go wide as Sarah emerges from her Japanese chrysalis looking daisy fresh and dressed to kill.

So to speak.

"The police were where?" she asks, tugging her mini skirt down over her ass by a whole three inches. The dress code brigade will probably send her home early for that look.

"Um," Glen glances over his shoulder, unwilling to make eye contact with his goddess.

"Spit it out, Penguin Man." Sarah's brow furrows as she scowls at him.

I have no idea the source of this nickname. He looks nothing like a penguin to me. Must be an inside joke, one on Glen instead of with him because he never appears pleased when she rolls it out. Maybe I should ask about its origins, but I don't particularly care.

Glen makes a whimpering sound but doesn't answer.

"Your house," I supply. Glen shoots me a grateful look. I'm somebody's savior, go figure.

Sarah digests the news then apparently shrugs it off. "Come on, Nic. I need to hit the can before first."

Our school, like many of the teachers within, is old, gray and haggard. It sits on a hilltop overlooking a lush country-side, an ugly blemish on the face of otherwise pristine land-scape. The main building is one sprawling story surrounded by a few scraggly trailers to hold the overflow classes that aren't considered important enough to warrant a room inside the original structure. Once upon a time, it was just meant to be a high school but then the housing market burst, people moved out of the area and the middle school ended up being split, with sixth grade conjoined with the elemen-tary level and seventh and eighth graders stuffed into our building as part of the junior/senior high school.

The seventh graders are puny compared to the seniors and have developed the survival habit of flattening them-selves against lockers or the walls so they aren't trampled. They all have the look of frightened deer and the upper-classmen smirk at them like cats toying with the mice they plan to eat.

Sarah's feigned nonchalance disappears when we reach the lavatory. A seventh-grade girl is washing her hands at the sink. She jumps when the door crashes open.

"Get. Out." Sarah's eyes narrow.

The girl obeys, leaving with the faucet still running.

"You okay?" It's the correct thing to ask even if it's obvious she isn't.

"Peachy." Sarah stalks into a stall. "God, Nic. Can we just leave this freaking place already?"

I have no intention of leaving and I'm certain Sarah doesn't want to go anywhere either. It's more of a game we play. "Where should we go?"

She's silent a minute, except for the typical bathroom

23

sounds. The toilet flushes and then she slides out of the stall, one hand on the door as if it's holding her up. "California."

I lean back between the hand dryers, crossing my arms over my chest. "And what will we do when we get there?"

"Find a bar. On the beach. Hook up with a couple of surfers."

I raise a brow. "Just you or am I included in this?"

"Bitch," she says playfully.

"Takes one to know one."

The bell rings, the warning one.

"Fuck," Sarah runs her fingers through her hair. "I gotta go. If I'm late again, Mrs. Gordon will kill me."

"I doubt that," I say and head off to my own homeroom.

My first class is Microsoft Word and Excel, a mixed class for sophomores, juniors, and seniors. I can't bother to give a shit about computers, but it was one of the few electives open to me. I'm not an artist nor do I much care about music. Computer work is drudgery, but it's better than pretending my soul has something to express.

That's for my free time.

There's someone sitting in my usual spot, facing the desktop, a senior by the size of him. His back is to me, but his shoulders are massive, his back broad.

We don't have assigned seats, so I shrug and look around for an open terminal. There's one directly behind his screen facing him and one at the other end of the room next to Glen. He waves to me, indicating the open spot.

I quickly circle the row and sit opposite the seat thief. I made the mistake of sitting beside Glen once and all he did was pepper me with questions about Sarah and tell me drawn-out stories about how they would play naked together in a plastic pool when they were toddlers. Back before her mother hooked up with her abusive husband. While he talked, I fantasized about luring Glen out behind the equipment shed, giving him a quick peck then stuffing his lifeless carcass in between the soccer cones and the lacrosse sticks. Temptation is best kept at a distance.

"Did I take your seat?" A deep masculine bass rumbles the question.

All the hairs stand on my arms at the sound of that voice. I don't realize he's talking to me until there is a tap against my foot. I tilt my head around the monitor so I can see him and freeze.

Bright green eyes, the color of new spring leaves stare back.

The wolf. Only he isn't a wolf any longer.

CHAPTER 3

A WOLF IN MAN'S CLOTHING

I t takes me a moment to realize he's waiting for an answer. By the time I recall the question—had he taken my seat—the final bell is ringing.

He flashes me a smile, even white teeth bared for just an instant, then he disappears behind his terminal. The announcements begin over the PA, but I tune them out.

How did he know that is where I typically sit? Why would he care?

The announcements end. Our teacher, Mr. Alcott, is a small man with a bald pate, horned rimmed glasses, and a push broom mustache. His clothes are always wrinkled, his manner perpetually exhausted. He rises and begins with attendance.

A foot taps against mine once. I look down and see the large boot belonging to the seat stealing wolf-man encroaching on my space. His legs are long. I have yet to see him standing, but I judge that he's over six feet tall, at least as a man. His footwear is not sensible hiking boots or even caterpillars. No, his boots are scuffed and black, like military combat boots. The tops disappear beneath well-worn and perfectly faded jeans. He doesn't move his foot. I can't tell if the action is deliberate or accidental.

"Nic Rutherford?" Mr. Alcott says my name in such a way that I know I missed the first call.

"Here," I mumble, sliding my foot away from the boot a bit.

The foot moves, slowly, creeping closer to my side as if in search of contact. Definitely deliberate. I shift away again.

The teacher proceeds on down the list and then switches to instruction mode like some sort of badly dressed robot.

"Today," Mr. Alcott drones in his perennially bland voice, forcing me to focus on the screen in front of me instead of the guy whose boot is once again touching mine. "I want you to start exercise three in creating spreadsheets."

I think about kicking the seat thief, then decide to just ignore the contact. It's not like he's touching me directly, just the material of his foot covering pressing against the material of mine. Even still, it feels…intimate. Much too familiar for a stranger.

Who is the wolf man? If we had a new student, Mr. Alcott would have introduced him. His face isn't one I've seen before. Not that I pay any particular attention to faces, unless they belong to one of my victims, but it's a small school. Everyone knows everyone else.

After creating my spreadsheet, I glance around the room to see if anyone is looking at the new kid, whispering about him. Nothing. Glen is picking his nose, his finger vanishing up the appendage to the second knuckle. The small girl beside him is studiously working on her spreadsheet. The two girls to my immediate right are texting, probably to each other. The boy on the end appears to be asleep. It's as if the wolf boy has always been here, a part of this class.

"Is there a problem, Ms. Rutherford?" Mr. Alcott has chosen today of all days to pretend to give a shit if we do the lesson. The textettes swiftly stash their bedazzled phones so they don't get confiscated.

"No." I don't feel embarrassed. If forced to name the emotion coursing through my body, it would be frustration. Why does no one else acknowledge the green-eyed newcomer?

Maybe only I can see him. It's an unsettling thought. Oracles, visionaries, any individuals who see differently from the population at large don't lead contented lives. Historically speaking, they were typically stoned to death, burned at the stake or locked away in some sort of asylum.

I have enough secrets already.

"Then let's get to work." With his mantle of feigned authority swathed about him once more, Mr. Alcott wanders back to his desk.

Throughout the rest of the period, I focus on the spreadsheet. Mental discipline is a skill I've worked hard to attain. The green-eyed boy taps his foot against mine a few more times until I tuck them beneath my chair.

The bell rings. All around me chairs scrape against the floor and out in the hall feet thunder to lockers or restrooms, the sounds of laughter mingles with a few shouts. Mr. Alcott, an unapologetic caffeine addict, beelines for the teacher's lounge for a hit before the next class. I dither with saving my work, hoping to catch the newcomer alone.

By the time I rise, the seat across from me is empty.

I stride over to the teacher's desk, and thumb through the attendance roll, searching shamelessly for a name I don't recognize.

It's there right on the first page, with a neat checkmark next to it to show he was present. *Aiden Jager.*

It must be him. I know all the other names listed, have known them for years. If he's on the list, other people can see him, too. So how come there's no gossip, no chatter about a new student?

It's almost as if he's been here all along.

"What the hell are you doing?" Sarah leans in the doorway to shout. "I'm pretty sure Alcott keeps all his meth in his trailer."

"Do you know Aiden Jager?" I ask as I join her in the hall.

She looks at me as though I'm an idiot. "Um, yeah. Don't you?"

I shake my head. "He just showed up in my Microsoft class."

"So? He probably transferred in." Sarah shrugs it off.

"This late in the semester?" I scan the halls to see if I can spot him. He's down to the left, right outside my civics classroom, talking to Jim Harris. Jim's a senior and captain of the football team, tall and muscled. This is the first opportunity I've had to see Aiden standing and my breathing patterns shift, coming in short, jerky inhales. He's roughly the same size and weight as Jim, but every part of him is…flawless. Though Jim is more classically handsome, blond hair, blue eyes, all aw-shucks Ma'am, he's obviously a normal. His nose is too long, and he has a few zits and his posture is horrendous.

Not Aiden though. There is not one imperfect thing about him. They are laughing and slapping hands in a way that indicates they've known each other for a long time.

"How long have you known him? Where does he live?"

Sarah gives me an odd look. "What's with the interrogation?" Then her face cracks. "No, wait. Don't tell me. You've finally spotted someone you wanna bone!"

"It's not like that." The words sound hollow, even to me. "There's something strange about him."

Sarah turns to face me, putting one hand on each of my

shoulders. "My wittle Nic is growing up. Is it time for the whole birds and bees chat? I'll put it on my calendar."

Sometimes Sarah pushes her luck.

I have to brush past Aiden to enter the classroom. He doesn't move at all when I pass. As though he wants the contact, minimal though it may be. I mutter an insincere, "'Scuse me," and take my usual seat beside Gretchen Hamill.

Gretchen has the unfortunate distinction of being the largest student in our high school. And one of the worst dressed. Her clothes always seem at least a size too small for her, as though whoever is buying them is trying to shame her into losing weight. She always looks uncomfortable. It must be tough, being obese as a teenager, especially at mealtimes. Insecure losers always hawk what's on her tray during lunch, as though it somehow affects them. If it's pizza and cookies, they roll their eyes in an *it figures* kind of way. If it's an apple and carrots, they snicker about her waiting too long to start the diet.

There's really no way to win with shits. Except for my way. And even I haven't kissed anyone just for being a garden variety asshole.

"Hey," I plop down next to Gretchen as the bell rings. "Do you know Aiden Jager?"

She nods, her baby-fine hair slipping from her ponytail holder. "Yeah, sure. Why?"

"How do you know him?" I press. When she frowns at me in confusion I clarify, "Where have you seen him before, specifically?"

She shrugs. "Just around school. Maybe in town a few times."

"Where in town? Can you recall a specific event?"

Gretchen squirms and I'm not sure if it's because of her skinny jeans that fit like sausage casings or my third degree. "I don't know. Around. What's it matter?"

Aiden, who's taken a seat diagonally in front of me, turns around and tosses me a wink.

"Never mind," I mutter and open my notebook.

He shows up in every one of my classes for the rest of the day. Health, English, math. In each class, I ask the students around me if they know him. Each one does, though they are unable to give specific examples. Not one teacher questions his presence. I'm not at all surprised to see him appear in chemistry, at the same work table.

I fidget beneath that green gaze, feeling hunted.

Ms. Delaney looks up briefly when the bell rings. "Do the series of experiments on page 198 of your textbooks. Take notes after each trial. Remember to wear your safety goggles."

"I hear you've been asking about me," Aiden says as he settles on the stool opposite me. His scent hits me like someone left a window open. Cedar, sage, and wildness. Breathing it in gives me a rush like I want to strip off my clothes and run naked through the woods.

With effort, I ignore his question and my own reaction, flipping through the text to the instructions and materials list. Bunsen burner, three flasks, tongs, ethanol, water and three strips of paper. I go to the cabinet to collect the materials needed. Already the room smells of gas from the burners.

I return to the table, where Aiden lounges, a predator playing at rest.

"You can ask me anything," he offers. "I promise I'll tell you the truth."

I raise an eyebrow at that, then put my safety goggles on. "I know enough already."

"Like what?" Again, those white teeth flash with the challenge.

I look around the room. The table full of jocks has

managed to light their text on fire. Ms. Delaney arrives with a fire extinguisher at the ready, a resigned expression on her haggard face. Across the room, there's a crash as someone knocks a beaker to the floor. No one is paying attention to us. Even so, I lower my voice.

"I know that you aren't what you appear to be."

The corner of his mouth twitches, the movement playful "And you are?"

I bite off the urge to ask what he knows about me. It won't do to look guilty. Instead, I refocus on the experiment.

One piece of paper goes into a beaker full of water, another into a beaker full of ethanol, and the third into a mixture of both.

I draw a chart in my notebook, labeling trial 1, trial 2 and trial 3. Aiden hasn't touched the green five star he carries. I have yet to see him open it in any class. For an odd moment, I wonder if it's a prop. Something visual to help him blend in as a student. The way my bait clothes help me blend in at a club or a rave.

The first piece of paper, the one soaked in water, doesn't burn. Shocker. The second one, the one immersed in pure ethanol ignites.

"Imagine that," Aiden drawls. "Alcohol is flammable."

Not bothering to answer, I use my tongs to retrieve the third piece of paper, the one soaked in the mixture of water and ethanol and hold it to the open flame. For a moment nothing happens, then a quick flare as the fire ignites the alcohol.

"Watch it!" Aiden barks.

Startled, I drop the paper. The water protects it, but my sleeve, which has gotten too close to the burner, alights.

I jump up, a scream working its way out of me, but before I can do anything, Aiden has a hold of my arm. There's a searing pain as though the fire has reached my skin, but it dulls to a warm glow of contact.

"You okay?" His hand falls away just as I'm getting used to the rare sensation of being touched.

I peer at the sleeve of my flannel. Scorched. The skin underneath it is unmarked.

I look up at him and my breathing goes all wonky again, though this time it might be from genuine fear. "What are you?"

"A wolf in man's clothing." The sardonic smile is back but it's hiding something. There's something lurking in the depths of those eyes. It's gone before I can name it.

The bell rings. He gives me one last wink before disappearing out into the hall.

I WOULDN'T DO WELL in prison. It's a fact that I'm reminded of every weekday at 2:15. The final bell is the sound of freedom, or at the very least a temporary reprieve. Society wonders why the school system seems broken, why incidents of violence, bullying, and suicides are on the rise for teens. A boundary is created, and a large group of individuals are crammed into it, forced to interact with one another. To cope with a schedule that strips away choices, simple matters like when to eat, when to pee, when to exercise and when to sit still and listen because the adults know best.

Isn't it amazing we can function at all?

When the bell rings, every cell in my body seems to exhale, a breath I have no awareness I've been holding until it expels in a great roaring *whoosh*. I roll up both sleeves to disguise the fire damage to my shirt on my way out of the room. A quick trip to the locker to discard my chemistry book and then I'm the first out the glass double doors, sucking in the sweet smell of freedom as the sun hits my face.

Cool mountain oxygen fills my lungs. I love fresh air and its medley of flavors. From the crisp fall wind scented with leaves and apples to the freezing stab of winter gusts. The sweet breeze of spring and even the damp heavy humid air of summer. The crackle of energy it carries just before a storm and the cold stillness before a snowfall when the world itself seems to be holding its breath. If I ever was to write poetry, it would be an ode to air.

Other students stream by me down the cracked concrete steps toward cars and busses, chatting and laughing, texting and bitching. I wait. No sign of Aiden. A feeling washes over me. I decide it is relief, not disappointment.

Sarah shoulder-checks me on the way down the stairs. "What's doing, Nic? Waiting for the short bus?"

"You're so funny. Oh wait, you just think you are." The banter is a solid distraction, a way to pretend I'm not looking for Aiden among the throngs of the freshly paroled. Curiosity isn't in my wheelhouse. I'm a planner, a meticulous researcher. Giving in to whims creates chaos and exacerbates risk, two things I try to avoid.

"C'mon slag, I'll give you a ride." Sarah heads to her POS and after one last glance around, I follow.

Our home isn't exactly on Sarah's way, but it's not unusual for her to drive me. She spends the least amount of time possible in her own home during any given day. And if Addy's still on the warpath over the license thing, better to have Sarah around as a buffer.

Puffy white clouds scud across the sky, and I can smell rain not far off. The wind is picking up so that the undersides of the new leaves are flashing us as we drive by. A storm brewing in the distance. Addy will need help at the clinic if she has a full house.

"Head for the office first," I instruct Sarah as we approach the first turn off to our property. She does, and I note that she has been uncharacteristically quiet on the ride. No obnoxious autotuned music, no quips or even complaints.

"Are you okay?"

"Fine." She nods, her eyes hidden behind little heart-shaped sunglasses. "You?"

"Fine." Since I'm lying I figure she is, too. I make a mental note to ask again later.

Mountain Veterinary Clinic is written in scrolling wrought iron above the stone archway. Sarah drives through it and parks in the gravel lot in front of the newly renovated barn that houses Addy's practice. The only other vehicle in the lot is the battered pick up that Addy drives around the property.

Chloe is sitting behind the tall reception desk, sorting through stacks of manila files. She looks up as the bell over the door jingles and grins when she sees us. Her scent is cloves and nutmeg, usually a sign of an easy day. "Hey girls, how was school?"

"Soul shattering as usual," I reply. "Looks like a storm's coming in. How many do we have?"

"Just two overnighters. Addy will bring them up to the house if it gets too bad. You want to stay for dinner, Sarah?"

"Who's cooking?" Sarah knows that the three of us rotate kitchen chores throughout the week.

It's my turn to cook, Addy's to clear and Chloe's to sit on her ass with a glass of red wine and channel surf. "I am."

Sarah wrinkles her nose. "Let me guess, rabbit pellets and cardboard?"

"Quinoa patties and green salad," I correct.

"Close enough. Think I'll pass. I should probably check in at home anyway." She hesitates for a moment and I know it's because she really doesn't want to go.

"Kitchen's open twenty-four/seven if you reconsider," Chloe says lightly.

This gets a smile from Sarah. "Thanks. We on for Club Yours tomorrow, Nic?"

I nod. Club Yours is our Saturday haunt. Full of college kids, which is why Sarah likes to go. Not the best hunting grounds since it's in town, but occasionally I pick up a stray who wanders into my territory. Mostly it's part of the ritual of going out and being seen, deepening the cover of normal teenager looking for some fun and excitement that my aunts and I have meticulously erected. "Sounds good."

Chloe watches Sarah back out of the lot then turns to me. "Issues at home?"

I nod. "The cops were there again last night. Joe's going to kill Sarah or her mother."

Chloe knows what I'm bucking for, a reason to take out Sarah's stepfather, my way. "Addy won't budge on it, Nic. It's too much of a risk. I'm sorry for her, you know I am. Perhaps the human authorities can do something?"

I shake my head. "Not unless Sarah or her mother report him and press charges. Right now, it's just neighbors phoning in complaints. It's not enough to get him out of their space."

Addy pushes her way through the swinging door. "Chloe, I need a hand back here."

Chloe gestures at the files. "I'm in the middle of this mess."

"These anal glands won't express themselves. The Fosters will be here at five and I don't want this dog leaking all over their upholstery."

"Ugh, way to glamour it up," Chloe grunts then holds up her Ombre manicure that ranges from pale pink to siren red. "And I just did my nails."

"I can take over the filing," I offer. It's a job I've done many times on weekends and during the summer.

"Yes, let Nic do it. She's better at it anyway." Addy leaves, knowing Chloe will follow.

"Thanks *so* much for that. Anal glands. Gods, how the mighty have fallen." With a dramatic sigh, Chloe disappears into the inner sanctum, the smell of burnt waffles trailing her.

I start with the files on the desk, checking to make sure that the day's updates have been properly logged and all fees are paid in full before storing them back beneath the desk. Then I pull the files for the following day and move on to the reminder calls. As the next day is Saturday, it's a brief list. As usual, Chloe was making a mountain out of a molehill, the work efficiently taken care of in under an hour. Her nails probably took twice as long.

I sit on the spinning desk chair, idly pushing in a ninety-degree arc first clockwise, then counterclockwise. Back and forth, back and forth. One eye on the road for the anal glands' owners. And for the wolf. The man. The man-wolf? The werewolf?

There's no such thing as a werewolf.

Yet Aiden said he was a wolf in man's clothing. He admitted it to me. What else could he possibly be? And how can I, the adopted child of the Fates with a toxic kiss, discount any possibility?

Especially after the fire incident. Slowly, I unroll the burnt edge of my shirt sleeve and examine it. It had caught fire, I'd felt the heat, the blistering burn on my skin. He'd extinguished it with nothing more than his hand. It wasn't possible. He had nothing to douse the flames, not water or fire-retardant chemicals. Yet I was whole, not marred in any visible way. So why do I feel different than before I'd walked into chemistry class? It's like his touch has altered me.

In no story I've ever read does a werewolf wield power over fire. But Aiden did. What could it mean?

I swivel the chair to face the computer and log into the clinic's files. Though I'm not expecting to find anything, I type in the last name Jager and hold my breath as the ancient machine hunts. Surprisingly, it comes up with a match. Emily Jager had come into the vet's office a week ago, bringing her new Labrador puppy for a round of vaccinations. New patient, no history of dog ownership. Could this Emily be in any way related to Aiden?

I scribble down the address and shut the screen down just as Chloe emerges from the back room, a disgusted look on her face.

"Filing's done. Can I borrow the truck? I need to run into town for something."

"Sure kid. Fill the tank while you're at it. Pick me up the latest trashy mags and something chocolate." She goes to her purse and fishes out a twenty.

"That won't fill the tank." I point out.

She grumbles and then hands over another twenty. "I want change."

"Change starts from within," I tell her.

She rolls her eyes at me. "Smartass."

It takes effort not to run for the truck. I want to be moving quickly, covering distance, finding out answers. Never have I felt so...out of control.

Not since I was six years old.

The storm breaks just as I finish pumping gas. I buy Chloe's magazines and a bag of M&Ms from the attached convenience store before heading to the address scribbled on the office stationery.

Emily Jager's home is a small brick ranch on a large lot off the county highway. The yard is fenced with split log rails and chicken wire. A decade-old Honda Civic is parked under the carport, safe from the rain coming down in fits and starts.

I idle at the curb, wondering what to do next. This is exactly why I don't act on impulse. My choices are limited. I can go knock on the door, ask if Aiden lives there or if Emily knows him. She might not. Jager isn't an unusual surname.

And if he's there? Then what? What can I say?

I jump as the passenger car door is yanked open. Aiden climbs in, his hair soaked from the now pouring rain.

I stare at him as he stares straight ahead through the windshield.

"You can't be here," he says.

"Why?" I ask, wondering if he'll keep his promise of telling me the truth.

"Just drive."

So, I do. The truck fishtails, and we speed on down the road into the encroaching darkness.

Questions and More Questions

I POINT the truck toward home, wondering what I'll do with Aiden once we get there. It might not be smart, taking him into my territory, but I have the advantage there. The wood chipper would be an option, bleached down after Paul Anderson and my guess is that Aiden could disappear just as readily as he had appeared.

Aiden's shoulders relax as we turn into the wooded drive. "You can't go there, Nic. You're not ready."

"Ready for what?" The cryptic statement has all the hairs rising on my arms.

He doesn't respond. Instead, he snatches up the bag of M&Ms. Tearing into it, he upends the package over his mouth, emptying it in five seconds flat.

I raise an eyebrow. "Did I say you could eat those?"

He chews, swallows and then smirks. "Better to ask forgiveness than beg permission. Do you have any more food?"

"What do I look like, an all you can eat buffet?"

He flashes me a lecherous grin. "Since you asked…."

Too late, I hear the double entendre. *Real smooth, Nic. He'll think you're trying to get in his pants.*

"Never mind. Here, go nuts." I reach across and pound the side of my fist against the dashboard compartment twice. It falls open, revealing my stash of chocolate protein bars.

Aiden helps himself, making short work of all five chocolate-covered snacks. "Thanks. I need something to take the edge off."

I shake my head. He's just downed about eight hundred calories, not out of the ordinary for a teenage boy. In fact, it's the first normal thing I've seen him do. "Look, I don't know who you are or what you're doing here, but I'll tell you once. Don't get in my way."

My warning doesn't appear to faze him. "Wouldn't dream of it. In fact, I'm here to help. Like I just did, saving your ass back there." He chucks a thumb in the direction of the brick ranch.

I divide my attention between him and the winding road. "Oh really? What was the danger?"

He wags one finger back and forth. "I told you, you're not ready."

"And I should believe you, why?"

"Because I'm here to help you." Green eyes, the same shade as the leaves dancing in the gusting wind, fix on me. There's something lurking in his eyes, something wicked and ancient. And powerful.

I turn back to the road. "Thanks, but I'm good."

"I know you are." There's some other meaning in his

words, a tone that is both new and familiar. If I didn't know better, I'd say he was…flirting with me.

I decide to ignore the innuendo and spell the situation out. "Look, I can handle things just fine on my own. So, I don't need or want your help."

His jaw clenches and a muscle jumps as if he's grinding his molars together. As though *I* am somehow frustrating *him*. "You're under the impression that I'm giving you a choice in the matter. I'm not."

His arrogance pisses me off. He may be a fire-snuffing wolf man, but I'm not in the market for a stalker or a sidekick, regardless of his abilities. "You said you'd tell me what I wanted to know. Well, I want to know who the hell you are and how you can do…what it is you can do."

"No, I said I would tell you the truth," he counters. "Big difference."

I slam on the brakes so hard that the truck skids to a stop sideways. "Okay, then get out." The rain picks up, pouring down onto the truck by the bucketful but I don't care.

He gives me a long look, then pops his door. "As my lady Nicneven desires."

My heart stops. It stills in my chest for a moment too long before staggering back to a regular rhythm. That name, I have never once heard it spoken aloud. Not by my aunts, not by any doctors or teachers. Most everyone believes my name is simply Nic, or perhaps that it's short for Nicole. Yet I know it's mine, have seen it in writing on my adoption papers. I feel the truth of it like a shadow lurking in a dark corner of my withered heart.

There's power in a name, power in knowing someone else's name, in wielding it like a weapon. Aiden might as well have fired a flaming arrow into my chest.

Aiden is outside, the rain soaking through his t-shirt and jeans his hand on the door, ready to shut it.

"Wait!" The cry tears from me, as though something important came forcibly detached. "How do you know that name?"

He stares at me a moment. "I have known it for centuries. When you first told it to me."

I blink at him. He looks seventeen, maybe eighteen. And I damn well know I am sixteen. Centuries? "That's...not possible."

"Perhaps, but it's the truth." He shuts the door and then jogs into the trees, moving through the rain like it's of no significance. Perhaps it isn't for him. He pulls his shirt over his head, drops it carelessly on the ground. He pauses long enough to yank off one boot and its accompanying sock, then the other. His hands go to his pants and I watch as his bare ass appears, and the denim is tossed aside. He turns back to me as shameless in the revealing as I am in the watching. He has nothing to be ashamed of, his body is perfect, like a statue come to life. Aiden nods once, as though acknowledging my voyeurism, then vanishes into the undergrowth.

I'm tempted to go after him and my reasons have nothing to do with the perfection of his naked form. My shaking hand grips the door handle. But I don't budge. I don't even breathe. There is no sound other than the steady drag of the windshield wipers across the glass and the constant drum of water falling as though the skies need to scour the ground clean of all that just happened.

Time passes, no idea how much. His cedar and sage scent lingers in the vehicle. My thoughts are like a flock of butter-flies, flitting around inside my skull but never perching long enough for me to grasp. A howl sounds in the distance, star-tling me back to awareness. The noise grounds me once more, I shiver, then shift the truck into drive and head for the house.

The Subaru is nowhere in sight. Addy and Chloe are still at the office. Good, I don't want them to see me so…shaken. It takes me a moment to find the right word to fit the feeling. It's a new sensation for me.

After parking the truck, I dart through the rain, pausing under the cover of the front porch to scan the trees. Nothing out of the ordinary. I know he's out there. Maybe as a man, more likely as the wolf. I can feel those green eyes on me, observing, taking in my every move. Turning my back on a predator of his caliber is one of the most challenging things I have ever done, but somehow, I manage it.

Once inside I lock the door, arm the security system, then hurry into the bathroom and turn on the shower. I kick my damp clothes toward the hamper and shiver as I wait for the water to come up to temperature. The bathroom is newly remodeled, but Chloe insisted on keeping the old fixtures like the Reganomics era shower head that yields better water pressure than the newer eco-friendly sorts. The pummeling of water on my back eases some of the tension in my stiff shoulder muscles.

I stand beneath the spray, my eyes closed, my thoughts in turmoil. My usual calm focus eludes me. I hunt for inner peace until the water turns tepid and forces me back to reality. With one fluffy blue towel swathing my wet hair and another circling my body, I pad barefoot into my bedroom. Extracting a set of Pilates pants, a tank, and hoodie, I add thick fluffy socks to the pile before dropping my towel.

A flash of lightning followed by a howl cuts through the drumming of rain on the roof. I'd almost forgotten that Aiden is out there, bare-assed and most likely in wolf form. Heart hammering, I duck into a crouching position, gaze sliding toward the window, half expecting to see the glow of green eyes peering in at me. Nothing there but the storm raging against the house.

Slowly, I stand until fully upright and then move toward the window. It's impossible for anyone to sneak up on the house. Besides the telltale gravel drive, the tree line is several hundred yards beyond the structure. When enabled, the security system sounds if the code isn't entered within thirty seconds of the motion detector being tripped, notifying all three of us via our phones that an unauthorized person is lurking on our property.

Cataloging the safeguards helps, but even with the rain cutting visibility down to less than a foot, all the hairs on my arms stand on end. I play bait often enough to know when I am being watched.

He's out there. Naked as I am. And he knows my name.

Though I have never experienced self-consciousness before, I wrap one arm over my bare breasts and use the other to snap the blinds shut before turning to dress.

Dressed, I move from my room into the kitchen where I rinse the quinoa, set a pot of water on to boil and extract lettuce, spinach, green onion and cucumber from the refrigerator. The familiar ritual of preparing dinner helps ground me. My body falls into the rhythm and my mind follows suit until I experience some of my usual detachment.

With the salad made and the quinoa cooling so I can work with it once the aunts arrive, I prowl through the house looking for something to occupy my thoughts and keep my hard-won calm. The spring chill still lingers so I build a fire in the hearth, glad someone—probably Addy— had the foresight to haul some logs in from the woodpile.

I strike a long-handled match and watch as the flame catches the newspaper that I've stuffed in around the small teepee of kindling. Of course, the flame reminds me of the one thing—person—I'm trying not to think about. My mental discipline has vanished since Aiden's arrival.

Giving in to the inevitable, I consider telling the aunts

about Aiden and what I've seen him do. The problem is I'm not sure what to say. He's new at school, yet I'm the only one who realizes it. I've seen him put out a fire and heal a burn with nothing more than his bare hand. He can transform into a wolf and knows my full name, a name no one else has ever spoken aloud and claims he met me centuries ago. And I'm pretty sure he was watching me dress. So that makes him an ancient, peeping, fire wielding werewolf?

And one more fact, I am oddly... drawn to him.

The problem is, I already know what Addy and Chloe will say. If he could appear without causing a stir, then he could vanish the same way. And if he's lurking in the woods outside my bedroom window watching me dress, there is a wood chipper with his name on it.

It's not attraction, my preoccupation with Aiden isn't rooted in hormones. I have never felt sexual desire for another person. Only the urge to hunt, to track, to kill the guilty who would prey on the weak. My fascination must be because he is so different, an unknown quantity in my typical sphere of operation. Other people are predictable. My victims, the townspeople, even the aunts. I say X, Chloe responds with Y, while Addy looks on in disapproval. All very clear cut. Aiden is a curiosity, the volatile variable introduced into a controlled experiment, nothing more.

My cell rings, freaking Hamster Dance blaring once again. I answer before my eye begins twitching. "What's up, Chloe?"

"Emergency came in about thirty minutes ago, a dog hit by a car. Addy's prepping for surgery now so we probably won't be back for dinner anytime soon. Go ahead and eat my M&M's."

A mental image of Aiden pops into my mind, long tanned throat working as he downs the candy. "Way ahead of you."

"You okay, sweets? You sound kind of off."

I physically shake myself and search for a plausible reason to be distracted. "I haven't heard from Sarah since she left."

"I'm sure she's fine." In the background, there's a crash and an accompanying string of oaths. "I've got to go, Nic. All hell's breaking loose. See you later."

I tap the end call button and check for texts from Sarah. Nothing. She might have left her phone on the car charger. She does that sometimes, especially when she's distracted by issues at home. I shoot her a quick message, inviting her over for a movie night, and then tap the phone against my leg.

Nicneven.

Slowly I raise my gaze upwards, to the loft where Addy and Chloe sleep. Before I am aware of deciding, I am up the stairs and standing in the aunt's spacious loft bedroom. The ceiling is vaulted to the apex of the roof, making the small space seem larger than it is. The twin beds are hand-carved from logs and are made up with matching green and red striped flannel comforters. At the end of each bed sits a heavy cedar trunk. Chloe's is strewn with discarded clothes and magazines, while Addy's stands bare. It is to Addy's side of the room that my willful feet take me, to the trunk where I know she keeps all her important documents and a few mementos.

After kneeling on the floor in front of the trunk, I lift the lid. The scent of pine and leather fills my senses. Some people might have experienced guilt or uncertainty about invading a family member's personal space. That's the upside of being a sixteen-year-old judge, jury, and executioner—no point in sweating the misdemeanors.

Even if Chloe hadn't left half her wardrobe strewn over her trunk I would know the neat piles and jigsaw-like fit of the items inside belong to Addy. The entire trunk is organized for maximum efficiency. Some of the items I recognize. A small hunk of concrete with the imprint of my much smaller hand that I don't remember making is wrapped in a thick yellow blanket that reeks of mothballs. That must have been made soon after they adopted me, maybe second grade.

I set the oversized paperweight back down, careful that it is swathed in the blanket the same way Addy had it situated and move on to the leather-bound book. At first blush, Addy doesn't come across as the sort of person who would keep a scrapbook. She's not nostalgic and doesn't talk about the past at all, unlike Chloe who likes to drink and reminisce about the days when they had real power to affect people's lives and shape the future.

The aged leather spine cracks a bit when I open it. The first page is somewhat sinister. There's no name, no personal information. Just a white page with a taut black line bisecting it. A quick glance might lead one to believe the line is drawn with ink or some other medium. But on closer inspection, it reveals itself to be a thread. The ends are taped down to the back of the page to keep the line perfectly straight. I'm not sure how much the Greeks got right about the sister Fates, but the thread tells me that at least some of the myth was based on fact.

In Greek mythology, the Moirai were the three sisters known to control the threads of fate. Clotho—Chloe as I know her—spins the threads of life for both mortals and gods. Lachesis is supposed to be the appointer, she who sets out the span of each life by measuring the length of the thread. And of course, Atropos—aka Addy—who cuts the thread, ending the life at its predetermined time.

I run one finger over the thread and feel it thrum with *something*. Power maybe, but definitely life. No indication what the thread means or, if the stories are to be believed, whose life it represents. If the life is over or has yet to begin. Unless I ask Addy, there is no way to know for certain. And even though I'm poking about in her private scrapbook, I don't have a death wish.

The next page contains a yellowed bit of parchment with odd symbols. Not Greek, I looked via Google and the symbols don't match any known characters in the Greek alphabet. It's an oddity, but not my main purpose for pawing through the book.

The third page holds the target of my hunt. The newspaper article is yellowed, the ink not as crisp as it once was, but still legible. I study my black and white image captured eleven years ago. My dirty six-year-old self stands frozen before a stone cottage. It's not one of the pretty picturesque ones being built as weekend homes by pretentious people. No, the cottage in the picture is an ancient ruin, the roof half caved in. I'd been clad in a ripped and dirty nightgown that had once been white, feet bare and every bit of visible skin is covered in filth.

I drink it in before turning my attention to the headline. It's in German, the entire article was clipped from a German paper, but the translation is clear in my mind.

Raised by wolves? Wild girl discovered living alone in the Black Forest. One hiker suffered a heart attack at the shock of her discovery.

I close my eyes and dredge up the memory...

My eyes open at the sound of their voices. Men, two of them on the approach to my hidden home. They are talking, laughing. I rise from the blanket on the floor and move to the window to get a better look. The sills are high, and I am short. No glass covering the openings, just crumbling shutters. I must stand on my tiptoes to see through them.

One wears an orange knit cap. The color is vivid against the moss and lichen-covered woods, the tree trunks black, giving the forest its name. The hat's color is obscene against the natural setting. It's the cap I spy first, like a bobbing fireball heading my way. The other one, his hat a more subdued but still an unnatural shade of blue looks my way. I duck low, heart pounding. Deep in my bones I know I've been seen.

They speak more quickly now, louder in German. I hear one phrase.

Hast du das gesehen. *Did you see that?*

Wo? *Where?*

Dort drüben im fenster. *Over there in the window.*

Their footfalls are soft on the forest floor. Not as soft as when I venture out in search of food or water from the nearby stream, but my feet are bare. They are wearing heavy-soled boots that trample the ferns beneath their tread.

They enter the cottage without bothering to knock. I watch as they squint, needing a moment to let their eyes adjust to the dim interior. They look like great misshapen beasts, large silhouettes weighed down with heavy packs. My heart pounds at the sight of them, two big dark shapes invading my space.

"Hallo?" *The one with the fireball hat spies me first and offered the greeting.*

"Hallo?" *I repeat. My voice sounds odd, rusty from disuse. I can't recall if I've ever spoken to anyone before. My memories before the last few days at the cottage are nonexistent.*

The one wearing the blue hat crouches down to my level. Ist hier jemand mit Ihnen?

Slowly I shake my head from side to side to indicate that I am alone. Have always been alone. Will always be alone....

The man with the blue hat shrugs out of his pack and removes a metal container from one side. He tries to hand it to me, but I shrink back, refusing to take his offering.

Es ist Wasser.

I point to the bucket I collected from the stream that morning. Wasser.

The one with the orange hat takes his pack off too and starts to dig through it. He moves forward. I press my back against the crumbling stone wall. Something about him smells...wrong. And, I don't like the way he's looking at me.

Bist du hungrig?

His pronunciation is off, and I realize German isn't his native language. I nod because it's been a long time since I've eaten and my stomach growls. If he has food to trade, I'll answer a few more questions.

He holds his hand out to me, large thick fingers around something in a brightly colored wrapper, although not as bright as his fireball hat. Slowly, I reach out, ready to snatch my hand away in case they grab me and try to drag me from my corner.

He doesn't move, though his eyes follow my every breath, reptilian gaze sweeping from head to toe. I take the offering, enjoying the way the package crinkles under my touch. I have never seen anything like it. Was ist das?

The one in the blue hat has large brown eyes like a deer. They grow even larger at my question. It's as if he can't believe I've never seen the thing before. After a moment of slack-jawed gaping, he answers, Schokoladentafel.

Schokoladentafel. *I repeat the word carefully, having never heard of a chocolate bar.*

They show me how to strip away the outer wrapping and demonstrate the way to break off a small piece of the dark interior. The one in the orange hat pops the piece he's broken off into his mouth and then chews, flashing me a smile as though demonstrating this is the correct way to enjoy the exotic food.

Dutifully, I copy his movements. The taste explodes on my tongue in a way that steals my breath. Sweet, so sweet. Sweeter than anything I've tasted before. No berry can compare with the melting sensation of sugar and cocoa coating my mouth. I grin at them and attack the rest of the bar.

Once it is gone and I am busy licking the melted bits from my fingers, I realize they've been speaking while I ate. The tone of the conversation turns to one of an argument. Four words is all it takes to pop the chocolate bliss bubble surrounding me.

Nimm sie bei uns. *Take her with us.*

Nein! *I* screech the word and tear past them, out the door and dashing through the trees before either one of them makes a grab for me. I hear their shouts from behind me but don't dare turn around to see if they are in pursuit. I cannot leave. Cannot, will not go with them. It is imperative that I stay at the cottage. That I wait.

Just like my memories from before the cottage, I have no recollection of where I go, how long I hide. Certain parts of my memory are fuzzed-out, like a telescope that has been knocked over and no longer focuses properly. Some bits are clear, others barely register.

Hours later, I creep through the door of the cottage, expecting to find the two men with their colorful hats long gone. I am half right. The one with the orange hat, the one with the chocolate and the reptilian eyes stayed behind. He is lying down on my pallet beneath the window.

"Hey there." His words are soft as though he doesn't wish to spook me. And I notice he switches to his mother tongue. "Do you speak English?"

I nod to indicate I could understand him, though my English is even rustier than my German.

"My friend's gone to get some help. So, I volunteered to hang out here and wait in case you came back. And here you are."

I bite my lip, unsure of what to do.

"How about you come on over here and sit for a spell." He gestures toward the bed, the pallet he occupies.

I shake my head, turning back to the door. Though I am exhausted, I would rather sleep beneath a hedge than share the cottage with fireball hat.

His words stop me. "Hey, I've got another chocolate bar. You know, Schokoladentafel?"

I still at the word and his grin is one of triumph. "If you come over here I'll share it with you."

I don't trust him, not at all, but I really want more of that rich decadent taste from before and my stomach is empty again. Soon the hunger pangs will start, and I will not be able to sleep. I approach him.

"Come on and sit next to me." He sits up, excitement visible on his face and pats the space next to him.

Hesitantly, I lower myself down, feet beneath me so I can jump up at any moment. He rewards me with half the candy bar. I grab it, this time ripping through the package like a rabid thing to get at the delicious food.

"Poor little mite, all alone here for who only knows how long." He shakes his head and reaches forward to stroke a hand down my tangled hair. "I'll make you a deal. How about I'll be nice to you and you be nice to me. We'll be friends."

"Friends?" I pause in my chocolate consumption, another foreign word. I have no Rosetta stone to help me translate.

"That's right, real good friends. You know what friends do?"

I shake my head. With no frame of reference, I am utterly clueless.

"Friends keep secrets. Like you want to stay here and pretend me and my buddy never stumbled across you, right?"

Slowly I nod. Yes, that is exactly what I want.

"Well, I can keep your secret. And maybe you and me can have one together."

I'm not paying attention to what he says, my eyes glued to the remaining half of the candy bar.

"Don't be greedy, sweet thang. You gotta work for it if you want more."

"Work?" I repeat, looking up into his face.

"That's right. But it won't even be like work since we're friends and all."

I watch him, trying to figure out what he means. His hand is moving from my hair until it strokes my cheek. I want to jerk my head away but don't because that candy bar is still in my mind.

"You ain't real bright, are you sweet thang?" He drawls, his excitement building to a fever pitch. "That's okay. Come here and I'll show you what you need to do."

He takes my hand and places it over his pants. I feel something there, something hard and squeeze eagerly, hoping it is another candy bar.

He groans then mutters. "That's it, sweet thang." His hands fumble for my nightdress, skin touching my own.

I spring up and shout "Nein," again, ready to run back out and lose myself in the forest. No candy is worth having his hands on me.

Only he has my dress gripped firmly in both hands. I struggle, but he holds me easily, shoving me down on the pallet and pinning me beneath his massive weight. He's still talking as he gropes me, his words a hiss in my ears. He slides the fabric of my clothing up over my dirty knees.

I begin to cry. Tears streak down my face as I shake my head from side to side. My small hands ball up into tight fists, but he pins them both in one of his massive ones.

My tears save me, though not through any decency on his part. He kisses them away, licking the salty wetness from my cheeks, then covering my mouth with his own to capture my screams.

His body bucks once, but it is not with the frantic need from before. He convulses on top of me. I scream even louder as his eyes roll in his head and a trickle of blood dribbles from his lips onto my face.

And then he goes totally and completely still, eyes glazing over with the fog of death.

I struggle and pant as I work my way out from under his heavy weight. Heart pounding, more tears mingling with the blood on my face. As soon as I am free I head for the door, but don't go far. One of the trees nearby has a hollow beneath it and my small body burrows inside like an animal going into a den to hibernate. I keep an eye out for the other man, the one with the blue knit cap, knowing instinctively that he will come back to collect his companion.

When he returns, he is not alone. Officials wearing similar clothes—uniforms I discover later—along with people from the newspaper. They swarm the house likes bees on a hive. More people show up. Some of them have food. From my hiding place, I see them eating. Food is my weakness. They catch me when I try to steal an apple from a woman's pack.

I reread the first line of German, my mind automatically translating. *Raised by wolves?* What I once thought was a fanciful description on the part of the writer, now seems like an eerie prediction. Is it possible that somehow, I was raised by wolves or werewolves? Is that how Aiden knows me? Had I once been part of his pack?

A thud downstairs snags my attention. I slam the book shut and place it back inside the trunk before flying to the stairs. I'm halfway down when I hear the noise again and realize the security alarm is going off on my phone.

Someone is trying to break in.

CHAPTER 4

CURSED

Slowly I creep to the door. It rattles in its frame as though something heavy slams against it, trying to knock it down. I don't have a weapon, I don't need one. Whoever is attempting to break in should be more afraid of me than I am of them.

Another thump and then all falls quiet. I reach for the handle, positioning my body so the door will conceal me long enough to leap out and plant a wet one on the intruder.

Heartbeat. Heartbeat. Heartbeat. I yank the handle.

When no knuckle dragger barges into the house, I peer around the door.

"Hey there." Aiden is standing there, naked and wet, one arm holding his left side. Blood oozes out from between his fingers. "Thought I'd drop by, see what was new."

"What happened to you?" I'm curious despite myself.

He takes a hesitant step forward. "May I come in?"

Now he asks? After trying to knock the door down? My gaze shifts from him to the tree line and I swear I see something move. "Is there something else out—?"

Aiden shoves me aside, barges in and slams the door. "Don't let them see you."

"Them? There's more than one?"

My phone blares Hamster Dance once more. Chloe, probably freaking out about the alarm notification. I reset it and then answer, not taking my eyes off Aiden. "What?"

"What's going on?" Chloe barks. "Do you need us?"

Something brushes my arm. Aiden's hand. Our gazes lock. He shakes his head, slowly, mouthing one word and for a moment I can almost hear him in my head. *No.*

"Nic?"

I have a choice. Trust the shape-changing stranger that claims he wants to help me or the aunts that have kept me in the dark for most of my life. Chloe and Addy are my wingmen, they're the ones that help me dispose of the bodies. Literally. But never have they spoken a word about why they help me, why they accept my deadly ability and my inborn need to hunt.

Aiden's green eyes are pleading and for a moment I think I hear his voice in my mind. *Trust me.*

If I'm wrong about the naked stranger, I can always kill him later.

"False alarm," I say, and Aiden's shoulders relax about an eighth of an inch. "I think it was a raccoon or something. The trash was tipped over by the back door."

"You're sure?" Chloe asks.

No. I think. "Yes," I say.

"Okay, well, we'll be home in a bit." In the background, I hear the animals yowling and making a racket. Chloe and Addy will most likely wait out the storm there.

I end the call and Aiden murmurs, "Thank you. I'm not their favorite person."

"You know Addy and Chloe?" Although why this surprises me I can't say.

"Mostly by reputation. Can I get a towel or something?" He shivers.

Right. He's naked and bleeding and in my space. "There's a blanket on the back of the couch. Go sit by the fire."

I leave him long enough to retrieve the first aid kit from the bathroom, along with a towel and a pair of gray sweatpants from Addy's closet. She's the tallest out of the three of us and the most likely to own anything that will fit him.

Aiden has the quilt draped over his shoulders, holding his hands out to the fire.

"Thanks," he murmurs when I hand him the pants and towel.

Our gazes lock and heat creeps up my cheeks. Am I blushing? Impossible, I don't do embarrassment. His nudity doesn't affect me at all. It's simply the heat from the fire.

Then why are you staring at him?

I turn my attention to the fire, giving him time to dry himself and pull the pants on and myself the opportunity to collect my wayward thoughts.

"Okay," he clears his throat.

I turn back toward him and almost smile at the sight. The pants are like clam diggers on his tall frame. The elastic bottoms ending halfway up his calves, but at least his man parts are no longer swinging freely in the breeze. His jaw clenches as he places the towel over his wound.

"Let me see," I order, unwilling to chance his refusal.

The towel lifts and I scoot closer, taking in the deep gash along his side. I reach forward to probe the injury and he hisses.

I withdraw my hand and look up into his pinched face. "I'll have to clean the wound. It's deep and will need stitches as well as a course of antibiotics. What happened?"

"You know how to do all that?" Judging by his tone, I've impressed him.

I shrug, noting that he's dodging my question. "Addy's a vet. I've picked up a few things."

A smile tugs the corners of his mouth up. "A vet? Maybe I should change back into a wolf."

"Then I'd have to shave the fur away. It would take too long."

His gaze searches my face, the skin crinkling between his eyebrows as he reads my expression. "It was a joke, Nic."

"I don't do jokes." I rise and move to the kitchen to heat some water. "There are some painkillers in the first aid kit."

"Painkillers don't work on me," he grunts and turns to see what I'm doing. "I metabolize them too fast. Same is true for alcohol."

"Sucks to be you." With the water on in the kettle, I have nothing to do but wait. "So, who's out there?"

I'm prepared for another dodge, another change of subject so he takes me off guard when his eyes grow distant and he murmurs, "the Wild Hunt."

I stare at him, again, that free-falling feeling of time lost. The Wild Hunt is a myth about a fearsome host of creatures from hell. Depending on the story's origin, it's a force of damned souls or perhaps unearthly creatures, an unstoppable army that snares unsuspecting mortals and enlists them into its ranks.

And Aiden thinks they are prowling beyond my front door? I don't know whether I should believe him or not. I don't want to believe him. In legend, the Wild Hunt claims evil souls.

Like, oh say the soul of a teenage serial killer.

I grip the countertop hard to keep my hands from shaking. My kiss can take down a full-grown man but against an army of the dead or otherworldly beings? I'd be no better off than a normal.

My stomach churns and I feel as though I might be sick. *This is fear.* The realization is unwelcome.

Behind me, the kettle starts to whistle, and the noise makes me flinch. I turn and fill a glass bowl with the hot water and let it stand on the counter. Aiden's gaze follows my every movement as I lay out the supplies I'll need and position a hardback chair for the best light.

I wash my hands thoroughly and don disposable gloves, then gesture for him to come sit in the chair so I can kneel next to him. Up close that wild cedar and sage scent is overpowering, fogging my thoughts. Ideally, I'd have him flat on his back, but just the thought of him in that position makes me go hot and cold. Too many feelings in too short a time and me, ill-equipped to deal with any of them.

I flush out the wound as best I can. He doesn't react, though his stomach muscles pull tighter as though bracing for impact. My hands shake a bit as I lay my gloved fingers against his taut flesh. This will hurt him, I realize and for some bizarre reason that bothers me.

I shake my head once. Why does it matter? He's already injured and without treatment, the wound will become infected. I'm helping him, an oddity itself. So why should the thought of causing him further pain bother me?

His hand covers mine. "It's okay, you don't have to."

"It needs to be done." I grit my teeth and make the first stitch to close the wound before either he or my own misgivings can talk me out of it.

He doesn't even twitch. I glance up, see his jaw is locked, though his gaze remains fixed on me.

"Okay?" I ask, wondering why I care.

Aiden swallows, then nods. "Keep going."

It takes twelve stitches to close the gash in his side, a deep cut that is too straight and free from crud to come from thorns or any nature debris on our property. It's from a blade, I realize with a jolt. A knife or sword edge. Slowly, I stand and turn away to dispose of the water.

"Thank you, Nic," Aiden says. His face is white, brows pinched from pain. Some fine sweat sheens on his forehead. The beginnings of a fever?

I strip off the gloves. "When was the last time you had a tetanus shot?"

"Never," he says.

I don't look at him as I dump the bloody water down the drain. "Are they after me? Because of what I am?"

"And what are you?" One corner of his mouth quirks up. "A teenage girl? A blonde?"

He wants me to say it. Say that I am a killer.

I just stare at him. If he doesn't know, I'm not going to enlighten him.

Aiden stands, one hand over his freshly stitched wound and pulls back the plaid drapes with the other. "No, they aren't pursuing you, Nic."

With nothing else to occupy my hands, I stuff them under my armpits to hide the shaking. "You sure about that?"

His gaze roves over the night darkened landscape another moment before letting the curtain fall back into place. "They're hunting me."

"You? Why?" And what sort of fresh hell did I invite into my home alongside him?

"It's a long story." He winces and heads into the kitchen. "Got anything to eat?"

Again, with the food. "Cooked quinoa. Green salad."

He casts me a dark look and heads to the sink to wash the blood from his hands. "That stuff will kill you."

Says the guy being stabbed by a myth. I pop up onto the counter while he prowls through the kitchen. He's thorough, opening every single cabinet and drawer, taking stock of the contents before moving on.

Watching him, so large, so shirtless in what I consider my space distracts me. It takes me a minute to figure out what question I most want him to answer. "You said you knew me from before. Did you mean another life? Like reincarnation?"

He, at last, settles on the fridge. A batch of egg salad, half an avocado and a brick of cheddar cheese in his hands. "No and yes. Bread?"

I point. "In the microwave. And what sort of an answer is no and yes?"

The light in his gaze shifts back to that amused look he wore during Chemistry class. "An honest one. Why the microwave?"

"We don't use it much and it keeps the bugs away." I'm starting to wonder if we're playing some sort of verbal sparring game. I strike, he parries then goes in for a hit. The one that leaves the ring with the most information wins.

I think about his last answer as he removes the rye bread along with a package of crackers. He snags a plate, going right to where they are kept in the cabinet next to the sink. Same with a knife. He slathers six slices of bread with egg salad, slices up the avocado and cheese and combines them with crackers and extracts an apple from the fruit bowl. After the way he attacked those M&Ms earlier, I half expect him to start wolfing—no pun intended—the makeshift meal down where he stands. Again, he surprises me. Plate prepared, he tidies away all the supplies, wipes down the counter with a dishrag and carries his bounty to the table. I follow him, grabbing two bottles of water from the fridge.

"Do you want some?" he offers me the plate first.

My stomach growls. He grins as if it's conspired with him to take me down a peg. The quinoa and salad will keep in the fridge.

I accept one-half of one of the sandwiches under his watchful gaze.

He waits until I've taken a bite before murmuring. "Trusting. I could have put anything in that."

The mouthful of food gets stuck in my throat. I swallow thickly, downing a good portion of the water before gasping, "Did you?"

Aiden shakes his head. "No. But it's a lesson you need to learn if you want to survive. Don't accept food or drink from anyone you don't know."

He makes it sound as if I'm some sort of mentally challenged child. "The food came out of my refrigerator and I watched you the whole time."

"I know, I felt your eyes on me." His voice is a low purr, making me sound like some sort of pervert.

"That's not what I meant." Another uncomfortable flush. Is the thermostat broken? I refuse to entertain the possibility that he's getting to me.

"It only takes half a second for a skilled assassin to slip poison into a meal, a little sleight of hand and misdirection and you're dead. From now on you make it yourself, or let me taste it first."

This amuses me. "So you can die instead?"

The three sections of sandwiches are gone. He extends his hand and offers me the remaining half. When I shake my head, he downs it in two bites, sips some water and then mutters. "Poisons can't kill me, at least not a small dose. Something that would cripple you might make me a little logy, but I'd shake it off. My metabolism burns through everything too quickly to let most toxins build up."

I stare at him a minute, thoughts racing. "What *are* you?"

"Cursed," his gaze falls back to his empty plate.

"And what am I? I mean, what am I to you?" This wasn't coming out well at all and I huff out a breath of frustration. "Why do you even care if I live or die?"

His lips part but a sound at the door has both of us

turning towards it. Over the wind I hear someone rapping crisply on the door, followed by Addy's voice. "Nic!"

I stand. "My aunts."

Aiden glances from me to the door. "I'll be close by if you need me."

"Nic, open the damn door!" Chloe this time. "It's freezing out here."

"You're leaving?"

"I won't be far." He hesitates a moment, reaching for my face and again, I swear I hear his voice in my mind.

I'll never leave you again.

I jerk back before he can make contact, my heart racing. The knocking outside turns to banging.

"Let them in." His hand drops to his waistband. My eyes go wide as he shucks the borrowed sweats and then turns… to the fireplace?

One minute he's a man, the next the enormous black wolf stares at me with Aiden's eyes. As I wonder how I'm going to explain the wolf to the aunts he steps into the roaring fire.

And vanishes.

I want to sink down onto the couch and get a grip, but the Fates are waiting.

He disappeared into the fire. The words echo through me as though I'm trying to convince myself that it really happened. Only a trace scent like burnt cedar chips remains.

I flick the deadbolt back and my aunts tumble inside, Chloe first and Addy who slams the door behind her.

I study the two of them with a frown. Chloe's manicure is completely wrecked, it looks as though she's been digging with her bare hands. Addy's clothing is ripped, her hair slipping from her no-nonsense braid. What looks like blood spatters her boots.

"What's happened?" I ask even as I think I know the answer.

It was the same thing that went after Aiden, why I'd had to stitch him up.

A shiver went through me at the thought of the words. *The Wild Hunt.*

"Nic," Chloe reaches me first, her face is devoid of color. "It's Sarah."

I frown, taken off guard by her tone as much as the words. "What about Sarah?"

Addy steps forward, grips me by the shoulders as though to keep me from toppling over. "There's been an accident."

My blood jolts to a halt as though it flash freezes in my veins. "What sort of accident?"

"A car wreck. One of the back roads was washed out during the storm. A tree came down."

Chloe won't meet my gaze, her eyes filling with tears.

Something twists inside my chest. "Is…is she going to be okay?"

"No, honey." It's the first time in memory that Addy's used any sort of endearment and that scares me more than anything else until she utters three words that stops the world from spinning like a little kid that halts a globe mid spiral. "She's already gone."

In the distance, thunder crashes and a wolf howls.

I ROLL onto my side when someone—Chloe because Addy would barge right in—raps lightly on my bedroom door. "Nic?"

"Yeah?" The numbers on the clock read nine of eight, a fact confirmed by the steady sunlight pressing against my still shut blinds.

Chloe pushes the door open but remains in the hall. "Do you want breakfast?"

I shake my head, letting my eyes slide shut to support my claim. "I'm too tired."

There's a pause as she digests my reply. I never skip meals, can't afford to let myself get hungry. Hungry equals hangry which equals irrational. Irrational leads to sloppy decisions. I also don't sleep in like a normal, the way Sarah does.

The way Sarah did.

The mental correction makes my hands clench into fists.

"No school?" Chloe tries.

"It's Saturday."

"Oh. Right." A floorboard creaks and I picture her there, hovering in the doorway shifting from foot to foot as she hunts for something else to say. "I forgot."

I sigh and toss the covers back. "What am I supposed to do?"

"What?" Chloe shakes her head. "What do you mean?"

"I mean, my cover is gone. The person that shielded me best is no longer an option. Am I supposed to mourn and wail publicly? How long until I can find someone else to act as a blind?"

Chloe's face tightens up as though she doesn't understand. "You want to *replace* Sarah?"

"I have to if I want to hunt. How long is it appropriate before I can make a new best friend?"

Chloe is looking at me as though she's never seen me before. "Nic, Sarah just died last night. She's not even in the ground yet." She says it in such a way that it's as though she's explaining the reality of the situation to me for the first time.

"Right, so after the funeral then." I sigh and flop back onto the bed.

Her head starts going back and forth. "You aren't this cold, Nic. Not even you could be so heartless."

There's a dry burn behind my eyes, as though the sockets have turned to sandpaper. "You know what I am."

Nicneven. Aiden's voice echoes in my thoughts.

Chloe huffs out a breath. "Right, well. I was going to stay home in case….

" She trails off.

In case what? I want to talk? In case I totally lose the shit I'm clinging to by a thread of fraying sanity?

"But since you're fine, I'll just go into the office." Her voice comes out dry and raspy.

"See you later." I pull the covers up over my head and wait.

There's a long silence. It's the watchfulness of a predator. No, not a predator, a parent animal, one worrying over the well-being of its offspring. A pregnant pause.

Then, mercifully, her footsteps retreat down the hall. Thirty seconds later the front door opens and then shuts with a good amount of force.

I throw the covers back but don't bother getting up. What's the point? I have nowhere to be, no one to hunt. It's expected that I mope and grieve and pull away from the rest of the world like a normal teenager would after her best friend dies.

Dies. It sounds so final. How come I've never thought of that before? Of death as being final? I've always seen it as getting rid of a problem, like setting out ant traps in the spring. I've seen their little corpses, all stuck in the gluey bait, writhing. Did Sarah writhe when her POS car wrapped around a fallen tree?

No. Addy made a point to tell me that Sarah had died instantly. Her neck broken, her spinal cord severed. No suffering, no understanding that the end is closing in, like my victims. Just here one second and gone the next.

Gone. My stomach turns over. It doesn't feel right, that

Sarah who loved to dance and fuck and eat like there is no tomorrow is just…no more.

And yet here I am. So full of nothing, consuming oxygen one breath at a time.

I roll over, look back at the clock. Fourteen hours, that's how long ago it had happened. What had she been doing, racing back here in the middle of that storm? Didn't she have enough sense to wait it out? She'd been near enough that the aunts had heard the sirens, had gone to investigate what had happened.

Had seen her body being pried from the wreckage.

Why didn't she answer her phone when I'd called? Had it been off or just out of reach?

"What the hell were you thinking, you stupid slag?" I mutter. Probably drinking. I got on her ass about the drinking and driving more than once, told her it was stupid, that she'd kill someone, never dreaming my words would be so prophetic.

Tired of the same useless thoughts that have been taking up space in my fuzzy brain for hours, I force my legs to swing over the side of the bed, my feet to hold up my weight as they hit the chill floor. The cold is a small bite of discomfort and I welcome it. Anything to help keep me grounded.

I shuffle to the bathroom and use the facilities by rote. I don't meet my eyes in the mirror as I wash my hands, then head to the kitchen.

The coffee maker is off, but it must be only just because steam seeps skyward like a dragon lying in wait. I pour the dregs of the pot into a mug. Though I usually take it with cream and sugar, I can't be bothered to retrieve either. The brew is strong. I swallow it one gulp after the next, dreading the last one because I don't know what comes next.

My phone rings, not Hamster Dance, thank fuck. No, it's the generic ringtone for people that don't call me on a regular basis. Someone, not me, bothered to charge it and it sits coiled by the electrical umbilicus that gives it life.

I unplug the phone and turn it face side up. The number is local but unfamiliar. Maybe a wrong number? I could ignore the call, but then I'd need to find something else to occupy my mind. Better to roll the dice.

"What?" My vocal cords are stiff. The word comes out sounding thin and reedy. I clear my throat and try again.

"Nic?" The male voice on the other end is hesitant, as though afraid he's disturbing me.

"Glen?" I ask even though I'm sure.

"Yeah. Did you hear?"

Another swallow before I manage to burp up a, "Yeah."

"I can't believe it," Glen says.

My lip has curled up in an involuntary sneer. "So, what? I'm supposed to cry on your shoulder? Or do you plan on crying on mine, maybe coping a feel while you're at it?"

"I…I…I…," he stutters.

"Spit it out," I growl.

"I was just wondering if you heard if they found her stepfather."

Everything stops. I hang onto the silence as though it's a solid thing. One deep breath, another and then a third, slow on the exhale. Glen, probably out of some dormant sense of self-preservation holds his tongue.

"Her stepfather is missing? Since when?"

"Last night. I just happened to be looking out my window—"

"You were spying on her," I supply.

He doesn't deny it. "And I saw Sarah run out of her house and get in her car. Joe was right behind her. He tried to get in the car after her, but she'd locked herself in."

There's a roaring in my ears. "What happened next?"

"She took off. I think she might have run over his foot because he was limping when he went for his truck."

"He drove off after her? Like he was chasing her?"

"I don't know. He just left after her."

"Was her mother's car there?"

"No. She was working last night. She works every Friday night."

Meaning Sarah had been alone with her predatory stepfather. "And he's still not back." I prod Glen, wanting to make sure I get all the information.

"I'm looking at her house right now. Her mom's there and her older sister. No sign of his pickup."

For the first time in my life, I want to kiss someone and wish it wouldn't be his undoing. "Thanks, Glen. I have to go."

"Go? Go where?"

I hang up without speaking the answer out loud. I close my eyes, imagining the scene Peeping Glen had witnessed. Sarah tearing ass out into the night. Had he hit her? Or had his attention turned sexual? Whatever it was, Sarah had been hell-bent on escaping him.

And she had. Permanently.

My throat closes until I can barely breathe. I suck in a sharp lungful of oxygen and then another. Once I am sure I won't pass out, I head to the bathroom, turn on the hot water and step beneath the spray. I need to spend the rest of the afternoon primping.

After all, a girl should always look her best when she goes out for a night on the town.

CHAPTER 5

A DISH BEST SERVED COLD

I don't bother to notify the aunts when I exit the house at sunset, leaving my phone behind so they have no way to track me and interfere. My plan is to let the night take me where it will. I don't want to waste time arguing. Like Aiden said, better to ask forgiveness than beg permission.

The nagging thought that I should have done this months ago offed the bastard despite Chloe and Addy's warnings, and then Sarah would still be alive, chases me into the truck.

Cool. I need to be cool about this hunt, as together as any other. I must be especially careful since my quarry knows my face. I can't give him the chance to go to ground with the knowledge that he's being hunted.

There are several dive bars in the high country. I don't bother heading to the one where Sarah's mother slings cheap whiskey and dollar drafts. Joe won't go there, too many people know him. I wonder if he feels guilty, or if he's even heard about her death. He could be passed out on a bathroom floor somewhere, drowning in his own vomit. Or he could have lost control of his vehicle in the storm, slammed into a telephone pole. It might be too late.

Hell, maybe Aiden's Wild Hunt absconded with his pervert ass.

It doesn't matter. Those thoughts get shoved aside because they don't help me. Instead, I smile and imagine there's a prickling sensation along the back of his neck, that gooseflesh ripples on his arms because somewhere deep down his body recognizes the feeling of being stalked. Hunted.

And soon to be caught.

My approach needs to be different, too. I can't lure him out, not when he knows me as Sarah's friend. No, I need to follow him, catch him alone and then do my thing. I won't take his license and I'll leave the body where it falls. If anyone asks where I was tonight I'll say out driving, lost in my grief. The aunts will know, but by then it'll be too late.

My knuckles are white on the steering wheel as I cruise the parking lot of the first watering hole. No sign of the rusted-out pickup. The tension mounts as I check out two more places without spotting my quarry.

If I were a drunk pervert that'd just chased an emotionally distraught teenager I had been abusing for years to her death, what seedy rock would I slither under?

The fourth bar is the scabbiest of them all, half the letters are broken in the neon sign so what should read Schmitty's Bar and Grill instead advertises Shitty BanG. The dirt lot is all cracked red clay, beer bottles, and cigarette butts. Surprising that the storm didn't wash more of the garbage away. Then again, this might just be from today's clientele. There, parked under a sickly-looking pine is the red POS truck I've been hunting.

Having memorized the plate months ago, just in case, I am confident it's the correct vehicle. I swing into the far side of the lot and back in. There are no streetlights, so once I shut off the engine, the truck is cloaked in shadow. It fits in here much better than I do. With my blonde hair and sixteen-year-old body, I will stick out like a sore thumb in the Shitty BanG.

Frustration gnaws at me. I want to do something, now.

Why didn't you do something before? Sarah's ghost whispers inside my mind. *Why didn't you save me?*

I swallow, shake my head. She isn't here, isn't with me on this hunt. It's only me and my prey.

But the question nags. I wanted to take him out, recognized the threat he posed to her all along. Maybe not a mortal threat, but I'd seen the way his gaze followed her, had seen the bruises she tried to cover. It isn't like I've never defied my aunts. My journal is proof of that. So why didn't I act sooner?

"It doesn't matter." I speak the words out loud to chase away the ghosts. "I'm acting now. And you can't stay in there forever." I clench my hands on the steering wheel until my knuckles turn white, and then relax them. This is all I can do, to go on from this moment and do my best. The past is set, but the future remains fluid, a river that is free to cut a new path. Loosing a breath, I settle in to wait.

Shitty BanG patrons arrive, the lot filling with cars and trucks, SUVs and motorcycles. Plenty of bodies in all shapes and sizes pass into the dive but none leave. With the engine off, the cab of the truck grows cold. There's a blanket in the backseat and I tuck under it, the weight comforting. After I warm sufficiently, I toss it aside. I can't get too comfortable and risk falling asleep. I might miss him. After tonight Chloe and Addy will have me on lockdown. It needs to happen tonight.

My mind wanders, but I am not alarmed. Part of the lie-in-wait method of hunting involves focus. Just like when I drive and let my gaze flick to the rearview or the clock on occasion, so it comes back sharper to the road ahead. To mindlessly stare out is to lose the sharp edge needed. I allow my focus to shift to another time and place. There is no controlling the memory. I let it wash over me.

I think back to the first real conversation I had with Sarah. I knew who she was of course, just like I knew names and faces of the other students at school. But it wasn't until partway through ninth grade that I really met the girl who was destined to be my best friend.

We are in the cafeteria, another lunch period winding down. Group discussions aren't my thing, so I sit by myself, trying to figure out how to fit in better when she plops down into the seat next to me, uninvited, shining an apple with the hem of her shirt and exposing her toned midriff. "Did you ever wonder what kind of sex made certain people?"

For a moment I'm unsure if she's talking to me, as it sounds like she's in the middle of a conversation. But there's no one else within striking distance. "What?"

"Look at Steve Smith over there. See?" Sarah points to a hulking football player with a distinct Cro-Magnon brow ridge. "I'm betting angry, I caught you looking at my sister's ass sex went into that mix."

I stare at Sarah as though seeing her for the first time. "Yeah?"

She nods, takes a bite of the apple and chews. "I've got this whole theory about it. Now take Harris Winslow," she does a chin jerk and despite myself, I can't help but follow her sightline to the boy with the perfectly parted hair and well-pressed pants. "Every fiber of his being practically screams missionary position. Lights off, pajama tops still on."

"And what about you?" I eye her ripped jeans and spaghetti strap black tank that shows more bra strap than it hides, the nose piercing, the sleeve of tattoos on her left arm that looked like a tangle of vines. If anyone is the least likely person to have a theory of any kind, it's the girl sitting in front of me. "What sort of sex made you?"

Her lips quirk up in a lazy smile. "Wild drunken orgy of course. Possibly a few hallucinogenics mixed in to spice things up."

Her grin is infectious, and I smile back. "On the ground?"

"Writhing in the mud like animals. My mom probably wasted out of her skull but taking it like a champ in every orifice. You know, her typical Friday night." Another bite of the apple with an accompanying eyebrow waggle.

I choke on my water.

She expels a laugh like air escaping a balloon. "Gotcha."

"You paint quite the mental picture."

"It's a gift." She polishes off the apple and chucks the core toward the large trash can, nearly pelting one of the mathletes in the head. The girl glares in our direction and without turning, Sarah gives her the one-fingered salute while asking me, "So, you wanna hang out after school?"

"Do I have a choice?"

She shrugs but because I'm watching for it, I see the brief flash of hurt. She looks away, makes to stand. "Whatever."

"You can come to my place." The words escape before I even think them through. I should give Addy and Chloe a heads up since I've never had a friend over before.

"Whatever," she says again, but this time the tone is different, lighter almost...relieved.

My mind jerks back to the present when the bar door opens and a lone figure stumbles out. The reason Sarah was relieved to have somewhere to go other than home. He staggers around the corner, not heading for his truck, but instead for the trees.

My pulse races. *Now, do it now.* The voice isn't Sarah's, but it doesn't seem to be mine, either. I make sure the interior light in the cab is switched off before slipping out the door and around the corner.

He is loud up ahead of me, crashing with little grace, causing enough of a racket that there is no way he can hear my silent footfalls. I stalk him, the sequence so different than my usual hunting, but at the same time the familiar feeling tears through me like a bolt of lightning down my spine.

One quick kiss, one moment of contact. Maybe I'll whisper *for Sarah* just as the light leaves his eyes. So that he knows. I don't allow myself to think about who will find him, who will tell Sarah's mother that she lost both her daughter and her husband in the same weekend. I have no room for doubt on this hunt. I need to be swifter than thought, stealthy as a shadow.

I need it done.

There, about twenty feet ahead of me, he stops. His back is to me. Without bothering to glance around, he unzips his fly and then the unmistakable sound of liquid on leaves, accompanied by his relieved groan. The back of his neck gleams in the moonlight and I prepare to dash forward and strike, quick as a snake.

A hand wraps around my waist, hauling me back into the darkness.

WHOEVER HOLDS ME IS STRONG, but not smart, since no hand covers my mouth. Not that it matters. I don't scream. Screaming would draw attention, the last thing I want. Instead, I fight. Kicking, thrashing, aiming for sensitive places. My elbow rams into a rock-hard midsection until pain ricochets through my funny bone. It's like bashing my elbow against a concrete wall. Tears well in my eyes but my foot stomps on a booted instep. My captor doesn't cry out, doesn't release me. Doesn't so much as flinch. Sweat coats my body when I am dragged around the corner of the building, away from my truck, from my prey, from all eyes. It's a silent fight for survival.

The reek of the Dumpster and the decay of leaves combine with rancid fryer grease fill my nose as I suck in air. "Who are you?" I hiss.

"Is it she?" The words come from the left, from the direction of the tree line and address my captor. "The one we seek?"

There is no verbal reply from the one that holds me, but the other, with the hissing sort of voice responds as though answered. "What is your name, girl?"

I don't answer. Though I peer into the dark, I see nothing but a shadowy outline. The speaker is of slight build, smaller in stature than I am but the voice has every hair on my neck standing on end. It's a male voice, at least I think it is, but those drawn out *s* sounds are unlike anything I've ever heard.

"Your name?" The speaker moves closer and I can see eyes glowing in the dark, orange eyes that burn like coals. The nose is misshapen, flat with elongated nostrils. And between bloodless lips a forked tongue emerges, flicking the air between us.

All thoughts of hunting, of secrecy, flees. I scream, throwing every bit of energy I have into making enough noise to be heard over the blaring pop-country crossover music emanating from Shitty BanG.

"Quiet," the snake man hisses. "Keep her quiet."

The one holding me shifts his grip to my neck and lifts me until my toes barely scrape the ground. The move cuts off my oxygen supply and my voice. I kick, trying my best to connect with something vital. My blows land with a dull thud and there isn't even a grunt of impact.

Who are these creatures? What are they? Little black dots

dance before my eyes as my brain gives birth to an incredible thought.

Not human.

The speaker with his ember eyes and prehensile tongue isn't just malformed. The one with super strength isn't just a lifter. These beings aren't *Homo sapiens*.

My vision tunnels. My struggles intensify as panic bubbles up. I can't afford to lose consciousness. These aren't the sort of monsters I'm used to dealing with. I've lost control and it's the most terrifying feeling I've ever experienced.

"Will you talk?" The snakelike one slithers closer. "Will you answer our questions?"

I can't respond, unable to speak or nod. My head lolls forward and my hands and legs go still as my vision tunnels.

"Drop her," the speaker commands.

The strong one opens his hands, allowing me to slip through as though I am nothing more than grains of sand. I crash onto the ground at his feet, wheezing in air through my bruised throat.

They wait, silent witnesses to my slow recovery. My lungs feel as if they will burst and my neck is on fire. I need to do something, to try and make lip to skin contact with one of them, no matter how repulsive.

And then get away before the other kills me outright.

"Your name." The snake man offers me a hand up.

That one. It'll have to be him, or her...it—revolting as I find the idea. I reach out to take the offered hand, ready my strength—

A growl rips through the night.

The creature's eyes go wide, confident manner slipping a moment before it's tackled into the dirt. Instinct kicks in and I roll away as a giant wolf pins the snakelike one to the ground. There's a hiss, it's fast but the wolf is faster, stronger as it tears the creature's throat wide.

He looks up at me, those leaf green eyes assessing. Aiden. The snake thing lies dead at his feet. I look away when I see a single drop of blood drip from his exposed fangs.

This might sound hypocritical as hell, but I don't do gore. My role ends at the takedown. It's Addy and Chloe that dispose of the body, sanitize the wood chipper. At first, I was too young and so I deferred to the Fates' decree. *Bodies lead to questions, whereas missing is open-ended. Don't worry, Nic. We'll take care of this.*

A sound snags my attention, like dry leaves being crumbled between leather gloves, only a thousand times louder. I look up and see the strong one falling to dusty pieces before my very eyes. "What the—?"

A warm hand lands on my shoulder. "Are you all right?"

Aiden is back in his human form. I missed his transformation. Somehow it doesn't feel real without witnessing the shift with my own eyes.

He shakes my shoulder a bit, as though trying to wake me. "Nic? Are you hurt?"

I glance up at him. There's blood on his mouth. Somehow, it's even more disturbing that way than on the wolf's muzzle. "No." The word comes out as more of a croak and I lick my lips.

"Good," his hand drops away from my arm. "We need to get out of here."

"We can't just…leave them here." All the times the aunts took care of the evidence would be wasted effort if the police discover this supernatural crime scene.

"I'll take care of it." Aiden tugs at my arm. "After you leave. But you need to go, now."

I stare at the remains and an involuntary shudder racks

my body, stemming from the scrap of shadow that passes for my soul. "What…are they?"

The noise from the Shitty BanG is drowned out by another sound, a sort of distant hum. "Minions. Of someone you don't want to meet. Now come *on*." There's a frantic edge in his voice, one of desperation and fear.

The noise grows louder, and the wind lifts my hair away from my face. It's a gale unlike any I have ever experienced, yet still somehow familiar. The aromas are wild, the same sort of wildness that is a part of Aiden's scent, but there are more layers carried on the wind. Every instinct I possess is clamoring that I should heed his advice and run. I obey, allowing him to pull me away from the inhuman remains, but I balk when instead of heading back into the parking lot, he veers into the trees.

Even naked, Aiden's speed is…inhuman. His every footfall silent. I have all the stealth of a tranquilized bear crashing through the underbrush. To keep up with him I trip over rocks and upthrust roots, dodge low hanging branches, barely avoid having my eyes poked out by leafless twigs. Every heartbeat ricochets in my temples, my breaths tear from me in ragged gasps. My companion doesn't even appear winded. His stride never breaks.

The sound grows thunderous, like giant boulders crashing together. I need to look back, to see what it is that pursues us.

Am afraid to look back because deep down I know.

Hounds bay, rabid in their pursuit and I realize the thunder is the pounding of invisible hoof beats.

The Wild Hunt.

CHAPTER 6

THE HUNT

iden veers sharply to the right, almost yanking my arm halfway out of the socket in his haste. "Here," he says, pressing against a giant oak. "Combine yourself with the tree."

"What?" I gasp.

"You need to combine your life force with that of the tree, let it absorb you." He places my palm flat against the rugged bark of the oak.

I stare up at him, confounded. He doesn't look insane. His gaze is fixed on where his hand covers mine against the tree trunk as though waiting for something to happen.

Behind us, a frantic series of yips and then a baying sound. The cry of a bird of prey and the great pounding of hooves. They are closing in fast, will be here in moments.

"They have our scent. This is the only way." Aiden insists.

"I don't know how." The fear rises within me. What will happen once the Hunt catches us? Will the dogs tear me apart? Or will they spirit me away to some sort of hellish afterlife?

Sarah, I'm sorry I let you down. I was such a lousy friend, using her for my cover. She deserved better, deserves to have her killer put down. I want to do one last thing to make amends, but it looks like my time is almost up…

"Nicneven," Aiden's voice is soft, the pressure from his hand steady. "Concentrate. Feel the life force of the tree. Let it become a part of you, let it pull you in."

My arm shakes. The panic grows, terror overwhelming me for the first time in my life I breathe the words, "I can't."

He ignores me, as though the admission of powerlessness didn't crack my very foundation. "You can, I've seen you do this a hundred times. Listen to it, feel it. Open yourself to it."

He's so sure and his confidence is rock solid. I suck in a slow breath, try to ignore the panic clawing through my intestines like a wild creature. Instead, I listen. It's the only portion of Aiden's instructions that makes any sense. The roar of the Hunt fills my ears, but I strain, search for any sound that a tree might make, try to focus exclusively on that. The wind rustling the budding leaves, the creak and groan of ancient branches that sway in the tempest. I sway along with it, closing my eyes, my hand warming against the trunk.

Against *my* trunk.

And then everything changes. I try to open my eyes and find I no longer have eyes. Moving is out of the question because my feet have morphed into roots. I can't see, speak, smell or taste but I feel more solid. There is a steadiness, a slow wisdom, and surety that ebbs through me. This tree has seen things come and go, passed seasons and decades all by standing tall and still. It soothes me, comforts me, lets me know I'll be all right while we are joined in this way. The tugging of the wind in the leaves, the richness of the nutrients in the soil. I am at once part of the tree and it is part of me, just like Aiden said.

Aiden.

I sense him nearby, not as part of the tree, part of me, but close. As is the Hunt. I feel it as my host would, a great disturbance in its otherwise tranquil environment. Again, that gnawing terror as I wonder if I will be able to separate myself from the tree if the ghostly horde carries Aiden away.

Or destroys him.

But the Hunt rides past the tree, past Aiden. I am sure he's still out there. Did he conceal himself from them somehow? Or maybe he joined with another tree?

Beyond my wood shelter, there is pawing and sniffing. And voices. Female voices. Crying out warlike epithets. Speaking a language that is both foreign and familiar.

"The hounds scent him," one says. Her voice is deep and smooth, like rich velvet.

"Brigit won't be happy if we return empty-handed." A different voice, higher in pitch with a sharply clipped tone. "She's been after him for months. Another failure won't sit well."

Horses whicker and the first speaker responds. "Failure is inevitable only until it is not. The Hunt never fails."

The brisk one barks out the order. "Come, we ride!"

The ground around my roots shakes as though under the onslaught of an earthquake. If I still had teeth I would grit them together, but the tree holds me immobile. That eerie wind gives one final tug against my upraised boughs and then they are gone.

And Aiden is there, with his hand pressed against my bark. "Nic, all clear."

I imagine myself separate from the tree, not allowing the what-ifs to get the best of me. The tree holds on to me. It's like trying to pry my entire body from a vat of tar inch by inch. I fight to reclaim my body, to be separate from the oak again. Its hold is desperately strong and a part of me wants to stay with that steady presence, stay where I am safe.

But I have a promise to keep.

One last pull and the oak bends to my will. There is a shift, and then I can breathe, can smell the cool night air, feel it caress my skin. I fall to the ground along with the other discarded leaves and twigs. Everything hurts, my body aches as if I've just come off a week of the flu.

"You okay?" Aiden crouches beside me, his hand resting on my shoulder.

I flinch at the sound of his voice. "Quit shouting."

"I'm not," he whispers but I clap my hands over my too sensitive ears.

I try to blink up at him but the starlight filtering through the canopy is bright as a spotlight and I throw an arm up to protect my vision. "What's wrong with me?"

He pats my back as though soothing a child but doesn't attempt to answer my question. I appreciate the restraint. Slowly, I relax, the stiffness leaching out of me. My hearing adjusts and I focus on each breath and listen to the music.

I never realized how rich and full of sounds nature could be. Frogs, what must be a million frogs not too far away. The splash of water over rocks from a nearby stream. Bugs flitting about, the hoot of an owl. It's a veritable symphony of the night.

The tension ebbs from my shoulders and slowly I sit up then try to open my eyes once more. The night sky doesn't blind me, which I suppose is a step in the right direction.

"Better?" Aiden's leaf green eyes assess me, the one word spoken on a soft exhale. His scent is overpowering with my too sharp nose. Cedar, sage and that unique hint of wildness on the wind. For a moment, I'm struck with the bizarre urge to curl up into his body and just breathe in the air around him, as though filling my lungs with his scent can fill my soul with his strength. The impulse frightens me more than the Hunt.

"Nic?"

I glance away, so he can't see the battle within. "What happened?"

"You joined with the tree in the manner of a dryad. Coming out again is a bitch, gives newbies major sensory overload. I wouldn't recommend doing it again except in cases of extreme emergency. And never the same tree."

Sensory overload, that sounds about right. "Where were you?"

"Nearby." As answers go, his is amazingly half-assed. I scowl at him, but he changes the subject. "You did well."

"They are hunting you," I say, though I don't bother to phrase it as a question. "Those women."

He doesn't bother to deny it. "Yes."

"They are part of the Wild Hunt?"

"The Unseelie commanders, yes."

"Unseelie?" It's not a term I'm familiar with, though the word stirs something within me. "What's that?"

"A faction of the fair folk. Half of the fey of the Unseelie Court of Alba."

"The fey? Do you mean fairies? You pissed off a bunch of fairies and they sent the Wild Hunt after you?"

He holds my gaze but offers nothing more.

"Who is Brigit?"

"No one you need to worry about." He reaches for my hand. "Come on. I'll see you home."

I pull away abruptly before he can touch me and get to my feet. "I'm fine on my own, thanks. Probably better off than if you come with me since you're a wanted man and all."

His hand drops to his side. "My only wish is to protect you, Nicneven."

Again with using my full name, wielding it like a weapon. No, not a weapon, but more of a tool, like a hammer to drive his point home. His use of my name is meant to pique my curiosity, to convince me to spend more time with him, if only to uncover the truth.

I don't miss the fact that his speech patterns have changed once more. His bearing is constantly in flux, sometimes very casual, at others formal and courtly.

As though he's pretending to be something he's not, but his real identity keeps peeking through. The bastard is trying to manipulate me.

One thing is clear. No one ever told him you don't play a player.

"And I've already explained this to you. I don't want or need your protection." I start walking, wondering if I'm even heading in the right direction but not really giving a shit.

"You have no idea what's out there." True to form, Aiden's dogging my heels.

I ignore him because really, what can I say? He's right, after tonight how can I argue? I have no clue what else is roaming these woods. The snake man and the one that crumbled into dust, a bunch of elven warrior women, never mind the naked shapeshifter hot on my heels.

And let's not forget the teenage serial killer on a mission.

That tree trick might come in handy in the future. A shudder steals over me when I think of how the tree clung to me, like the adhesive on a bandage, tearing little bits of me away as though desperate to hang on to whatever it could. I decide to use it again only as a last resort.

We reach the stream. It's wider than I thought but shallow. I don't remember crossing in when we were running, but the chase might have blotted it from my mind. Maybe we leaped over it at a narrower point? I glance left and then right, relatively sure I am heading the wrong way, but my pride refuses to ask Aiden for help after insisting I didn't need him.

I sit down on the bank and unlace my boots.

Aiden crouches beside me. Completely unselfconscious that he's still naked. Even though I don't feel any sort of attraction to him, it's hard not to look, like a car crash on the highway. Anyone would look. I should just look since he insists on parading around in front of me in the raw. Just look and get it over with and maybe he'll kindly fuck off.

Eyes on my bootlaces, I clear my throat and ask, "Doesn't that bother you?"

"What?"

I gesture at his naked body. "Being without clothes."

He shakes his head. "I've spent most of my life skyclad, as the wolf and as a man. It's the wearing of garments that feels unnatural now."

Most of his life? That would explain the lack of tan lines. I don't want to ask any more than I want to look, but the words slip out. "Where the hell are you from that people don't expect you to wear clothes?"

"Underhill. And not people, the fey."

"So, you're telling me, what. That you're a fairy from a magical kingdom?"

"Technically it's a queendom." He shakes his head. "That's not where I was born, only where I lived for a time. My circumstances were …unusual."

From his tone, I deduce his words are an understatement. I don't believe him, though my rational mind has yet to offer any sort of explanation to the night's events. Aiden had promised not to lie to me, but is it a lie if he believes the nonsense he spews? "And how did you come to live with the fairies?"

He shakes his head, a shaggy lock of hair falling over his eyes. "It's a long story and we have been here too long. You need to go home and stay there."

"Don't tell me what to do." I yank off my socks and stuff them in my boots and then head into the stream. The water is icy on my bare feet, the rocks sharp. "I came out tonight for a purpose and I mean to see it through."

Aiden remains on the bank but raises his voice loud enough so that I can hear him over the splashing. "I'm sorry about Sarah."

My boots fall from my nerveless fingers and hit the water with a splash.

I AM FROZEN, the water washing over my feet and ankles. There is a sucking sensation, as though I am being slowly devoured by the stream, just another rock for it to dull down over time.

Aiden rises to his full height. "It wasn't your fault."

"You know nothing about Sarah." I shake my head. "Or me."

"You couldn't have done anything," he insists.

I won't talk to Aiden about this. I refuse to, but again, something deeper within me overrides my will. "I could have killed him."

"He wasn't for you to kill."

I shake my head. "You sound like Addy. I knew what was happening to her. I should have stopped it before...while it could have helped her."

"He wasn't one of yours," he repeats the sentiment, speaks the words as though he understands.

He can't. But the way he's looking at me—is that pity in his gaze? "What's it to you? I saw you rip a guy's throat out with your teeth not even an hour ago."

Aiden doesn't flinch at the reminder. A stone-cold killer, no remorse, just like me. "Why risk exposure? So he doesn't hurt anyone else? Or to punish him for hurting you?"

I turn back around, determined to tackle the stream and get away from him. "He can't hurt me."

"Sarah is dead, Nic. Taking her stepfather out won't bring her back."

The words hit me with the impact of bullets. I lose my footing and fall to my hands and knees in the water. He's right, I know he's right. Nothing will bring her back, nothing I do or don't do will fix what has been broken.

Behind me, there is splashing and then a hand reaches out for me. "Come with me."

I look at the proffered hand while my own slowly freeze. The urge takes me to just lie down in the stream, let the frigid water numb me back to where I was yesterday before I saw him.

Before Sarah died.

"Nic, please."

I glare up at him, all the bitterness twisting my insides finding an exterior target. "Why do you care, huh?"

His expression is soft. "Because I hate to see you in pain."

Pain. That's what I've been feeling since the aunts told me what happened. Not physical pain, like a burn or a cut, but emotional anguish, mental torment.

Sarah is gone. *Gone.* Never coming back. The tightness in my chest constricts my lungs until I can barely breathe.

"Let me help you," Aiden whispers. "Please."

I take his hand. That flash of heat rushes through me. Awareness of him, of myself and that I've just agreed to something more than a hand out of the water.

Connection, burrowing deep, filling a small part of the echoing cavern inside me.

Aiden helps me out of the stream, then goes back for my forgotten boots. I lay back on the ground, lacking the energy to get up, to go find Joe and make him pay. To dry myself.

My jeans are soaked to mid-thigh, my hands and feet freezing.

My black heart, broken.

Not a clean break either, not something to be set like a fractured bone. How strange that I'd never thought I possessed a heart until it shattered into a million pieces.

"You can walk, or I can carry you." His tone has changed again, making it clear that there isn't a third option.

"I'll walk."

My boots hit the ground with a *thunk* about a foot away from my head. "I'd recommend you put them on."

"They're soaked through."

His gaze doesn't waver, his voice solid as steel. "Better than walking barefoot back to the lot and getting your feet torn up. You can take them off as soon as you're in the truck."

I stare at him for a minute. He stares right back. Ignoring the saturated socks, I pull on the boots.

The playfulness is gone, as is the formality. He's a man with a purpose now and I get the feeling this is the true Aiden.

A survivor on a mission.

Again, he helps me up, this time, not releasing my hand. Each step is accompanied by an unpleasant squish, but Aiden cuts a clear course and we are back at my truck in under fifteen minutes.

"Keys?" he holds out a hand.

I balk at handing them over. I've gotten this far, I can drive home. "I'll take it from here."

He studies me a moment, then nods and steps back. "I need to clean up the mess, but I'll be right behind you. If you want company, leave your bedroom window open."

I blink, a little shocked that he would just throw it out there. "I don't... that is, I'm not...."

A grin steals over his face. "I don't mean for sex, Nic. I

89

was talking about answers. I'm sure you have questions after tonight."

"Good, that's uh, good. Because sex isn't on the table. Like ever. I'm asexual."

I've never told anyone that before. Explaining that I don't experience physical attraction to others is complicated and making such a claim leads to questions, or even worse, comes across as a challenge.

Aiden's eyebrows lift. "You're not attracted to me?"

I stand there in my soggy boots and shake my head. "No."

"Or anyone else? Ever?"

"I only use sexual attraction as a weapon to entice others, but I don't experience it myself."

He smiles then. "Good."

"Pardon?"

"It's good that you've made yourself so clear. You aren't interested in me sexually. It's good to know where I stand. Be sure to let me know if that changes."

I eye him suspiciously. "It won't. So, don't think you can convert me or whatever."

"I have no intention of converting you or whatever." He opens the truck door. "Time to go."

What the hell does that mean? That *he's* not attracted to me? Why does the thought fill me with disappointment? And why am I worrying about such stupid shit?

I climb in the truck and reach out to shut the door. Where naked Aiden stood a moment before there is now only the large black wolf.

He stares at me with hungry green eyes.

I shiver and slam the door shut with him safely on the other side.

Addy and Chloe are waiting on the porch when I drive up. Chloe is parked in her Hampton Bay wicker chaise with a scruffy looking marmalade cat on her lap. Addy stands at the railing, knuckles turning white. Even from several yards away I can tell she is so angry she is practically vibrating with rage.

"Where the hell have you been?" She asks the second I have one wet foot on the ground.

"Out. I needed to get out." Normally I would be a bit careful with Addy being in such a lather, but the nonstop emotion and unearthly events have taken a toll.

"Out? You think that works as an explanation?" Addy's eyes narrow on my wet clothes. "Did you kill him and dump his body in a river?"

For a moment, I have no idea who she means. Then it snaps back, the whole point of my outing. "No."

"Tell me the truth," she gets right in my face.

"Addy, back off," Chloe rises from her chair, still holding the cat, her expression worried.

"She deliberately disobeyed us," Addy snaps, not taking her eyes from me. "Went out on her own after a target that we said—"

"I know what she's done," Chloe interrupts. "But we need to be calm and decide how best to handle this."

My heart sinks. They don't believe me. Don't believe I didn't kill Joe.

"Were you seen?" Addy rests her hands on my shoulders as though preparing to shake me.

I shove her. "Aren't you supposed to be goddesses of Fate? Don't you know whether someone is alive or dead?"

"It's not like we have supernatural lo-jack." Chloe's tone is dry. "It doesn't work that way."

"Well, how the hell would I know? You never tell me anything!" My voice rises to a shout. I've never actually shouted before, let alone at them.

Addy keeps her distance, but her tone is no less volatile.

"This is not the time for some sort of temper tantrum. Did you or did you not go after that man?"

"I did."

Both sisters flinch. "Where is he?" Addy demands.

Something inside my chest withers. I thought that they were on my side, that our odd little family unit fit together because we were all well off-center. The Fates and their adopted serial killer. But looking at the two of them as they stare me down, it dawns on me that it's never been the three of us against the world. It's the two of them keeping most of the world safe from me.

"Nic?" Chloe sets the cat down and it scurries off the porch.

"Probably passed out in some public restroom. I repeat *I didn't kill him*. Why don't you believe me?"

"Birds need to fly. Fish need to swim. You need to kill. It's Mother Nature at her most basic." Addy utters each sentence matter-of-factly.

"Are you saying that I'm an *addict*? Is this some sort of fucked up intervention?" And only yesterday she was arguing that I wasn't a serial killer.

"Let's forgo the drama," Addy growls. "Did you not have the opportunity to take him out?"

"I was interrupted."

"And you expect us to believe that would dissuade you? Gods, Nic! I swear, sometimes you are more trouble than you're worth."

My hands ball into fists. Every muscle shakes. Words come out a low warble that grows louder on each syllable. "I have had *plenty* of opportunities. Dozens, maybe hundreds. I should have taken him out months ago. But I didn't, because of you, your paranoia and fretting. If you think I'm so much trouble, then maybe I should be locked away where I can't hurt anyone else!"

"Nic," Chloe tries, but I ignore her, ignore both of them and storm into the house, slamming the screen door behind me.

I wait until I'm in the shower—where I know they won't follow—to let the tears fall.

CHAPTER 7

THOSE WHO LIE DOWN WITH WOLVES

Another sleepless night awaits me. Though bone-weary, I lie on my side and stare at the window and have a debate on whether to open it. Aiden promised me answers. More than the aunts have ever done. He also seemed relieved when I told him I wasn't attracted to him and he vowed not to try anything. If I trust him and he goes back on his word, I can always smooch him.

Except he knew what I intended to do to Joe. Somehow, he was aware I staked out the Shitty BanG to commit murder. I knew he had been watching me, but had he seen everything I'd done? And, even more disturbing, did he have some sort of defense against my Goodnight Kiss?

That thought causes my lungs to constrict. Imagine, locking lips with someone and not seeing him or her die immediately afterward. Kissing someone because I want to, not to kill, but to demonstrate affection. I've never thought it possible, that someone somewhere would be immune to me. Picturing it makes me shiver.

I haven't been completely honest with Aiden because I don't know if I am fully asexual. That label fits me better than any other. Except maybe for monster. Serial killers don't have sexual feelings, though they do often sustain physical relationships as part of their cover. Mostly, they get their jollies from the kill. But for me, the hunt is about justice, not release. Though I've never experienced sexual lust for another person, not the way it's portrayed on television or online or even at school—where the post-adolescent mating dance is a daily occurrence—I have a hypothesis that it's in me to develop those sorts of feelings.

A hypothesis with no way to prove it. It would have to be someone I trust with the truth about myself. Someone who is also immune to the deadlier effects of my lips. And someone that wants me sexually, even though I wouldn't reciprocate those feelings from the start and is willing to take the risk. An unlikely trifecta for the perfect test subject. Hard to believe potential dates will line up to test for immunity when I've had a hundred percent success rate.

One kiss equals one dead body on the ground.

With chances so slim, I've never seen a relationship as a possibility. Like a chemistry experiment, where the correct combination of elements yields a particular result, but change just one thing and it doesn't work right. But maybe I ruled it out too soon. After all, I've cried twice in one day and came home without offing a target. Miracles do happen.

I wish I could talk to Sarah about this. About all of it. Why didn't I trust her enough when I had the chance? A day ago, I might have tried talking to Chloe, or even to Addy. Not now. My support network is completely decimated.

I probably should know exactly how much Aiden knows about me before I decide anything. Maybe he doesn't know that my kiss is deadly, only that I am a killer. It seems unlikely because he seems to know everything else about me. But there is a chance.

"Screw it," I grumble. Shoving the blankets aside, I storm

to the window and throw the thing up and then stand back to wait.

At first, there is nothing other than the occasional raindrop hitting the metal porch roof as the wind shakes moisture from the leaves. And then light appears at the tree line. Not electric lights but more like embers smoldering from a fire. Thousands of little sparks drift in through the holes in the screen, landing about five feet from me and begin to take shape.

A familiar shape.

Once the last particle joins with the whole there's a white flash and Aiden stands before me, a man once more.

"What are you?" There is no accusation in my voice, only curiosity.

"Tired." He sits wearily on my bed and rubs his eyes. "Pants?"

The ones I'd snagged for him the night before are draped over the seat of my desk chair. I reach for them and toss them to him, then offer my back. Even if he isn't affected by nudity, the last thing I need is Addy walking in here to find him naked on my bed with me eye-humping him. One brawl with a Fate a day is plenty. My gaze drifts to the door to make sure the latch is secure, and I hunt for something benign to say. "When was the last time you slept?"

There is some rustling of fabric then he responds. "The first night you saw me."

I frown. "That was three days ago."

He places a hand on my shoulder. "Got anything to eat?"

I turn around and check to make sure he's covered before moving to the nightstand. Somehow, I knew he was going to ask about food. The bottom drawer holds my secret chocolate stash. Boxes of cookies, cupcakes, Kit Kat, Hershey bars, both with and sans almonds. I try to eat healthy, but chocolate isn't something I'm willing to do without.

"Whoa, the motherlode." Aiden's eyes go wide. "Is there a reason you have all this in here?"

"If I left it in the kitchen, Chloe would decimate it within minutes. She's an unrepentant chocoholic with the nose of a bloodhound." I snag a Kit Kat for myself and gesture to the drawer. "Help yourself."

Aiden studies me a moment, then shrugs and selects a package of cupcakes. "One of the Fates is a chocoholic. Learn something new every day."

I sit in the chair across the room and nibble on the candy. He appears content to eat in silence, which allows me time to gather my thoughts. After the cupcakes, he devours half the chocolate bars, only the ones without almonds, and the entire box of cookies. He stuffs all the wrappers into the cookie box, crumples that into a passable ball shape and tosses it into the trash can on the far side of my desk in a perfect arc.

"Nice shot," I comment. "I usually have to bank it off the wall."

"One of my many talents." He shuts the bottom drawer and then, without asking, opens the top drawer and begins to snoop. Finding nothing of interest, he heads to my book-shelf. I try to swallow my mouthful of chocolate, so I can protest, but he already has the diary out. It looks ridiculous in his big hands, all fluffy, pink and girly. He examines it with a frown. "Doesn't seem like your style."

The chocolate is stuck in my throat and it's an effort not to tear the thing out of his hands before he tries to open it. Did I secure the lock? "Put it back."

One eyebrow arches but he does as he's told. "Can't imagine what you'd write in there. Dear diary, today I daydreamed about kissing my math teacher and watching him twitch and die."

So, he does know everything. I force a smile, unwilling to

let my true terror show. Only Chloe and Addy have ever known so much about me. "He should have let up on the quadratic equation."

As though sensing I need a minute to digest, Aiden continues to peruse my bookshelf. He's a tactile explorer, not content to simply read the titles on display. One long finger grazes down the spine of each book in turn. He selects one on heathen traditions and mythos and opens it up. Flips a few pages, frowns and slams it shut. Replaces it carefully on the shelf before turning to face me.

"So, go ahead and ask your questions. I'll do my best to answer them."

"Why now when you weren't willing to say much yesterday?"

He props himself on the edge of my desk, hands braced on either side. "Because someone is looking for you. That means you aren't hidden anymore."

I think back to my almost abduction. "Those...creatures that you killed. Were they part of the Wild Hunt?"

He shakes his head. "No. Nor are they part of the Unseelie Court. A different faction altogether." His eyebrows draw down as though trying to puzzle something out. "I still don't know how they found out who you are."

"Who do *you* think I am?" This strikes me as the most important question to ask. He knows my secret and isn't afraid to be alone with me in my territory. I need to know what he wants and what I can do to convince him to keep his mouth shut.

Instead of answering, he picks up my cell phone and begins typing. He doesn't ask for a password, shouldn't have been able to use the thing because it was locked with my fingerprint, but when he hands it over to me, I see he's opened a webpage. I glance from it to him and back again before reading aloud.

"Nicneven, Queen of the Unseelie Court and leader of the Wild Hunt." My voice doesn't shake, it is flat and devoid of all emotion. He's insane. I have a wolf shifting, fire wielding madman in my bedroom, wearing my aunt's pants. "That doesn't make any sense."

Aiden returns to the bed, stretches out with his arms behind his head. "Most of what you'll find online is misinformation, but occasionally the humans stumble over a kernel of truth. For instance, some also believe you to be a witch goddess of some kind."

"But that's not the case?" One eyebrow quirks up in challenge.

He shakes his head. "Witches have to generate magic with spells and potions. The fey magic comes from the elements."

"You're saying I'm one of the fey? A fairy queen? How is that possible?"

"I don't know the particulars."

"How convenient." I stare at the photo at the top of the article. It's of a dark-haired woman with green skin seated haughtily upon a throne of bones. Her expression is cruel and cunning. "I look nothing like this."

He shrugs. "You could if you wanted to."

I blink. "Come again?"

"If you used glamour." He answers my question with one of his own. "What powers have manifested so far?"

"Powers?" I shake my head.

He sits up, those muscles in his abdomen contracting with the movement. I note his wound from the night before is barely visible. Does he possess rapid healing abilities, too? "As a Queen of the Unseelie, you can use any of your subject's powers whenever you chose."

"You mean I can do more than just the tree thing?"

Aiden nods. "That gift is from the dryads. If you chose

99

you could breathe underwater like a water horse, shriek like the banshees, shrink in size like the pixies."

"Aren't pixies good fairies? I'd think they'd belong to the Seelie court."

"The fey courts aren't divided into good and evil subspecies. Mortals are notorious for prejudice against all they fear and that's their classification. It makes it easier for them to deal with the world in terms of good vs evil. Gnomes are not all kindly little garden dwellers any more than satyrs are lust-filled beasts, though there are certainly some that fit the mold. In fact, I know a century-old satyr who is still a virgin. Everybody's different." His answers are smooth. He believes what he's telling me.

I try to come up with a question to stump him, to see how deep his delusion goes. "Where's the dividing line then? What's the actual difference between Seelie and Unseelie?"

"It's more of a location-based boundary, different realms where they ended up and established the courts. Of course, over the centuries other cultural differences cropped up. Seelie fey tend to live alongside humans whereas Unseelie fey want to be left the hell alone. And they sometimes eat those that don't abide by their wishes."

"And how can I be queen of these…more hostile fairies when I don't even know they exist. It's not like I ran for office."

"Yours is an inherited title, one of four. Each of you controls one of the four elements. Yours is air because that's how the Wild Hunt travels, on the gusts of the north wind. Brigit is the other Queen of the Unseelie. Mistress of the Mantel. Her element is fire. She reigns half the year, from the first day of spring through Samhain. You tire more easily once spring arrives, right?"

I suck in a breath. "How do you know that?"

He gives me a small smile. "I remember it's not your season. A sizable portion of your magic shifts to her. You are weakest at midsummer, strongest at midwinter. The opposite is true for Brigit. Right now, you are officially off duty until Samhain though you still retain your innate powers and can still tap into those from your subjects."

"And the Seelie Courts? Earth and Water?"

"Soladin, Brigit's Seelie counterpart is the Lord of the Land. He's one of the god Pan's bastard sons. He's relatively new to the title, having inherited it from one of his older brothers. We don't hear much from his court. If he's anything like his dad he's far too busy plowing every field that comes along. Wardon co-rules at the same time you do. He's Master of the Waves. Too bad he never manages to master his own arrogance."

His story, the way it blends seamlessly with the bits and pieces I know of my history…can he be right? "But I'm only sixteen. I've never ruled, never even seen a fey."

"Not in this life," he agrees.

I huff out a breath. "Aren't fairies immortal?"

"Forever young," he corrects. "Doesn't mean they can't die. Or be killed." Something in his voice grows quiet, his gaze loses focus.

Just when I think his story can't get any stranger. "You're talking about me. Saying that what, I've been reincarnated?"

"It's…complicated." He stifles a yawn, the fatigue evident in every line of his skin. "I need to crash. May I sleep here tonight?"

Disappointment fills me. He's just revealed a few pieces of a puzzle, but not nearly enough to see how they fit together or to give me a clear picture. But he does look ready to pass out. "The Hunt won't find you here?"

He shakes his head. "The Fates have a protection ward in

place around the property. It's like a secret room no one from Underhill can detect. You're officially off the fey grid."

Something else they've never bothered to tell me. "Just answer one more question. Do my aunts...the Fates...know what I am?"

He hesitates. "When you were born, they were charged with protecting and raising you, so yes, they know."

And they never told me. I turn away, unable to bear his gaze. "I'll get you some blankets."

"Don't bother." Aiden heads for the bathroom, leaving the door open a crack. A moment later the sweats are tossed out and land in a heap. Another heartbeat and the large black wolf pads into the room launches himself up, turns around twice at the foot of the bed and then lies down with a groan, taking up more than half the mattress.

"I meant you could sleep on the floor." I grouse.

His eyes close, a sure signal that he won't budge anytime soon.

"At least move to one side." I shove him with negligible effect and then give up and head for the bathroom to brush my teeth.

When I return, I see he's repositioned himself, sprawling long ways across the left side, using two-thirds of mattress real estate. All I can think is I'm glad my bed is a queen.

Just like me, apparently.

I pick up the sweats, drape them over the chair, then shut off the light. Maybe I should have some sort of apprehension about climbing into bed with a full-grown wolf. He might be nuts, but he appears harmless, his big furry chest rising and falling in a steady rhythm. Besides, if he wants to tear my throat out he could do so at any time.

I slip beneath the covers, sure all I've learned will spin around in my mind and keep me up all night. But fatigue and mental overload demand their due and I drift off as soon as my head hits the pillow.

I WAKE to find myself in another bed, a larger bed, with Aiden's body pressed against mine. Not Aiden the wolf though. Aiden the man has his arms wrapped around me in a very familiar way. One tucked under the curve of my waist with his big warm palm pressed into my midsection, the other draped protectively over me as though physically shielding my body with his own. His front is pressed tightly against my back, his face is buried in my hair, his breathing deep and even.

We are both skyclad, covered only with soft furs.

Sunlight filters through gauzy curtains that look like cobwebs. The windows beyond are thrown open to allow the spring breeze in. From my position, I see a body of water, possibly a lake, the surface sparkling like diamonds in the sun. Beyond great green rolling hills stretch to the horizon. The room smells warm and sweet like honeysuckle and fresh grass, rich earth. And Aiden. The morning is ripe with possibility.

I turn my head and look at him, a smile on my lips. My handsome consort. To think, I used to dread the coming of spring and all it meant. Now I long for it, for the time of year when I can just be. Be with him. Be me with no other worries or courtly drama plaguing me.

His eyes open, that vivid green just as breathtaking as it had been the first time I saw it, centuries ago. "My queen. What is thy bidding?"

"None of that, not today." I slap playfully at him. "I just want to enjoy us."

His perfect lips curve up in a grin. "As her highness commands."

Without warning he dives beneath the covers, his hands tickling my exposed flesh. I shriek and swat at him, laughing with my playful lover until I am breathless. Only then do the light touches deepen into familiar caresses. My gasps for breath morph into groans of pleasure as he kisses his way down my stomach to...

I sit bolt upright in an entirely different bed, the familiar room still dark, a cry on my lips.

Beside me Aiden—still a wolf—lifts his head and tilts it to one side as though asking me what's wrong.

"Nothing," I shake my head to clear the image from my mind. Of him as a man. As my lover, my consort. It felt so real. "It's just a dream."

I say the words to convince myself as much as to convince him. Just a dream. Brought on by his vivid imagination and my meandering thoughts about sex. If I'm not careful, he will suck me completely into his fantasy world.

Aiden stares at me a moment as though challenging my claim that everything's all right. His scrutiny along with the imagined intimacy makes me squirm.

"Go back to sleep," I snap.

With a groan, he lowers his head and shuts his eyes. After a moment I force myself to do the same.

This time I know it's a dream from the beginning because I'm looking in the mirror. The face isn't mine but it's not the green-skinned woman either. My hair is longer, so long I could sit on it if I chose. A woman—fairy judging by the gossamer wings—stands behind me a hairbrush in one hand, weaving it into two corn silk plaits, one over each ear.

"You're with the Hunt tonight, my queen?" she asks.

"Yes."

"What time shall I tell your nobles to arrive?"

I glare at her reflection in the mirror. "When I damn well please. Now leave me."

She fastens the second braid, falls into a hasty curtsy while murmuring, "As her majesty wishes."

I sit straight, waiting for her to exit my chamber. The part of me that is still Nic notes the click of her heels on the stone floor, feels the warmth of the overlarge fireplace roaring with a blazing inferno, the sounds of merrymaking from somewhere not too far off. The scents are dark and rich, familiar and foreign.

My eyes—icy blue still though somehow different—go to my reflection, studying the perfect features without pleasure. Everything is sharper, from the jut of my chin to the point of my ears. I've never given much thought to blemishes, but my skin is as smooth as a porcelain dish, as though it's never known a pimple. The small hairs on the back of my neck lift and I whip my gaze towards the crackling in the hearth. My pulse quickens, and I can't shake the feeling that something momentous is about to happen...

The scene shifts. I am on horseback, my knees guiding my steed through the autumn night. Fall wind fills my lungs, harvest scents in my nose. My mount's hooves don't touch the ground but glide on currents of air. Behind me, the Wild Hunt surges forward, my trusted commanders flanking me on either side, whooping and shouting out warnings to the mortals below. Our prey is across the Veil, the villain whose time has come. He is a predator that preys on the weak of his own species. Young boys have disappeared from the village and the elders have left out offerings for the fair folk, asking for protection.

They will get vengeance instead.

I raise my sword and slice, creating an opening in a fabric that cannot be seen with the naked eye, then ride through.

Distance is no obstacle for us, we can cross leagues in half a heartbeat, oceans in a few strides. We will capture and consume his polluted soul. Justice will be done.

I live for these moments. When I can play with moonlight and stalk with shadows. Not the posturing of court, certainly not receiving the Unseelie nobles as my sister does. Brigit enjoys taking males betwixt her legs. Whether they are fucking her for her status, for her favors, or for the chance to be named her new consort and have the rank and power that title carries. I have never selected a consort, only accept the males during my fertile time for the sake of procreation, as duty demands. I crave only my trusted warriors at my back, the wind tugging at my hair and the music of the night in my ears.

It's a shame I'll have to go back, to accept them into myself for the entirety of the day. I spotted them on my way to the stables, lining up outside that antechamber where I will have to receive them each in turn.

"My queen," it is Freda, my second in command. "Is aught amiss?"

"I am right where I wish to be," I tell her honestly. Then, curling my fingers in my mount's mane I surge ahead, preparing to bring the Hunt down to a field near our prey's homestead.

Silent as phantoms, the Hunt slows to a stop. No candlelight burns within the small hut but there is light coming from the barn. Our well-trained hounds pause alongside the horse, their growls fading to stillness.

"Shall we go in for him?" Nahini, the newest member of our ranks, whispers.

We could ride through the walls, completely unseen and snatch the prey up. But this night I want to take my time, to enjoy claiming the soul of the damned. I shake my head and dismount. "I will fetch him."

"My queen?" Freda arches one blond eyebrow.

I hold up a hand to forestall her inquiry. Her mount whickers low and shifts as though picking up on his rider's agitation, but she wisely holds her tongue. I stalk forward, eager to find the villain and end him once and for all.

The man is passed out in a pile of hay, an empty bottle that smells strongly of spirits discarded at his feet. He won't even be a challenge.

I reach for him, ready to seize him by his throat when I hear a noise from a darkened corner. It sounds like a moan of pain.

Frowning, I leave the drunkard and head toward the dark. A boy is tied there, a collar around his throat. No, not a boy, a man, though a young one. He is half-starved with all his ribs visible, arms and legs looking like sticks. He is dirty and bloody from head to toe and from the looks of things, he's been horribly beaten.

I should leave him here, take what I came for and ride off. Even as I think it, he makes that noise again, not an exclamation of pain, but of heartbreak. A soul wound. My own recognizes it as the sound it makes every month during my fertile time. Weariness of spirit, a pain from within, that cannot be so easily assessed. The sound of one that's been forced to endure unwanted sexual desire. The sound of a rape victim.

My lip curls in revulsion, not at him, but at what has been done to him.

One eyelid cracks open, a bright green iris barely visible between eyelashes crusted with blood. "Kill me, please."

I've heard that request before, from countless victims that would rather die than endure the agony of life. I usually grant their wish, smirking all the while knowing that death isn't a reprieve. But this young man isn't mine to dispatch. I try to read him, come up empty. He's not a mortal, but somehow, he's been captured and used by one. How?

"Please," his voice is soft as he begs. "Have mercy on me."

Pain radiates off him in waves, his eyes dull with it.

"Why do you wish to die?" I ask.

"Because," he coughs, blood spattering the dirt by my boots. "I don't deserve to live."

He might die anyway. Before I think better of it, I unsheathe my sword, the silvery blade singing as it comes to life, glowing with a purple light. Seelenverkäufer, the soul reaper, is the blade of the Unseelie, of the Hunt. My weapon, tied to my life force and those collected with it. It is said to contain a fraction of spirit from all those it has felled in battle. His eyes remain open and fix on the blade, on me, as though wishing to see death coming. A warrior's heart lurks in that sunken chest.

Before I can think better of it I raise the blade and swing down with all the force I can muster, the razor's edge singing a mournful dirge as it cuts through the air to its target.

.

CHAPTER 8

SECOND CHANCES

One thought wakes me from my fitful dreams. It forces my eyes open as adrenaline dumps into my bloodstream.

Somehow, I'd been brought back from the dead.

And if I was resurrected, Sarah could be as well.

It's also the best way to test if Aiden is telling the truth. I have no doubt that he's some sort of supernatural creature. I've witnessed the displays of his power. It doesn't mean he's telling me the truth about myself though. That I'm a queen of the fey and I died and was brought back. The best test I can think of is to see if the same can be done for Sarah.

Sitting up, I glance around but there is no sign of man or beast, though I do hear the shower running. Unwilling to wait for him to finish, I throw back the covers and head into the bathroom. It's not like he's shy and if he's going to strut around naked all the time, I'd better get used to it.

I spy him through the steamy glass doors. Aiden stands under the spray, both palms resting flat on the shower wall. Every muscle is taut with tension, his head bent down, his eyes closed as though in defeat.

For a moment I flashback to that bizarre dream, of finding a half-starved Aiden chained up and begging for death. Obviously, he is still very much alive. So, did that mean I'd spared him? Or had it just been a vivid product of my imagination?

Either way he has the answers I need and waiting patiently is not in my nature.

Raising a hand, I rap smartly on the glass door. "I have a question."

He jumps a small motion which is oddly satisfying to me. Aiden always puts me at a disadvantage so seeing him startle levels the playing field a bit.

Water drips from his shaggy dark hair and he has a light growth of stubble on his chin. He looks cranky and not thrilled to see me. Very different from that first dream. "Can't it wait?"

"No." I reach for a towel and tap my toe while he shuts off the water.

He slides back the shower door and reaches for the towel. "What is it then?"

"Sarah. I want to know how to bring her back."

He stills in mid swipe. "You can't."

"You said I have all this power I could tap into. Another fairy out there somewhere could—"

He shakes his head rapidly and water spatters my pajamas. "Not over life and death."

"Well, who brought me back?"

"It's different, you were an immortal made mortal. Sarah was just a mortal."

I get in his face. "Sarah was not just an anything and her life was cut short."

To his credit, he looks abashed. "Apologies. I didn't mean to insult your friend."

"So, who did it? You said the Fates took charge of me. Were they involved?"

"In a way," he hedges.

I put my hands on my hips, ready to chew him out when there is a knock on my bedroom door, followed by Chloe's raised voice. "Nic?"

I curse and wave at Aiden. "Shoot. I need to deal with her."

He opens his mouth, most likely to argue and I add, "Don't move."

I slip through the bathroom door and shut it behind me and then stride to the bedroom door. Chloe stands there holding a tray. Her scent is sharp, like licorice, which informs me that she's feeling apprehensive. She frowns and studies my pajamas and obvious bed head. "I thought I heard the shower going."

"Just waiting for it to warm up. Is that for me?" I gesture to the tray.

She nods. "You didn't eat anything last night."

It's apparent she's gone out of her way. There are doughnuts and Danish from the bakery in town as well as fresh fruit, whole-grain toast with jam and coffee. My stomach is in knots, but Aiden will appreciate the meal. I take it from her and mutter thanks.

"Addy needs me at the clinic. You'll stay in the house?"

"Are you asking if I'm going to go hunting again?"

She rolls her eyes and offers a self-deprecating grin. "Subtle, huh?"

"I have nowhere to be."

She turns and then hesitates. "About last night. It's not that we don't trust you. And Addy didn't mean what she said."

It's a struggle not to flinch at the remembered words. *More trouble than you're worth.*

"We're just so worried about you," Chloe finishes.

"You didn't believe me." I wrap my arms around myself. "Neither of you."

"We want to. You had such a rough start in life and you've had so much to deal with, what with your ability and all. And losing Sarah can't be easy. I know what it's like to lose someone close to me."

I look away from the naked pain on her face. If my plan works, I won't have lost her for much longer.

Her tone brightens. "Will you come by the clinic later? Those pesky files are stacking up again."

I force a smile. "Maybe. Thanks again for breakfast."

"Anytime kid." She pats me once on the shoulder and then picks up a cat carrier and leaves.

I go to the window, watch her load the cat and then climb into the truck. Only when the dust has settled do I set down the tray and return to the bathroom to find Aiden in the same position as when I left. *Exactly* the same position, fingers clenched around the towel at his waist, lips parted as though he flash froze that way. Something is very off.

"What's with you?" I ask.

He doesn't even blink.

What sort of game is he playing? "Aiden, tell me what's going on."

"You told me not to move," he huffs the words out like a puff of air, his lips tight as though fighting some sort of invisible hold. "So, I can't."

Not possible. "You mean, you have to do whatever I say?"

He doesn't budge but he glares at me in pure exasperation.

"Move now," I say, feeling odd. "Any way you want."

He releases a breath and sags a bit. "Thanks. And to answer your question, not whatever you say. It's whatever you command. If you order me to stop breathing, I'll have to do it."

I stare at him, uncomprehendingly. "How? Why?"

He shakes his head. "It's a long story. Do I smell food?"

"Breakfast. The house is empty. Go—," I was about to say go help yourself, but rephrased before the words come out as an order. "You can help yourself."

He sends me a sheepish smile that conveys his gratitude. "Thanks. I'm starving."

Needing a minute to myself, I wait until he leaves the bathroom and turn on the water in the sink. How many times did I inadvertently command him since we met? I remember his hasty exit from the truck. I had ordered him to get out, hadn't I? He didn't want to go, it had been pouring rain, but I'd commanded him. And he'd been forced to obey.

As my lady desires.

There had been other times, too. He'd dropped my journal like it was hot when I'd told him to put it back.

The dream—memory? —of the two of us in bed on that lazy spring morning comes roaring back. *As her highness commands.*

Oh, no. Oh *shit*.

Though my stomach is empty, bile churns up. I lunge for the toilet and fall to my knees, retching.

He was *my* consort. *My* lover. That's how I—the me in the dream—had thought of him. Like a possession. A belonging. A well-earned prize. Had I freed him from those iron fetters only to enslave him in another way? Did I put some sort of mystical compulsion on him, something so strong that it outlasted my first lifetime?

No wonder he'd grinned when I told him I was asexual. After our previous relationship, it must be a relief to know he won't be forced to…service me.

If it's true, I am no better than those I hunt.

I flush and sag against the wall, banging my head softly against the plaster. *What a mess.*

A soft knock on the bathroom door. "Nic? You okay?"

"Fine." My voice comes out as a croak. "Just going to brush my teeth. Do…whatever."

I squeeze a quarter of the tube of pale blue toothpaste out and brush my teeth thoroughly. Then floss. Then chug half the bottle of mouthwash. The overload of spearmint does nothing to settle my squishy stomach, but at least my mouth feels clean, even if nothing else does.

I stare at my reflection in the mirror. I need to ask him about it, long story or not. A niggling voice in the back of my head insists I should plot a way to use this new discovery to my best advantage. If I tell him to leave me alone forever, he'll have to do it. Problem solved. If I order him to help me find a way to resurrect Sarah, he won't fight me on it.

But can I really do that? Force him to do things he doesn't want to do? My insides twist again. I brace my hands on the sink and hold my own gaze in the mirror.

"You," I tell the blonde girl staring back at me, "Are not a rapist."

Saying it aloud makes me feel a bit steadier. I take a deep breath and repeat the statement.

Another tap on the door, followed by the rattle of a handle. "What's going on in there?"

"Keep your pants on," I bark, and then instantly regret it. "Sorry, I didn't mean it that way."

I open the door to find a grinning Aiden toying with the waistband of the sweats. "Does that mean you want me to take my pants off?" he asks, thumb tracing along the elastic band of said pants suggestively.

"No!" I bark and then shut my eyes. "I mean, I'd appreciate it if you wear them, but go ahead and do whatever you like. It's your choice."

His grin widens. "You're really freaked out about this, aren't you?"

"Yes, I am! I could kill you by accident."

He throws his head back and laughs. It's a full-throated guffaw that seems to come from deep within him.

"Stop that," I snap, but instantly regret it when the sound breaks off. "Sorry. What I mean is, what's so funny?"

There's a sparkle in his leaf green eyes. "You don't see the delicious irony? You've been toying with the idea of killing me since you first saw me. But now you're afraid you might do so by accident?"

Heat crawls up my neck and I stare at the carpet, not wanting him to see the confirmation in my gaze. "I never seriously would have gone through with it unless you'd attacked me or someone helpless. That's my rule."

Aiden curls one large finger beneath my chin, forcing my eyes to meet his own. "One, you won't kill me by accident. So, get that out of your head. And two, since when does a single life matter so much to you?"

If there'd been any harshness or accusation in his words I might have used my newfound ability and told him to literally go kick rocks. There is no condemnation in his voice, only curiosity.

He'd promised me honesty and, after all, I might have put him through in my last life, I feel the need to return the favor. "Since Sarah."

He nods as though he understands. "You asked before about a way to bring her back. Do you still want to know how?"

My heart flutters in my chest like a fledgling bird ready to leave the nest. "There's really a way?"

He nods. "Yes. The magic is beyond you, beyond even the Fates. And there's a steep price."

"But you know someone who can do it?" I ignore his warnings. There's no price I won't pay for Sarah's return.

"I could tell you about it. While we eat." He offers me a hand and after only a brief hesitation, I take it. His calloused palm scrapes against mine and again that sense of connection sweeps through me. With his free hand, he balances the tray and we head to the dining room table together

Aiden sets the tray down. He releases his hold on me only to pull out a ladder-back chair. It's such a civilized gesture, almost foreign in my everyday world. Not to mention totally out of character with a being that spends most of his time running naked through the woods. I murmur thanks and sit and then wait for him to settle across the big farm table. I want to know about our relationship before—his relationship with my previous self—but I am unsure how to ask. And though I am eager to discover what we need to do to retrieve Sarah, I'm hesitant to say anything that might come across as a command. What do normals discuss over breakfast? I study the still full pastry box and pour myself a cup of coffee. "I'm surprised there's any food left."

He feigns an indignant expression, which contradicts the air of mischief. "Did you think I'd eat you out of house and home?"

I answer with a shrug and attempt to match his bantering tone as I pass him the coffee carafe. "Well, I did set a wolf loose in our kitchen."

"I'm not without manners. Except when ordered to be so." A secret smile steals across his face.

Not touching that one with a ten-foot pole. "Were you born a wolf? Or a man?"

The smile vanishes, and his expression grows a little darker, a cloud passing over the sun. "Neither. I was born a god."

I blink. "A god? As in all-powerful, omnipotent, religious deity?"

"Not exactly." He offers me the pastry box and I snag a strawberry Danish.

I consider what I've seen him do. "Either you were a shape-shifting god or one with an affinity for wielding fire. And Aiden is a Gaelic name."

One corner of his mouth twitches up. "Very good. It means little flame. That's not the name I was born with, but I took it as my own. Fire wielding is in my blood, so it seemed appropriate."

"How did you become," I have no words to accurately describe him and settle for a vague, "What you are now?"

"It was a punishment." Anticipating my next question, he adds. "Not for anything I did."

"Then what—?"

"In order to bring Sarah back," he interrupts, his tone more forceful than I've heard. "We need to talk to a giant. And it just so happens that I know one."

"A giant?" Though it's exhausting repeating everything he says, I can't seem to break the habit.

"Giants are the oldest creatures in the world and they have knowledge that no one else does."

I nod slowly. "So where do we find a giant?"

"Beyond the Veil."

At my blank look, he elaborates. "Magic is hidden from the human world by an invisible magical cloak. It's transparent, separating the world you know from Underhill, the realm of the fey and other magical creatures. The Veil originally protected the humans from being wiped out entirely but in recent years it has also kept magic from discovery by humankind. That's why there aren't a thousand videos of fairies and shape changers and other magic wielders online."

"Where did it come from?"

He shrugs. "It's always been there, undetectable unless you know what to look for. It's light and moveable and ever-changing. Think of it like a curtain blowing in the breeze."

Instantly I recall that dream again. The soft gusts of air scented with spring. His hands exploring my body. I survey him closely. Had his word choice been deliberate? Did he somehow know about the dream? He doesn't look as though he's needling me, but he keeps his emotions in check.

I shift in my suddenly uncomfortable seat and set down my uneaten Danish. "So, how do we get to the other side of this magical barrier?"

"With use of an In-Between."

"A what?"

"A space that is partway between this world and Under-hill, like a fold in the fabric of the Veil. A place of transition. If you can shrink us small enough we can look for a fairy ring or we can wait until midnight. In the heartbeat between one day and the next, the entire world becomes an In-Between as though the fabric of the Veil parts."

"What about your house?" I ask as something snaps into place. "Is it an In-Between, too?"

"Yes. It's a direct passage from the heart of the Unseelie Court." He reaches for the last slice of toast. "But it's not the best idea."

"Is that why you warned me off when I showed up there?"

Aiden nods. "It's an official channel and leads directly to the court. All crossings are monitored. We still don't know which faction was after you and the Hunt is still on my trail. We're better off flying under the radar. Aren't you hungry?" He gestures to the forgotten Danish.

I shake my head and push the plate across the table. "You can have it if you want. So, fairy ring or midnight are the only real choices?"

He nods but doesn't take the pastry. "I recommend the

fairy ring. We won't risk passing by the Hunt and it'll be good for you to practice borrowing abilities."

With the bonus that we would be gone before Chloe and Addy came home. "All right. How long will we be gone?"

He hesitates. "Time moves differently in Underhill, not anything steady you can clock. We might be gone for what feels like a few days, only to discover that centuries have passed."

My mouth falls open. "*Centuries?*"

A solemn nod. "The world might look very different on this side of the Veil when you come back. Are you sure you want to do this?"

I swallow. My throat is suddenly bone-dry. Centuries. I could save Sarah, only to return her to a world she won't remember, all her family and friends long since turned to dust. Although in the case of her stepfather, that's a bonus.

"There's more," Aiden adds quietly. "You're safe here. Hidden. No responsibilities beyond your own life. It's what the old you, the Nicneven I knew before, wanted most of all. The freedom to live without court demands or intrigue bogging her down."

I thought of Addy and Chloe's reaction last night, of how they didn't believe me when I told them I hadn't killed Joe. They'd been dismayed at the thought, at the same time they were ready to swoop in and help hide the evidence. *More trouble than you're worth.* Maybe it would give them a measure of peace to live without the responsibility of cleaning up after me for a few—hundred—years.

I hadn't done what I could for Sarah before and she'd paid the price. She never had the chance to leave our small mountain town the way she'd always dreamed, to see the world. I owe her. "I need to do this, whatever the cost."

Aiden leans back in his chair and nods once. "Then pack a bag. I'll go find our exit."

❄

I PACK ALL the protein bars from the cupboard, about a week's worth for me, a day's for Aiden, and the remaining candy from the nightstand stash. A change of clothes that I squeeze into a zippered plastic bag to keep watertight and free from potential melting chocolate stains. A spare toothbrush and toothpaste, hairbrush and a bar of soap. Plus, a tiny First-Aid kit. I have no idea what conditions will be beyond the Veil, but I've always been fastidious and don't plan to "rough it" any more than necessary.

Essentials packed, I add a small framed photo of me and Sarah from last summer. Chloe had taken it, though we hadn't known it at the time. We were lying on beach towels, side by side at the lake. Sarah had on her cat-eye sunglasses and I wore a Carolina Panthers ball cap. Though I can't recall what we'd been talking about, both of our faces are animated, full of life.

We'd be that way again if I have anything to say about it.

I pick up the pink fuzzy diary and hold it for several long moments. Leaving it behind feels like a mistake. The aunts will tear my room apart for any clue to where I've gone. They will certainly find this and most likely destroy it. Part of me desperately wants to pack it, to have it with me. But we need to travel light and I don't want to risk losing it.

In the end, I dig a hole beneath my bedroom window and bury it several feet underground, then set a potted rosemary bush on top.

Task complete, I take one last look around the room. Without conscience thought I pull the copy of Norse myths from the shelf, the same one Aiden frowned at last night. Before I can question the impulse, I shove it in my backpack.

"All set?" Aiden appears as I'm cinching the strings. Again, there is no noise from his footfalls, as though he pads on wolf feet even while in human form.

I nod and pull the pack over my shoulders, so my hands will be free. "Did you find what you were looking for?"

"Several. Spring is the best time for fairy rings, what with all the restless fairies crossing through the Veil, hunting for food or entertainment."

I grab two metal water bottles from the fridge, use the bicycle clips to secure them to either side of my pack and then follow Aiden out into the woods. The earth is soft and smells of loam and new plant life. Old leaves and sticks snap beneath my boots and I look back to see one set of footprints —mine. Aiden's progress goes utterly unmarked. How can he avoid every dry twig without leaving a single trace?

The air is still but heavy with the threat of more rain. The scrubbier trees give way to birches and pines, and maybe it's my imagination but it feels as if they are calling to me. As though they know I can meld with them. A shiver runs through me. I spent hours climbing trees when the aunts had first brought me to this place, swung from the branches and napped in their shade. I doubt I'll ever see them as such inno-cent props again.

Aiden climbs one of the steeper slopes and stops. "Here."

I glance down and spy a circle of beige capped mush-rooms. "This?"

He nods and moves to stand on the opposite side of the ring so he's looking me in the eyes. "Do your thing."

I cast him a dark look. "I don't know what my thing is, remember?"

He doesn't appear fazed. "It's like with the tree. You need to focus on what you want to have happen. Envision us small enough to fit in the middle of those mushrooms. Not so small that we float away in the breeze though. Without wings, we'd have no control where we would end up."

Panic grips me. It's not a feeling I enjoy though I am becoming more accustomed to it. "You're telling me I could overshoot this? Shrink us down too far?"

"Don't think about what could go wrong," he cautions.

"Then you shouldn't have suggested it," I snap.

His voice is steady, soothing. "You need to picture the end result, those mushrooms as tall as trees, and us meeting in the middle of them. Only there can we find a fold in the Veil."

I release a huge lungful of air. "I don't know if I can do this."

"You can." Aiden's faith in me is absolute. "Think of it like borrowing powers from your subjects, the same as borrowing a pencil from another student. Not yours to keep, but it's a tool you need to get the job done. And as soon as it is, you'll give the tool back to the rightful owner."

He's so sure, and his belief in me, in my abilities, boosts my confidence. I nod once then close my eyes. The red-gold light from the sun strikes my face and I lift my chin, letting the world that is fade.

Imagine us three inches tall. Small enough to enter the fairy ring, to cross through the Veil. To save Sarah.

You can do this. I don't know if Aiden says the words aloud or I hear them in my mind. I reach out across the ring, not physically, but mentally and sense him there, purple and red outlines in the shape of a man.

We need to be smaller, to be three inches tall.

Behind my lids, the light flickers, blue and purple sparks exploding like fireworks.

Three inches tall. Three inches tall. Three inches tall.

The wind lifts my hair away from my face and there is a noise, like the roaring of an oncoming train.

I open my eyes and the world I know is gone.

CHAPTER 9

BEYOND THE VEIL

I blink and look around, trying to figure out what happened to the field. It appears I've transported myself into some sort of jungle. The bright sunlight is blocked out by oversized greenery. I turn in a slow circle, wondering how I screwed up. No sign of Aiden, the field, the fairy ring. The air is much denser here, so wet it's almost tropical. Had I somehow borrowed the wrong power and transported myself to the Amazon?

Up ahead, what looks like a mile off, I spy something large and beige. A structure of some sort?

Then it hits me. I'd done it. My body shrank in size and what looked to me like a forest canopy was really the un-mowed field I'd been standing in, as seen from a bug's perspective. What I thought was tropical humidity is really morning dew that has yet to evaporate. The brown shapes in the distance are those of the mushrooms.

Jubilation fills me and a grin spreads over my face. It had worked. Sort of. I was much smaller than the three inches I'd intended. And there is no sign of Aiden. Where could he be?

He'd been standing across the ring. And if those mushrooms were a mile off from me, then Aiden is two miles directly in front of me.

Making sure my backpack is secure, I stride off toward the mushroom. Considering his persistence to dog me, Aiden will probably meet me there. It amazes me how much space exists between blades of grass, like walking through a well-planned grove. The terrain is rough and uneven, the red clay almost like mud as it sticks to my boots. A huge mound rises before me, a half-buried stone poking up from the ground. The mushroom stalk is just on the other side of it. If I go around, it might take longer, or I could miss Aiden altogether.

Decided, I find a toe hold and start climbing. The stone is rough against my palms, but it's craggy enough to allow me plenty of hand and toe holds.

I am halfway up when I hear a strange buzzing sound.

"Nic!" Aiden's voice calls out. "Where are you?"

"On the rock outside of the ring."

"Stay where you are!" he hollers.

The buzzing is growing louder, almost deafening. "What's that noise?"

"There's a nest of mud wasps inside the ring. Make us big again and we'll find somewhere else."

"You're kidding, right?" I can't see his face, can't see anything but the planes and angles of the stone I'm still traversing but he must be joking. "I barely made it work *this* time."

"They could kill you at this size!" There is a grunt and a thud. "Make us big again. We can wait until midnight."

To hell with that. Finally, I reach the summit of my own personal peak and poke my head over the top. The sight before me is like something out of a dream. Aiden is in between two wasps, a sharpened stick in each hand. He twirls them like makeshift spears. I gape as a wasp dive-bombs him and he thrusts with one spear at the other while tucking into a roll to avoid the charge. A third wasp hovers in the background, as though waiting to strike the killing blow.

I scramble up and over the rock, half sliding, half free-falling down the other side on my butt. I hit the ground with a thump, my teeth clacking together hard. Aiden jabs one of his spears into a dive-bombing wasp. It freezes in midflight and falls to the ground, impaled like bug kabob.

Scrambling to my feet, I scan for my own weapon and instead see a flutter of movement. Something sparkles, like sunlight on water. And then it fades, reality solid once more.

But then five feet away there is another ripple. It's exactly as Aiden described it, like fabric fluttering in an invisible breeze. The air in the disturbance is different too, rich with exotic aromas, spices and the wildness I am coming to associate with Aiden.

Aiden spears the second wasp and glances over his shoulder. "Run!" he shouts.

"Look out!" I shriek at the same time. The third wasp dive bombs him. Aiden whirls around, extracting the spear from the nearby corpse. He wrenches it free and pivots to face the attack only to be stuck through his left shoulder by the stinger.

"No," I shriek as he falls to his knees in the dirt.

The wasp thrashes, its stinger breaking loose and flies off.

"Aiden!" I run to catch him before he falls on his face and impales himself even deeper. He sags in my grip, deadweight.

I would know.

"No, no, no, no, no," I repeat the word like a mantra as I lie him down on his back. The stinger rises obscenely from his arm like a lance. I want to pull it out, but fear that removing it will only cause him to bleed out faster. What if it pierced his heart? He can't die, he *can't*. He's my guide.

Without him, I might wind up stuck at my minuscule size forever. "Don't die."

"Won't," the word rasps from deep within his chest. He's still alive but from the sounds of things, won't be for long.

The medical kit in my bag is all but useless when faced with such a grievous injury.

More buzzing in the distance. The rest of the nest, coming to finish us off.

"What do I do, what do I do?" I glance around, as though the answer might present itself.

The shimmer appears again, about twenty feet away. It fades. Then returns at no more than fifteen feet.

The wasps crest the cap of the mushroom, what looks like twenty of them. There's no way I can fight them off on my own.

But if we can cross through the Veil....

The shimmer is heading in our direction, that rich scent of loam and heat and spice growing stronger. Ten feet away I see the ripple. "Come on." Somehow, I manage to get Aiden to his feet, stinger and all. He's heavy, staggering but I'm used to hefting bodies twice my size. "Our ride's here."

Five feet away the airwaves like heat lines coming off a grill. I hold tight to him and squeeze my eyes shut as the wasps dive down for us, the lead one aiming right for my head.

The ripple engulfs us.

THERE IS DARKNESS FOR A MOMENT, like the darkest night with no moon or stars, no man-made light. I still have a hold of Aiden, still, hear his shallow panting breaths, but I can't see him at all. Pinpricks of multicolored light appear. Deep purple, bright blue, flawless white, sunshine yellow, petal pink and ruby red wink into existence. Beneath my feet, there is something solid, not solid like the ground but solid like the hull of a boat. Whatever it rests on, I can't see. Except I see no sides or railings. The air is still and calm, without breeze or scent. Different than the smells I detected before we crossed. It's as though the world has been put on pause.

The stars, not our vessel, begin to move. Shooting out and down into long lines across the sky, fading before new ones appeared.

"Where are we?" Though I don't intend to whisper, my voice comes out softly.

"The Star Ferry." Aiden's voice sounds a little stronger. "It's okay, we're safe for the moment. We're crossing an In-Between. You can let go."

Belatedly I realize I'm still holding on to him and command myself to release him. Without my assistance, he sags to the deck. I kneel, my hands fluttering like butterflies. "What do I do?"

Aiden's hands wrap around the end of the stinger. "Help me pull this damn thing out."

"Are you sure that's safe? That you won't bleed to death?"

"I told you," he pants through clenched teeth. "I can't die like that."

"If you're sure." At least one of us is. I reach for the stinger and yank it back. Aiden grunts as the end impaling him slides out of his shoulder. He crumples onto the deck, panting and shaking. Blood spills from the wound, along with sickly yellow pus.

I drop the stinger to the deck and then shrug off my backpack. My portable medical kit may be flimsy, but it's better than nothing.

But when I move to rip open a sterile bandage Aiden gasps. "Save it. Food."

"You want to eat?"

In the glistening starlight, I can see sweat forming on his brow. "Faster metabolism means faster healing. But I need fuel."

Taking him at his word, I replace the medical supplies and unwrap three protein bars. He takes all three at once and downs them one at a time. Then closes his eyes.

"Incredible," I breathe. The pus evaporates, the blood slows, and the wound starts to knit itself back together. "How come this didn't happen the other night?"

"The Wild Hunt poison their blades to stunt the immortal healing process." Aiden's eyes are closed, his face tight with exhaustion. "This is much simpler to heal."

After removing the water bottles from the sides of my backpack, I lift his head and slide the pack beneath for support. He blinks up at me, the rainbow of colors reflected in his eyes.

I uncap one of the water bottles and hold it to his lips. "You need to drink."

Green irises fix on me while he does as I've suggested and then murmurs, "Thank you."

I quirk one eyebrow at him. "For the food, the water, or for saving your life?"

His lips twitch. "None of the above, actually. I was thanking you for not ordering me to drink, for letting me have a choice."

"I'm trying to be careful about that," I admit.

"Why?" There is no mocking in his tone, he is genuinely curious.

"Because. I would never want anyone to have that kind of control over me. How did it happen anyway?"

His eyes slide shut. "I pledged my fealty to you, Nicneven, as Queen of the Unseelie. The obedience is a side effect of an immortal vow that intense."

"Did you know that would happen when you made your pledge?"

He nods, eyes still hidden.

I shake my head, unable to understand. "Then why go through with it in the first place?"

Aiden doesn't respond, though he is breathing. I watch the steady rise and fall of his chest. He's asleep. Or maybe he's feigning unconsciousness, so he doesn't have to answer my question.

I sit beside him and stare up at the lines of color streaking past. The Star Ferry. So, this is what lies beyond the Veil. People have used that term to describe what happens after death. Several mythologies and religions describe a tunnel or a crossing of some sort. In others, a ferryman transports the soul across rivers to its final resting place. Were any of them talking about this place?

Only we weren't dead and as far as I can tell there is no ferryman. There is nothing guiding the movement of the skies, our passage through this In Between.

I lose track of how long it stretches on. Aiden sleeps beside me and from time to time I check on the progress of his shoulder. It looks as though it had never been damaged. Behind closed eyelids, his eyes dart back and forth and I wonder what sort of things fill his dreams.

Who is he? And why had he been willing to take on an immortal life of forced obedience to pledge his loyalty to one of the two Unseelie queens? Out of gratitude that she—that I —saved his life?

But that makes no sense. If my dreams were real, and the more I see the more I believe they are memories from my past life, he hadn't begged me to free him, he'd begged me to kill him. So why the life debt?

I take a sip from my own water bottle, careful to conserve

it. After an endless time, I stretch out on the deck beside Aiden and prop my hands beneath my head. Music fills my ears, not a song I know, but a chorus that seems to fit with the changing of the colors above and my lids grow heavy, the adrenaline from our encounter with the wasps leaving my system.

I dream of Sarah.

"Don't take this the wrong way, but you're different than I thought you'd be."

We lay in a field beneath a hundred-year-old oak, its leaves turning golden in the late summer sun. I turn from my contemplation of the tree to meet her gaze. "Oh yeah? How did you think I'd be?"

Sarah shrugs, looking slightly uncomfortable for the first time in memory. "You know, sort of basic."

"Basic?" I blink, unsure of how to react. Is it an insult?

She makes a frustrated noise. "Cookie cutter. All Northface gear and Ugg boots and pumpkin spice lattes which you take pictures of and post on Instagram with the hashtag #PSL."

Do people really do that? What the fuck is the point? To cover my ignorance I deadpan, "I have never once ordered a pumpkin spice latte."

She laughs, as I've intended. "Well, I know that now. It's just this vibe you put off. Like you're exactly like everyone else."

Just what I've been aiming for. Although she's seeing behind the façade, so I need to keep an eye on her.

"Instead you're just who you are, no apologies, zero fucks given." She gets up and heads to the edge of the stream, dipping her sparkly blue toenails in the water. "You're probably the least judgmental person I've ever met."

The irony makes my lips twitch. I'm not just the judge, I'm the jury and the executioner.

I close my eyes and smile at the memory of my last kill. It had been a woman, a horrible woman with Munchausen syndrome by proxy. She lived in Raleigh and the aunts and I had been following the story for months.

She'd poisoned her own son repeatedly because she craved the attention having a sick child brought her. Eventually, his system had shut down and he had died. Her lawyer had gotten her off on a technicality, something about the collection of evidence. And she had another child at home, a little girl.

I'd approached her in a supermarket parking lot, offering my sympathy and support. Late at night with the cloak of darkness at my back, with the aunts nearby and ready to help should the need arise, I'd gone in for a hug before she knew what was happening, pressed my lips to the side of her neck.

That judgment had been especially satisfying. A judgment Sarah knew nothing about.

"Nic, wake up." Someone calls softly. The voice pulls me away from my dreams, away from my memories. I don't want to go.

"Nic." This time fingers stroke down my cheek accompanies the summons. "We're here."

I blink to see Aiden leaning over me, the stars beyond his head stationary multihued dots once more. His hand is still on my cheek, the moment ripe with intimacy.

His shoulder is completely healed, his eyes once again bright as new leaves. "You fell asleep."

My face feels hot and I turn away from his touch. "Didn't mean to."

"I wasn't criticizing." Aiden helps me to my feet and then adds, "It's all right, you know. You don't always have to be on high alert."

"Habit." It's the only explanation I can offer. He's reattached the water bottles to my backpack. He hands it over then picks up the stinger, still coated with his blood.

"What are you going to do with that?"

He shrugs. "It's better than sticks in case we run into any more trouble. Come on."

I'm about to ask how we get off when I see the gangplank that has appeared on the far side of the ferry. "Where did that come from?"

"Magic." There is mischief in his gaze as he offers me a hand. "Let's go."

The gangplank stretches on through the dark for what feels like miles. I have no idea how Aiden can see as the stars above us appear to be winking out one by one.

Just as I wonder if we'll end up stumbling off the gangplank into the void, a shimmer appears that ripples the same as the one we crossed in the fairy ring. Here, the Veil does resemble an ethereal curtain, refracting the light from the few remaining stars.

Aiden looks back at me. "You ready for this?"

No, I'm not. But what choice do I have, really? I nod. He squeezes my hand once before releasing it and pulling the Veil aside. Aiden gestures for me to step through and after only a slight hesitation, I do.

Firelight greets me, casting an orange glow from torches mounted on roughly carved stone walls. The torches are very high above us, each stone the size of a house. Shadows dance and play as Aiden passes through the Veil behind me, as though we've been brought in on an invisible gust of wind.

"Where are we?" It appears like we've entered Medieval Times or some other sort of themed tourist trap. Just done on a much larger scale.

"The hall of giants. Welcome to Underhill, my queen."

CHAPTER 10

THE HALL OF GIANTS

"**A**re we still minuscule?" I turn in a slow circle, taking in our full surroundings.

Aiden shakes his head. "No, those powers you borrowed would have been returned the second you crossed Beyond the Veil. Although...." He tilts his head to the side in a very canine type gesture. "It appears some things are still out of proportion."

"What?" I frown and then glance down at my chest, where he's looking. And yelp. "What the hell?"

My breasts are enormous. The bra I'm wearing—a respectable 36 B—can no longer contain them. They strain against the fabric of my tank top, the shirt now stretching obscenely. "How...?"

"Fairy magic always takes a toll in Underhill." Aiden doesn't bother to hide his grin. "As prices go though, this is one of the better deals I've seen struck."

I need to get the damn bra off, it's strangling me. The thought of freeboobing it with that wolfish gaze watching my every move is almost as uncomfortable. "Turn around."

Aiden pivots and I reach behind myself to unfasten the catches when he comes full circle. "I said turn around."

"And I complied. Followed your order to the letter."

"You know what I meant," I snap, too wigged out by the changes in my body to be overly concerned that I'm barking commands at him. Are they still growing? The strain is unbearable, and I feel as though the bra is about to cut me in half.

Aiden's smile fades. "Nic, calm down."

His words have the opposite effect. "Calm down? Easy for you to say. No parts of your anatomy have gone berserk!"

"Turn around," he repeats the command to me.

"Why?" Unlike him, I have zero compulsion to obey.

"I want to help you. I promise not to do anything that makes you uncomfortable and you know you have the power to stop me, right?"

I nod.

He makes a spinning gesture with one finger. "Now turn around."

I turn and stiffen when he pulls up the back of my tank top. The chill air of the corridor hits my skin, making me shiver.

"Easy." He talks to me like he's gentling a wild animal. "Just one quick tug and it'll be better."

He does as he says and the pressure eases. I take a full breath and then reach for the straps, only to encounter his fingers already working them down the length of my arms.

I glance over my shoulder, meet those fathomless green eyes.

"Better?" he asks.

I nod and tug the straps free from his fingers. "I got it from here."

A soft chuckle rasps out. "No thanks required."

"Thanks?" I murmur as I work the final strap free and wad the now useless bra up in my hand.

"It didn't even occur to you did it?" Aiden sounds—for lack of a better word—testy. "The more things change the more they remain the same."

"And what's that supposed to mean?" My tone is distracted, my thoughts on my chest. With no better use for the bra, I stuff it in the side pouch of my backpack. Will I ever fit into it again? Will my body ever go back to normal or am I stuck with these megaboobs for the rest of my life? They must be at least DD if not larger, the imbalance awkward on my petite frame. Try as I might, I can't imagine running with these boulders attached to my chest.

"It means, your royal highness," his snide tone makes it clear he's patronizing me. "That you may be in a different body but you're the same spoiled brat you've always been."

I glance over at him, frowning at his sudden shift in attitude. "What's your problem?"

His lips part as though to respond but then he glances away. "Never mind."

I study him closely, hands clenched into fists, a muscle jumping in his jaw. "You're really angry," I say with mild surprise.

He nods once, not meeting my gaze.

"Because I didn't say thank you?" I rise, unbalanced by my new top-heavy state. Aiden automatically steps closer, his hands on my shoulders, steadying me.

He doesn't answer so I say, "Thank you. And I'm sorry."

The last part gets his attention. He meets my gaze, dark brows pulling close. "Sorry?"

"I ordered you to turn around. I'd just promised not to do that but in my panic over what was happening, it slipped out. I'll try to be more careful."

He tilts his head to the side, the maneuver so reminiscent

of the wolf. "I did it to show you that you don't have to be careful. Even with your ability to command me I usually find a way to circumnavigate the order. To follow it but not follow it. Disobedience and mischief are in my blood."

"What does that mean?"

He's about to respond when the ground quakes beneath our feet. I crash into him, knocking him off-balance, though he regains it before we both fall. The room steadies momentarily before another quake erupts.

"We need to hide," he hisses. "Now."

I'd been wrong, I can run with the megaboobs, especially when Aiden's yanking on my arm. "What's happening?" I gasp.

"Someone's coming." Each quake lasts longer, the intensity more extreme until my teeth rattle together.

The light dawns. "Those are footsteps. *Giant* footsteps."

"Right," Aiden heads for a divot in the stone where the mortar is chipped away, the divot creating a small cave to us.

"But aren't we looking for a giant?"

"A specific giant. We have no idea who is heading this way. Giants are extremely difficult under the best of circumstances. Now come *on*."

He yanks me into the cleft and then presses into me until I am secure between the wall and his body. His forehead rests on my shoulder, his thighs press into mine, my newly enlarged breasts smash directly against his chest. Air can't pass between the two of us.

"Ssshhh," he mutters in my ear when I struggle. "Giants are nearsighted, but they have exceptional senses of smell and hearing. And human is their favorite meal. Best stay still."

I want to argue that he shouldn't be so close, but am unsettled enough by the thought of being eaten to put up with his nearness. Sage and cedar threaten to swamp my olfactory sense with each inhale. He showered in my bathroom, with my soap and shampoo so how can he possibly still smell so unique? His body radiates heat to an astounding degree. With my back pressing against the cold stone, the sensation is like facing a campfire on a frigid night, half my body overheated, half-frozen to the bone.

The quaking stops suddenly. Over Aiden's shoulder, I spy bare feet the size of aircraft carriers leading into legs that resemble nothing more than enormous tree trunks. From our hiding place I see up to about mid-thigh, enough to ascertain that one, the giant is nude, and two, I don't want to see any more.

A sound emerges from far above our heads, like air being sucked into a vacuum. It's breathing?

"Come out, little flame. I know you're here."

"Whatever happens," Aiden breathes into my ear. "Stay hidden."

My hands are trapped between us and I clench them into fists. I am about to ask him what he intends to do when he darts from our hiding place to face off against a giant.

I'm too terrified to move, to breathe or to make a sound. Aiden looks minuscule beside that overlarge foot, his entire body no bigger than the giant's smallest toe. I thought my deadly kiss gave me power, but my ability is nothing when compared to the massive size of the giant.

"Greetings, Angrboda," Aiden calls up to the giant. "I have come in search of you."

The walls shake again, this time with the sound of giant laughter. "Really? The last time I saw you, you promised to... what was it again? Oh yes, find a way to end my miserable existence. Is that your purpose here?"

Aiden doesn't react at all, not even a flinch. "Can you blame me? After what you did to my family?"

Another rasping chuckle booms through the hall. "I did nothing to you, little flame. Nor to your mother or brother. And to your father…well, he got exactly what he wanted."

Aiden's hands clench into fists, his shoulders tight with tension. "I have not come here to rehash our difference of opinion, Hag of the Ironwood. Tell me, is my grandmother here?"

"Laufey is forbidden from setting foot in these halls," Angrboda says. "She is banished for her crimes against our kind. I can tell you where you can find her. For a price."

"The debt is paid in blood," Aiden points to a spot on his left arm. There is a blaze of flame and I flinch, barely covering my mouth quickly enough to stifle the sound of surprise in my throat.

When the flame disappears, a mark remains on his skin.

"The debt is paid in blood," Angrboda repeats, her tone more subdued. "Go to the swamp at the edge of the dead forest. There you will find what you seek."

Aiden waves a hand over his arm again. Another spurt of flame and the marking vanishes. He doesn't move, doesn't turn to look back at me, doesn't take his eyes from the giant. I wait, afraid to breathe too deeply or move an inch.

After what feels like an eternity, the giant lumbers off, ground quaking beneath her massive weight. I stay where I am, feet rooted as deeply as when I joined with the tree.

Finally, Aiden calls out. "You can come out, Nic."

Slowly, so slowly, I'm barely aware of it, I creep from my hiding place. For his part, Aiden doesn't budge an inch, hands still clenching at his sides, shoulders still rigid, jaw set.

"Who was that?"

"No one important." He turns and begins striding off in the opposite direction from the one the giantess took. "We have a very long walk ahead of us. It would make sense to leave by way of the kitchen, stock up on a few provisions before we depart."

I scurry to catch up and place a hand on his back. "You called her the Hag of the Ironwood."

"Only because whore of Babylon is already taken," he spits.

I peer at his arm. Though he's moving quickly, it's obvious that whatever mark had appeared is invisible once more. "It sounded like she was getting ready to broker a deal, but then you showed her some sort of marking and she just changed her mind."

"A rune," he corrects without looking my way. "I showed her a rune, a blood debt given to me by one of her kin."

"Who? And why isn't it always visible?" I lay a hand on his arm, over the spot where the rune had been.

"What's with the interrogation?" Aiden yanks his hand away, as though my touch burns him.

"I'm trying to understand what just happened here. She spoke of your grandmother. Is she a giant, too? Is that who we seek?"

Though his features still appear tight, his shoulders relax somewhat, now that my questions no longer focus on Angrboda. "She's who we came here to find. If anyone knows how to resurrect a mortal, it'll be Laufey."

"That name sounds familiar." Angrboda's too for that matter, though I can't place where I've heard either.

"Yes, she's a giant. Though she is weaker, smaller and slenderer than most of the others. The Needle of the Forest."

"When was the last time you saw her?"

"A few centuries."

I blink at him. "It's been centuries since you've seen your own grandmother?"

"My family isn't all that close." And then low, almost under his breath he adds, "Not anymore."

His mood seems dark, his gaze unfocused and I decide it's better not to ask anything else for the time being.

The scents emanating from the direction of what I presume to be the kitchen are unlike anything I've ever experienced. Fresh bread, roasted garlic, pies, and cakes and overwhelming it all is meat. Metric tons of it, salted and spiced. My stomach lurches and it takes all my effort not to vomit.

We hide behind the folds of a huge tapestry and watch the activity in the kitchen. Enormous cooks move about, not with the forceful stride of Angrboda, but with more a heavy shuffling gait. Their movements are slow but purposeful.

"I can't go in there." I swallow hard, put off by the odor of cooking flesh.

Aiden's stomach growls, loudly. Obviously, he's an omnivore. "You have to, the door to the outside is at the far end of the kitchen."

"Of course it is." I huff out a fast breath, then nod once. "Okay. But if I upchuck, don't say I didn't warn you."

Aiden peers around the fabric. "All clear. Breathe through your nose and run. I'll get you out and go back in for the food. Ready?"

How much meat would it take to feed a castle full of giants? Herds of cattle, flocks of chickens and ducks. So much meat. I stagger, woozy from the smell. Sticking around here won't help me in the long run. I gag and then cover my mouth with the sleeve of my flannel shirt and give him a nod.

Aiden clasps my other hand. It's not like the other times when his thumb and forefinger ensnared my wrist to pull me along. No, this time he laces his fingers through mine, so our digits are interwoven. "On the count of three. One, two, three!"

He tosses the fabric aside and we burst forth, the equivalent of mice scurrying through a human kitchen.

The cooking giants are smaller than Angrboda and more cowed. Their chatter booms off the stone walls, but I focus on keeping the scents out of my nose, and can only mute one sense at a time.

We weave feet and dodge tables, narrowly avoiding getting cooked alive when a cauldron of bubbling water overboils. Aiden yanks me to the side before the liquid can touch me, the motion so fast that I stumble, unbalanced by my megaboobs.

He doesn't miss a beat, scooping me up and tossing me over his shoulder in a fireman's carry. Air *whooshes* out of my lungs at the impact of his hard shoulder into my midsection. My backpack jounces against the back of my skull with Aiden's every step and my hair falls in such a way that it completely blocks my sight of anything but the floor. We must be close, just a few more steps….

"EEK!" Someone shrieks and drops a wooden spoon the size of a Mack truck.

Aiden curses low under his breath and increases his speed. We've been spotted.

"Quick, catch them!" Another voice, one that rings with a tone accustomed to giving orders and having them obeyed, barks. "Human would make an excellent soup."

A shudder washes through me.

There is a flurry of motion and Aiden zigs then zags in rapid succession. We zoom past a massive table leg and then duck beneath some sort of shelving. I hear the clattering of utensils, the cries of agitated giants. The space below me grows dim. And then Aiden sets me down, a hand over my mouth cupping but not connecting with my lips.

I meet the green gaze that glows in the dim lighting. He

puts one finger to his own lips in the universal shushing gesture. I nod once. Aiden withdraws his hand.

We are inside some sort of cabinet or pantry. Bags of potatoes line one wall, jars of jam and preserves are crammed into the one above.

They didn't see where we went.

I start and look at Aiden, wondering if he spoke or if I cracked my head at some point. He's staring right at me and again I hear his voice in my head.

We need to find a place to hide, to wait out the search. He gestures with his thumb to a bushel of giant-sized apples, just to make it clear that yes, he really is somehow communicating with me telepathically.

I try to send him a message, but with no idea where to start, end up nodding to indicate that yes, hunkering down seems like the right thing to do.

We walk over to the basket and begin to climb. The weave is tight and makes for perfect foot and hand holds, but my disproportionate upper body keeps getting in the way, impairing my reach and keeping me from hugging the contours of the basket in a way that feels natural. My head crests the top until I can see into the basket. My panting breaths are so loud I fear the giants will hear them even through the closed door.

Take your time. I'm enjoying the view.

Inhaling sharply through my nose, I glare down at Aiden. He smiles wolfishly up at me, then flicks his gaze to my backside, no more than six inches from his face.

Prick, I think. He laughs a little. Is it possible he heard?

As much fun as this is.... He props one hand under my backside and pushes. His strength is incredible, and I topple over the edge into the apple basket. A moment later he joins me, though his landing is much more dignified.

Don't ever do that again. I glare up at him from my prone position atop a giant-sized Granny Smith.

He nods once. Message received.

I close my eyes in exhaustion. And frustration. Again, I didn't mean to issue an order, but again my temper got the best of me. Two days ago, I didn't even think I *possessed* a temper but now it's controlling me.

Aiden hunkers down beside me, I can feel his heat, sense his nearness even before he mentally sends me a one-word question.

Hungry?

I nod without opening my eyes.

Warmth and light flickers beyond my closed lids. Curious, I open my eyes and see Aiden transforming, well partly transforming. His right hand is engulfed in blinding white light. I squint to protect my vision, but then it is done. Where his human hand had been only a moment ago, there is a wolf's paw equipped with razor-sharp claws.

Claws he then uses to cut away sections from a nearby apple. The slices are even and precise. Using his still human hand he plucks one free and gives it to me.

Took me a century to master a partial change. He flashes a grin at me. *But it's better than a Swiss Army knife.*

I take the apple, which is roughly the size of a toaster, though my gaze is fixed on him. Just when I think I've seen the strangest thing possible, something else knocks the moment out of first place.

Hesitant, I touch the sliced fruit to the tip of my tongue. Will Giant apples taste any different than the ones I'm used to? Familiar flavor explodes on my taste buds and I take a small bite. The apple is juicy and sweet with just a little sharpness. I eat while Aiden proceeds to slice up more and pile it beside me.

This is fine for now. He thinks when he's decimated the left side of the apple. *But I'm going to look for something that will travel a little better. Rest awhile.*

He turns to climb from the basket to explore the next shelf up, but I take hold of his arm.

Thank you. The thought is deliberate and clear, the first one I send to him that isn't prickling with hostile energy.

He smiles and nods, placing the wolf paw over his heart. *As my lady desires.*

Then he leaps up, snags the shelf that had been six feet above his head and uses that incredible upper body strength to pull himself up onto the next shelf.

I eat my fill of the apple and do my best to get my head around all that has happened. My thoughts are muddled though, too many feelings coming on too fast for me to process. It's as though I've gone my entire life in an emotional void and now that the sentiments have a toe hold, they are making up for the lost time.

I must have dozed off because the next thing I know, light is flooding into the basket and a giant hand reaches for me.

I scramble upwards, but the uneven surface of the apples is like climbing slick rocks and humongous fingers close around me as a voice like thunder booms.

"Gotcha," it says.

CHAPTER 11

WHAT'S ON THE MENU

Terror consumes me as that massive hand blots out the light. The thought of being thrust into a boiling stewpot or spitted and roasted over an open flame, like the wild boar I'd seen when we first entered the kitchen, turns my insides to jelly. Aiden said giants consider humans a rare delicacy. Will they chop off my head and then use bits and pieces of me in several different dishes? Or will I be cooked whole?

I thrash in my captor's grip as he moves away from the pantry. Away from Aiden. My heart feels on the verge of explosion, it's pumping so hard. Perhaps I'll have a massive coronary before the giant reaches his destination. Never have I been so powerless, not even when the snake man and his clay cohort had me. At least then I had a plan, to kiss and run like hell.

To kiss.

Frantically, I whip my head toward the giant's thumb—the digit closest to my face—and press my lips against it. For a moment nothing happens. Then the forward momentum of the giant halts.

"What?" the voice sounds faintly surprised for a moment before its owner crashes to the ground.

Cocooned as I am inside his palm, the impact is buffered, though my insides feel as though I've just gotten off a roller coaster. The apple is threatening a comeback. From outside my fleshy prison, I hear booming shouts as all the kitchen giants come to investigate their downed comrade.

Out. I need to wriggle my way out of his hold before anyone checks his hand. There is light between two fingers, the grip not completely tight. I shove myself toward it and manage to squeeze both hands through the opening. I use them to push his fingers further apart and create a larger gap, one big enough for me to escape through. It's slow going, his fingers are heavy as tree limbs and completely uncooperative. His body is still warm. Sweat forms on my brow as I struggle. It slides down between my breasts and soaks my shirt until the fabric clings.

A loud sound erupts, like a hundred buzzsaws in concert. I freeze, my nose and mouth inches from the relatively fresh air of the kitchen.

"I'll be jiggered, Bil fell asleep standing up." One of the other giants exclaims.

What? Is it possible that my kiss, while toxic to humans, is only the giant equivalent of NyQuil?

"Well, how you like that?" Another gives the body a kick, jostling me to the point I fear being snapped in half more than discovery. "Decides to take a nap and leaves us with all the ruttin' work."

"All right you lot," another voice booms. "Nuff of this standing around. We got a supper to put on the table."

There is much grumbling about Bil and about work in general as the giants lumber back to their duties.

"And as for you," the voice with the ring of command

moves closer. "Would serve you right if I left you here, drunken sot."

Yes. Please, just leave him here. Preferably unattended.

Instead, the head cook crouches down and holds a small vial under my captor's nose. The snoring pauses and then the hand I am in is flung violently upward as if to beat back the odor.

The palm uncurls, and I drop to the floor, landing on my right side and slamming into the hard stone with enough force the breath is knocked from my lungs.

"Wha—?" Bil struggles up, nearly crushing me with his elbow. I roll under a nearby shelving unit, so I am at least partly hidden from their view.

"Were you at the fairy wine again?" The head cook demands.

"No!" Bil's big face scrunches up in confusion. "I caught one of them humans. It was in the pantry."

The head cook carries a wooden spoon and he whaps Bil over the back of the head with the flat side. "Idiot. Don't you think if we kept humans in the pantry we would have something better to serve than truffle pie? Now come on, I'm demoting you to dishes 'til either your head clears or your fingers bleed, whatever happens first."

I lay my head down and take a deep breath. Or try to. Searing pain radiates from my right side, at the spot of impact. I must have a cracked rib, as every inhale sends a new spike of agony through me. Running or any kind of swift movement is completely out of the question.

Panting in shallow breaths I assess my situation. My kiss isn't deadly to the giants, though it will knock them out. Of course, the chances of me surviving another encounter like the one with Bil aren't good. What if next time it's my spine that breaks?

I can wait here for Aiden to find me. Perhaps he's on his

way even now. I struggle to send him a telepathic message and let him know where I am, but there is no reply. Perhaps he is too far away for it to work. Or he's ignoring me. What if he decides I'm more trouble than I'm worth, just like Addy and Chloe?

No, better not to count on Aiden staging some sort of rescue. I still don't know what he wants from me, but it's entirely possible he's come to the conclusion I'm not worth the effort.

His loss.

Considering my injury and relative ineffectiveness of my kiss against the giants, my best plan would be to wait until the activity in the kitchen dies down and sneak out the back. I just need to remain hidden until the meal is finished. Which might be a problem. As hiding spots go, mine isn't the greatest. The giants are clumsy, constantly spilling things or knocking them over. All it would take is a giant dropping something, bending down to pick it up and I would be in the soup—literally.

White-hot pain lances through my body as I struggle upright, my eyes hunting for the best place to take cover. Not the pantry or a pot or anywhere else. Someplace they won't go poking about and preferably, someplace close by.

Just then a large bare foot comes into view. Angling my head up, I watch as the giant, this one female, drops something into a nearby bin. Garbage.

Of course. If I hide in the garbage, eventually one of the giants will take it, and me along with it, outside. Exactly where I want to go. Still, I hesitate, shuddering in revulsion at the thought of being buried alive by giant-sized food scraps. No other option presents itself though. It's my only real chance.

Standing is an effort and my steps are slow. I stick to the shadows of the table, my gait an unsteady hobble. Giants move past, but none of them spy me creeping along. The smell of rotting food grows stronger. My teeth sink into my lower lip. If there is any other way to escape, it eludes me. Into the garbage, I must go.

The bin is several football fields high and I hunt for a way to get up to the opening, preferably one that won't cause me any extra agony. The bin itself is all smooth sides and nothing dangles over the rim. Even if I'd been in any sort of shape to climb, there is nothing to assist me.

Except for my untapped reserve of talents.

My poisonous kiss won't help me, neither will shrinking and there are no trees to meld with. But from what Aiden told me, I can tap into any Unseelie power I choose— for a price. And though I've never seen an actual fairy, they are often depicted with wings.

My hands cover my chest and I grimace. Hopefully, my boobs won't get any bigger. Or what if something else grows this time? My nose? Or my feet? I could end up looking like a pornstar hobbit.

Still better than being giant soup.

"Wings," I mutter, closing my eyes to envision the result, as I did with the tree, with the shrinking. I don't picture light and wispy wings, but those I know will work, those of a bird, with large black feathers. I see them in my head, stretching out on either side of me, large enough to lift my weight and then a little bit more. Birds have hollow bones. Their lack of density is what allows them to fly. On impulse, I imagine my own bones as hollow. Even if I am caught, at least the giants will be cheated out of my marrow.

A burning sensation spreads across my back, the skin stretching, changing to my will. Without opening my eyes, I shrug out of my backpack, clutching it in my left hand, with my right arm still pressed against my damaged ribs.

When I open my eyes, the first thing I notice is that the

pain in my ribs is missing. Not better, but gone as though it'd never been. Frowning, I lift my shirt to inspect the skin, but there is no bruising, no sign of any injury.

Something soft and light brushes my cheek. I look up and see large black feathers each the size of my forearm. I shift my back muscles and sure enough, I have wings that stretch out to about six feet across. The shape is soft, gentle and round at the tops to mimic the arch of my shoulders.

I can feel each wing jutting from my shoulder blades. The sensation is odd, almost as though something foreign has been attached to my body, but at the same time altogether familiar. I focus on spreading them out wide, as wide as they can go. The feathers flutter, a few falling out as I shake them. Next up, flapping.

At first, it's slow going. I get the left wing to move but the right doesn't budge. More feathers shake free, the motion loosening them. At this rate, I'll have bald wings before I get an inch off the ground.

Feeling foolish but not knowing what else to do, I set my backpack down and then stretch my arms out, one on either side and mimic the flapping motion. If it works with my arms, there's no reason it can't with my wings.

The left side slows, and the right takes up the rhythm. My gaze flicks upward to my target, the rim of the trash barrel. My feet leave the floor as my speed increases. Hastily, I look around for giants, but their focus is elsewhere.

Two feet up and then four, ten, I steadily climb up, eyes on my destination. A smile bursts free and I want to crow in victory, to swoop and sore, that is until I overshoot the garbage can by a good twenty feet.

With a curse, I twist in midair and divebomb the trash. Not knowing how to stop, I fold the wings in and drop like deadweight into a bed of wilted lettuce.

I made it. Unbelievably, against all odds, all logic, I grew wings and flew. Not gracefully or prettily. The end result is what matters. The reek of discarded room temperature food makes me gag, but the refuse provides ample cover.

Unfortunately, my pack is still where I'd discarded it, beneath the work table. Everything I own on this side of the Veil is in that pack. The extra layer of clothing, the food and water might mean the difference between life and death once I make it outside the warmth of the kitchen.

My graceless dismount leaves me deep enough in the bin that I can't see over the rim. Crawling over enormous chicken bones, rotting melon, stale bread crusts and gelatinous things I do my best not to think about until I reach a browning head of cabbage that abuts the side. Three quick flicks of my wings and I land easily atop it with only a short stumble.

Using a stray cabbage leaf for camouflage, I crouch down so none of the giants moving nearby spot me and assess the risk. I want the pack but can't control the wings well enough to make a round trip a sure thing. As I debate, sparks drift down toward my belongings. I want to scream, fearing all my stuff will be burned to ash until the embers coalesce into Aiden's human body. He picks up the pack, a frown marring his perfect features, then looks up.

Our eyes meet, and his bare shoulders shake with silent laughter.

I give him the finger. He grins widely before shifting to glowing coals and floating upwards. He forms beside me with my belongings secure in his hands.

"Nice," he says, stroking a finger down the wings. "What magic did you use to grow these?"

"These were the magic." I frown. "I could have sworn I had at least one broken rib, but as soon as I grew the wings, the pain went away."

"Dare airson aisling." Aiden studies the wings with awe, reaching out to stroke a hand over one.

"What did you just say?" I shiver beneath the unexpected touch.

Aiden notes the reaction with a small smile, before withdrawing his hand. "It's Gaelic. It means dare for a dream. Underhill sometimes rewards magic wielders for taking unfathomable chances. A healing like you experienced, the return of something precious thought forever lost, the development of a new skill or ability. The stories are infrequent, but it has been known to happen. She's a fickle beast and no one knows why she rewards some that take risks but punishes others."

I stare at him a moment, letting the information sink in. "You speak of Underhill as though it's a person, not a place."

"She's both. Just because some fleas take up residence on your dog, doesn't mean your dog is any less a living creature with a will of her own, right? The fleas don't dictate what the dog does any more than the unaging dictate Underhill's actions."

I raise a brow at him. "In your analogy, we're the fleas?"

He stoops down and picks up one of my newly fallen feathers, examining it closely. "Some sort of pests. By the way, your majesty, you don't smell so great. And you appear to be molting. Why are we hanging out in the refuse?"

Briefly, I explain my thoughts about hiding and having the giants take us where we want to go.

Aiden tucks the feather behind his ear and his brows pull together. "But how come you didn't wait for me? I could have transported you as easily as I did your pack. You took a significant risk and it paid off, but still."

"I didn't know if you'd come find me. I've caused you a lot of trouble and if I were you, I wouldn't bother."

His lips part. I turn away before he can respond.

Suddenly feeling exposed, I gesture to the sloping side of the cabbage. "Since you're here now, we should find better cover than a wilted leaf. Come on."

I try to put the backpack on over my shoulders, but the wings are in the way. Resigning myself to carrying it, I crouch down and try to tuck my wings in so they don't snag on anything sharp.

Aiden crouches beside me, placing a hand over the pack. "Nic, look at me."

I don't want to, but his hand is in the way and while I can order him to remove it if I choose, my discomfort isn't a good reason to abuse the power I wield over him. With a sigh, I meet his gaze.

"You are worth the trouble," he says, green eyes bright. "And I will always come for you."

"Well, I know I'm worth it. It's the rest of the world with the problem with what I do, not me." I snap. Then the rest of his words register. "Why? I haven't been very nice to you in this life or from the sounds of things, in the past. I don't understand."

He rises and holds out a hand. "You never have. But that's all right because I understand you. All you need to do is trust me."

"You'd be better off asking for the moon on a silver platter," I grumble. "I don't trust anyone. I know better."

"*Dare airson aisling,*" Aiden says softly.

Dare for a dream.

I let him take the backpack and scan the waste for a decent hiding spot. There's a cracked pewter mug on the opposite side of the can, turned on its side. It's large enough to hold both of us and offers some protection from any further layers of garbage.

Aiden spots it at the same time I do. Swinging my pack

over one shoulder, he holds out a hand. "Do you want to fly us over there, or should I?"

I glance at him. "We're not going to walk?"

"Through the garbage for what looks like half a mile?" He quirks a brow at me as if asking if I'm serious.

"I'm not that good with the flying," I admit. Plus, more feathers have fallen out just in the short while we've been talking. He might be right about the molting.

"With your permission then?"

I nod in agreement. Then my body...comes apart. There's no other way to describe it. All the pieces that makeup me, Nic Rutherford, separate. It starts at the extremities and works its way inwards, my feet within my boots, my fingers just disperse into embers. It's not an unpleasant feeling so much as an unnerving one. My body dissolves like salt in water. My gaze flicks to Aiden before my eyes are caught up in the magic. He too is coming apart, the bits and pieces of him also undone and sparking to life.

The transformation is painless and freeing in a way. Gravity no longer holds me down, all the fragments of me are free to go where they will. And yet there is something that keeps all the free-floating parts on track. Whether it's coming from Aiden or myself, I have no idea.

Then my senses abandon me. They're not muted like when I joined with the oak, just no longer there. I don't smell the garbage and that might be a relief if not for the fact that I can't see or hear or touch anything either. I am, I exist, but all the tethers to my mortal flesh are gone.

Is this what death feels like? Awareness still intact but no more input from the world around you? No more danger or pain... just being. People who've claimed near-death experience talk about floating above their bodies. Did Sarah feel this weightless freedom, too?

Then we are solidifying inside the cup. The same process

is done in reverse. My center mass, head chest stomach. Then my legs and moving steadily down to my feet. A few stray bits swirl around my face as I am put back together. Lastly my hands, first the left and then the right, still connected to his.

"You okay?" Aiden squeezes my newly reformed hand.

"That was…" I shake my head, having no words for such an ineffable experience.

"You get used to it. At least I did." Aiden pulls me deeper into the cup and sits. "Come on, nothing to do now but wait for them to take out the trash."

I sit beside him, my back hitting directly against the bottom of the cup. "My wings are gone."

Aiden looks down at me, the feather is still tucked behind his ear. He plucks it free and gives it to me. "Magic is always temporary. By the way, your other imbalance corrected itself."

"Huh?" I glance down and notice that my chest is back to normal. "Oh, thank *god*."

"Which one?" Aiden murmurs and closes his eyes before I can ask him to explain.

CHAPTER 12

OUT WITH THE TRASH

Though fatigued enough to sleep, between the unsettling dreams and unpleasant changes I found upon waking, I don't want to chance a nap. With nothing to do but wait, I study the feather Aiden had rescued and imagine what will happen next. We need to find Laufey and figure out how to resurrect Sarah. Somehow, I doubt either task will be as simple as it sounds.

After an interminable amount of time, there is a shift in the bin. I put a hand out, but the next jolt sends me sprawling. I tumble into Aiden, pinning him to the bottom of the cup. Reflexively, his arms go around me, though his eyes remain closed.

"You can let me go," I whisper even though it's doubtful the giant carrying the bin can hear me.

"Never," he breathes, a small smile on his lips and then his mouth is on mine.

No no no no no!

Every cell in my body freezes, my brain screams out a denial. I expect him to go limp at any moment. And in that instant, assured of his demise, I kiss him back, fully, as the only means I have to say goodbye.

The kiss is sweet and gentle, so different than any of the rugged attacks I've experienced before. Aiden's heat radiates into me, warming places I had no idea had been frozen solid until they begin thawing. His hands move along my now wingless back in a tender caress. My fingers curl against his bare chest, memorizing the feel, the closeness of him for the first, and what I am sure will be the last time.

But his body doesn't twitch in death throes, his arms don't sag to the side, his eyes don't glaze over. Instead he moves into me, pressing himself intimately against me as his hands grow bolder, tangling in my hair, cupping the nape of my neck, caressing my face. His scent overpowers my senses, cedar and sage shoving the pervasive garbage odor away. I revel in his wildness, his heat and crave more. I am losing myself in him, in this, and panic begins to well within me.

Then the world spins upside down, the sensation of free falling. Aiden and I are violently separated as the trash is upended. I see him for a moment, tumbling out of our temporary sanctuary before I lose track of him in the chaos. My head cracks against the opposite side of the cup with a dizzying thump before my body slides down at an angle to the rim. I manage to grab hold of the edge and stop my free fall, but it doesn't matter as the cup is also falling. Either my body will be crushed on impact or the cup and the ton of garbage above it will flatten me.

"Nic, hang on!"

Out of the corner of my eye I see Aiden making his way toward me, seeming to climb up an ever-shifting staircase, leaping from one piece of debris to the next, flashing between his fire form and his human one. He lands in a crouch from a spinning half rotten potato and pushes off instantly before my nerveless fingers lose their grip….

And then we are both floating upwards in a shower of sparks.

Up and up and up we drift on a breeze I neither feel nor scent but know is there all the same. Aiden guides us out past the giant's rubbish heap, over a body of water to the far edge of the shore beyond before finally bringing us back to earth.

I hit the ground on my left side, hard enough to knock all the air from my lungs.

"You okay?" Aiden crouches down beside me.

"Give me a minute," I wheeze, taking stock of my recently disassembled, then reconnected form.

"Take all the time you need." Aiden stands and moves away, for which I am grateful. Too much is happening too fast and I can barely keep up.

There is a moment during a hunt where time slows, where every breath takes millennia, every heartbeat an eon. I've grown used to the odd sensation, even learned to use it to my advantage.

But this is different.

"What just happened?" I ask Aiden.

"You mean, other than us getting chucked out with yesterday's garbage?"

I nod.

He sighs.

"And don't tell me it's complicated," I snap.

Both his eyebrows ascend. "Well, it is."

When I glare at him he adds, "To put it simply, I sped us up, so we could beat time before we were flattened."

I stare at him. "How is that even possible?"

"Nic, I don't know." He plunks down beside me and scrubs a hand over his face. "What is it with you and understanding everything? You never used to care how something worked, only if it did."

I sit up and scowl at him. "I'm not the same person you

knew, Aiden. I don't know who she was and have no idea how to be her. All I know how to be is me. Don't ask me to apologize for that."

He stares at me for a long moment, as though trying to puzzle me out. "Time can only move in one direction, forward. But in Underhill that forward momentum isn't assigned to every creature in the same way and it's possible to...detach from it. It's like a trick of the light. If time doesn't have a firm grasp on you, you can slip its hold. Temporarily. Eventually, the demands of the physical body will want to sync back up with standard time. Does that make sense?"

In a weird sort of way, it does. "And how are you still alive. Is that a trick, too?"

He blinks. "What are you talking about?"

"I know you said kissing me couldn't kill you, but I felled a giant earlier by just brushing my lips against his skin. It doesn't make sense that you're still alive." I stand up and stalk toward my pack which had fallen some distance away. I don't want anything out of it, but it's something to focus on other than the tempest of feelings roiling inside me.

Aiden grabs my arm and spins me to face him, brows furrowed in confusion. "I thought that was a dream. I didn't mean to actually..." He stops and tilts his head in that wolf like way and says with wonder in his voice, "I'm still alive."

I expel an exasperated breath. "That's what I just said!"

"That means you wanted the kiss."

"What?" I yank my arm free and he lets me go, though he's obviously reluctant to do so. "I thought you said I couldn't kill you?"

He shifts his weight, looking almost as uneasy as I feel. "When did I say that?"

"In my room, yesterday." Or had it been the day before? "You said I couldn't kill you by accident."

He shakes his head. "No, I said you couldn't kill me with a

159

misspoken order. Your kiss is different, it could kill any creature if you meant for it to happen. Even a giant, though it
would drain you."

I stare at him. "So why aren't you dead right now?"

"I told you, you must have wanted me to kiss you. There's
no other explanation."

When I start to shake my head, he holds my face in his
hands. "Nic, it's all right. You can control it when you want
to. Didn't anyone ever tell you that?"

I think back to my panic, my longing for him not to die.
Had that affected my deadly kiss? "No."

"It's a weapon in your arsenal, but much like a sword, you
can keep it sheathed so it can't hurt anyone."

I can control it? My head keeps shaking back and forth
until I'm sure it'll fall off.

Aiden appears to sense my panic because he releases me
and takes a step back hands held up in front of him. "It was
an accident. I'll sleep in wolf form to make sure it doesn't
happen again, all right?"

I can't look at him anymore. I grab my backpack and head
to the water. "I'm sick of smelling like garbage. I need to get
cleaned up."

He's not saying anything, just watching me closely.

I hesitate at the water's edge, still unwilling to strip in
front of him. "There's not anything lurking in here that will
eat me, right?"

Aiden shakes his head. "No, just a few bioluminescent
creatures. I wouldn't drink it though, unless you want your
insides to glow."

"Okay." Still I wait for him to turn his back.

He stares at me, clears his throat. "We'll camp here
tonight. I'll get some wood for a fire." He dusts off the
battered sweats which I get the distinct impression he's

holding onto for my comfort more than his, and heads into the dark trees.

I don't wait to see if he's spying on me, just retrieve the bar of soap from my pack, shuck my clothes and head into the lake. The water is cool, but since I've lived most of my life in a mountain town, frigid water is something I've developed a tolerance against. Little blue green lights flick up as my feet disturb the sandy bottom. The largest would fit on the head of a pin. I watch their zigzag movement, fascinated as they flit about in the water, before resettling.

That minor distraction over, I focus on soaping myself up. The bar I packed is plant based and though I'm relatively confident it won't harm the little critters in the lake, I use only enough to get the stink of garbage off my body and out of my hair.

Everything I thought I knew about myself, about my world, is changing. Aiden had been right, I did want to kiss him. Not because I desire him, I still don't feel any sort of sexual attraction for him, but more from curiosity. And I hadn't wanted him to die. Were those needs enough to stay my toxic kiss?

They must be otherwise Aiden never would have made it out of the cup. And neither would I. The rules of Underhill are so different than what I am used to. I am no longer the hunter, the biggest baddest killer around. Yet somehow, I was a queen of this realm, of the Unseelie Court. I commanded the Wild Hunt. That must have meant I'd mastered the secrets of Underhill.

And if I did it once, I can do it again.

A close splash breaks me from my reverie. Water ripples out and Aiden's wolf head pops above the surface, surrounded by the glow of even more bioluminescent creatures. He dog paddles in a circle, looking more like a goofy Labrador than a big bad wolf.

A smirk pulls at my lips. "You look ridiculous."

I could swear he grins at me before paddling deeper into the water, a bioluminescent trail in his wake.

I turn back to the shore, not at all surprised to see a roaring fire. What I am surprised to see is the blanket that is spread out beside it, a towel folded neatly on top. Where had all that come from?

I dry myself with the towel and sit wrapped in the folds of fabric, glad for the fire's warmth and light to examine the blanket. It's a patchwork quilt, hand crafted with skill. Neither Chloe nor Addy were seamstresses but there were a few women in town that made such things. One had given Addy such a gift when the Fate had saved her Great Dane after the creature had been mauled by a bear.

I study the blanket closer, swearing the white and blue pattern with the little pink flowers was the same pattern. Could it actually *be* the same quilt?

Turning back to the discarded towel, I eyeball that as well. It looks like the rose-colored ones that hang in our bathroom. I didn't pack either item. Were they some sort of creation Aiden had summoned to comfort me? Or had he somehow brought these specific things across the Veil?

At that moment, Aiden charges up out of the water, dripping bioluminescent droplets from his shaggy black coat. Then he does exactly what I expect, and shakes. I get the blanket up as a shield just in time. It's a long, thorough motion which starts at his snout and carries all the way down his spine to his tail.

Again, I find myself chuckling at his antics. The ferocious man eater that plays like a puppy.

"You smell like wet dog." I get to my feet, blanket still swathed around me, and carry the towel to him. Even post-shake he's soggy and saturated. "I bet you air dry as well as a pair of jeans."

He lifts his head and closes his eyes as I rub the damp towel over his saturated fur.

"I don't know how you got these things," I mutter to him. "But I'm glad you did. Thanks."

Green eyes open. Aiden doesn't say anything, he can't in this form but in my head I hear, *your wish is my command.*

"How come you couldn't hear me earlier? When the giant grabbed me. Was there too much distance between us?"

No. Distance isn't a factor with telepathy. I didn't realize you were gone at first, my attention was on stocking up our supplies.

"Supplies?" I frown, glancing from the towel to the blanket. "You mean things like these?"

No, these came from your farmhouse.

"You transported them here?" He can do that? "Why didn't you just take us out that way?"

It doesn't work that way, not on living beings. Aiden shook again, though this time it mostly fluffed out his coat. *It'll be about a three-day trek to find Laufey.*

"Your grandmother." I add.

Yes.

The towel is completely saturated, unable to hold another drop. I spread it out on a nearby branch to dry. The branch is already coated with a glowing pink mossy like substance. The leaves are pinkish purple, and rustle in the light breeze coming off the lake. Reaching out, I touch the moss, find it soft and springy beneath my fingers. Is it bioluminescent, too? From what I recall about creatures that put off that sort of light, they usually dwell in darkness, like at the bottom of the sea. Odd, to find them here, at the edge of a moonlit forest.

Aiden continues to stare into the fire. After a moment of studying the trees growing at the water's edge, I resettle on the ground, still wearing only the blanket. "Were the two of you close growing up?"

Aiden lies down, paws stretched toward the blaze. *No. She and my father didn't get along. I didn't meet her until I...left home.*

I don't miss his careful word choice or the sadness in those green eyes. He looks lost, or as lost as a wolf can look and once again I mentally flash back to the dream where I found him chained and begging for death. Had that happened? I want to ask, but he already looks off. He's my only guide in this strange place and it's not worth the risk to upset him. He'd mentioned his punishment happened before he left home as well. I wonder if one has to do with the other, but Aiden is thinking at me again.

She took me in. Taught me how to change my form, to control the wolf within and without. She is very wise and gentle, especially for a giant.

I study him in the firelight, ears forward, body tense. "You don't like talking about your past, do you?"

His head turns in my direction. *No.*

It's my turn to stare into the flames. "I get that. I was... found in a ramshackle cottage in the woods. Abandoned and living alone."

That wasn't supposed to happen. Aiden's eyes are bright. *I should have been there to protect you.*

I pick up a deep brown stick and snap it in half. "Do you know how I got there? Who left me there? I mean, reincarnate or not, someone raised me from infancy. I'd like to know who it was, why they abandoned me and why I can't remember them at all."

I wish I could tell you. For a wolf, his expression looks truly regretful.

"Did I ever tell you...?" I toss the stick onto the fire, the greenwood smoking slightly. "Who my parents were?"

Yes.

I look over at him. He stares back, unblinking. Waiting.

I suck in a deep breath. Aiden will tell me if I ask. But do I want to know? After all, if I'm reincarnated, I must have had two sets of parents, four people that I can't remember at all. Had the second set been the ones to raise me and then leave me in the Black Forest?

"I don't think I want to know that now," I say.

It might be my imagination, but for a moment it appears the wolf is relieved.

You should get some rest. We'll set out at first light.

I nod and lie down facing the fire. The flames dance behind my closed eyelids. After a moment, Aiden, now mostly dry, lies against my back, protecting it.

Though I still don't know why.

"Kill me, please."

With my sword raised, I study the youth with the green eyes, read the intenseness of his request.

"Why?" I ask.

"I don't deserve to live." There is no hesitation in his voice, his conviction is absolute.

"And you deserve death?" I ask him. "As a punishment or a mercy?"

"Both." He shifts slightly, wincing in pain. "And neither."

Even bound and weakened, obviously ill used by the filth at my back, I sense power radiating from his withered form. Strength, guile and a weariness so heavy he wears it like a shroud. He sincerely wants to die. Should I grant his wish?

I raise my sword. He smiles, not an overlarge gesture, just the smallest twitch of his cracked lips. Without further rumination, I swing, the blade singing as it splits the air and slices the chain that binds him in one, smooth stroke.

His smile dies as he stares up at me. "Why?"

I turn and toss my braid over my shoulder.

"Why?" he calls again, his voice raspy.

Chains rattle and I picture him getting to his feet. I crouch over my victim, the bastard that had chained and raped the young man at my back, adding to what was an already top-heavy sentence. He lets out a snort and tosses an arm up. He smells of horse manure and unwashed flesh and some sort of nasty homebrew that kills humans almost as effectively as I do.

Almost. But not fast enough.

I kiss him lightly, unwilling to touch his flesh more than necessary, but with more potency, more feeling than I've ever managed before. I rise and watch the bastard's eyes open, watch as he starts to twitch, his gelatinous body that has caused so much harm, shuddering, racked with unfathomable pain. The young man I've freed comes to stand beside me, his green eyes wide as he watches the bastard thrash.

Foam bubbles from his fleshy lips, runs down his unshaven chin. I spit to the side, trying to get the taste of him out of my mouth.

His eyes shift to the captive as though pleading for help. The sight enrages me past the point of sense and I crouch beside him, grabbing his jaw and forcing him to look at my face.

"Don't look at him, filth. Look at me, your executioner. Do you know what awaits you? Ice in your blood, your bones frozen and your flesh being peeled off in strips slowly, over a century. You are mine now."

One final shudder and it is done.

I rise, wiping my hand on my cloak, then turn to the green-eyed youth. "Do you still long for death? Because that is what it looks like." I point to the corpse. "There is no reprieve, no chance to make things right. Just an end."

He stares at me a long moment, then suddenly grabs me, and presses his lips to mine.

I start at the assault, the way his hand fists on my braid, holding me in place. I wonder if he thinks kissing me would be like running himself through with my sword, some form of suicide.

So, I kiss him back. All the rage at what had been done to him, what would be done to me when I return to my court, bubbling forth. It is not a kiss of tender affection, rather one of desperate hungers and unnatural desires. Hot and ravenous and full of self-loathing. And understanding. Teeth clack, tongues duel. Two damaged souls collide with maximum impact.

He breaks away abruptly, gaze down, posture submissive. "Forgive me, my lady."

"I am not your lady," I tell his profile. "You don't like your life? Find a way to fix it. Brave souls seek something worth dying for and then devote every breath to living for it."

"What do you live for?" he asks, green eyes stark.

"The Hunt." I turn and stride from the barn before he can utter another word.

"What happened?" Freda frowns, her winged helmet reflecting the moonlight. "You were gone a long while."

"It's done now." I settle myself on my mount's back, my sword sheathed, my temper still high. "Let's go."

"Look," Nahini points back in the direction of the barn.

I turn in time to see fire blazing within, all the dry hay and weathered boards catching. Flames lick out of the window, through cracks in the boards.

I start, about to rush back in for the foolish young man, when a large black wolf streaks from the building, heading toward the woods.

My mount rears. I steady her with a sharp word, following the wolf. I see him pause at the tree line, green eyes glowing in the firelight.

"My queen?" Freda asks.

I stare at the wolf. He stares back. Something passes between us, electric as a bolt of lightning. It's him, somehow, I know it's him.

"We ride." I tell my warriors, then under my breath utter one word. "Godspeed."

CHAPTER 13

THE DEAD FOREST

Morning light reveals more information about our surroundings. Namely that the woods beyond our secluded bank are comprised of gnarled leafless trees, cracks in the ground and a yellow gray haze that stretches beyond my sightline. The air around me is sweet and cool, but there's the scent of rotting things coming from that direction.

"The Dead Forest." Aiden, once again in human form grubby sweatpants and all, crouches beside me. He holds the water bottle out and I reach for it with one hand, the other securing the quilt around my body as I sit up.

"Apt name," I take a small sip, trying to conserve the water for our upcoming journey. "It doesn't look like anything lives there."

"If a creature tries to build a home in the deadwood, it doesn't last very long. The land is cursed, the soil toxic. I'd advise you to go around it, since I don't know how it will affect a human."

"How long would it take to go around it?"

"A few weeks."

Not time I'm willing to sacrifice. "I'll chance it."

I take another small drink and try not to stare at Aiden, the dream fresh in my mind. His face appears so different than it had, gaunt and hollow as if like the forest before me he was little more than a haphazard pile of skeletal remains.

Why did he want to die so badly? The drive had been strong enough that he'd kissed me, even after he saw what could happen. Sexual assault may make a person suicidal, but he'd displayed no signs of shame relating to his physical condition. He hadn't tried to cover his nudity or the signs of abuse, had met and held my gaze as both a human and a wolf. No, there must be more to Aiden that I didn't know yet.

"We should get going," Aiden says now. "We don't want to be in there come nightfall."

"I need to get dressed."

He nods and then presents his back. I crouch beside my bag and extract the spare set of clothing from the Ziploc bag, glad to have something other than the smelly discards from yesterday.

The breeze off the lake is chilly and I shiver when I drop my blanket. As always, Aiden appears unaffected. "Don't you ever get cold?"

"I'm descended from a fire deity," His tone is soft, his gaze still on the dead forest. "Flames are in my blood, and it keeps me warm, regardless of the ambient temperature."

"Must be nice," I pull on my underwear and jeans as well as yesterday's bra, that once again fits.

"Press up against me," Aiden suggests.

I pause with my tank top over my head. "No."

"It'll warm you."

"And if that's not the oldest line in the book," I mutter into the fabric.

He makes a disgusted sound. "Nic, what will it take to

convince you that not every suggestion is some sort of attempt to get into your pants?"

I'm about to retort when I note the defeated set of his shoulders. He was sexually abused. Regardless of what our relationship had been in the past, it's possible he no longer wants that kind of connection. Instead of a waspish rejoinder, I murmur a soft, "I don't know. Giving people the benefit of the doubt isn't my strong suit."

"I'm trying to be honest with you. To open up," he swallows audibly. "It's not easy for me either, you know. There was a time when you knew everything there is to know about me. And I knew you. Feeling as though I know you even though you don't remember me...," he shakes his head.

Hesitantly, I reach forward and put a hand on his shoulder until he turns to face me. "You lost a friend, too. Didn't you? The way I lost Sarah?"

"Friend isn't the right word. We were close, we understood one another. Accepted each other as we were, faults and all." Then correctly reading my next question he adds. "And yes, we did have a physical relationship."

"Consensual?" I need to know for sure.

"Yes. Neither one of us is a rapist, Nic." He exhales wearily. "You're *right* there. I scent you. I recognize you. But you're so different. Cold. Suspicious. Untrusting. When was the last time you laughed?"

"Never." I don't laugh, not the way he means. Sure, I possess a certain wry amusement, a sharp wit, but that's not the same as watching others lose themselves in good humor.

"You used to," he says quietly. "Until all the breath went out of you. Joy effervesced from you like rays of light."

I break eye contact and pull on my flannel shirt. "I can't be who you want me to be, Aiden."

"It's not about what I want. You're hiding from yourself."

Socks, shoes, and then I close the pack and fling it over my shoulder. "Well, you'd know about that, wouldn't you?"

He frowns. "What do you mean?"

"Isn't that why you wanted to die when I first met you? Because you were ashamed of who you were, what you'd done?"

It's a wild shot in the dark, but it hits him center mass. His jaw drops, and he staggers back a step. "You remember that night?"

I pivot toward the deadwood. "No. Are we going or not?"

Aiden grabs my arm, his grip loose but unshakable. "Tell me how you know about that."

The hot temper that keeps flaring inside me is going to get me in trouble. "I dreamed it, okay? I didn't even know if it really happened until I saw your reaction."

Aiden's grip on my arm tightens and I see him swallow. "Then maybe the rest of your life will come back. In time."

I search that bright green gaze, wondering what exactly he is feeling. Some sort of deep emotional response though the feelings shift too fast for me to read them. Surprise, possibly relief. Followed by caution.

"Come on," his hand slides down my arm until he can take my hand and leads me into the blighted forest. "We have a lot of ground to cover."

Maybe it's just my imagination but his steps seem heavier. As though the possibility of me remembering my former life has added a burden that he must carry.

The question is, why?

THE LIGHT IS different in the Dead Forest, muted by a sickly yellow haze. The sour smell grows stronger, like rotting piles of lemons and sulfur. Soon my sneakers are coated in a tarlike substance that drips from thorny vines, the only thing that seems to flourish within its borders. The vines aren't passive either. They reach out, trying to trip us or to stab those razor-sharp thorns into my flesh. Aiden, back in wolf shape, blazes the trail ahead, using teeth and claws to fight our way through.

It's slow going. Aside from the vines and the tree roots there are bones. Small bones which might have belonged to birds or squirrels. Medium sized bones like those of a four-legged creature, all the flesh rotted away. Large human sized bones mix in too, a femur here, a ball and socket joint there. At one point we cross over a smooth mound, what I assume is a natural rise in terrain turns out to be a giant-sized cranium, vines weaving in and out of its eye sockets.

Enough thorns can take down even a giant. Aiden pauses on top of the skull and does a slow survey of the land around us. *Are you familiar with stories of fairies putting humans to sleep for hundreds of years?*

I nod, and he continues. *The vines of the deadwood have been used for just such a purpose. Ground down into powder and mixed into a drink.*

Why are the vines so predatory? Though I could speak aloud, having Aiden in wolf form is good practice for my telepathy.

They don't know when their next meal will happen by. The thorns don't kill, they only put creatures to sleep. A long, deep dreamless sleep. Anything that reaches that state here will be slowly digested to feed the forest. Only the desperate cross the deadwood. And even they should never cross it alone. Come on, I can see the path ahead.

Aiden charges back into the undergrowth and after a swig from the dwindling contents of the last water bottle, I follow.

The vines, I note as the afternoon wears on, have some

sort of collective intelligence. One will rise to tangle in my back foot even as another dive bombs the spot where my torso lands. Aiden charges back every time, claws slashing the vines to ribbons. But there are always more to take their place.

We're being followed.

All the hair rises on my nape as Aiden's voice echoes in my mind. *By who?*

The vines. The wolf hunches low, as though ready to attack. *The forest knows we're almost out and it doesn't want to let us go.*

A slithering, like that of a thousand snakes.

I can't fight them all. Aiden whirls, mentally screaming one word at me. *Run!*

We both take off at a sprint, vines shooting up from the toxic soil, intent on felling us. Though Aiden could out distance me easily, he stays by my side, taking down any vines that come too close.

In the distance I can see the sun sinking, down and down and down. Now I understand why Aiden wanted to make it through this horrible place before dark.

One succeeds in tripping me and I go down hard on hands and knees. My palms slam into something sharp. I lift the hand to examine even as I scramble back upright. "I've been stuck."

Another jab through my jeans, leaving a bloody furrow in my upper thigh.

Aiden bites the vine in half before it can strike again. *Get on my back.*

I do as he says, my limbs already sluggish. A yawn escapes but my adrenaline spikes. I don't want to fall asleep in this horrible place to be digested and feed the dead forest for the rest of my life.

Aiden turns to face the vines and a giant fireball erupts

from him, clearing the vines on all sides. He doesn't even wait for the flames to die down as he charges for the edge.

Finally, as the sun dips below the western horizon, we stumble out of the deadwood. The line demarcating the Dead Forest from the swampland beyond is clear, the ground softer, loamier, the greenery lush and the air moist instead of thick with the rotten citrus and sulfur smell that had been burning in my nose all day. The vines, which had been trailing us for the better part of an hour, slither back to their toxic home, deprived of their prize.

My strength goes out of me all at once and I slide down Aiden's back, collapsing onto the moss at his feet.

Nic!

I roll to my side, too exhausted to keep my eyes open. A blinding flash of light and then warm hands are on me, pulling the thorn still embedded in my palm free. Blood pools out, too much blood for that small wound. Aiden dumps the last of the bottled water on it as well as the scratch on my thigh. I hiss. The water might as well be acid, the burning is so intense.

His arms curl around me. There is a sense of weightlessness as he lifts me. My head lolls against his hard chest.

"Hold on Nic," Aiden urges as he starts off into the swamp. "Don't go to sleep just yet."

I try to nod but my head must weigh a thousand pounds. Moving it is out of the question.

"Talk to me," he urges, his speed increasing. He is barefoot and weighed down with me and my pack and even after a day of hiking through less than ideal conditions, his breaths are even. "Tell me a happy memory."

I frown, my concentration muddy. "Birthday."

"Your birthday?" He ducks under a low hanging branch.

I shake my head. "Don't know when my birthday is."

"You were originally born on the night of Samhain. October 31, by your calendar."

I smile dreamily. "Like the fall. Feels like a beginning."

"Whose birthday was it?"

Birthday? Right, the memory I'd dredged up for him. "Chloe's. We crashed a bachelorette party in Nashville. Women were so drunk, they didn't even notice us follow them onto the party bus."

A soft chuckle echoes in his chest. I can feel it reverberate against my cheek. "From what I've seen of human women, they can get pretty wild. How old were you?"

"Fourteen. They wouldn't let me in the all-male review."

"I should hope not. You stayed on the bus?" He leapt over a particularly soggy patch.

"With the driver. He was bad, one of mine. It didn't even take him five minutes to come after me."

Aiden swore. "How is this a happy memory?"

My eyebrows pull together. "Because, the aunts let me hunt. Knew I needed to do it, accepted the world would be better off without a man that preyed on intoxicated women. It was Chloe's birthday, but she gave me the gift and Addy helped hide the evidence. That was before..." I swallow, my throat tight.

"Before what?"

I close my eyes, lulled by his warmth, the strong cedar and sage scent of him. "Tired."

"No, Nic. Stay awake." Aiden jostles me hard. Fatigue overwhelms me, and I don't protest his rough handling. "Damn it, you can't succumb to the poison."

He sets me down on the ground and leans over me, his hands on my shoulders, shaking me. "Nic, please. Fight it. If you go to sleep now, I don't know if I can wake you in your lifetime. You could die without ever regaining consciousness."

My eyelids flutter. I want to stand, to move but my limbs are ungainly and out of my control. I utter two words I've never said before. "Help me."

"I will," Aiden insists but I can tell from the edge in his voice he doesn't know how.

"Burn me," I curl onto my side.

"What?" his hands fall away. "I can't."

"You have to," a yawn breaks me away from the thought, so wide it makes my jaw pop. "Pain is the only way to keep me from falling asleep."

There is no sound for a moment. The damp ground of the swamp seeps into my clothing, rocks and sticks poke at me but even the discomfort isn't enough to fight back the wave of sleep coming for me.

Aiden's hand wraps around my forearm in a tight grip. "Forgive me."

At first his hand is just warm, then hot. I try to shift away as the heat expands. Smoke curls away from the point of contact. A scream tears from my throat as agony rips through my arm. I jerk, but he holds on tight. The smell of cooked meat wafts up, making the experience that much more surreal. Tears pour down my face, my wordless scream making my throat hoarse.

Then, right before I am about to pass out, Aiden lets go. I fall back, cradling my throbbing arm. The pain is worse than any I've ever felt. I can't stop the flow of tears.

Behind me, Aiden has his head in his hands and is rocking back and forth. In my head I hear him chanting, *I'm sorry, I'm sorry I'm sorry.*

The urge to comfort him wells up in me. He's suffering now, the anguish in his mental voice is evident. The desire to help him is...odd and I do want to give into it, but it's not strong enough to overcome the pain of the burn. Nerves are singing out all over my body, the sense of wrongness setting off every alarm bell in my brain. I can't touch the wound directly, but visual inspection shows a hand print seared into my skin, somewhere between a first and second-degree burn.

"Well, what do we have here?" A new voice asks.

Through my tears, I see a new pair of feet and a mud-spattered skirt hem.

A reed basket is deposited on the ground beside me, as well as a rusty lantern and then the owner of the feet crouches down to inspect my arm. I try to pull away, to protect the damaged flesh, but her grip is like iron.

"This looks painful. Were the two of you fighting?"

"He had to," I gasp, my voice like a puff of smoke. "To keep me awake."

"You came through the deadwood, didn't you? Foolish child." From her tone I can't tell if she means me or Aiden. She reaches into the basket, rummages and snaps off something green and holds it out to me. "Aloe Vera. Probably better that you apply it."

I hold out a shaking hand and she squeezes the plant until a cool gel oozes out of it. I am slow bringing the clear substance up to my arm, afraid it'll make the pain worse. But the first touch soothes the damaged skin, cooling the over-heated flesh. I use up what she gave me and reach out for more. She obliges, then gets up and carrying her lantern, steps over me to check Aiden.

"I don't see any sign of a wound." She says, placing her long white fingers against his forehead. "No blood or bruising."

I sit up. Dizziness and nausea well up, but I fight them back, focusing on the slim figure crouched by Aiden's side. Her hair is long and falls in red-gold curls, her clothes plain and unadorned. Like Aiden her feet are bare. "I don't think he is hurt, at least not physically."

She puts two fingers against a spot on his neck, probably checking his pulse. "You said he had to hurt you. Is he the cause of that burn?"

I nod. She stares at me with eyes the same color as Aiden's. "You're Laufey?"

"No time for introductions, girl. Help me get him back to my house."

I move so that my good side is propped against Aiden and drape his arm over my shoulder. He weighs about as much as the two of us combined "Do you know what's wrong with him?"

"Mental trauma," she grunts, hefting him with much more ease than I did, even stopping to collect her basket. "You ever hear the expression this will hurt me more than it hurts you?"

When I nod she goes on, "Well, for someone like Aiden, that is a literal statement. Hurting you damaged him and he wouldn't have done it if there had been any other recourse."

I want to ask more questions, about her and Aiden and our surroundings, but keeping in line with her sure quick steps drains my already low reserves.

Finally, we come to a dock. Tethered to the end is a small rowboat.

"Don't just stand there girl, climb in." Laufey shifts all of Aiden's weight to herself, freeing me enough to step into the boat.

I do, taking my pack with me and settling it in the bow of the boat. Laufey hands over her basket, the lantern and then physically lifts Aiden and places him on the bottom of the boat, his head in my lap.

"How...?" I ask, awed by her strength.

"You forget, I'm a giant, girl. I could have carried both of you if I needed to. Better that you walk though, shake off the last of the thorn's effects."

"You don't look like a giant." Or a grandmother.

"And you don't look like a fairy queen bloody and sweating, but here we are." Her tone is light, breezy but I get the hint of bitterness lurking beneath the easy manner. "Keep him still while we row. Touch his skin. Let him hear your voice. Smell you."

"Smell me?" I blink up at her.

"So that he knows you're all right. It's his worry over you that put him in this fugue. You're the only one who can reassure him enough to come out of it."

Though I don't understand, Laufey appears deadly serious. I hold out a fistful of my hair and bend down, the blond waves trailing across Aiden's face.

"Why does he care so much that he hurt me? He barely even knows me."

Laufey's green eyes, so like Aiden's, pierce me to the spot. "Because you're his mate."

CHAPTER 14

THE NEEDLE OF THE FOREST

"Is mate?" I shake my head back and forth in incomprehension, sending even more hair across Aiden's lower jaw so it sticks in the dark stubble growing there. "No."

"Fool girl, why else would he have gone to the trouble of resurrecting your sorry carcass?" Laufey holds a stick about ten feet long and skinny as the handle of a rake. She plunges it into the water until it hits the bottom. I see it reverberate in her hand. She pushes off, our small craft leaving the safety of the shore.

"*Aiden* resurrected me? He told me only the giants have the knowledge to do that sort of magic."

"The giants have the knowledge," Laufey yanks on her pole until the muddy end breaks the surface, then thrusts it with a barely leashed violence back into the water. "That doesn't mean any of us have the inclination to interfere. You, little Queen, had been betrayed and murdered. And no one cared, not one wretched soul in your entire court, save for my grandson."

My gaze falls to Aiden's still slack face, all the odd things he's said to me clicking into place. *My only wish is to protect you, Nicneven. I hate to see you in pain. As my lady desires.*

"What does that even mean?"

"To you? That you can order him about and he will have to obey your every command. That he will fight for you, carve off pieces of himself for you and even find a way to die for you if you will it. For him, it means nothing but endless suffering. Even now, I see it in your expression girl. The avarice for power, the desire to use this latest information to your advantage."

Even despite the swampy air, my throat is completely dry. "I won't—"

"You will." She cuts me off with a steely glare that sees all the way to my blackened soul. "When you want something badly enough, you will use him and discard him, the way you did before."

I want to know more about before, but it's clear she doesn't intend to elaborate. "You don't like me very much." I don't phrase it as a question.

"No," she agrees. "There's not much there to like. What he sees in you is unique to him."

I gesture to the burn on my arm. "Then why bother to help me?"

"Aiden was bringing you here for some reason. He won't understand if I leave you to rot, the way I want to. Foolish child." This time there isn't any doubt that she means Aiden, the harsh words softened by the fond way she looks upon him.

I look down at Aiden. Maybe it's my imagination, but the tightness of his jaw appears to relax a little and his breathing seems more even than before. His eyes remain closed but at least he looks like he's sleeping, not dead.

Caretaking isn't my strong suit. I've never had to comfort another person. The Fates never get sick and injuries from animal bites or farm work are patched up and then ignored. Sarah when her romances inevitably went south came to me, but she liked to bitch about all the reasons she was better off without the bastard. My role involved nodding and making sympathetic noises while spooning out ice cream.

With Aiden, I don't know where to put my hands. Finally, I settle for one on his shoulder and the other stroking his hair, the way I would pet an affectionate animal from Addy's clinic. There's no evidence it helps, but neither Aiden nor Laufey protest so I keep up a steady rhythm.

"Up ahead," Laufey says. It's the longest sentence she's uttered in half an hour.

I glance up, but full dark has set in and my eyes can't make out anything beyond the glow of the small lantern.

"Listen," Laufey stills, lifting her pole out of the water and setting it down inside the small vessel.

Without the sound of rowing, the night becomes uncomfortably still. There are no frogs, I realize with some surprise. No buzzing of insects, or chirping of birds. Just a steady lap of water against stone and my own ragged breaths.

"What—?" I begin but she holds up a hand to silence me. Then, over the quiet water comes a mournful tune. The sound is difficult to pinpoint, and I strain my ears as the music creeps inside me. Some sort of stringed instrument, possibly a violin, in the hands of a master musician. In the swamp? It makes no sense.

Though I have no ear for music, the haunting melody invades me, seems to caress my frazzled nerves. The stinging pain in my arm is forgotten, Aiden and Laufey vanish from my thoughts as the music fills my mind, my soul. So lonely, whoever is playing must be so lonely, a kindred spirit, lost with only the violin for solace.

I don't realize I'm standing until I am yanked back down by a hand that covers my mouth. I struggle, needing to get to the musician, to find out who it is and why they play such sad notes but the iron grip on my mouth won't budge.

Then there is a splash. The music cuts off abruptly and my struggles cease.

"Look," Laufey loosens her grip and leans to peer into the black depths of the swamp. I mimic her, seeing ripples from whatever it was she threw overboard. And then about two feet away, a hideous head emerges. Hair the texture of seaweed, skin the color of dying moss and yellow eyes that glow brighter than our lantern. Eyes that devour. One three-fingered hand appears, holding a small, thin object aloft. It glints in a shaft of moonlight. A needle.

The yellow-eyed creature watches us go, its unnerving stare following us around the next bend. Only when it is completely out of sight, does Laufey exhale audibly.

"What was that?"

"Nøkken."

At my blank look, she frowns. "A water horse, if you prefer."

That didn't look like any horse I'd ever seen. "That was what was playing the music?"

When she nods, I voice my next question. "Why did you throw a needle to it?"

"Metal objects buy passage from the Nøkken. Any bits of iron or steel will do. Think of it like a toll."

"You mean if we hadn't paid it wouldn't have let us continue?"

Laufey cast me a withering stare. "If we hadn't paid, it would be digesting you right now."

"Is there anything in this place that *doesn't* want to eat me?"

A soft chuckle escapes her. "Girl, you're human. Even the creatures that won't actually eat you crave a taste of your flesh."

A shudder racks my body. "Aiden told me about the division between the courts, the fey that want to eat humans and those that don't. Why are we such a delicacy?"

"Having never eaten a human, I couldn't say. Vegetarian."

"Me too."

She blinks at me in surprise, then tips back her head and laughs. "Oh, that is good. The Unseelie queen is a born-again vegetarian. The Norns are not without a sense of irony."

Norns. The three sister goddesses charged with guarding the Well of Fate. I'd always thought of them as a Germanic version of the Fates. Although maybe they weren't just a similar myth, but the same three women. Sure, their names were different, but many cultures had different names for things. Could it be possible that Chloe and Addy were the Norns charged with guarding the Well? "Do you know what happened to the third sister?" I ask Laufey.

"She was executed long ago." Leaf green eyes grow hard.

"Executed? Why?"

"For tampering with destiny. It is really their only crime. The Norns are a law unto themselves, they go where they wish, do what they wish, but they must uphold the will of the cosmos. Humans can change their own fate, gods can change their own fate, but the Norns cannot."

"But they are like super goddesses, aren't they? Who could kill one of the Fates—err…Norns?"

A small smile curves her lips. "Why, the other two of course."

AFTER WHAT FEELS LIKE AN AGE, the boat finally pulls up to a crooked dock. I look up to see a massive water wheel churning slowly and beyond it, what looks like an abandoned house with a tree growing out of its roof. Not any sort of tree I recognize. It's massive, the trunk is visible through the open windows, the bark a gray-brown that blends seamlessly into the dim lighting of the swamp. Branches as thick as my thighs stretch out to cover the remaining bits of the roof.

"Home sweet home," Laufey steps easily from the boat to the rickety dock. I watch as she bends down and ties an expert knot around one rotting post, tethering the rowboat in place. Then she steps back in and helps me pull Aiden to his feet.

His eyes are open now, I can see them reflecting the lantern light, but he doesn't appear to be tracking us or anything else.

The air is cool and damp and smells of green and growing things. It seeps through my clothes and down to my marrow even as sweat beads my brow. I struggle beneath Aiden's weight, taking one shambling step and then another toward the literal treehouse.

"I'm home!" Laufey calls out in greeting as we cross the threshold.

At first, I wonder whom she is addressing, but am too bogged down by Aiden and my own saturated clothing to care.

Then I see dozens of little brown creatures, no larger than my thumb, scuttling together to form a larger shape. Like the way that Aiden's sparks can pull apart and come together, yet I get the impression that each of these beings is an individual, even as they solidify into a short, stout woman.

"Was wondering when ye'd be home." The woman kisses Laufey affectionately on the cheek, then moves to help us with Aiden. "And what's happened to your youngen this time, pet?"

"Life," Laufey grunts. "Let's get him to the table."

Between the three of us, we manage to hoist Aiden onto a large flat table made of stone.

"Get him out of those rags. I need to make sure he isn't otherwise damaged. Laufey barks and it takes me a moment to realize she's addressing me.

"Um," I slide a look to the remains of the muddy tattered sweats. "I'm not really comfortable—"

Laufey talks over me. "Fern, stoke the fire, put on a kettle of hot water, get some clean linens and my medicine chest."

Fern nods once and then scatters, or at least the bits of her scatter in different directions. I see a few of the twig-like creatures carrying wood to the fire, others struggling with a cauldron of water as still others flit up into the tree.

"What are you waiting for, an engraved invitation?" Laufey turns to a water pump and begins scrubbing her hands like a surgeon. "Undress him."

Can I really protest when Fern, who appears to be the ultimate multitasker, is doing everything else? My insistence that Aiden burn me was what got him into this. I need to help.

"Sorry about this," I say to Aiden and reach for the band of the sweats on either side of his narrow hips. "Your grandmother is insisting I strip you. She's a real peach by the way."

Behind me, Laufey barks out a laugh but stifles it quickly.

Taking a deep breath, I tug the fabric down. It's not a gentle or painless process, especially with his body inert. There is much tugging and lifting, rolling him to one side and then the other. Heat scalds my face as more and more skin is uncovered and I force my gaze away from between his legs, concentrating on the task and feeling like a grade A perv.

Finally, the fabric is free. No sooner is he naked than Fern —at least one-fifth of Fern—drapes a blanket over him, preserving his modesty.

"Child, you are as red as a ripe tomato," Laufey comments. "One would think you've never seen his naked form before. Don't you know shape changers prefer to be skyclad?"

"I've been doing my best not to." I hold the grubby sweats up. "He has no other clothes, so he's been making do with these."

Fern reassembles, her tasks complete. I don't miss the odd look that passes between her and Aiden's grandmother. I wonder for a moment if they can speak telepathically the way Aiden can, but dismiss it as they move into position, Fern on his left, Laufey standing regally at the head of the table. Fern reaches her bark colored hands to hold him still as Laufey takes three deep breaths. Theirs is a sort of mind-reading that speaks of years of familiarity and the deepest sort of trust. I'd seen Chloe and Addy work together that way to save a wounded Rottweiler. Needs being anticipated, every action focused on the task at hand.

"What are you going to do to him?" I ask as Laufey's palms begin to pulse with a soft, blue light. The glow isn't steady. Instead, it throbs like a heartbeat.

"Patch his mind back together, if he'll let me. Come closer girl, let him feel your presence."

I want to inquire about the process—how does one repair a shattered mind on a dining room table—but it's clear all her concentration is on her grandson.

"Take his hands," Laufey instructs.

Fern immediately picks up Aiden's limp left hand and I clutch his right. The warmth of his skin assures me that he'll live, at least. The question is, will he be Aiden again, or just a shell of the man I'm only just coming to know?

The pulsing in Laufey's hands spreads up to her elbow, the flashes of blue growing brighter. Her eyes slide closed, as though whatever she is doing is beyond sight.

Sweat beads her forehead and small tremors rack her form.

"Easy, Fe," Fern croons, still holding Aiden, but eyes on Laufey. "You know what can happen if you spread yourself too thin."

"No worries, my love." Laufey grates. "I know what I'm doing."

"Stubborn old bat," Fern says with affection.

Laufey smiles slightly.

"What can happen?" I whisper. The question slips out, but I don't take it back. If they can flirt and tease, they can keep me looped in.

Fern's gray eyes flicker in the blue lighting. "Patching a broken mind requires a deft hand for the healer and an ardent desire to live from the patient. If the healer stretches her abilities too far, she risks losing her consciousness in her patient."

I swallow. "And what about if the patient doesn't want to live?"

"A mind that doesn't want to heal could kill the healer who touches it."

My hand squeezes Aiden's. In my dreams, he'd wanted to die. I can only hope that is no longer his wish.

Stay with me. I think the words, staring down at his face. *Please.*

Laufey jerks as though she's been struck. Her head whips to me, eyes going wide. "What did you do?"

"Nothing?" The word comes out as a question because I'm not sure. "Why? What's wrong?"

She staggers back and the light winks out. Fern drops Aiden's hand and catches Laufey before she falls. "Fe, what's wrong?"

"He just...." Laufey shakes her head as though trying to

clear it. "The only way to describe it is that he slammed the door in my face."

Nic?

I start when I hear his voice in my head. *Aiden? Can you hear me? Are you hurt?*

"What's going on, girl?" Laufey snaps, yanking her arm free of Fern and staggering back to the table.

"I can hear him. In my head." I squeeze Aiden's hand tighter and repeat my question.

Are you? The mental voice sounds small, wary and tired, like an exhausted and frightened child. *I hurt you.*

I squeeze his hand tightly. *Yes, because you needed to but I'm fine now. You saved me. Are you ready to wake up?*

No answer.

"This means he'll be all right, doesn't it?" I look up at his grandmother who is frowning down at him worriedly.

"I don't know." She shakes her head.

"But surely if he's talking to Nic, he's not shattered." Fern comes to stand by her side.

"It's not Aiden she's talking to." Laufey leans down and pulls one of Aiden's eyelids up. "She speaks to the wolf. Bind him to the table."

"What?" I ask, and then shrink back when vines grow up out of the floor, wrapping themselves around Aiden's body. "What are you doing?"

"Keeping him from attacking us." Laufey snaps. "That wolf is uncontrollable and deadly."

"No, he isn't." I shake my head. "I've been around Aiden's wolf plenty and he never once hurt me."

"That's because it was my grandson in control of the beast, a control it took him centuries to build, brick by brick. To master the hunger, the need for blood, for killing. The beast within is insatiable." Laufey snaps at me. "Even the gods fear wolves like the one in Aiden."

Fern moves to stand between me and Aiden's grand-mother, acting as a physical buffer between the two of us. "Try to understand, Nic. It will destroy Aiden entirely if he harmed one of us. This is a simple precaution, to keep everyone safe."

I look down at Aiden again, bound by vines and tree limbs thicker than my thighs. Unable to accept what they are telling me. "Is the wolf really so bad?"

Laufey opens her mouth to form a retort when thunder booms outside. No, not thunder, but the sound of a thousand horse hooves.

Fern disintegrates into her smaller components, then reforms by the window. Her big eyes grow bigger, and she sways on her feet. "It's the Wild Hunt."

"They're after Aiden." I reach out and put a hand on his forehead, where sweat starts to bead. "They were tracking him in my world, too."

"I'll be roasting in Hel before they take him." Laufey storms out the door.

I hurry to the window and stand at Fern's side. Together we watch as Aiden's grandmother approaches the mounted warriors.

They are everywhere, horses and hounds, foot soldiers holding black banners. This isn't a hunting party, it's an army, one that looks more than ready to do battle. And Aiden's grandmother strides right up to it, as though she too is preparing for combat.

I blink as between one step and the next Laufey's head goes from an even six feet up to the edge of the roof. Then with another, above it. "Is she *growing?*"

"She is a giant," Fern's tone is brisk. "She loosed her grip on her glamour to remind those women with whom they are dealing."

The sight is impressive. By the time she reaches the front

line, her head is taller than the tallest tree. Her skirts swish as she moves, breaking limbs off trees and making the ground quake. I wouldn't fuck with her.

"Stand down, old woman." One of the mounted warriors rides forward, her voice authoritative. I recognize it from the woods behind the bar. "We are not here to do battle with you."

"It is you who will stand down." Laufey's voice booms out and I see several of the foot soldiers clap their hands over their ears. "You have no business on my land. Be gone."

"You harbor one we seek." The rider removes her winged helmet and I see a long blonde braid slip out before her perfect face is revealed. Freda, my second.

Before I am aware of making the decision, I stride to the door.

"Nic," Fern's twiggy fingers curve around my arm, stopping me on the threshold. "You can't go out there. You're human. If you interfere with the Hunt, they'll spirit you away."

I shake her off. "Let me go."

"Think of Aiden," Fern begs. "How will he react if he wakes up to find you gone?"

I glance back at the table, where Aiden is bound by greenery. "Better than if his grandmother dies or he is captured by the Hunt. I need to confront them."

She swallows and then releases me. "All right."

My pack is by the door, right where Laufey dropped it. I scoop it up and stride out into the clearing to meet my fate.

CHAPTER 15

TRUCE

They don't appear to notice me at first. Laufey's humongous back is to me and the warriors of the Hunt have eyes only for her. I approach slowly, heart working overtime, still not sure what compelled me out into the open when I could have easily hidden within the relative safety of the house.

Survival is my main instinct, and here I am, playing fast and loose with it.

Another warrior dismounts and removes her brass helm. A riot of black braids falls around her elegant dark-skinned face. Nahini, the tribal wise woman and third in command of the Wild Hunt. Her face and that of Freda's are as familiar as my own.

All around us, the swamp quiets, just like the woods when the Hunt chased us. Without the hoof beats or shouts from the hunters, the unearthly host is deadly still. Not a whicker from a horse or a shift in the saddle. The hounds stand ready to attack but don't pant or bark.

"Great Laufey," Nahini approaches with gloved hands out in front. "Your grandson swore allegiance to the queen of the

Unseelie. Brigit seeks him to keep his word. It is a matter of honor."

"He has broken no vow." Laufey points directly at me. "There is the queen he serves."

I start as all eyes shift toward me. Guess someone had noticed me.

"What trickery is this?" There is no recognition in Freda's face as her icy blue eyes narrow on me. "You would try to pass off a human as an immortal queen?"

But Nahini frowns and moves closer to inspect me. She stops when we are about ten feet apart. Hairless brows pull together. "Nicneven?"

"You can't possibly think—" Freda snaps.

"Look with your heart, sister. Not your mind." Nahini moves even closer. "It is her. You know my face, don't you?"

I nod, just once, afraid to make any large gestures.

"The ones from Beyond the Veil," Nahini says to Freda. "We have no record of where they came from. She's been collecting them. The great Nicneven hunts true!"

She gestures toward the rear of the host, where the foot soldiers stand. The ghostly horde of the wicked dead, those who will serve until the end of time. They part as though great hands shove them away, clearing a path.

I see Paul Anderson first, my most recent victim. Then the woman from Raleigh that'd poisoned her own son. That handsy party bus driver. The German hiker from the Black Forest, the one who'd tried to rape me when I was six years old. They are all here, their eyes unseeing, their forms flickering in the swamp lights. Condemned to death with a kiss, no choice but to serve the Wild Hunt forever.

I didn't just kill them. I've damned their immortal souls.

Hashtag #Stillnotsorry.

"My queen," Nahini drops to one knee before me. "I am yours to command."

Though I have watched people die on their knees, something about this subservience feels wrong. "Get up. I'm not a queen anymore."

Freda frowns from where her second still crouches before me. "How is it possible?"

"All things are possible," Laufey says. She's been shrinking until she stands at the same height I first saw her. "Just because one can doesn't mean one should. But as you can see, my grandson has broken no oath and Queen Brigit can shove off if she claims otherwise."

Freda shakes her head, her golden braid slithering like a serpent across her armor. "A test then, to prove she is Nicneven."

I have no confidence that I can pass a test posed by the acting leader of the Wild Hunt. My memories are from dreams, not actuality. I shoot a glance at Laufey, who simply nods. "So be it."

"Where do I hail from?" Freda stands chin raised in defiance.

I stare at her for an endless moment, scrutinizing her features, her stance, and manner. The pose is familiar. It's there, a spark of remembrance, a glimmer of a memory. I fan it the same way I would when building a fire, tending it carefully so that it will catch and grow. I smell the ice on the wind, the temperatures well below freezing, the tang of the sea.

"A small fishing village in what is today considered Norway." I don't know where the answer comes from, but instinctively I know it is right.

Freda crosses her arms over her breastplate, not convinced yet. "When did we meet?"

Now that I've placed her and mentally set the stage, the action unfurls, like a movie I saw long ago. "You trapped one of the low creatures of my court. Gave it its life in exchange for bringing you to the reigning queen." The words come slowly, with them, the memory of a skinny teenage girl kneeling at the base of the Shadow Throne. "There you offered to serve me in exchange for eternal life."

Her expression gives away nothing. Freda might have a better poker face than I do. "Why would I make such a bargain?"

"You were to be married to a man who had killed his last two wives. You didn't want to, but he had wealth and your father was greedy."

"And you granted my request," Freda nods.

I sense the trap, letting the story unfold in my mind. "No. I didn't." Though I'd wanted to, had felt a kinship immediately with the brave girl who would sell herself to the Queen of the Elphame rather than live the small, sorrowful life that the Fates dealt her. But I couldn't show weakness before the court, for word of any sympathy would be perceived as weakness.

"I let you return home, where your father married you off to the brute. That night, the Hunt came for him before he could land his first blow. And you were accidentally swept up in the furious host." Though it had been no accident. Once a human experiences the Wild Hunt, that human's soul belongs to the Hunt. But without my deadly kiss to mark her as one of the damned, Freda's life could continue as one of Nicneven's Nymphs.

Freda's bright blue eyes shone with tears, not of sadness, I realize, but of pleasure. "It's really you."

I shrug, trying to disguise my trembling hands. Up until this moment, I might have been able to convince myself that Aiden was influencing my memories, as they all had something to do with him. But my memories of Freda were as clear as those of Sarah in my mind. And undeniably mine. "I suppose it is."

Freda removes her stiff black leather gloves and reaches out to touch my face. I don't flinch under the contact. Her skin is cool against mine, like the frost of that icy northern village settled into her bones. I see the questions in her eyes, but then steely resolve takes over. Then she too drops to her knees.

Behind them, the entire host does the same.

A soft laugh from Laufey and she puts a hand on my shoulder. "The Wild Hunt is yours to command, Nicneven."

I stare out at the kneeling sea of bodies, both living and dead. My friends, my victims. A heady rush shoots down my spine. For most of my life I have known power, have wielded it over my contemporaries. A secret strength. But now I control an unstoppable army. What will I do with them?

"On your feet." This bowing thing is unsettling.

Almost as one, they rise.

"Aiden," I say. "You must stop hunting Aiden."

"Yes, my queen." The response echoes through the night.

I look to Laufey, wondering what ought to come next. She gives me a shrug.

"If I may, my queen," Nahini offers. "What should we tell Queen Brigit as to why we have stopped hunting her consort?"

Her consort? My blood superheats in my veins, my hands clenching into fists. He was *my* consort. Or, he had been. And she what, appropriated him the way she did the Hunt?

"Easy girl," Laufey again puts a hand on my shoulder. "Rein in your temper."

"I never used to have a temper," I grumble.

"Perhaps it would be best if Brigit doesn't realize you command the Hunt," Freda suggests. "Or that you are back. Until you are ready to return."

"Return? As in rule?" I'd come to Underhill to save Sarah, not to reclaim the Shadow Throne.

"Not now, of course." Nahini soothes. That's her place in the hierarchy of the Hunt, the moderator, the voice of reason. "Come Samhain."

"Brigit has ruled year-round for almost two decades," Freda argues. "Nicneven has always been stronger, even in her down cycle and with the Hunt at her back, I see no need to wait."

I can see plenty of reasons, the first being I have no interest in ruling over a court of fey that would rather eat me than talk to me. "I'm human, the Unseelie won't accept me."

"If you no longer rule, you no longer command the Hunt," Nahini says almost apologetically. "And the wolf's life is forfeit."

"Like hell it is." A snarl rips out of Laufey.

"But you can win your immortality," Freda waves off my mortal state as though stating a pesky detail. "I did. Nahini as well. We can coach you, prepare you for the gauntlet."

I glance back and forth between the two of them, wondering what I had done in my previous life that they would have such absolute faith in me.

Nahini looks up at the clouds scudding over the moon. "If we are to cross the Veil this night we should take our leave."

Freda curses. "We'll return in three days' time to begin your training for the gantlet."

My gaze sweeps to Laufey who stands as though still ready to do battle. "Will you promise not to hunt Aiden again until after this...gauntlet?"

Perhaps he would recover enough that we could run before their return.

"I vow it." Freda places a hand over her heart and bows.

"On my honor." Nahini steps closer, her shy smile so at odds with her warrior's stance. She puts one hand on either side of my arm, then bows her forehead until it touches my own. Then, just loud enough for me to hear she murmurs, "It is good to see you, my queen. You have been missed."

A lump forms in my throat, as though I'm seeing Sarah again. These women had been my friends, and although my memories of them are vague, it's still there, almost like watching characters from a favorite movie come to life. "It's good to see you, too."

Freda doesn't stand on ceremony, instead, she wraps me in a bear hug, all that raw emotion practically overwhelming me. She doesn't say anything, doesn't need to, I can feel her giddiness, her relief as though the emotions are my own.

They don't prolong the goodbye, instead, each woman pivots and side by side, they stride for their horses. The entire Wild Hunt is still as stone as they settle their mounts. Freda draws her sword, the one I remember from my dream and cuts the night air in a giant slash. An otherworldly breeze funnels through the space where she made her mark. Freda's pale white horse rears and then takes off at a gallop and vanishes. Nahini follows behind her and then the living host, male and female, hounds and horses, birds of prey all more beautiful than any known to man. I see the dead coalescing into nothing more than lights, the souls of the damned traveling fast as thought.

Three heartbeats later, the swamp around us is still.

"Where did they go?" I turn to Laufey.

She lets out a breath that could be mistaken for a hurricane's gust. "Through the Veil. *Seelenverkäufer* can cut it at any point and create a rift directly between Underhill and the mortal world."

"How?" I expect her to say magic so am surprised when she offers a more detailed explanation.

"The Veil is made up of spirits. The sword contains fragments of souls from the slain. It tricks the Veil, for lack of a better word."

"The Veil is sentient?" Chills rack my body at the thought.

"Not on the same level as you and I are. Not even in the same way Underhill is. It's more animal instinct, the bits that remain after a tree has fallen, or a stream has run dry, but there are still damp patches. Not human spirits, like the damned in the Hunt, but all souls are made of the same basic material.

"*Seelenverkäufer* contains the same instincts and for a short while, it can fool the Veil into believing the area it cuts through is still covered by the webwork of spirit. Eventually, the souls will discover the defect and knit up the gap, like beavers filling the leak in a dam. By that point though, the Hunt is long gone."

"Do souls ever get trapped in the Veil? People's souls I mean."

She nods. "Yes, which is why it's dangerous to cross without a weapon like *Seelenverkäufer*. When you crossed with my grandson, which way did you come?"

"Through a fairy ring."

She waves that off. "I mean, what was the transition in the other place? A bridge? A tunnel?"

"A ferry."

"Did you see lights like multihued shooting stars?"

When I nod she continues, "Those are the spirits of the Veil. If you'd fallen off that ferry, your soul would be consumed by those spirits, become part of the Veil."

An involuntary shudder courses through me. And I'd fallen asleep on the ferry, believing we were safe.

Laufey places one long-fingered hand on my shoulder, turning me back toward her treehouse. "That was very brave, revealing yourself to the Hunt to save Aiden. Did you know they wouldn't hurt you?"

"No." My memories of Freda had come charging back

only after she had removed her helmet. I'm just lucky that Nahini had recognized me.

"Then why leave the house?"

I look up at her. How to explain when I barely understand it myself. "I didn't want you to face them alone."

She blinks, as though I've said the last thing she expected. "I don't know whether you're terribly brave or terribly foolish."

"Both, according to my aunts."

Laufey laughs at that and then gestures to the house. "Let's go in. Fern will be beside herself with worry. For you see, I am also both terribly brave and terribly foolish, so you are in good company."

As Laufey predicts, Fern is atwitter, all wringing knobby knuckles and barely able to hold herself together. While Laufey explains what happened with the Hunt, I move to the table where Aiden still lies trapped by roots.

I took care of the Hunt. They won't be chasing after you for a bit. I tell him.

No reply, though his head moves slightly.

"No change, Fern?" Laufey takes up a spot on the other side of the table. With a casual gesture that speaks to deep affection, she runs her hand over his sweat-dampened hair.

"None." Fern shakes her head sadly. "Should I try spooning some broth into him? He needs to keep up his strength."

Laufey catches my eye. "Let Nic feed him if she wishes."

Her show of trust moves me. Funny, I never would have thought gaining the trust of someone that hadn't liked me at all a few hours ago would feel so…satisfying. And physically caring for another? Out of the question a week ago. But

Aiden has done so much for me. He brought me back from the freaking dead. Spooning a little broth into him is the least I can do. "I would, thank you."

Fern looks back and forth between us. "Well, how would you like to get cleaned up while the broth heats? Laufey can show you to the spare room while I get the supper on."

Laufey grunts and gestures for me to follow. Her steps are sure and light, belying no trace of the giantess within.

"Why don't you live in the castle with the others?" I ask as we ascend the spiral staircase around the tree.

"They banished me ages ago." Her tone is grim, and I notice her knuckles turn white where they grip the railing. Did I hit a nerve?

Never one to give up my advantage I ask, "Why?"

She shoots me a scathing look. "You are a curious sort."

I don't bother to deny it or apologize for the probing question. "Because of your relationship with Fern?"

She snorts. "No one cares about that. Nor did they care when Aiden's grandsire raped me and planted a child in my womb because some mystic told him I was to be the mother of his line. Giants are much like your Unseelie Court, doing what they wish, whenever and to whomever, they wish and not caring overmuch who is hurt. This will be your room."

Raped. She had been raped, forcibly impregnated. This creature that grew taller than trees, who'd faced down the Wild Hunt on her own. So, too had Aiden, if my dream-memories were accurate. The wolf inside him, the one that terrified Laufey and Fern, hadn't protected him. He could turn to embers and slip through a screen but still, he had been held captive, shackled somehow, and violated.

My stomach twists. Even creatures as powerful as they aren't completely safe.

Laufey pushes through a tangle of swamp moss and reaches for a small stone door. It scrapes on the floor, rattling me out of the dull fog of horror. She ducks down and into the room. The door is only about five feet high and swallowing the bile that had crept up my throat, I force myself to follow. The small space beyond the door looks more like a forest glen than a room in a building. A hammock swings between two young beech trees and cool clear water spills down over rocks into a pool large enough to bathe in. Stars twinkle overhead, the night sky visible through the lush canopy of the tree. The air is sweet and ripe with the rich scent of night-blooming flowers.

I glance down at my filth encrusted clothing. Mud and sweat stain this set, while the others smell of giant refuse. "Do you mind if I wash my clothes out in the pool?"

"Here are some clean clothes." Laufey reaches into nothing. One moment her arm is complete, then it vanishes at the elbow. A second later it reappears, holding a bundle of cloth. She shakes it out, revealing a long-sleeved shapeless dress the color of oatmeal. The cut is simple, and I can tell the hem will hit me mid-calf. She reaches through the invisible air again and pulls out a pair of sandals.

I frown. "Where did that come from?"

"My storage room."

"These look like they will fit me perfectly." She couldn't have just had them on hand.

Laufey nods. "Beings come to me for knowledge and healing. I barter with them and they trade me goods for my services. I take whatever is offered. If it made its way to my door, it's meant for me, even if I can't see why yet."

I examine the fabric, spy the label at the neckline. "This came from my world."

"Almost everything here does. We have no textiles, no industry. If we want resources, they need to come from beyond the Veil."

At my sharp glance, she elaborates. "You ever have something go missing? A spoon? A jar of peanut butter? Most likely it was a poor fey trying to feed his family. The courtiers, ones with stronger magic, like that of *Seelenverkäufer* can open portals into banquet halls, wedding receptions, and hotel kitchens anywhere on the globe. They can pick and choose, while the poorer subsist from whatever is within grabbing distance, through their own fairy rings and the In-Between at Midnight. In ancient times, humans left offerings out for the fey, but that tradition is almost extinct. The species here have been living off humans for millennia, like remora feasting off a shark's leftovers." She pauses and taps her chin. "Of course, some just eat the humans, though that practice is…frowned upon."

"Because it's wrong?"

"Because it's too easy to get caught. Better hurry and wash up. Fern will fret if the broth overboils." Laufey pushes out through the moss, though she leaves the stone door open.

I stare after her. Will I ever get my bearings in this mixed-up place? The water beckons and while I desperately crave some alone time to sort through all I've learned, I strip off my clothes instead. I haven't bathed since the bioluminescent lake and feel as though layers of filth cling to my skin. Once naked, I retrieve my soap and shampoo from my bag. The book of Norse mythology falls out, and I set it aside, still unsure of why I brought it.

The clear pool is an inviting lukewarm temperature and I wade in up to my hips. Lingering beneath the waterfall is tempting, but my stomach growls. My meager stash from the backpack is getting low, and there has been no sign of the food Aiden filched from the giants. Though asking for more than they'd already given galls me, I might have to beg a small meal off Laufey and Fern.

With no towel, I use my soiled plaid shirt to wick away the water, I comb my damp hair, then braid it haphazardly before slipping the dress on. The cloth is soft, some sort of woven knit fabric. The sensual feel is almost decadent against my bare flesh. Laufey hadn't bothered to provide undergarments and the dress is long. After a moment's hesitation, I decided to go *al fresco* rather than put the dirty items back on.

I rinse all my own clothing in the waterfall then hang it to dry over a tree branch before heading back down the spiral stairs. Though I've only been gone a few minutes, the room has been transformed. Aiden, while still tied down, sleeps in a massive four-poster bed before the fire. A plush armchair has been pulled up beside it and the steaming broth sits on a low table in a mug that looks like an upside-down acorn. On a piece of cloth beside it lies a rough-hewn wooden spoon.

"Eat yours first," Fern advises as she sets a loaf of sliced brown bread and butter down beside the mug along with a wooden knife. "You need to keep your strength up."

I smile in thanks and pick up a piece of the still-warm bread.

Fern pulls up a stool beside me and produces a basket of knitting. "The broth is vegetable-based, so no meat. Laufey mentioned you are vegetarian?"

"Thank you and yes, have been all my life."

She chuckles, it's a warm sound, like water bubbling over stones in a sunlit stream. "The Fates have an odd sense of irony. A man-eating wolf mated to a vegetarian."

"That's how they raised me. Not that they were morally against meat," Or killing. I take a bite of the bread. It's warm with a crusty exterior and a soft interior. "This is very good."

"My own recipe." She smiles. "My mother taught it to me and I passed it on to my own children."

"You have children?"

Her expression grows sad. "Had. Two girls. They were killed in the uprising at the topside palace when—"

She meets my gaze and the breadsticks in my throat. "The uprising when I was killed, you mean."

Fern nods. "They were house sprites in the topside palace, where the Unseelie Queen resides during her off-seasons."

My appetite is gone but I force myself to sip some of the broth, knowing if I don't eat, I'll regret it later. "And Laufey couldn't bring them back to life? The way I was brought back?"

Fern shakes her head as though even the suggestion is blasphemous. "Even if it were possible, it wouldn't really be them."

When I frown she says, "You of all people know what it's like, to have a past life interfering with your present. Urges that make no sense, memories that aren't your own. Dreams that are so vivid they drive you mad. Trapped forever stuck between who you were and who you long to be. No, they could come back, but they wouldn't be my girls again." She meets and holds my eyes and in her unwavering stare, I see the same sort of strength as I'd witnessed in her lover. The kind that could only stem from moral conviction and absolute certainty. "Would you wish this sort of life on anyone else?"

CHAPTER 16

REVELATIONS

Aiden finishes my cup of broth and two more, one spoonful at a time. Though I try to communicate telepathically with him several times, it's like looking for someone in a fogbank. Occasionally, I feel as though his mind brushes against my own, but he doesn't respond to my voice.

Fern sits with me the entire time, her three knuckled fingers clicking the knitting needles with superhuman speed. She finishes almost two-thirds of a blue and green blanket before packing up her yarn and standing from her stool. "If you don't need anything else, I think I'll head to bed."

"Will Laufey be down again tonight?" I hadn't seen Aiden's grandmother since she showed me to the guest room.

Fern shakes her head. "She's probably fast asleep. Dropping and reestablishing her glamour always drains her." She moves to a low chest and lifts the lid. Removes a finished afghan like the one she'd been knitting, this one in red and orange. She hands it to me with a smile. "In case you get cold."

"I appreciate it. Thank you." I've uttered those words more since stepping foot into this house than I have in my entire existence. The odd thing is, I don't know whether that says more about me or my life to date.

Alone once more with Aiden, I stare at his sleeping face and wonder how to reach him. With no one else in the room, I speak out loud.

"The burn on my arm is almost healed." I'd examined it while bathing and was surprised to see nothing more than some mild redness. "It doesn't hurt at all."

Behind his closed lids his eyes dart back and forth. What is he dreaming about?

"Please wake up," I whisper silently. "The Hunt will be back in a few days and if I don't agree to become queen again, to run their gauntlet, they are going to take you back to Brigit."

If what Freda and Nahini says is true, he'd been Brigit's consort as well as my own. Again, that searing stab of rage bubbles in my veins. "What are you doing to me, Aiden? Why did you come looking for me? What is it you want?"

No answer.

Frustrated tears sting my eyes. I wipe roughly at them and then move to stand before the fire. Though my memories are full of holes, the thought of becoming an Unseelie Queen ties my insides in knots. My reaction to the Hunt is different. Part of me feels as though I belong with Freda and Nahini, leading the unearthly host, punishing the wicked. I've always been a hunter, even when it's the prey that chases me.

I damned Paul Anderson and those like him with my Goodnight Kiss. Perhaps I could go back, return to the mortal world and keep hunting the way I always had. Addy and Chloe will be pissed, but they'll get over it eventually.

But what about Sarah? My inner voice prompts. *What about Aiden? Will you just abandon them to their fate?*

"There's nothing I can do about that," I mutter.

"Of course, there is," a female voice says.

I frown, glancing around. The voice hadn't sounded like Laufey or Fern. The notes were younger, sultrier. "Hello?"

A hand breaks through the fire. Small and pale, delicate, with a live snake encircling the wrist. "Come with me."

Say what now? I kneel. "I don't even know who you are."

"Hel." The voice responds, soft and crooning. "I've been watching you, Nicneven."

No that isn't a little bit creepy. "Hell? Isn't that a place?"

The snake writhes. The hand turns over, one finger curling and uncurling in a beckoning motion. "It's both. Come with me."

"Why should I?"

"Because I can help you remember. Like the dreams I sent to help guide you."

I shake my head, backing away from the hand, all the hairs standing on the back of my neck. My instincts are screaming at me to run. I don't trust this woman. "Why don't you come talk to me here?"

"I'm trapped in my queendom. Much like you can't cross the Veil back to your own world without an In-Between, I can't fully cross into Underhill."

Her answer is far too convenient. "No thanks. I don't want to risk getting trapped, too."

"You won't be," her voice is full of surety.

My heart pounds. The craving for information goes deep. I yearn to know whatever this ethereal being will tell me.

Again, the hand reaches out and I know she's not going to say anything more until I agree to go with her.

Swallowing, I lean down and reach for the ghostly hand. Hesitate.

Behind me, there is a thunderous roar. A crash.

I whirl in time to see Aiden fighting his way free of the vines.

"Quickly," Hel prompts, her hand flailing. "Before he gets loose."

"Aiden won't hurt me." The words don't sound at all confident. He looks mad, green eyes glowing, lips pulled back to expose his teeth. Another flash and then the man is gone. The wolf stands ready to spring.

"Aiden," I try, hoping to see him settle down. "It's me. It's Nic."

Saliva drips from his mouth, all his hackles stand on end. There is no recognition in his gaze, it's all animal, all predator about to strike.

I take a step back and raise my hands to ward him off. Something wraps around my bare ankle. I glance down, see the serpent that had been coiled around Hel's wrist now tethers me to her. She grips its tail, gives a yank. I fall to my knees and she drags me into the flames and down into the dark.

My head cracks against a stone floor and for a moment, all I see are stars swimming in darkness. The stench is overpowering, like rotting food left out to mold. I sit up, gagging from the reek of it. The air tastes acrid, as though we're in a musty room that hasn't been exposed to the elements since its construction a millennium ago.

"Forgive the deception. And the landing."

"Deception?" I ask, rubbing at the sore spot at the back of my head.

"Your wolf sleeps still. An illusion to persuade you to come closer so my pet could ensnare you."

Then a face appears.

Well, half a face.

On the left, she is a pretty young woman, probably about

my own age. Long dark hair like a river of night, blue eye the color of the ocean, flushed apple cheek, aristocratic nose, and full red lips. The right side of her face is withered like that of a mummy, the skull visible through shriveled skin, the cartilage of the nose missing, the teeth exposed. Her body is covered by a cloak so there's no making out her shape. I can't tell if the disfigurement is isolated to her face or spread throughout her whole body.

I've seen plenty of fresh corpses. But none of them have moved. Or spoken to me. A scream tears its way up through my throat and I scramble away from the horror.

"Apologies." It's the same voice that came from the fire. That lovely hand and a skeletal one reach up to the hood on the back of her robe and tugs it forward, covering her face. "I forget that the living have such a negative reaction to my appearance."

"Where am I?" I glance around the space. Logs burn green on a hearth. It's the only sign of color in the room. The rest of the chamber—it's too large with too many columns to be called a room—is gray, monochrome. The carved columns, the long table, the stone steps and dais atop them, even the throne is the same bleak hue.

Except it's made from neatly arranged bleached bones.

"You are in my realm." Hel glides towards the table, intentionally putting distance between us. "I would offer you something to drink, but that would trap you here forever."

The snake releases its hold on me and slithers after her. "Why have you brought me here?"

"You need to know a few things." Hel reaches down her living hand and the snake curls around her in a gesture that is almost loving. "I sent my sentries to Midgard to find you after I heard you were reborn. All but two have returned. I don't suppose you came across them?"

I watch as she pours a ruby red liquid into a gray chalice

and takes a sip. "Um no…" Then I recall the attackers behind the Shitty BanG. "Wait, the snake-like creature and the man-made of stone? They work for you?"

She dips her hood in what I suppose passes for a nod. "He was a golem, one of the protectors of the dead. The snake-like creature, as you call him, is a Naga. Not deep thinkers by any means, but they follow orders well enough."

I scramble to my feet, keeping my back to the wall. "Why did you send them after me?"

"I wanted to see if the rumors were true, that an immortal queen had been reborn as a mortal. As I said, I can't leave my home here, so the next logical step was to bring you to me. I also would like to offer you a deal."

"What kind of deal?"

Hel sets down her goblet and turns toward me. The deep folds of her hood conceal her startling face. "An exchange. My information for the souls you bound to the Wild Hunt. They belong here, with me, not roaming the worlds."

"Worlds?" Something else dawns on me. "Wait, did you say you sent your sentries to *Midgard?*"

Another bob of her cloaked head and a book appears in her hands.

With a start, I recognize my copy of Norse myths, the same one from my pack. "How?"

"Like the fair folk, I can grab what I need from other worlds unless it has a will of its own." She opens the book, seemingly at random and offers it to me.

I take it. The book is open to a picture of Yggdrasil, the World Tree.

Hel's skeletal finger points to the lowest realm depicted beneath the roots. "We are here. Here is your mortal world." That boney digit moves up to the middle part of the tree, seeming to stop in the center.

I stare at it, information clicking into place. Laufey had

called my aunts Norns, not Fates. Laufey for that matter was also mentioned in myths. I flip through the book, hunting for her name. There it is in black and white. The Needle of the Forest.

I look from the book up to the shaded space where Hel's face should be. "She's your grandmother, too, isn't she?"

Another bob of fabric. "I'm his half-sister, by way of our father."

"Loki." I let out a deep breath as it all comes together. "Loki is your father. Aiden's father."

A soft chuckle escapes her, though it holds no humor. "Sire is perhaps a better word, as he is a selfish short-sighted ass that thinks only of his own glory. But yes, we are biologically related, Váli and I."

"Váli?" I ask, frowning. "I don't remember reading about him."

The book in my hand starts flipping pages all on its own.

"I have duties to attend to. I'll leave you to read." A hand—her human one—lands on my shoulder. "We'll talk again soon."

With a start, I wake as something strikes my foot.

I jerk fully awake in my armchair and blink at the dying fire. On the four-poster Aiden sleeps soundly. Had it all been some sort of nightmare?

I stare down at the book at my feet, open to one of the last chapters, regarding the punishment of Loki, the trickster god.

Slowly, I reach down and pick it up. After one final glance at the fire, I sit back to read.

IT'S A TRAGIC STORY, the gist of which does tickle my memory. After much duplicity and trickery, the other gods decided they'd had enough of Loki's foolishness. As punishment for his involvement in the death of the beloved god Balder, Loki is captured, and his entire legitimate family brought to a cave in the Underworld. There, Váli, the older son by way of his wife Sigyn, is transformed into a wolf. The crazed beast shredded the younger son, Nari. The boy's entrails are used to bind the trickster god to the rocks beneath a venomous serpent. Sigyn is given a bowl to hold over her husband's head, to keep the venom from striking him, but every time she turns to empty the bowl, the venom splashes the god and the worlds quake from his agony.

The book says nothing about what happened to the wolf who'd been forced to murder his own brother. It assumes that he had been killed, too.

I stare at the figure on the bed. What if he hadn't? What if he managed to escape? Had to live with the horror of what he'd done, what had been done to him.

Aiden said he'd been born a god. And his transformation to a wolf had been a punishment, though not for anything he'd done.

Kill me, please. The Aiden in my dreams had begged. *I don't deserve to live.*

Guilt. That was why he'd allowed himself to be chained, beaten, violated. Guilt over murdering his little brother. Was that also why Laufey had been banished by the other giants? Because of her son's wicked deeds?

It explains so much, Aiden's self-loathing, why he doesn't like to talk about where he comes from or who his father is. Why Laufey, with all her power, fears the wolf within him.

If it killed his little brother, it's capable of anything.

Setting the book aside, I stand and stretch my throbbing back muscles. My head feels too light, as though it will float up off my shoulders at any sudden movement. Aiden groans in his sleep, thrashing against the vines. Is he dreaming of the scene I just read about?

So many questions, I have so many questions and only he possesses the answers.

Why did you bring me back? I think at him.

The thrashing stops and his brow furrows. *Nic?*

Yes. I take his hand, trying to forge a connection that will draw him out of his self-imposed prison. *I'm right here. We're at your grandmother's.*

Sweat beads his brow. *It's not safe for you.*

What isn't?

Me. That one-word echoes through my mind. It pulses like a wound, throbbing with anguish. *I'm losing control.*

Of the wolf? I tamp the thought down before I can project it to him, not wanting to mention the beast or what it might do. *I can take care of myself.* I squeeze his hand again, hard. *Remember? I'm a badass hunter of men.*

His lips twitch as though a smile is trying to break free. *Yes.*

I hesitate a moment, fighting the impulse to brush his lips with my own. So many years fearing my gift, that I would unintentionally hurt someone with a gesture of affection. But never have I allowed fear to dictate my actions. I kissed Aiden before and he didn't die, both in the dream and in our reality.

Slowly, I lean down and press my mouth to his.

Heartbeat. Heartbeat. Heartbeat. I pull back.

His eyes flash open, the green glowing in the dim room and Aiden's wolf looks out at me. There is no sign of recognition on his face. We are two predators, sizing each other up. Its gaze falls to my lips and a low growl fills the space between us.

I want to back off completely, the sound is clearly meant

as a warning. But instinct, my well-honed instinct, screams that I don't want to give him an inch.

"Back down," I say, my own words a growl.

He bares his teeth, a snarl ripping past his lips.

"Nic?" Laufey appears, wearing a long white dressing gown, an edge in her voice.

He jerks at the sound, the warning rumble ripping through the quiet room.

"I got this," I say to her, my eyes still locked with his. "Stay away."

"He'll kill you." She is convinced of this, I can hear it in her voice. "He killed his own brother."

"He won't hurt me." That's what got him into this state, burning me. To save me, yes, but the act also brought the wolf out to kill the threat that harmed the one it protects. I've seen it in the veterinary clinic, mother dogs injuring the humans that would help them to protect their pups. I know it, my instinct knows it. I need to convince the wolf I'm not in any danger, so it releases its hold on Aiden. "Just stay back."

Thankfully, she does. In the quiet, I hear her bare feet scraping against the floor as she retreats.

"Now it's just you and me," I say to Aiden's wolf.

The snarling stops, though his unblinking stare doesn't waver. I press my advantage and climb up onto the four-poster beside him and throw one leg over him, my body pinning his. He growls again but the sound is less of a warning this time, more like an automatic response. I grip his hair with my hands and pull lightly, staring down into his eyes and think the words at him even as I say them out loud. "Let go."

He raises his face, though he can't go far, not with the vines and me pinning him in place. He moves towards my neck and for a terrifying moment, I think I've made a mistake—that he's going to rip my throat out as I saw him do to the snake creature. But his goal is the hair that has unraveled from my haphazard braid. His chest rises once on a slow inhale and when he breathes out, I can feel the tension leave him entirely.

We stay that way for countless moments and then he sags back against the bed. I breathe in his cedar and sage scent, feel his chest rise and fall beneath me. After a while he sighs, the sound human, not the animal. I look up. Sweat beads his forehead as though a fever has broken. His features are pinched and exhausted, his stubble rough but there is a stillness about him. The tension seeps from him, his rigid posture sags and his lids flutter closed.

"Aiden?" I ask, just to make sure.

"Yeah," the word is hoarse, his throat dry.

I release the grip I have on his hair and call out to his grandmother. "It's okay. He's back."

She and Fern bustle in, recrimination for the foolish chances I took from Laufey, a flurry of multitasking from Fern.

"Girl, you don't have the sense the gods gave an opossum prick," the giantess snaps at me. "Stubborn, foolhardy child."

"I think I'm growing on her," I say to Aiden.

A dry chuckle escapes, but then morphs into a series of coughs. I realize I'm still sitting on him, completely nude beneath the borrowed dress that has ridden up to mid-thigh. My face flames. In front of his grandmother and her significant other no less.

Aiden catches my gaze, amusement in his eyes. The coughing grows worse. Oh yeah, he picked up that nugget of thought all right.

Carefully, I slither off him as Fern—part of her anyway—arrives with a cup of water.

Laufey releases the bindings and helps Aiden sit upright so he can drink.

I slink off the bed, surreptitiously shaking the fabric of my dress back down, then make my excuses. "I'm beat. See you all in the morning."

"Nic," Aiden reaches out and takes my hand. "Thank you."

His calloused palm on my skin feels… right. I shrug out of his hold. "Night."

Picking up the book and the afghan Fern had given me to cover it, I head for the stairs without a backward glance.

"She's such an odd, prickly sort," I hear Laufey grouse.

"That she is." There's a note of whimsy in Aiden's voice. "I wouldn't have her any other way."

You don't get to have her at all, I mentally correct him and stomp to my room.

Downstairs the coughing fit resumes.

CHAPTER 17

PAST AND PRESENT

I am in the kitchen of the little stone cottage in the meadow. Time's almost up. The signs of the change are everywhere. The weather has turned chill, the morning dew is slowly being replaced by light frost that is gone the instant the sun kisses it. At night Aiden and I see the fog of our breath when we walk the forest path back home.

Autumn approaches.

Never have I been so reluctant for the change of seasons, to see the return of my strength, the waning of the daylight hours. It means loss, the loss of this haven. No more lazy days lounging in bed. No more plunging into the cool mountain lake at the top of the ridge or running naked through the fields to dry off. No more time.

My hands are covered in flour and I hum a tune without words as I plunge them into the bread mixture. It is something I've seen the mortal women do when they go about their daily chores. It's easier to pretend than it is to face reality.

The back door swings open and Aiden comes in, carrying an armload of firewood. He wears only jeans lifted from nearby mortals, his sweat-slick skin betraying the labor he's put into building up the fire. It isn't necessary. He could easily conjure flames perfect for my baking project, just as easily as I could wave my hand and collect the deadwood of the forest and transport it to our hearth. But he's abiding my command—to use no magic unless it is necessary.

To see if we can live as the mortals do.

I eye his body hungrily, my teeth sinking into the fleshy part of my lower lip as I watch the shift and pull of muscles beneath his skin. He looks like a god, a fire deity when cast in shadows from the flickering firelight. I can never tell him this, he wouldn't appreciate the reminder of where he comes from. But I see it and remember for him.

He turns, catching me staring and smirks. "How goes the task?"

I frown down at the bowl of glop, lift it up in my hands. It slithers through my fingers in a gelatinous mass. "Does this seem correct?"

He moves forward, wraps his arms around me and rests his chin on my shoulder. "Not in the slightest."

I sag, dropping the mess back in the bowl. Another meal, ruined. If we truly were mortal we would have starved by now. "I don't understand. Even the dullest human peasant is capable of making bread. Why not I?"

"You were born to be a queen." His lips brush the exposed skin of my shoulder. "No one taught you how to live without magic or servants."

I turn in his arms until we are staring each other in the eyes. "Do you think it's wrong for me to want to do this? Be honest." The last two words come out equipped with the ring of command.

He hesitates, and I can see the wheels turning in his clever mind. "I think you are who you are. Pretending to be something else won't change your nature. Nor would I want you to change."

"A diplomatic answer," I grumble. His knuckles brush the underside of my jawbone, wiping away the flour that had somehow wound up there. I grip his hand, holding it tightly. "It's our last night."

"I know."

"I don't want to go back."

Aiden looks away, his gaze on the fire. "You must."

I shove him away. "Why must you always remind me of my duty and obligations?"

He squares his shoulders, lifts his chin. "I am consort to the queen. It is part of my role to support her highness, and help her rule in whatever way I can."

"The queen." Not me. My title, the only thing anyone ever sees, ever wants of me. Frustrated tears well up and I turn away to hide my pain. By tomorrow night, I will shove it all down, will be haughty, cold, unaffected. Everything the Unseelie Queen ought to be. The Ice Bitch.

But summer has spoiled me. Tricked me into thinking that I might be more than just the figurehead. That my value might come in who I am, not what I can do for someone else.

Aiden enfolds me in his arms again, pressing his body flush against mine. "I'm sorry I caused you pain."

He didn't. I would never give him that power over me. "My situation causes me pain, not you."

He hesitates. "Is it the others?"

The other men, the Unseelie nobles that once a month, line up by the dozens for their shot at impregnating the queen, becoming consort and father to the heir. My stomach turns over when I think of the last ritual, held two weeks before the end of winter.

"I've never liked the thought of being a broodmare," I mutter.

His arms tighten around me. I am his mate. He detests sharing me almost as much as I loathe being used. "You are queen. Put an end to it."

He makes it sound so simple. "There must be an heir. Brigit already has three."

"So, let one of hers take over your place."

"The Hunt will never accept commands of a summer fey. It is

for them as much as for me that I must submit to it." I touch his hand lightly. "Unless...you change your mind."

He freezes, his entire body going still. "I can't."

"Aiden—"

"I won't be a father, Nicneven. Please don't ask it of me."

"But it would solve everything." I could order him of course, command him to remove the contraceptive charm he wears tethered around his wrist and attempt to impregnate me. To keep trying until he is successful. Until we can be together in all ways, to rule together.

But I want him to agree on his own. To choose me over his fear, his stubborn pride.

He is silent for a long time. "I can't risk it, not even for you. Passing on this curse to another generation, or worse, siring progeny that will side with my father in the last battle. Ragnorok is coming. You know I can't. Please accept this limitation, love. I beg you."

I grind my teeth together. "Then nothing will change. You will have to share me and be replaced once another sires an heir to the Shadow Throne."

"As my lady desires." Again, his lips find my neck. "I have you now and that's what matters."

If only now was enough.

He senses my mood, seeks to distract me. One hand flattens over my belly as the other lifts the hem of my skirt travels up the expanse of one thigh until it finds the slick flesh between my legs. My head falls back against his shoulder, my breath coming out in soft, quick pants as his clever fingers part my nether lips and stroke with quick perfect pressure, bringing me to the brink.

"Please," I pant, gripping his wrist, right above that blasted contraceptive charm. "Please."

"As my lady desires," he repeats, wickedness threading through his tone....

I wake in the hammock, panting and on the edge of a

cataclysmic orgasm. My thighs press together, my body overstimulated and strung so taut I feel as though my bones will snap like dry twigs.

My blood pumps, my breasts tingle. Arousal. I'm in the throes of full-blown sexual stimulation and seconds from culmination. I want to finish it, to let the pleasure wash over me. I refuse to finish it.

"Damn you Hel," I huff. "What's the point of these dreams?"

Of course, there is no answer. Even if the halfdead guardian of the underworld can hear me, I doubt she would give me a reason for messing with my sleep.

The book on Norse mythology lays open to the chapter I'd been reading before I dozed off. I pluck it up and set it on a nearby outcropping of rock, then strip my dress and wade into the water, not to bathe so much as to cool my body down.

I dive deep, touch the sandy bottom at the center of the pool and then shoot back to the surface. Again. The water isn't cold enough to break the haze of lust but at least I'm no longer on the ragged edge.

On the third dive, my mind has cleared enough to think about something other than the pleasure I've denied myself. Like the fact that I'd been fucking untold members of the Unseelie Court, trying to sustain some sort of fey legacy. That I'd threatened Aiden with being replaced in my bed if he didn't do the job first. Uck.

No wonder I'm asexual this time around. Had more than enough of the beast with two backs during my last go.

Even more difficult to admit. I didn't like the woman I had been. Utterly helpless without her sword or magic. I couldn't even make bread. My thought processes were too narrow, rigid and unbending. And I'd thought about ordering Aiden to impregnate me against his wishes.

Just no.

I break the surface again. Someone is standing at the edge of the water. Naked.

"Aiden," I gasp and almost go under in my hurry to pivot away from him. "What are you doing here?"

"Sorry," he says, sounding not at all sorry. "Fern said I should ask if you want breakfast."

"Naked?" I face the waterfall, sure his keen gaze can see everything through the clear water.

"Well, you could go down naked if you wanted. Give the old gals a thrill. Given their preferences, I'm sure they'd appreciate it. I know I would." Amusement laces his tone.

"No, I mean why are *you* naked?"

"Can't find my sweats." There's a splash. "And I really need a bath."

"Wait a second," I choke, on water or my own saliva, I'm not sure which.

"I'd come in as the wolf, but you complained about the scent last time." He's enjoying himself, the beast. "Besides, it doesn't matter because you're not attracted to me, right?"

"Right." The word comes out thin and reedy. Of course, now I remember being attracted to him and that in no way gives me the squicky sensation that I thought it would. The memory of his lips against my neck, his hand working between my legs….

I risk a peek over to the left, where I can hear him cutting through the water like a shark. Power and grace radiate from those sleek muscles. Godlike, I'd thought in the dream and godlike he is in appearance, in motion.

A cursed god. One that sees me as his mate.

I tread water as he laps the perimeter of the pool, disappearing for a few seconds beneath the waterfall and then reemerging and continuing to swim.

I want to say something, there are so many questions that

only he can answer. Yet between the intimacy of the night before and the erotic dream that shames even as it titillates, I can't seem to find the words.

"You're quiet." Aiden pauses after his second lap. "Is everything all right?"

"I should be asking you that." It's a remark meant to cover my own discomfort.

He pushes dark wet hair out of his face, tilts his head to the side as though to indicate I haven't fooled him. "I'm fine, thanks to you. Can I ask you a question?"

"Sure," I strive for nonchalance but fail epically.

He moves closer, though there are still several spans between us. "How did you know what to do? With me?"

I shake my head. "I didn't, not really. It's not like there was a set of instructions tattooed on you or anything."

Aiden frowns. "You weren't afraid to challenge him though? The wolf?"

I splash water at him. "What a stupid question. *Of course* I was afraid. I've been nothing but afraid since I came here and the more I remember, the more terrified I am."

Aiden's staring at me as though he's never seen me before. "You've remembered more?"

"Bits and pieces. Please turn around so I can get out."

He does as I request. "Tell me what else you remember. Specifically."

I scurry from the pool and over to the hammock. There's no towel so I wrap myself in the afghan as I consider how to answer. "Freda and Nahini. Riding with The Hunt."

"That makes sense." In the pool, Aiden's still facing the waterfall. "The Wild Hunt was always the most important part of your life. You sacrificed much for it, for them."

"You sound bitter," I observe, slithering into my dress.

"Of course I'm bitter. If not for The Hunt you never would have—," he breaks off abruptly.

225

My heart pounds. "Never would have what?"

"Nothing." Aiden heads for the shore and strides out with none of the modesty I'd experienced.

For once I'm not put off by his nudity and stride to catch his wrist. "What, Aiden? What did I do?" My gaze travels to his arm, to where I remember the contraceptive charm from my dream.

It isn't there.

Dawning horror. I look up into those forest green eyes, see the flash of betrayal there, the wounded pride. I'd thought about it, the old Nic had. She'd wanted an heir, wanted Aiden to father it.

His free hand goes to my face, though he doesn't touch me. "You remember that, too. Don't you?"

"Not all of it. Just a single discussion."

He laughs, shakes his head. "Discussion implies there was more than one side's point of view being considered. That you cared what I wanted."

"I did care," I say. "I remember that much."

He pulls away and heads for the door. "Not enough."

AIDEN IS NOWHERE in sight when I come down the spiral staircase to the main floor.

"Oh good, Nic." Fern bustles forward. "I'm going to need your help. It seems the other two have abandoned us. Probably brooding in the swamp, as though there aren't a million things to be done."

She gestures for me to sit. The bed has once again been transformed into a table. She places an acorn mug before me, along with a plate made up of unfinished pine. There are green things on the plate that look sort of like under-ripe berries.

I pick one up and try to squish it between my fingers. It doesn't budge. "Are you sure this is safe for humans? Certain kinds of berries are poison to us."

Fern puffs up indignantly, momentarily flitting apart. "Yes, I'm sure. Do you think I make a habit of poisoning my houseguests? Besides, they aren't berries, they're swamp nuts."

Swamp nuts. Oh, that sounds much better. I give them a tentative sniff. Like the scent of a jockstrap after August football camp. Anything with the word swamp and nut in it was destined to be a culinary masterpiece. A smile flits over my face as I recall how Sarah had reacted to my chia pudding.

"My word, I do believe that's the first time I've seen you smile." Fern pats my shoulder. "Eat up, they are very high in protein and you're going to need your strength."

Crossing my fingers, I pop a swamp nut into my mouth and chew. It's got a rich buttery flavor, sort of like a macadamia nut, but a little saltier. "What's happening today?"

"I promised to instruct. A brood of eight. It totally slipped my mind until I woke this morning. Of course, when I told Laufey, she headed for the hills. Never been a fan of youngens, even fawn kits."

"You want me to help you babysit?" I stare at her uncomprehendingly.

"Well, you're a human teenager. As I understand it, that's a popular first job for your ilk."

"Yes, but not usually for the ones that kill full-grown people on a regular basis." I wave my hands in frustration.

"Oh, it's not like there is much to it. Just keep them from impaling themselves with sharp sticks."

My hands had grown clammy and I almost drop the fragrant mug of herbal tea. "Um...?"

A knock on the front door. "That'll be them now."

Fern flits apart and then recombines by the door and flings it wide. "Hello, Brooke dear. How are you?"

A blonde creature stands on the other side, surrounded by her offspring. They are all naked from the waist up, and mostly human-looking save their pointy ears and too large eyes. From the waist down, they are still naked, although equipped with deer legs. "Fern, thank you *so* much." The woman ushers the miniature versions of herself inside.

They descend like a wave crashing onto the shore, spreading out in every direction at once. The clopping of hooves on the stairs, on the floor, as they scurry about. One even climbs inside the empty iron kettle before his mother hauls him back out.

"Dale, stop that." She sets him down and he bounds off, looking for more mischief. "He's taken to hiding, lately, so don't be surprised if he turns up in odd places." She offers me a strained smile. "Sorry, I didn't catch your name."

"Nic," I say, unsure whether to offer my hand or not.

"She's a family friend." Fern has two of the fawns hanging upside down by the legs. They giggle as their bodies swing back and forth like this is the best game ever.

"Well, I'm glad you have help. Thank you again for doing this. I'll be back an hour before sundown. Kits, behave!"

"Enjoy yourself!" Fern calls out, sets her giggling handfuls down and then turns to me. "Don't just stand there, girl. Round them up!"

"For execution?" I shout. The noise level has increased a thousand-fold.

"For activities." Fern pats my shoulder. "Go on, you get the ones upstairs."

"I—," she's gone before I have a chance to protest.

I find three of the fawn kits in my room. One is swinging in the hammock, its little spotted legs dangling through the holes. "I stuck!" it screeches in a high-pitched whine.

Two others are in the pool, shoving and splashing. My serene space has been transformed into a theme park.

"I stuck!" the one in the hammock flails like a worm on a hook.

"You two, out of the water before you drown one another," I shout even as I pluck the screecher out of my hammock. "Come downstairs so we can do some activities. Doesn't that sound like fun?"

"Fun!" the splashers resume the game with glee.

"Fun," I echo hollowly, understanding for the first time why certain animals eat their young. And I'd wanted a child in my last life? I must have been insane.

Eventually, after I'm soaked to the knees, I manage to usher all three of the fawns out of my room, sliding the great bolder into place. No doubt they could work their way past it but at least it would slow them down.

"Ah, there you all are." Fern has somehow managed to organize the rest of the brood at the table around an arts and crafts activity. There is much stickiness and bits of nature strewn everywhere.

"Can anyone find the healing moss?" Fern asks.

Hooves stamp and human hands scrabble, each proffering a stringy yellow-green moss.

"Very good," Fern nods. "Glen, can you tell me what sorts of wounds the healing moss is best for treating?"

"Venomous animal bites." The one I suppose is Glen answers promptly.

Fern nods with approval. "Excellent. Go ahead and glue that to your paper. Can anyone tell me what bark from the Great Tree is used for?" She gestures to the large tree that grows in the middle of her house.

Another hand shoots up, this time the smallest child. "Time travel spells and enchantments."

"Very good, Glade. But please wait until I call on you."

I sit at the far end and grab a piece of paper.

The fawn next to me looks surprised. "Are you going to make a project, too?"

I nod and uncap a marker. "I've got a lot to learn. Pass me the glue."

The kits all giggle but the glue comes my way.

CHAPTER 18

WHAT'S IN AN OATH

Brooke arrives just as the sun touches the hills to the west and not a moment too soon.

"I hope they weren't too much trouble," Brooke takes a sleeping Dale from my arms.

I open my mouth to reply when I feel a sharp jab in the ribs from a mini Fern. I glance at the rest of her and she sends me a warning look even as she replies, "Not at all."

Maybe not for her. After the project, Fern and I gathered the kits and took them on a nature walk through the swamp. Though I'd been hoping to catch sight of Aiden, there had been no trace of man or beast. Fern had pointed out many more helpful plants with magical properties which I'd scribbled on my Underhill crib sheet. Knowing my surroundings had always been essential to me and learning more about the swamp made me feel a little less like prey.

We made the kits lunch and settled the youngest down before the fireplace for a nap, while the older kits went out to help Fern tend her garden. The problem was, the little ones didn't want to nap.

"Tell us a story." Glade popped a finger in her mouth and looked at me with large, expectant eyes.

"I'm not the best storyteller."

This results in a full-blown tantrum. Screeching like a tea kettle along with shouts of "I want a story," that could wake even the dead.

In the end, I'd stumbled my way through a bastardized version of *The Sleeping Beauty*.

"Let me get this straight. The prince fought the dragon and the princess slept through the whole thing?" Dale asked. "That doesn't seem fair."

That kid…err kit, was growing on me.

"Well, thanks again." Brooke rounds up her brood with the efficiency of a drill sergeant and marches them out the door.

I flop into the armchair by the fire. "Stick a fork in me. I'm done."

"Be careful who you say that to," Fern cautions. "There are plenty around here who'll take you up on such an offer."

I grimace. "How could I forget?"

Fern smiles and pats my shoulder. "You do look all done in. Why don't you head up to your room for a little rest before dinner?"

I take in the mess around the house. Twigs, moss, and leaves everywhere. The rustic bowls and plates we'd used at lunch stacked by the iron cauldron Fern uses for washing up. Muddy hoof prints on the wood floor. The place looks as though it has been tossed by the mob and trampled by wildebeests. "Let me help you clean up."

She blinks in obvious surprise and then smiles. "Oh, that's very sweet of you dear, but I'll be leaving clean-up for Laufey. It's our understanding, you see. She has no direct contact with the kits, but she does the tidying afterward. As soon as she sees Brooke pass the third rise to the west, she'll head home. It's become something of a game, I see how much work the kits can make for her."

"How devious. I wholly approve." My back aches and my temples throb. "Okay then, if you're sure. I have a little reading to do anyway."

Fern nods. "I'll call you when supper is ready. Or when Aiden returns."

So, my surreptitious glances on our walk hadn't gone unnoticed. "Thank you."

I trudge wearily up the stairs and shove the boulder aside. Though the pool looks inviting, I don't plan on getting caught in the raw again. This morning had been a near enough miss.

Instead, I pick up the book of Norse myths and lie back in my hammock. I'm starting to think of the tome as an index for my adventures. I've only read the chapter about Aiden, Váli—whoever, the previous night. Now, I hunt for the people I've encountered.

The first I come across is the giantess Laufey, the Needle of the Forest. I scroll back to the beginning of the paragraph and read aloud. "Mother of Loki, the trickster deity. In fact, Loki is often referred to in Eddic poetry as Loki Laufeyjarson, or son of Laufey. The consort of Loki's father, Farbauti. The descriptor needle because she is believed to be both slender and weak."

A snort escapes. Can't believe everything you read.

I skim the next few pages. Laufey didn't raise Loki. The book doesn't say why. In fact, the next mention of him is when he becomes a blood brother to Odin, the All-Father. His trickery and mischievousness get him and the gods of the Aesir into trouble time and again. Often, the same duplicitous mind also bailed them out of sticky situations, usually under threat of death or dismemberment.

"Loki fathered three children with the giantess Angrboda," I read aloud. "Her name means foreboding or the bringer of woe. Also called the Hag of the Ironwood of Jotunheim, she is recognizable by hair the color of dried blood. The products of their union were monstrous. The great wolf, Fenrir, destined to swallow the world. The Midgard Serpent, Jormungand that encircles the realm of Midgard. And Hel, the appointed ruler of Niflheim, or the underworld for the dishonorable dead. She was chosen for this position by the All-Father because her half-dead appearance made her more comfortable with the dead than with the living."

I shut the book and stare into the waterfall. The giantess in the castle. Aiden had called her the Hag of the Ironwood. And if she had three children with Aiden's father that meant Hel was her daughter. As well as Aiden's half-sister.

I'm not the kind of girl prone to fantastic imagination or building fantasy worlds to escape reality. My reality has always been bloody and harsh, but I could always tell the difference between real and not real. Is it possible that the new boy at school is really the cursed son of a Norse god? That his grandmother is a giant? And all the people I've hunted are trapped forever in service to the fabled Wild Hunt? That Sarah is dead, and Aiden's half-sister is the goddess of the underworld?

That I am the reincarnated Queen of the Elphame, rightful heir to the Shadow Throne of the Unseelie Court?

It's too much, too unbelievable. I pride myself on cool logic. But what logical explanation is there for my current location? The things I've seen and done? For the scars from the thorns that nearly killed me, from the almost healed burns in the shape of Aiden's hand?

For my growing attachment to him.

I let out a shaky breath. Damn it, Aiden is just like Sarah, a chigger burrowing beneath my skin so deep that I can't root out. I can't ignore the response he drags out of me.

Sarah made me feel like a person, not just a killer. I crossed the Veil in hopes of getting her back. And last night, last night I would have died if Aiden's wolf hadn't backed down. I knew the risks, understood the danger and had put myself in harm's way.

"Would the real Nic please step forward," I grumble.

What the hell is it about him? The powers? His dogged determination to help me whether I want it or not? Some sort of weird payback since he went to the trouble of reincarnating me? The answers prove elusive, much like Aiden himself.

A tap on the stone door breaks me out of my thoughts. "Come in," I call, not bothering to get up.

Laufey pushes through the vines, a smile on her face. "I hear you helped Fern babysit the fawn kits. From the look of things, they were wound up today." She frowns at the book in my hands.

I hold it up for her inspection. "How much of this is real?"

"All of it. None of it. It depends on whom you ask."

"I'm asking you."

She exhales audibly. "Tell me, why are you here?"

The question startles me. "Because Aiden brought me."

She perches on one of the boulders by the water's edge. "But why? From what my grandson tells me, the old Nicneven was only interested in her own situation, an attitude that gave him no small amount of heartache. Do you know what it's like, watching someone you love be used by a selfish person?"

I look away. "That's not me. Not who I am. I don't use people." Even as I whisper the words they stick in my throat.

"No, you just kill them."

No denying the truth. "I do."

"And you enjoy it. The act of killing brought you satisfaction?"

"I thought it did." Again, I meet her eyes. "Every kill connected me to my victims in a way I've never experienced before. It connected me with myself. I was doing something good, something no one else could or would do. It felt...right."

"But you had to hide what you are, what you can do. Because the humans wouldn't accept your sort of vigilante justice. And tell me, have you killed anyone since you came here to Underhill?"

"No."

"No one? Not any of the beings who threatened you?"

I shake my head.

"You risked yourself for me with The Hunt. You risked your life to bring Aiden back last night. Not typical behaviors of an incredibly selfish person."

I sit up, no longer at ease in the hammock.

"What about that friend of yours? The one you want to bring back?"

Blood pounds in my ears. "Can you do it? Can you bring Sarah back, the way you did for me?"

She answers my question with one of her own, her green eyes narrowing. "Why do you want this so badly?"

"She never had a chance to really live."

"I didn't ask why she deserves to come back, I want to know why you've taken it upon yourself to bring her back."

My head shakes back and forth. "Because if I don't who else will? She was no one of significance."

"She must have been to you," Laufey counters softly. "Like you were to my grandson."

"So, will you help me?"

"I'm actually sorry to say that I can't." It's her turn to look away. "I would like to help you, Nic. But it's not in my power to do so."

I stare at her blankly. It had all been for nothing?

Laufey stands, shaking her drab skirt out around her legs. "Come down to dinner."

My stomach is in knots. "I'm not hungry."

She sighs and heads out of the room, only to turn by the door. "For what it's worth, I think you're an impressive young woman. You would have to be, to overcome the obstacles of your former life and risk yourself the way you have. I know the Norns. They would have resources, wealth. And there are no better protectors in all the nine worlds. So why leave all that and come here, to Underhill to be hunted?"

"I had a friend," I swallow. "Who deserved better than the hand she was dealt."

"You still do," she says softly.

I sit in the hammock until the brightness of the meadow room fades to a creamsicle-esque twilight. I'm a puppet whose strings have been severed, a discarded mannequin with no purpose. My only thought is on a loop as I stare at the bubbling water.

Sarah, I'm sorry.

I did nothing for her, not in life when she wanted to run to California. Nothing to prevent or even avenge her death. I'd let Aiden stop me. No, not Aiden, he'd talked me down, but I'd let him. The blame for it is squarely on my shoulders because I didn't want to get caught. Was too afraid of human prisons or what they'd do to me if they found out about my Goodnight Kiss.

Though I'm lacking the details, from my most recent dream and his reaction concerning The Hunt, it's obvious that I'd betrayed Aiden on my last go.

I'm self-centered, I know this. It's who I am. How is it fair that a creature like me gets two chances to screw up life and Sarah didn't even get a full one?

It was easier when I pretended they didn't matter, not Sarah, not Aiden or even Chloe and Addy. They were just background characters, props to support my narrative. But now….

I wipe at the wet streak on my cheek. Now they matter.

The pity party is getting ugly. I have nowhere to go, no resources, no family or friends. I can't ask any more from Laufey and Fern and even if Aiden had returned, which he hadn't, I refuse to accept anything more from him. Who knows how much time has passed in the mortal realm? Even if the Fates don't age, I can't ask them to take me back. I'm still more trouble than I'm worth to them.

I can't go back, can't stay still. That leaves me with only one option. The Wild Hunt and the Unseelie Court. My memories from my last life convey that one had been my escape, the other my prison. Freda said they'd return in three nights. Perhaps I could make myself useful again for a few days, help Laufey and Fern until they came for me.

That leaves one loose end, one thread I need to disentangle.

I'd rolled the collage I'd made into a tube, so it would fit in my backpack. Hefting myself out of the hammock I move over to retrieve it. There isn't enough light in the meadow room to read the inscriptions. I head for the stairs.

Fern and Laufey are sitting at the stone table amidst half-filled bowls of steamed roots and roasted nuts. Laufey has her back to me, but Fern grins widely as she tells her an animated story about adventures in gardening with the kits. She pauses and smiles up at me. "There you are. Your dinner will be like ice."

"I'm not hungry," I say. It's the truth. "I have a question

though, about the sap you spoke of earlier. From this tree." I pointed to the one growing in the middle of their house.

"Yes?" Fern tilts her head to the side in a birdlike manner.

"If I understood the lesson correctly, you said it can be brewed into a syrup that will break any magical connection."

Laufey turns to look at me. "What of it?"

I take a deep breath. "In my last life, Aiden made an oath to me. One that has superseded my death and compels him to obey my every command. I was wondering, could the syrup break that oath? Free him from my control?"

The two women exchange a glance.

"It's possible," Laufey says at length. "Though there's no guarantee."

"Have you talked to Aiden about this?" Fern wrings her hands, her brows creased together.

"I haven't seen him since this morning."

"He gave you that oath of his own free will," Laufey speaks slowly. "It was made from trust and devotion."

"I know. And I think I abused that trust." I shake my head. "I spent my life punishing those who prey on the weak. I'm not comfortable having that sort of compulsive power over anyone."

Fern works her lower lip. "I'd be happy to make the syrup, but he must be the one to choose to undo it. Are you sure this is what he wants?"

I huff out a breath. "Honestly, I don't have a clue what he wants from me."

Another exchange of glances between them.

"What?" I ask.

"You're his mate," Laufey says slowly. "Even if we manage to break his oath, that bond remains."

"I don't even know what that means. I've had dreams about what our relationship was like before and I can't give that to him."

Fern stands up. "I'll get started on the syrup. You go find him, talk things out. If you both come back and say you want to try to break the oath, we can do it."

I frown. "Where should I look for him?"

Laufey exhales a mighty breath. "There's a cave, a few miles to the west. He used to stay there, back when he was still learning how to control the wolf. I'll take you there."

"Careful, Fe," Fern cautions. "There's blood on the moon tonight. Trouble is coming our way."

Laufey rolls her eyes as she stands from the table. "You are a superstitious old bat at times, my love. Nic, grab a cloak from the peg. It's cold out tonight and you weigh next to nothing."

"Just let me grab my backpack." In case I decide to cross the Veil at midnight, a thought I don't vocalize. At least in the mortal world, I have an advantage of the Goodnight Kiss. And there aren't nearly as many beings who want to eat me.

Laufey sets off at a brisk pace. The sun is gone, but the moon rises full. With a glowing halo around its shining face, it casts a silvery light on the well-worn path through Fern's garden and out into the woods beyond. The borrowed cloak is rough homespun, not nearly as soft as my native cotton, but it does provide plenty of warmth against the biting wind.

We walk in silence, with me trying my best to keep up with her long-limbed strides. Occasionally, she pauses to check my progress before resuming the brisk pace. I'm glad for the physical demands, it keeps me from obsessing about what I will say to Aiden when I see him.

Should I apologize for what I'd done in my past life? There are memories that connect me with the Nicneven I was before. Riding with the Wild Hunt. There are others that shame me, like my thoughts of ordering Aiden to remove his contraceptive charm. And others still that spin me all around until I'm dizzy. Like the ones where he touched me, kissed me, wanted me.

And I wanted him back.

"For what it's worth," Laufey interrupts my brooding. "I don't think he'll agree to break the oath."

"What makes you say that?" The ground between us is steep and I use my hands to pull myself up. "I'd think he'd want to be free of me."

"Maybe the old you," Laufey offers her hand and after a brief hesitation, I take it. "The Unseelie Queen who did nothing but take what she wanted. But I saw the way he looked at you last night. Even without some mystical compulsion, I'd wager he would do whatever you ask, regardless of the risk."

I shake my head. "If not for his tie to me, the old me, he wouldn't bother with me. Not the way I am now. Our past is the only thing we have in common and it's a past I can't fully remember." A past in which he had a very good reason to hate me.

"We'll see," is all Laufey says. "The cave is up there."

She points. Up ahead, there is the flickering of firelight. And a man-shaped shadow cast on the wall.

I stare at it, feeling the knot of snakes in my belly shift and doubts surface.

"What if he doesn't want to see me?" He'd stayed away all day.

"Only one way to find out." Laufey turns and within three steps, vanishes into the darkened forest.

CHAPTER 19

DARE FOR A DREAM

My entrance into the cave is neither quiet nor graceful. I trip on a root and end up sprawling in the dirt at Aiden's feet.

"Are you hurt?" He crouches down beside me, a frown pulling his dark brows into a deep V shape.

"Fine, though I doubt I'll get my wilderness merit badge anytime soon." My cheeks are hot from more than the roaring fire.

He grins and helps me rise. "I never know what you're going to say or do next."

His hands are warm on mine and I can't help recalling how hot they blazed when he burned me. I should fear his touch, what he can do, yet I can't seem to let go. And that scares me more than any pain—real or imagined.

His smile fades as he searches my face and he is the first to break contact. The moment stretches out awkwardly, neither of us speaking, the silence tense. I concentrate on dusting myself off and notice he's once again wearing the ratty sweatpants that I'd removed from him the day before.

The question comes out automatically. "Where did you find those?"

"The trash out behind the house." He makes a face. "They didn't smell too great, but I washed them in the river earlier."

"You went Dumpster diving for clothes? Your grandmother has a whole supernatural storage room. Couldn't you just borrow something from there?"

A shrug is my only answer. He turns away, facing the fire once more. "I prefer these. What are you doing out here, Nic?"

"Looking for you." I glance around the cave, again seeking a subject to glom onto. The fire pit is set beneath a crack in the rock above, large enough to vent the smoke. I run my hand along one smooth wall. "This feels too even to be a natural cave."

"That's because it was carved by magic. Laufey's magic. Why were you looking for me? Is something wrong?"

I don't answer him. Instead, my attention drifts to shackles bolted into the far side of the wall. Long chains lead to four cuffs about three inches wide. I move closer until I can crouch down to examine them, lifting one cuff and the great chain that dangles from it. The weight is incredible. There's also a tickle in the back of my sinuses which I am beginning to equate with magic use. "She told me you stayed here while you were learning to master your wolf."

He moves closer, takes the shackles from me. "That's right."

I try to read his expression, but he has it closely guarded. "They chained you up?"

A nod. "There are also bars to seal the entrance, though they aren't active any longer."

I stand and face him, wrapping my arms around myself to ward off a sudden chill. "Why would they do that to you?"

"I asked them to. To help me." He drops the chain and it

hits the stone with a deafening clang. "You never saw what I was like in those days. In control one minute then rage would crash through me with no provocation. No one was safe around me, not even those I loved."

He moves to turn away, but I reach out. My hand lands on his stiff shoulder. "You're talking about your brother."

He closes his eyes, guilt emanating from him in waves. It's answer enough.

"Please tell me what happened." My voice is soft, as though the power of it alone might break him.

Aiden stares at me for a beat, then down at where my hand touches him. A muscle jumps in his jaw. "I don't talk about this. Not ever. Not even with you."

He's carried the burden, the guilt, by himself for centuries. "Maybe you should."

He turns his head, so he is facing the fire, hands fisting and relaxing. "My father is Loki, son of the giants Laufey and Farbauti, sworn blood brother to Odin. He's a trickster, selfish and scheming. He arranged for the death of the beloved god Balder. I'm sure you read that much in your book."

When I nod he continues, "What it didn't mention is that I knew none of this. To me, he was just…Dad. A fun dad. He spent time with me and with Nari, took us fishing in Midgard, hunting in the Vanir lands, exploring here in Underhill. He loved to laugh, to play pranks, wasn't afraid to make a fool of himself for our amusement. I think that might be why Mom loves him so, even after everything."

"It sounds like an idyllic childhood."

His tone is wistful. "When he was around, he was the best father I can imagine." He turns away from the fire.

"And when he wasn't around?"

He squares his shoulders as though preparing for battle, then turns to face me. "You saw Angrboda. His consort, well one of them anyway. His jealousy over the Aesir prevented him from any sort of true loyalty. He went to a seer to find out how he could destroy them. She told him to father monstrous children with the giantess. Those children would bring about Ragnorok, the end of the nine worlds. It didn't matter to him that Mom cried herself to sleep every night he was gone, that I had to look after Nari in his absence. I read to him, tucked him in at night. Went to him when he had nightmares. Taught him to command the fire, the gift that my father passed down to all his children. Things a father should have done for his youngest son."

I don't speak, afraid to interrupt. After a moment he swallows and continues.

"I think Odin and the others would have let him go if not for Balder's death. They forgave him for all the other schemes and plots. But his role in the death of Balder was the beginning of the end."

I shiver. "They caught him in the act?"

Aiden shakes his head. "He admitted to it, to finding the mistletoe, the one tiny plant Frigg hadn't wrangled a promise not to harm her son. Of giving it to the blind god, Hodr. Dad always was a sloppy drunk. When he sobered up he knew they would be after him. And instead of warning us, of telling me to take our mother and Nari away from the wrath of the gods, he ran. Like a coward, he left us to save his own skin."

A laugh that is completely devoid of amusement. "Not that it did him much good. Thor and the others caught him anyway. And when we were summoned to that cave, well, we knew he would be punished, but we had no idea what was about to happen. Mom was told to bring a bowl, the largest she had. I still remember the panicked look in his eyes when they dragged him in, still sopping wet from the river and trapped in a mystical net. He'd always looked larger than life to me, but in that moment, I saw him for exactly what he was, a small and petty being."

"How old were you?" The book hadn't been specific on those details.

He meets my eyes, green fire reflected in his. "The same age you are now. Nari had just turned eight."

I squeeze his arm. It's an involuntary reflex on my part, an urge that I can't trace, can't ignore.

"I shoved Nari behind me and I challenged them, challenged the gods. I don't even remember what I said. All I knew was that he had fucked up royally this time. I thought if I could show bravery in the face of his cowardice, they might be lenient, on him, on us. The Norse gods value courage above all the other noble virtues. But it didn't matter, their minds were made up."

His eyes close and a single tear tracks down the side of his face. "After that it gets fuzzy. They brought forth my transformation power, one I didn't even know I possessed and changed me into the wolf. I was essentially shoved to the back. My will no longer mattered, my body was unfamiliar—not my own. I could still see through its eyes, but I couldn't control anything...couldn't stop it when it turned and caught sight of Nari...."

He stops swallows. "After it was over, they dragged me from the cave, presumably to kill me, too. The Aesir fear the wolf. They wouldn't have let me go. But the instincts for survival rode me hard. I bit and clawed and scratched until I got free and then I ran, faster than I'd ever dreamed, the taste of his blood still in my mouth."

His brother's blood. The brother he had protected and nurtured and had been forced to destroy. Now I understand why he'd sought out that bastard, let himself be captured and used. Why he thought he deserved to die.

"It wasn't your fault." Conviction rings in my tone.

"How would you know?" The question comes out thick and raspy as if the words are choking him.

"Because I've been killing since I was six years old. And that first time, it was by accident. Every time since I set out knowing what I could do, with the intent to kill any that would try to harm me. They were guilty of unspeakable crimes. But the first time, I didn't realize what I could do. I killed a man."

The firelight brings out flecks of gold in his bright green eyes. "What happened?"

My arms tighten about myself, the damp of the cave seeping into my bones. I'd never spoken the words out loud. Addy and Chloe must have known, but we never talked about it. "A man tried to rape me."

His hands clench into fists. "I should have been there. Should have been with you, watching over you, protecting you."

"I made it out okay," I tell him. "That's all that matters."

He does a slow once over my body, gaze taking in my rigid stance, the white-knuckled grip I have on my arms. "Are you so sure about that?"

I don't like what he's implying. His scrutiny unsettles me further. Dropping my arms, I lift my chin to meet his challenge head-on. "Look, hunting is a part of who I am, just like it is for your wolf. The only difference is, I trust my instincts."

He shakes his head, his shoulders tight. "You killed a predator who was trying to hurt you. I killed an innocent child. One I was supposed to protect. Out of the two of us, only one of us is a monster."

I reach for his hands. It isn't a calculated move, or even one I think about. Yet it feels natural to touch him as I try to convince him of something I realized the night before. Aiden needs to accept his wolf if he is ever to find peace. "Your wolf isn't a monster, it's an animal. Someone else used you as a weapon. Killing your brother was not your choice, it was theirs. You couldn't stop it."

His response is another shake of the head. I squeeze his hands. "Aiden, look at me. You couldn't have done anything differently, couldn't control it. They used you horribly. You were a child. You did nothing wrong. It could have just as easily been your brother that was turned into the wolf and you the one who'd died. Would you want him to blame himself if your positions had been reversed?"

He stares at me, unblinking, his brow furrowing. "Why did you have to be like this?"

"Like what?" I frown.

A muscle jumps in his jaw. "So different."

My heart sinks. Why do those words hurt so much? Because I knew how much he cared for the old Nicneven? The one he made an unbreakable vow to obey? Even though I don't want that mystical compulsion between us, a sick sort of jealousy twists my stomach. He loved her—me—that much and I have come back different. And here I'd been thinking that I was pretty fucking nifty. Laufey even said I made great strides. I won her cantankerous old ass over. Yet he prefers Nicneven 1.0. Ouch.

I turn away, unable to hold his gaze. "Sorry to disappoint."

He catches my arm, turns me back around. "I'm not disappointed."

A snort escapes. "Yeah right."

"I'll admit, it took me by surprise at first, how much you've changed. The way you stand, the way you speak, your mannerisms are all different. The fact that you remembered nothing, didn't remember me at all...it hurt. You were my world for centuries, I had you memorized and for days I searched for similarities, any similarities between you and the Nicneven I'd pledged myself to so long ago. Your scent and the fact that the Fates are your guardians told me it was really you, but it felt as though I'd lost you all over again."

My lips part but he covers them with his hand. I can't stifle a flinch, but when he doesn't keel over, I relax.

His hand falls away. "Let me finish."

I inhale and then nod. "Okay."

"You're so much more than you were. And I feel…disloyal just thinking it."

What? "Disloyal? Why?"

"You…the old you, were my mate. You were strong and smart, courageous and beautiful. I felt lucky just to be near you. But…" He trails off, swallows and then glances away as though ashamed. "I didn't actually like you."

I stare at him, uncomprehending. "You didn't like me?"

"You were so cold, ruthless and ambitious. Brave yes, but there was no compassion for anyone. No softness or gentleness. You only cared about yourself and what you wanted."

"I'm still like that," I protest. "I'm still selfish and cold."

"Really? Is that why you're in Underhill, trying to bring your friend back to life? Is that why you risked yourself last night to hold me together mentally, to talk my wolf down?" He shakes his head. "The Nicneven I knew before never would have done any of those things."

I lick my lips. "So, you're saying I came back better? That now you like me?"

He answers with a slow nod. A charming flush stains the skin along his cheekbones. "It's unworthy of me to say so but yes. I prefer you like this, with your sneaky dark humor, your cunning and sense of vigilante justice. You're a punisher of evil deeds, yet somehow your compassion for those you care about shines through."

My heart thunders in my chest. He prefers me, modern Nic the teenage serial killer to Nicneven the Unseelie Queen who wielded the power of the Wild Hunt.

"I dared to hope," Aiden moves in slowly until he can tilt my chin up. Our eyes meet, our gazes lock. "That you would find a measure of peace and contentment in this life since it eluded you in your last one. And that you would choose to share that life with me."

I'm finding it difficult to breathe but somehow, I manage to whisper, *"Dare airson aisling?"* Dare for a dream.

A soft smile plays across his lips and he nods. "You have always been a dream that is worth any risk."

The moment stretches out, a big lazy cat that is completely content to linger. My awareness of him increases. Time seems to slow as every detail sharpens, like those moments right before I strike. I make note of everything, the sweep of his dark hair. The hungry look in his green eyes. The scent of cedar and sage that beckons me closer. The way he licks those perfect lips. I wet my own lips in response.

"Nic," he whispers.

My gaze sweeps down his body as my awareness grows and the heat builds. Not external heat from Aiden or from the fire but my own internal furnace blazes. Where moments before I'd been cold, now my temperature spikes. Desire. I'm feeling desire, not a desire for food or rest or a kill, but for another person.

For Aiden.

My brows draw together. "You told me once to let you know if my lack of attraction for you changed."

"And has it?" His breaths are sharp and jagged.

I am mesmerized by the sight of his bare chest rising and falling. He is all male perfection but this time I see it not as just aesthetically pleasing. No, I'm fighting urges to touch and stroke, to explore his body with my hands. With my mouth.

Where would I start?

The stubble along his chin, days' worth of growth. It'll

prickle my fingertips. The ghost of the sensation makes me shiver, as though I am touching him already. The air between us is charged, like a great storm growing closer, on the brink, an instant from being unleashed upon the world below.

"I don't know…." I swallow, hunting, not for game but for words, the right words. Words to make him understand things I can barely comprehend myself. "I don't know if I can be what you need me to be."

He cups my face, his big hands gentle. "You are already everything I could ever want."

It's too much, his acceptance of me, of what I am willing and able to give him. For the first time in my life, I initiate a kiss, not for punishment. For pleasure. Despite all my experience, it isn't a smooth thing. Our teeth click, our noses bump. But he is as hungry for me as I am for him. My fingers find that stubble and marvel at the contrast between the roughness and the softness of his mouth.

The hands cradling my face move downward, exploring the column of my neck, sweeping along my collarbones. In a deft move, he undoes the knot in my cloak and the fabric puddles on the ground.

I pull him down on top of it, intent on my own exploration of his body. I want his weight on me, want to feel his bare skin sliding along my own. Though the images in my mind are a jumble, my flesh knows his. Though I've never been touched this way, my body instinctively accepts that Aiden can give me what I need.

He is hard everywhere. All lean ropey muscle covered by smooth skin. The expanse of his back enthralls me even as I take a deeper taste of his mouth. His tongue tangles with my own. His hands sweep over my belly until my hips fit snuggly against his. I feel him there through those sweats that any sane person would have rejected for suitable clothing. He is hard and thick. Ready.

He pulls back, a question in his eyes. "Tell me if this is what you want."

My breaths come out in rough pants, my pulse thundering in my ears. Whether the attraction has developed naturally over the course of days spent working together or is some sort of remnant from my last life, I don't know. Neither do I care. My only concern is the urge I feel, the ache deep inside to touch and be touched.

It is that uncontrollable need that terrifies me.

"I'm...not sure," I breathe.

I expect disappointment or regret to flash across his face. Instead, he smiles, his expression full of understanding. And devotion. "Then we'll go no further until you are."

"I might never be," I feel it's only fair to warn him. "Part of me is screaming not to waste this opportunity, that I should see it through to the end because these feelings might not ever crop up again."

He shifts and settles his weight alongside me, propping his head up on one elbow so he can hold my gaze. "I don't think that'll be the case."

"But if it is?" I push, though I'm not sure why it matters.

"Then it is," he says simply.

I shake my head. "How can you be so...accepting of whatever I give you?"

He glowers, though amusement dances in his eyes. "You make me sound like a dog contenting itself with scraps."

I raise one eyebrow and he laughs. "Okay, maybe that's fair. And accurate on some level. But what you fail to realize Nic, is that I'm content to be with you. As we are now. Would I like to share more with you as we did in the past? Yes. But sex isn't a deal-breaker for me."

He's serious. "Let me get this straight. You just want to be with me? Nothing else?"

His thumb skims my cheek. "Is that so difficult to believe?"

Yes, I think. I swallow and say, "I've been told I'm not worth the trouble."

Another smile. He rolls onto his back, pulling me flush into his side so that my head rests on his shoulder and his legs tangle with mine. "Then it's my job to make you believe otherwise."

"Oh, I know it," I tell him. He squeezes me tighter. "I'm awesome as is."

"You are." I can hear the steady thrum of his heartbeat. My back is to the fire, my front pressed against him so that I am warm all over. The desire is still there, to touch him, so I do, letting my fingers explore his face, his chest, mapping his body to add to the flesh memories, just in case I never feel this way again.

Eventually, the glow of warmth and his steady breaths lull me into total relaxation. I melt into him and my eyes drift shut.

MY DREAMS ARE, thankfully, forgettable. I awake and the first thing I see is Aiden's perfect face, relaxed in sleep. It's a different sort of slumber than when he was wrestling the wolf. His features are peaceful, not pulled taut and his eyes aren't darting behind shut lids. He appears younger, more vulnerable.

And after last night, much more appealing.

I shift within his grasp, one he has maintained throughout the night, his arms around my body, holding me close. As though I am a commodity so precious he couldn't bear to lose me. He had always held me that way, according to the memory fragments lodged in my mind. Close to him with his body as a shield to guard me even as he rests.

My fingers push a lock of dark hair off his smooth forehead. It's odd, the warm feelings in my chest as I watch him. Without the worry of if he'll be all right, if the wolf will arise and kill me, I can assess the blooming attraction between us. Perhaps it comes from remembering a time when we were intimate. Perhaps it's because I know I can now control the toxin emitted from my kiss, that I won't hurt Aiden unintentionally.

At least not with a kiss.

I remember the first one we shared. Fear of what might happen distracted me from the pleasure of his lips. And last night, with him looking at me, the intensity had blotted out all the small moments.

Now I savor them, the dark fans of his lashes. The shadows under his cheekbones. The thick stubble growing on his chin, the way his lips are parted softly with each breath.

He's done amazing things, personal sacrifices I never thought any being capable of, and he's done them for me. This cave for example. Though he didn't say so, I knew this is where he'd run to after I'd freed him. From one prison to another, so he could learn control over his wolf. So that he could come back to me, to be by my side. Every step, every heartbeat has been for me, to defend me. I never wanted a protector, never needed one, but his unyielding devotion to me and me alone, that superseded even my death….

Even if his physical perfection didn't close the deal, his dogged altruism would.

I crave a first kiss to remember, to cling to no matter what comes next. Here at the beginning of whatever we are, the moment needs to be marked. Regardless of the next step, or the tangled mess of our past, at least we'll have this between us.

One perfect kiss.

Slowly, I move until my upper body hovers above his. His arms tighten, then slide down my back. Sometime during the night, my hair came free of its braid. It falls in a curtain around the two of us. Beneath the thin fabric of my dress, my breasts flatten against his bare chest as I lean down. My heart thunders in anticipation. Will his eyes flash open in surprise? Or will he let out one of those soul-deep groans that tells me he is experiencing more pleasure than he ever has before?

I lick my lips. Close my eyes.

"Stop!" the shriek comes from the mouth of the cave.

I whip my head around, just as Aiden's eyes flash open.

My jaw drops. No. It can't be.

A snarl rumbles out of Aiden and he moves in an instant. One second, I am poised atop him, the next I am peering over his shoulder.

At the shocked faces of my aunts.

CHAPTER 20

BETRAYAL

"**N**ic," Chloe is the first to recover. She looks the same as always, red hair spilling down her back in a crimson wave, blue eyes bright. Though not with mischief. No. With fear. "Nic, he isn't one of yours."

I stare at her, feel the skin between my eyebrows crinkling in confusion. It takes me a moment to believe they are truly here, in Underhill. That they crossed the Veil to find me. And another longer moment to realize what she means.

"I'm not...that is, I wasn't...." I shake my head.

"She wasn't going to kill me." Aiden hasn't budged, still bodily blocking me from Addy and Chloe. "Nic wouldn't do that."

Addy's brown gaze narrows on him. "You're that cursed godling that brought her to us as a babe and begged us for our protection."

"He's my grandson." It's Laufey's voice this time. I almost overlook her, where she's skulking in the shadows near the mouth of the cave. For a giant, she is masterful at hiding in plain sight.

Addy whips her head to Laufey. "We had a deal, giant. The girl is ours to raise."

"You two know each other?" I try to shove Aiden aside but it's like moving a block of granite. "Wait, what deal?"

Chloe and Addy ignore me, their gazes fix on Laufey. As I watch, their eyes begin to swirl, brown and blue disappearing into a silvery gray nothingness. In unison they begin to speak, but not in their normal voices. There is no inflection no personality. It is more like they are reciting some sort of chant. "You have tampered with fate. Given life and stolen a soul from the underworld. Your hubris must be punished."

"Only me." Laufey hesitates, her gaze flicking toward us before returning to my aunts. She raises her chin. "He has been punished enough by you bitches."

Again, in unison, my aunts speak three damning words. "So be it."

"Punishment?" I ask. It's all happening too fast. Only a moment ago I was about to enjoy the first planned kiss of my life and now my aunts have appeared from out of nowhere and they are going to punish Laufey. "What are you talking about? What are you going to do to her?"

No one answers me. Wind whips through the cave, an eerie gust that carries something more than ozone. Clouds form just outside, congregating into a black cloak that blots out the early morning sun. Energy crackles, sparking in the space around the Fates.

"No," Aiden cries and moves.

But he isn't fast enough.

A lightning bolt streaks down and hits Laufey square in the chest. She flies back about ten feet, arms pin-wheeling, body in free fall down to the bottom of the hill.

Aiden charges after her and I'm half a heartbeat behind.

"Nic," I can hear Addy and Chloe calling my name, but I

ignore them, my focus on getting to Laufey, on helping Aiden.

She is at the base of the incline, lying face down in a narrow stream. The water runs red beyond where her body is. Overhead the sinister clouds my aunts have summoned part and the sun shines down like the freak storm never occurred.

"No no no," Aiden chants as he falls to his knees beside her, turning her body so that he can cradle her in his lap. "Oh gods, no."

Her dress is charred black around where the bolt struck, blood oozing out. Her eyes stay shut, each breath a wheeze of air that barely moves her chest.

"Is she…?" The word dead lodges in my throat.

Aiden bends down and touches his forehead to his grandmother's. "She's alive, just barely."

I hear their footfalls then. Slow and careful coming down the hill behind us. Addy speaks in her brisk way. "Stand aside. Let us finish this."

My hands clench into fists and I round on them. "Why?"

"Nic, she tampered with fate when she brought you back," Addy explains, cool and calm, her eyes back to normal. "We can't allow a creature with that sort of ability to exist. It would destroy the natural order."

"You're saying I should have stayed dead then?" I rage. "You should take it out on me, not her."

"Nic," It's Chloe who speaks, her voice soft and pleading for understanding. "Nic, that's not what we mean at all. We can't have her do it again. It's a power that can't exist, the one to tamper with destiny."

"She isn't going to." My throat is tight and the words hurt as I force them out. "I asked but she said there isn't a way to bring Sarah back. She isn't going to interfere with your precious natural order!"

"It's not a risk we are willing to take." Addy's eyes flash. "Now, let's be done with this so we can go home."

She reaches for me, but I jerk away. "You can't be serious. You want to kill an innocent woman in front of me, a woman that essentially gave me life and you expect me to just sit on the sidelines and then go home with you?"

They exchange a glance as though I've confused them. I probably have. After all those nights I stalked and hunted, that they cleaned up my mess.

"You don't belong here, Nic." Chloe implores.

"I don't belong anywhere!" I shout at them. "Don't you get it? I'm not a fairy queen or leader of the Wild Hunt. I'm not your daughter, no matter what paperwork you have that says otherwise. You raised me to murder! I should be in prison because I'm a mortal that kills other mortals. I should be dead because I died in my last life or because I was abandoned in the Black Forest at six years old, with no food, no one to explain anything to me but I'm right here! Don't talk to me about where I don't belong because I have no home, no family, no place. All I have are a head full of messed up memories and a killing power."

Aiden puts a hand on my shoulder. I hadn't heard him come up behind me. "You belong with me."

"We had a deal," Addy practically snarls at him. "You were supposed to leave her be."

"And the three of you were supposed to protect her." Aiden doesn't back down. "You need to tell her who abandoned her in that cottage in the woods."

Addy stills. Chloe's eyes grow bright, her scent that of scorched earth. "We had no control over her actions. We thought one would suffice as a guardian—"

"One?" I cut her off and stare between the two of them. "One what?"

Aiden takes my hand in his, urges me to face him. "One sister. One Fate."

I stare at him, uncomprehendingly. "What are you talking about? I didn't meet them until after I was found."

"How dare you?" Addy shakes with barely suppressed rage. "How dare you interfere?"

"You were supposed to protect her in my stead." Aiden's green eyes flash with barely harnessed fury. "I trusted you with her. After all the three of you have done to me—"

"We've done nothing," Chloe tries to break in. "It's the Well of Fate that we guard,

the balance—"

"Don't talk to me about balance." Aiden is a juggernaut, his rage unstoppable. "Not after all you've taken from me. Even after all that loss and pain, I trusted you with her, to raise and protect her. Who better than the women even the gods fear to keep her safe?"

He laughs and it's a hollow sound. "Instead, you abandoned her to a fate worse than death. Leave her to starve, to be savaged by brutes. You are no better than the mortals she hunts."

It clicks into place, the severed thread in Addy's album. Laufey telling me about how the Norns had to punish one of their own for tampering with fate. With *my* fate. I stagger and would have fallen if Aiden didn't have a firm grip on me. My voice is thinner than that strand as I ask, "The third sister?"

"Nic, please," Chloe implores. "We had no way of knowing what she'd do."

"She sees the future," I respond in a deadened tone. Addy has always born the burden of knowing. It's what makes her so surly.

Addy sighs. "Not all of it. Not sudden choices. And once a course is set, we can't intervene."

"Your sister made a choice to abandon me in the woods, to wipe my memories. And you didn't interfere."

"We came for you as soon as we could." Chloe's voice holds a pleading tone.

More trouble than you're worth. "I'm sorry you were hampered with me all these years. Sorry you had to kill your own sister because of it. I don't know why you didn't just let her off the hook."

"To do so would collapse the Veil and send the worlds spiraling into chaos. There can be no trust in us when one of our own is untrustworthy. What she did reflects poorly on us all." For once Addy doesn't sound self-righteous, only sad. "She was our sister, the third part of our soul. But fate cannot be tampered with, even by us."

On the ground behind us, Laufey gags and Aiden rushes back to her side. I glare at the sisters who'd given me so much and then crouch beside him, putting Laufey's head in my lap. Her cheeks are hollow, her lips cracked as though she's been without water for days.

"We need to get her back to the house," Aiden says. "To Fern."

"Take her. I'll deal with them."

I can tell he doesn't want to leave me but worry for his grandmother fights with his instinct to watch over me.

"They won't hurt me." But I couldn't say the same for him or for Laufey.

He nods once and then lifts her up in a gentle hold and takes off for the woods.

"Nic—"

"Just go," I whirl on Addy and Chloe. "You say you can't interfere with a set course. I decided to leave you, leave the farm. To never see the two of you again."

"You don't mean that." There are tears in Chloe's eyes. "We're your family."

I shake my head. "You never were, not really."

Addy puts an arm around her sister. Her own eyes are dry, though her expression is sad. "Then we'll leave you to your fate."

A chill goes through me. "What does that mean?"

She reaches into her pocket and extracts a ring of keys, tosses them to me. "The farm is yours, as is the clinic and our vehicles. Everything is registered in your name. You'll find all the paperwork you need in the safe in my office. The combination is the day we adopted you."

I stare stupidly down at the keys. "You're just going to abandon your lives there?"

"We were the best guardians we knew how to be," Chloe wipes her eyes, steps forward and takes my hand. Her scent is bittersweet, like burned brownies. "We made mistakes along the way. But we did our best. I know it's not in your nature, but do you think maybe someday, you could forgive us?"

I look away, put the keys in my pocket. "What is it you always say? Forgiveness is for quitters?"

Her hands fall to her sides. "Right. Knew that was going to bite me on the ass one day."

Addy puts a hand on her sister's slumped shoulders. "May fate be kind, Nic. We will never forget you."

I close my eyes and turn toward the path Aiden took.

And don't look back.

I SIT outside on the dock overlooking the swamp, waiting for Aiden, for news of Laufey's condition. He'd come out to tell me that Fern had been in the middle of preparing a poultice for the wound and that it was too soon to tell if the giantess would pull through.

What he didn't say is that this is all my fault.

He doesn't have to say it. I know it in my bones, like an ache brought on by a savage fever. If I hadn't been so determined to bring Sarah back, Aiden never would have brought me here and my aunts never would have come looking for me.

The Fates. They were never my aunts, never more than temporary guardians.

The keys form a large bulge in my pocket. The farm is mine. I know I'll return there and find no trace of either of them. Not Chloe's hairbrush on the bathroom sink or Addy's glasses by her nightstand. Not the handmade quilt Chloe likes to snuggle under on cold nights or the scrapbook Addy keeps in the chest at the foot of her bed. All personal touches will be eradicated like they'd never been.

His footfalls are soft but still audible. I turn and look up into his red-rimmed eyes, a jolt of fear passing through me. "How is she?"

He crouches down beside me. "She'll make it."

My head feels too heavy and I let it drop so that my hair hides my face from him. "I'm so sorry, Aiden. I never should have insisted you bring me here."

His hands reach up, part my hair curtain and tuck several strands behind my ear. "It's not your fault."

"Did I command you to bring me back?" The question has been gnawing at me ever since I'd found out he had a hand in resurrecting me. "Is that why you did it?"

He frowns. "No. I brought you back because you never should have died, Nic. You were supposed to be an immortal queen."

I look away.

He clears his throat. "And because it was my fault."

"What? How could it be your fault?"

"I...left. We had a fight. The Hunt was out. It was my job

263

to protect you when they rode. But I was angry, and I left you alone."

I turn so I can face him fully. "What did we fight about?"

He stares out over the swamp, at the flitting light from the will-o'-the-wisps bobbing just above the murky water. "It doesn't matter."

"It does," I insist, my gaze falling to his wrist, where the contraceptive charm had once resided. "I want to know what went wrong before so I don't make the same mistakes."

"Believe me, you won't," his chuckle is darker than the midday shadows.

I put my hand over his, a gentle touch of connection, one I never would have considered making a few days ago. "Please. I need to know."

He sits fully so that his thigh presses against mine. His feet dangle over the edge of the dock. It strikes me that this is such a normal thing to do, sit side by side with your boyfriend and look out over the water. Just two teenagers wasting time together. Only he's not my boyfriend or a teenager. He's a cursed god who is beholden to me. And I doubt any couple in history has had a conversation like the one we're about to have.

"Okay, well first off, the mistakes weren't yours. They were mine. I knew you required offspring, that you hated the attention of the fey noblemen. It's law that any monarch who fails to produce heirs with their chosen consort must accept the attention of any fey noble who seeks them out at the appropriate times. For all intents and purposes, you couldn't say no."

My hands ball up at my sides. "All monarchs? The kings, too?"

He nods. "Yes. The lines of succession are critical to the survival of all fey. Most enjoy that aspect of ruling. Loyalty to a partner is a foreign concept for the fey. They don't mate for life and change partners as often as they change clothes. Sex is for power and personal gain as much as it is for pleasure."

"But I was different." My dreams had indicated that much.

"You were the ice queen."

A new memory surfaces, murmurs in the court as I pass sentence. "You're being kind. What they actually called me was the Ice Bitch." Just as Sarah had.

He doesn't deny it. "Colder than winter's heart, lacking the wild passions of the fey, immovable logic, ruthless in your ongoing pursuit of justice. It's why you were given command of the Wild Hunt. Nothing to…distract you."

At least not until him. I don't speak the words aloud but from the vividness of my memories, from the fact that I'd chosen Aiden to be my lover, I knew very well that he had been a distraction.

He inhales, his chest expanding before he continues. "The answer was simple, at least for you. If you had a child, had my child, all the rest of it would stop. The line of succession would remain intact."

"It sounds medieval." The words slip out.

"It's older than medieval, older than mankind. And if you think humans are slow to accept change, the fey are like carts stuck in the mud. Roll half an inch forward, then half an inch back. Only the combined ruling of both Seelie and Unseelie courts, all four royals, can change the law. And getting four royals to agree on anything is like asking time to stop churning forward."

"If they're half as stubborn as I am, I can see it."

"You were trapped by your obligations to your people and your crown. Once a month, on the moon of conception, I was forced to let you go to the fey nobles who craved my position at your side. Knowing full well that if you did conceive with one of them, I would be forced to leave."

A muscle jumps in his jaw as he stares out over the water.

"Those nights were almost as difficult for me as they were for you. I hated the idea of others touching you, loving your body as I did. Of *knowing* you in that way. The thought made the wolf rise to the fore. Even if the mortal part of me understood, the wolf could only sense that his mate was unhappy. I'd have to run for the entire night, just so I wouldn't slaughter them all. I never told you that before. Figured it was hard enough on you without worrying if I was going to lose it and destroy the entire court. There were times when I wanted to, believe me."

I do. His sincerity is etched in every line of his perfect face, much as I'm sure mine is a mask of revulsion. Moon of conception. Ick.

He sighs. "Even though I was eaten up with guilt and jealousy, I kept hoping that you would get what you needed so that it would end, and you could be at peace. Even if it meant I had to leave."

My brows draw down. "Why would you have to leave?"

"Once a royal consort has been replaced, they are banished from court. In the distant past, they were killed for not performing their duty, but that was one of the few laws the royals agreed to change."

"How generous." I can't keep the bite of sarcasm from my tone.

"It's not much of a pension plan," Aiden's lips twitch, but then he sobers. "The Unseelie Court is a treacherous place. All of Underhill is. I knew that going in, but in the end, I didn't have a choice."

"Because I was your mate?" I shake my head. "I don't even know what that means."

"It means my wolf will fight for you. Die for you. But that's not why I sought you out. Nic, from the first moment I saw you, you gave me a reason to live. I admired what you were, what the Wild Hunt stands for. Bringers of justice to the unjust. You were fearless, even when you were full of fear for yourself. Your position, your people came first. I needed to be part of that, a part of your life, if only for a little while."

His thumb skims lightly over my knuckles. "But I couldn't be a father, couldn't pass on Loki's genes to a new generation. What monstrous abilities would they possess? As a royal of the Unseelie court, they could tap into all the powers of the fey. What if they side with my father during Ragnorok? It could mean the end of the world."

I stare at him, trying to comprehend the sorts of abilities he described. The sort of worries that kept him up at night.

"We were trapped, me by my shitty genetics and you by your shitty job requirements. There was no way out without one of us compromising who we were to give the other what they needed."

"Did I order you to impregnate me?" If he says yes, I will vomit.

"No." He doesn't say it the way I'd been hoping he would, with a small smile on his lips and amusement dancing in his gaze. As though I'm fretting over nothing. He speaks the lone word as though I'd betrayed his trust in another way, a darker way that I have yet to imagine.

Dread coils in my stomach but I need to hear it all. "Please tell me."

He takes my hand, twines my fingers through his, as though he needs the connection, the reminder that I am right there beside him, not haunting his memories. "The last night that you...had to leave me, I went out for a run. I crossed dozens of leagues trying to calm the wolf. All my hackles were up. I knew it would come to a head soon. Even if I wasn't to be replaced and forced to leave, the wolf was getting harder to control. The knowledge that you were with someone else drove him mad, made him crave a kill.

"I was exhausted and half-crazed when I came back to

our chamber. Then I smelled the blood. Your blood. You were in the bath, you usually were, afterward. Washing their scents away. But your face…." He shakes his head, exhales.

"Someone hit me?"

"Someone beat you bloody," he corrects, his hand squeezing mine lightly. "Broke your nose, your eye was swollen shut. Your lovely skin mottled red and purple until you were practically disfigured. One of them had done it. The scent was nearly gone but I could have tracked him across the Veil, never mind to the outer hall. I ripped him to shreds before he could say one word. And I left my contraceptive charm on top of his tattered remains. Before the moon rose on the new month, you were with child."

My hand goes to my stomach. It's a ridiculous reflex, one I have no hope of fighting. "I was pregnant when I died?"

Aiden looks back down at the water. "Yes. And that's why we fought."

"Because you regretted your decision?" After all the reasons he'd stated that he didn't want children, how could I blame him for his feelings?

"No, because you forced my hand."

How? He said he'd come to me willingly. Was it because I'd been savaged, and he felt the need to protect me and wound up resenting me for it? That didn't sound like the Aiden I've been getting to know. He took more than his fair share of responsibility for every action and reaction. "I don't understand."

He opens his mouth to elaborate when there is a ripping sound, like a great bolt of fabric being rent in two. Aiden is on his feet before I can blink, facing not back toward the land, but out over the swamp. "Get behind me," he snarls.

I see black claws curl from his fingers and his eyes glow with emerald fire. Every hair on my arms stands on end.

"What is it?" I ask, even as the familiar shape of a sword

appears. It's blazing with an orange glow as it arcs down in a wide swath. Then the first rider appears. Freda, helmet decorated with falcon wings and riding a snow-white stallion and behind her, Nahini on her chestnut mare. Mounted fairies, charging hounds and undead foot soldiers make their way out of the tear and cross the water, all traveling on air between the glow from the will-o-the-wisps.

The Wild Hunt is back.

CHAPTER 21

A PLACE FOR MISFITS

Freda's mount steps from the nothingness three inches above the surface of the swamp to solid ground without a pause. "Greetings my queen. Wolf." She nods tersely at Aiden.

His claws are still out, and he bares his fangs at her. "You can't have her."

Freda tosses her long golden braid. "As I have told you many times before, the Unseelie Queen is not your property. You cannot dictate where she chooses to ride. Perhaps you need a reminder." She holds *Seelenverkäufer* out, her smile a challenge.

"You will not hurt him," I push past Aiden, the oddest sense of déjà vu sweeping through me. "Stop this, both of you. Aiden, you need to back down, now."

It's not a command but my tone is stern, so he knows I mean business.

He tenses, but slowly, gradually, the claws retract.

"My queen." Nahini, always the more formal of the two, dismounts and goes down on one knee before me.

"Don't please. I'm not a queen." I reach down and offer her a hand up.

"At least not yet," Freda smirks, her look a challenge.

"I thought you said three days." I turn to her. "It hasn't even been two."

"Time moves differently beyond the Veil." Aiden reminds me.

"Right." I've been putting off thinking about what would happen when they returned. So many other things have required my attention.

"If it is acceptable to you, we will dismiss the host to set up camp." Nahini gestures to encompass the remainder of the army. They have gone still as death itself, even the hounds.

I nod. "Go ahead."

The living fey separate from the rest, trotting their mounts to the land, the hounds at their heels. One huge man has a large falcon perched on his shoulder, and the name Alric flits through my mind as he passes me.

"Go find a place to set up camp," Freda says to one slight girl with a long red braid and pointed ears. She looks to be about twelve. "Wait for my signal."

"Yes, mother." The girl dips her head respectfully.

"Mother?" I blink.

"You know I could never say no to a nymph in my bed." Freda grins.

"A nymph?" Nahini raises one perfectly arched brow.

Freda winks at me. "There might have been more than one. You play you pay, am I right, Nicneven?"

Beside me, I feel Aiden tense.

I look out at the rest of the company, the disembodied souls. "What about them?"

With a wave of her hand, Nahini flicks a glowing sort of

light out over the undead. The mist rises off the swamp, consuming them from the ground up even as they seem to melt down into it. The ghostly entourage blends with it until I can no longer make out individual forms, just wisps of putty-colored fog on the water.

"They will remain here until summoned." Nahini leads her horse forward. "Where are we being quartered?"

"Um…?" My teeth sink into my bottom lip. I don't look to Aiden. Somehow doing so in their presence feels wrong. He has been my guide through Underhill, but I'm supposed to be a leader to these warriors. At the same time, I have brought an army to Laufey and Fern's doorstep, not once but twice, and right on the heels of Chloe and Addy's brutal attack. Miss Manners would not approve. "Well, we can't stay here."

Aiden touches the sleeve of my dress lightly. "You have lands in the mortal realm."

I glance up at him, surprised. "You mean the farm?"

His face is like stone, not a man who looks like he enjoys what he's suggesting. "The protections will still be in place, it's isolated and there is enough space for the Hunt to set up their summer camp without detection."

I open my mouth, then close it once more. What choice do I have? "All right. The farm then."

Freda whistles and the little elven redhead runs to her side. "Gather them again. We cross the Veil once more."

The small girl's blue eyes sparkle with excitement. "Yes, mother."

Nahini is busy urging the mist to reform into the dead members of The Hunt. One large man—a spirit of a man anyhow—seems to glower at her. It's the kind of look you give to someone who got you out of bed the moment after your head hits the pillow.

Aiden pulls me aside as the Wild Hunt reassembles. "I'll need a few days here."

I blink up at him. "You're not coming with us?"

He traces the backs of his fingers down my cheek. "Not yet. I do not wish to leave them alone here until Laufey is fully recovered."

Of course, he would want to stay. I should have thought of it myself, but I never considered the possibility of going back without him. Going anywhere without him. In a very short time, Aiden has become a permanent fixture in my life. "Do what you gotta do."

He searches my face. "Promise me something. You will not leave the farm until I return."

"What? I'll need to go out. If for nothing else than to get groceries to feed an army." Well, half an army anyway.

"Send someone in your stead. The Hunt and the enchantments the Fates placed over the residence will keep you safe. I found you when you left to hunt. Others could do the same, especially once Brigit learns that you are alive. When the Hunt no longer responds to her summons."

I meet his bright green gaze. "One day soon, we're going to have to talk about Brigit and how you seem to know so much about her."

"We will," he agrees, his expression giving away nothing. "Soon. I will miss you, Nic."

My lips turn up in a small smile. "Don't be too long. You're my guide through all this."

He nods, his eyes somber. "It's been my privilege. And my pleasure."

"My queen?" Freda is mounted once again and extends her hand down to me. I grasp it and she pulls me up. I swing my leg over until I am mounted firmly behind her.

Aiden steps back farther onto the dock, still near but clearly out of reach.

"Didn't take him long to slither his way back into your

bed," Freda grumbles as she turns her pearl-colored mare around in midair.

"We're not sleeping together," I inform her, though I'm not sure why. Divulging personal information isn't something I do. Ever. Yet something about Freda's straight-to-the-heart-of-it manner emboldens me.

"If you want my advice, you'll keep it that way." Freda turns her mount to the east and slashes the air with *Seelenverkäufer*. The tear appears, glowing and pulsing like a raw wound.

"Why do you dislike him?" I turn to look back at Aiden. He stands there on the dock, watching me, his expression is unreadable.

She sheaths the sword. "Because he's fickle. Swearing allegiance to you, then Brigit, then you again. A true companion of the heart should be loyal, don't you think?"

My head whips around to meet her gaze. "He swore allegiance to Brigit? An actual oath?"

"Before the entire court, just as he did for you."

I turn to look back at where Aiden still stands and part my lips. If he had to obey her, the same way he did me... possibilities whirl in my mind.

But then Freda's horse pushes its nose through the tear. There is a great roaring, like the heart of a storm followed by a sucking sensation as though my body is a cherry at the bottom of a milkshake and some giant is trying to pull me up through a straw. Freda spurs the mare into a gallop as we pass back through the Veil. When I look again, Aiden is nowhere in sight.

THERE IS no ferry this time, no shooting starlight from the

souls that maintain the Veil. One moment we are surrounded by the humid air of the swamp and the next the cool fresh mountain breeze surrounds us. Freda's horse gallops on invisible currents of air. In the distance, lightning flashes as dark clouds stack up. A storm is coming, the energy crackles through me, making all the hairs on my arm stand on end.

Riding with the Wild Hunt is both terrifying and exhilarating. Just like in my dreams, wind whips at my hair, tugging it every which way. The clamor of the army behind me abandoned whoops, barks and bays and the cry of the falcon I'd seen earlier. I barely stifle my own urge to throw back my head and shout out along with them. Energy pulses between the living members of the unearthly host. We are one, connected beneath the stars.

"You'll have to direct me from here," Freda turns her helmeted head, the wings nearly poking me in the eye. "I don't know exactly where we're going."

I look down, hoping to spot anything familiar. Of course, I've never had an aerial view of my hometown before. The houses and stores are all tiny pinpricks of light, the people no larger than ants.

"Can't they hear us?" I shout to her and gesture down at the tiny scuttling beings.

"If they do, they'll dismiss it as noise from the approaching thunderheads. Does anything look familiar, my queen? The storm front will be upon us soon and I would prefer not to dodge lightning."

"There." I point at a winding road that bends out from the center of town. "Follow that to the east, through the trees."

Freda does. It's difficult to judge distance but I keep the road in my sights. The main road dumps out into a gravel drive and then I see the farm. First Addy's clinic, the abandoned building that used to be for seasonal workers to bunk, and then finally the farmhouse. The only home I've ever known.

No lights shine from the windows, no smoke rises from the chimney. My throat constricts. They really are gone.

Freda's mount touches down lightly, the steed shifting from running on air to solid earth without losing a step. Nahini draws up her own reins, the motion as natural to her as drawing breath. Behind us, the rest of the Wild Hunt lands with barely a rustle of grass.

"My queen?" Freda peers over her shoulder at me and with a start, I realize she's waiting for me to climb down. I do, with much less grace than she exhibits a moment later, but at least I don't land on my ass in the dirt.

"Fascinating," Nahini removes her helmet, her plethora of braids spilling free. "We've traveled past this place a dozen times when searching for the wolf, yet I never saw it. I can feel the magic protecting it. It throbs like a pulse in the air. No wonder he eluded us."

A memory flashes in my mind. Nahini, though I hadn't known her name at the time. She throws herself between me and the man I'd come to claim. They have made camp away from the rest of their village, intentionally. Plants and herbs lay strewn about and the man on the pallet sweats with fever. Firelight dances off *Seelenverkäufer* and reflects in her dark eyes as she glares at me. "You shall not have him."

I could shove her aside easily but pause. "He is damaged, child. Sick."

She bares her teeth. "He's my brother."

Her fierceness, her loyalty burns as bright as their campfire. Not a trait I see often.

"He's hurt others," I say. "Innocents. He belongs with the Hunt."

She shakes her head. "He's all I have."

"My queen, allow me to dispatch them both." Freda,

always eager to prove her devotion with bloodshed, steps forward.

I raise my hand in silent command and move closer to the pallet. The half-naked man thrashes, his eyes dart behind closed lids. I sheath my blade and I bend down to touch him, but the sister is there, gripping my gauntleted wrist. "No."

"Release her," I hear Freda's blade scrape free of her scabbard.

I meet the sister's fierce gaze. "Peace, child. I only intend to ascertain his condition. I will not harm him. None of us will harm either of you." The yet goes unspoken.

She searches me from the crown of a braid pinned atop my head to the mud on my boots. I get the feeling that she can see inside me, is reading my intent. Her shoulders relax slightly, the adrenaline leaving her system.

"Stand down, Freda," I tell my second. "There is no danger here."

After the slightest hesitation, she does.

The dark girl swallows and then let's go of my wrist.

I touch the forehead of the man, and it's like touching fire. "The fever rages within him. He will die this night."

"He won't," she shoves me aside and places a wet cloth on his forehead. Her eyes are wet though no tears escape. "I won't let him go."

I watch for a moment as her nimble fingers crumble dried herbs into a clay pot and then set it over the fire. Her skill is obvious, she must have been trained as the tribal wise woman or healer. But her brother's misdeeds, his perversion, have forced her from her people.

And her loyalty to him kept her by his side.

I crouch down next to her as she spoons water past his cracked lips. "Even your remarkable will and all the love in your heart won't win this battle. But there is a way you can stay with him."

"How?" Her face is bleak. She has been at this many days.

"Join us. Join the Wild Hunt as your brother must."

She doesn't recoil. "You aren't human."

"No, but my second is." I gesture to Freda. "She is an immortal being now, like me. And like you will be if you join us. Your brother will die. You will live, but my way, the two of you can be together. And you never have to worry that he will hurt an innocent again. You can help us stop others from hurting innocents."

I see the shadows in her dark eyes, the worry there. She knows what her brother is, knows it and loves him anyway. A human flaw, the capacity to love, one I am glad not to possess.

"Will it hurt him?" she asks with a fearful look at the weapon strapped to my hip.

I can at will increase the potency of my kiss, kill him within a heartbeat. "It doesn't have to. You will join us then?"

She swallows, nods once. "I will."

"And I will be proud to have you as part of my ranks. We will be your family." I bend down and press my lips lightly against her brother's, sealing his fate with my most toxic kiss….

"My queen? Is aught amiss?" Nahini is frowning at me now.

I shake my head, then gaze past her, to the deathly ranks where her brother stands. He was wrong in life, like all the dead of the Hunt are, but Nahini's love for him is pure and true and has survived for a century after his death. For those we hunt, we are a scourge, a tsunami that can't be stopped. An afterlife sentence. But for me, for Freda and Nahini it's about loyalty. Family. A place in the world where misfits belong and can protect those that need it most.

"Perhaps we should set up camp?" Nahini suggests.

I nod. "Sure, wherever you think is best."

She surveys the open field where we stopped, about an acre from the house. "Down there by the stream will do."

"Not too close, it tends to flood this time of year. And we need to make sure both the gates are closed." The last thing I want is for locals to stumble across the Hunt.

"We'll see to it." Freda mounts again and gestures for her daughter to climb on with her. They vanish between one step and the next.

Nahini dismisses the dead and they disperse into the fog, whatever fibers that hold them together dissolving into nothingness.

The living host begins to break out tents. Some of the fey soldiers collect stones and dig fire pits. There is talk now and laughter. Fey armor is set aside for polishing. It's a camp much like any other. It's difficult to believe this many people could travel and stand as quietly as I've seen them do.

"My queen?" I turn to find the male with the falcon. His eyes are brown with flecks of gold, his hair as pale blond as my own.

"Alric, right?" I try the name that registered when I'd first spotted him

His smile is soft and as brilliant as the dawn sun. "You remember me?"

"Only your name, I'm afraid. What can I do for you?"

He clears his throat. "It's the animals. The hounds and birds of prey. Typically, I set up a tent for them beside my own but with the approaching storms, I was wondering if there is anywhere else I might keep them. Somewhere with better shelter?" A flush stains his cheeks all the way to the tips of his pointed ears.

"I have just the place. If you'll gather them together."

He whistles once, sharply and within seconds is surrounded by hounds on the ground and birds in the sky.

"Wow," I breathe. I've seen well-trained dogs, but never so

many at one time, and never the birds. "You must have a way with wild creatures."

"I'm a Spriggan. We have a unique connection to speak with all varieties of fauna. Shall we ride?" He gestures to his horse.

"Um, it's not far. Just down the hill." I point to the well-worn path towards the clinic. "So, when you say speak with them you don't mean like having a conversation, like the way we are doing now?"

Alric falls into step beside me with the hounds trailing in our wake. "Not in the same way. Animals think differently from humans or fey. They aren't bogged down by memories of the past or desires for the future. All they see is the now."

"I envy them." I sigh.

"As do I." Alric again offers that radiant smile. "Try it."

"Try what?"

"Talking to one of them. Swift, to me."

A sleek black hound breaks formation and takes a place beside Alric. "This is Swift, the fastest hound in the Hunt. Not even your wolf can outrun her. She is a good breeder, has spawned two litters, but running is her joy." Pride laces his every word.

"Oh, I can't," the protest bubbles up.

He raises one ash blond brow. "You are the Unseelie Queen. My powers are at your disposal."

"Right." Now that I am no longer in Underhill, hopefully, I won't experience any bizarre consequences from fumbling with magic. I turn to the dog and smile. She sits and waits, not panting or wagging, just staring.

Run. I think at her.

Nothing happens.

"Try picturing the command," Alric urges. "Animals put together pictures, not just from sight but from sound and scent, the feel of the wind, the taste of the water. See in your mind what you want her to do and imagine the sensations that go along with it."

I nod. After taking a deep breath, I try again, this time picturing Swift running down the hill to the door of the clinic. I see her ears flapping, her tongue out to taste the breeze as she runs full tilt, feel the impact of the ground beneath her paws.

She takes off at a sprint, charging down the hill so quickly she is nothing but a black blur. Alric closes his eyes and a moment later the rest of our entourage follows Swift down the hill to the door of the clinic.

"Amazing." My body tingles with the sensations Swift experienced on her dash down the hill. My heart pounds as though I had been the one running and my breaths are uneven, almost ragged. "Can you feel all of them at once?"

He nods. "Yes, I had to train to focus on one at a time though. When we go into battle, I must be able to filter out the different messages."

"Battle?" I ask, but the thundering of hooves on pavement draws our attention away.

Freda and her daughter draw up beside Alric's pack.

"Who gave you permission to leave camp?" she barks.

For a moment I think she's talking to me, but then I see her gaze fix on Alric, who grows tense beside me.

"The queen said—," he begins but she cuts him off.

"You do not break from camp in the mortal realm without direct permission from me or the Second. Is that clear?" she seethes.

His gaze flashes anger but he lifts his chin and says, "Forgive me, First."

"We wanted to secure the animals before the storm hits," I intervene. "I was showing him where. He was just doing his job."

Freda blinks as though she forgot I am standing here and

I can sense Alric's gaze on me. I feel as though I've walked into the middle of a marital spat and stuck my nose where it doesn't belong.

Freda squares her shoulders, eyes flashing, and I know I made a mistake. "The storm approaches. We best get to it."

CHAPTER 22

TRAINING

"What exactly is this gauntlet I'm supposed to run?" I direct my question to Nahini since Freda's been chilly with me ever since the incident with Alric.

The entire afternoon has been chaos. First, Alric, appalled because I'd intended for him to put his beloved hounds and birds in cages the way humans do.

"Would you put a friend in a cage?" He'd asked as he strokes the white breast of a hawk.

I answered honestly. "I don't have any friends, other than Aiden and there are times he needs to be restrained."

He'd shut down entirely. In the end, I retrieved every linen and the spare cot Addy had sometimes slept on when she had a touch and go case and left him to hash the animal quartering out as he saw fit.

Freda awaited me outside, her gaze as stormy as the skies above. When I tried to apologize, she held up a hand.

"It's your job to lead The Hunt, not mine. I have grown used to command with the queen issuing orders from the court. It won't happen again."

She turned and climbed aboard her steed and hasn't spoken a word to me since.

Apparently, immortals sulk as often as mortals.

And when I invited her and Nahini to stay in the house with me, they exchanged an appalled look. "Only the royal consort, direct blood lineage, and servants share a roof with royalty."

"Why?"

"Cohabitating is for lovers. The current ones and the honored ones that have yielded offspring."

Great, more people who thought every invitation would lead to sex. What, did I have the reputation of being some sort of nymphomaniac in my last life?

"What about food then?" I ask. "Surely you'll stay for a meal."

That seems acceptable to them until they realize I intend to do the cooking.

"Majesty," Nahini's dark eyes are wide. "You have a host of servants to cook for you."

I find a veggie lasagna stashed in the freezer and peel off the aluminum foil to nuke it. "Actually, I don't. It's fine, I do this all the time."

Another unreadable glance between them.

"Oh, come on," I snap. "You were both mortal once, you know what it's like. You have to fend for yourself."

"But you're the queen," Nahini protests.

I am getting very tired of hearing that.

"It's not really cooking. Just reheating." I explain how the microwave heats things up.

"Incredible," Nahini launches into a multitude of questions about how a microwave works, who created it and other bizarre inquiries I can't answer.

"We should steal some," Freda says to Nahini as I set the steaming lasagna on the table. "Carry them back across the

Veil to the court. It will win us many favors with the province lords."

Images of them looting a Best Buy flash through my mind. "You need electricity to make it work."

Nahini frowns. "Where is Electra City? I have never heard of such a place."

Mental forehead smack. "It's not a place. Electricity is how we power our homes now. Like the lights." I point over at the Tiffany lamp on the sideboard.

They exchange another look. "But you still have candles and fireplaces."

I nod. "For when the power goes out."

"Whose power?" Nahini asks.

"I need a drink." It's not something I ever thought I'd say. Sarah had liked to drink, more accurately she'd liked to get drunk. I'd always been her wingman, the straight arrow. Alcohol equals slower reaction times and poor choices, two things I avoid while hunting. But if I am going to make it through this meal without kissing someone, I need an assist. Besides, average my past and present lives together and I am well over twenty-one.

Chloe is a wine lover and she keeps several bottles of Rosa Regale in the fridge at any given time. I grab one, pop the cork and swig straight from the bottle, before passing it to Nahini.

Her eyes light up as she samples the bubbly red. "'Tis better than fairy wine."

"Tell me about the gauntlet," I repeat my earlier question. "What are the challenges like?"

"It's different for everyone. The gauntlet exists in the catacombs in the very heart of Underhill. The tests are crafted to make you face your worst fears." Freda finally looks me in the eye as she says this. "We are forbidden to speak of our time in the gauntlet. Suffice it to say, it finds your mental, physical and emotional limitations and then pushes you well beyond them. Many who enter never return."

"It's designed to ensure those who pass truly know what they are giving up. That they really want to be immortal and will sacrifice anything to attain their goal," Nahini adds.

I snag the bottle from Freda and take another swig before passing it back to Nahini. Great, I'm not even sure I want to be immortal and the test is designed to weed out the lackluster applicants.

"How can I prepare for an unknowable test?" I fork up some lasagna but don't taste it.

"We'll do our best to see that you are both physically and mentally ready," Nahini reassures me. "This is delightful, is there more?"

With a start, I realize she's polished off the bottle of wine. "In the fridge. Help yourself."

She retrieves the remaining two bottles, passes one to Freda and keeps the other for herself.

"We'll start your training in the morning. At first light." Freda finishes her food and then rises, leaving the unopened wine standing on the table. "I should check on the camp, make sure all is as it should be."

I watch her go.

"Did something occur?" Nahini asks tentatively.

Briefly, I sum up the incident with Alric.

"Ah," she nods as though that makes perfect sense. "She and Alric have a complicated history."

"Who doesn't?" I grumble. My thoughts focus on Aiden.

She smiles and pops the cork on the last bottle. "Alric's father is part of the gentry, a province lord of Unseelie lands. He was Brigit's consort for a time. One of his half-siblings is even in line for the Fire Throne. They are pure fairy blood and Freda is an immortal human, not fey."

"So?" I'm doing more drinking than eating, but it feels right. I go with it.

"Not all of the courtiers are as accepting of humans as you were. You are." She corrects, her brows drawing together with a frown.

"I'm having trouble with the tenses, too. But that's Alric's father's prejudice, not his."

The beads in Nahini's hair click together as she shakes her head. "It's not so simple. Alric was assigned to do a tour with the Hunt. After his campaign is over he is expected to take his father's place at court." Her eyes seem to be willing me to connect the dots.

I flinch when it hits me. "You mean, to try and become a consort. *My* consort."

She passes me the bottle. "Correct."

"And when she saw us together earlier, she was jealous." I shake my head.

I blow out a sigh. Maybe it's the wine, maybe it's because I know Nahini's loyalty runs deeper than an underground river, but I decide to open up to her. "Do I have to do this? Can't it go back to being what it was, me hunting on my own, capturing souls for the Wild Hunt? I'm not cut out to be queen."

"Nicneven," she pats my hand once, a comforting gesture. "You were born for this. You are needed on the Shadow Throne, needed to rule. There hasn't been a winter Queen of the Elphame for almost two decades. The balance must be restored."

"Why though? Why can't Brigit do it all?"

"Because she is your opposite. All sun makes a desert. And because you are the leader of the Wild Hunt." She shifts, clearly uncomfortable. "Freda didn't want me to tell you this, but you should know. There has been talk at the court of disbanding the Hunt."

"What? Why?"

"Brigit has never cared what souls we reap for the Hunt. She has used us more like her personal guard, which enrages the Seelie kings. Your leadership, your temperance kept the Hunt focused on seeking out damaged souls. Souls like my brother. Brigit just orders us to make quota at the same time she diverts us on personal errands, like tracking the wolf. Our resources are stretched too thin. We aren't meant to ride in summer, but to rest. For everything there is a season and the Hunt was tied to your season. We haven't had a proper summer rest since you left us."

"Why was she after Aiden?" I ask, afraid of the answer but needing to know it anyway.

Nahini rises. "That is for him to tell you. I must away. Pleasant dreams, my queen."

I watch her leave and then, ignoring the dishes, move to sit before the fireplace with the half-empty bottle. The fire is dying so I turn and snag a log to add to the pile. A stack of newspapers is piled up neatly next to the kindling. I lift the top one, dated the day Aiden and I had left for Underhill. Addy always stacks the newest paper at the top, just a quirk of her OCD. So. Barely any time has passed in the mortal realm. I'm about to set it aside when the headline catches my notice.

Local teen killed in freak car accident.

I begin to read.

Sarah Larkin, age sixteen died Friday night after her vehicle was crushed beneath a tree during a torrential downpour. Funeral services will be held graveside Monday at 2 PM.

I fling the paper on the fire, tears welling in my eyes. Never have I felt like this before, like my best isn't good enough.

"I'm sorry, Sarah," I murmur and reach for the wine bottle. "I don't know what else I can do."

A LOUD CLATTERING jerks me from dreams that fade away as soon as the light touches them. I look up to see Freda standing at the open door, a bold silhouette like a Viking girl pinup with the rising sun behind her "Time for training."

My head throbs like an exposed heart, the light from the clear morning sending stabbing needles into my brain. My words come out as a croak. "Shut the door,"

She slams it and stalks inside, all restless energy, a predator waiting for her chance to strike. "We must begin if we're to get you ready before Samhain."

In contrast, my head is full of fog, my brain fuzzy, my mouth tastes like the floor mat at the vet clinic. "Freda, about, Alric."

"I don't wish to speak of it," she seethes. "He is nothing to me."

"Okay," I rub my eyes, hoping to clear the haze away. "But I still won't sleep with him."

She is pacing the length of the couch and casts me a disbelieving look. "When you become queen again, you won't have a choice."

"Then I won't become queen again." I struggle up, so I can meet her gaze.

That halts her in mid-step. "What? But you are the queen."

"I'm as mortal as you once were. And I'm also asexual."

She tilts her head, the gesture akin to something from Alric's hawk. "What is that? One who reproduces like a plant?"

I groan. "No. I'm not attracted to other people. Or fey."

"What of your wolf?" She sits in the chair beside me. "Are the two of you not involved again?"

"Not sexually. Not really. I have…feelings for Aiden. But

they're sort of a mess. I'm not sure if they are my feelings or my memories, you know?"

"No, I don't."

I didn't really expect her to understand something I am still struggling with myself. "Look, all you need to know is I want nothing to do with this consort business. I'm not some broodmare for the Unseelie court. If they want me to rule, then they get me, not my lineage. And whatever happens with Aiden and me is our own business. No one else's. Got it?"

She stares at me for a long time and then a smile splits her face. "And I thought you were formidable before. I believe you, Nicneven. You will be a queen for the ages. But not until after you train."

"Give me a minute." I stagger toward the bathroom, my tongue practically stuck to the roof of my mouth. The wrath of grapes indeed. The shower looks incredibly inviting, especially after days without. I can just imagine Freda storming in and dragging me naked and dripping out to practice, so I settle for brushing my teeth and popping two aspirin for the pain.

I'd slept in plaid pajama pants and a tank top, so I move to my bedroom to find something a little sturdier for whatever training involves. Judging from the muscle definition on both Freda and Nahini, it wouldn't be a walk in the park.

I emerge fully dressed in jeans and a flannel shirt with sturdy boots on my feet and my hair braided back so it won't get in my way. Freda is pawing through the fridge, much the same way Aiden did. I feel a pang at his absence and my hand rises to rub over the hollow spot in my chest.

"To think," she muses. "All this food just steps away. Sometimes with the Hunt, we ride days without food or drink."

I feel immediately guilty for not offering more to the

troops. "Did everyone eat last night? You can take whatever you need from the house to feed them." Aiden said I shouldn't leave but internet shopping could fill in whatever gaps there might be in the pantry.

Freda bows. "Many thanks. I will let the battalion commanders know."

"I don't remember much about leading the Hunt. I will need your guidance."

Her expression is pleased. "I am your First. Your right-hand battle commander. I will always do what needs to be done for you and for the Wild Hunt. Now, to the sparring ring."

The angle of the sun is changing, the light growing brighter. The scents of damp earth and fresh-cut grass greet me. Home. I really am home. Water drips from the bright green leaves overhead and mist rises from the ground. I shiver and wonder if I'm walking through a soul or maybe several of them.

Freda leads me to a field not far from where Aiden and I crossed the Veil. In the distance, the Wild Hunt's campsite is visible, though few are up and moving so early. There is a crumbling stone wall where Nahini is already perched, legs dangling carelessly over the edge. I get the feeling that if the wall collapses, she will be well away from it.

An array of weapons is laid out on the ground before her. I stare from the black hilted sword to the crossbow, the mace and several other things I can't identify.

"Which one is for me?"

"All of them." Freda bends down and sweeps up a sword and flings it at me.

I hit the ground as the blade whizzes past where my chest had been. It lands with a dull thump a foot behind me. The two of them burst out laughing.

I glare and pull myself up and dust off my clothes. "What the hell? I'm mortal, remember?"

Nahini bites her lip. "It's a dull blade, my queen. A practice sword. It won't cut you."

"Could have told me that before you threw it," I grumble and move to pick up the defunct blade. It's heavy, probably at least ten pounds and unwieldy. I need two hands to have any control over it. Just as Nahini said, the edges are rounded, like a pencil that hasn't been sharpened for a while.

"One hand," Freda draws *Seelenverkäufer* and demonstrates how she wants me to stand. "Like so."

I do my best to mimic her, positioned sideways, blade raised at an angle across my body. "Don't I need a shield or something?"

Nahini shakes her head. "A shield only adds to the weight you must carry. You're not a soldier going into battle, you're a hunter. An assassin. Speed is your best advantage."

Freda turns slightly, pivoting one leg so her feet are shoulder-width apart and changing the angle of her blade. I copy her, feeling clumsy in comparison to her lithe movements.

"Now lunge." She demonstrates, flowing into a new form, sword extended as though spearing some invisible enemy in the gut. "And retreat before they know what's hit them." She resumes the first form, again standing sideways.

I try, the maneuver nowhere near as elegant as hers.

"Again," Freda backs up to assess.

I repeat the three steps she showed me. Defense, ready and attack stances. The second time is harder, the weight of the blade drags my arms down. When I get into the attack lunge, Freda casually swings *Seelenverkäufer* down to connect with my blade, about an inch from my hand. The reverberation stings, jarring all the bones up to my shoulder. My sword falls from nerveless fingers.

"Ouch," I shake my arm out, trying to bring the feeling back.

"Don't ever drop your weapon," Freda uses the blade of *Seelenverkäufer* to flick the practice sword up until she can catch it by the hilt. She then uses the two blades to create a scissors effect with one on either side of my neck. "' Lest it be used against you."

I swallow, afraid to nod or speak in case whatever passes for my soul gets sucked into the mystical blade.

She moves back and tosses the practice sword to me. "Again."

I repeat the stances, my feet finding the rhythm better this time. The attack comes not from Freda on the third pose, but from Nahini on the second. Her crescent-shaped blade is at my throat before I'm even aware she's moved off the wall.

"And never assume your enemy is alone," Freda says as Nahini releases me.

"Like deer." I nod.

They stare at me blankly.

"It's something you learn driving in rural areas. If you see one deer, always assume there's another so you don't speed up when the first one crosses the road in front of you, or you might hit the second one."

"Ah," Nahini says. "Yes, like that. Except deer won't have weapons and you want to hit them."

Sword practice goes on for hours. The stances grow more familiar and I manage to keep my sword when Freda makes contact, though I am never fast enough to prevent Nahini from catching me unaware. The woman moves at the speed of thought.

"How do you do that?" I ask her at one point.

"How do you kill with a kiss?" she responds.

I shake my head. "I don't know. It's just something I've always been able to do."

"Same is true for me. We all have our gifts, my queen."

As the sun hits its zenith, Freda departs to check on the camp and Nahini and I return to the house. Though the temperature is in the low seventies, my body drips with sweat, and my bones ache, the muscles spasming out of control.

"I didn't even get to the other weapons." I grouse in frustration.

"Take a few moments to rest," Nahini advises. "We will work on your mental skills after midday repast."

I nod and stumble off to the shower. The warm water is delectable against my skin and I feel as though I'm rinsing days of filth down the drain with every swipe of the washcloth.

Wearing only my bathrobe, I pad into my bedroom and fall face-first onto the mattress.

A knock sounds on my door.

"What?" My response is muffled by the covers.

The door opens with that familiar creek and Nahini steps in, carrying a tray. I scent the aroma of bean and barley soup. "I used your wavy box to heat it." She beams with pride.

"Microwave," I correct. My stomach growls at the delightful fragrance of herbs. The soup recipe is one of the few things Addy cooks well and she would make vats of it at a time, canning what we couldn't eat immediately in mason jars. "Where did you find that?"

"In the other unit."

When I frown, she sets the tray on my nightstand and holds up her hand about six inches above her own head. "Large white box about this tall. You have one in the other room to store the winter's chill."

I blink. "You mean the refrigerator? We don't have

another one." Even as I say it, I remember there had been an ancient unit in the abandoned outbuilding on the opposite side of the property from the vet's office. "Was it in a ramshackle building with the roof caved in?"

She nods. "I have a few of the spirits repairing the structure now. It will make a fine headquarters for our summer campsite."

I sit up and reach for one of the bowls of soup. "You really are planning to stay through the summer?"

She nods. "The queen—that is Queen Brigit—will dispatch us at her leisure. Freda and I discussed it and it seems wise to continue to obey her orders until you are ready to face her. She must believe she still maintains control of the Hunt. But she makes no arrangements for our food or lodgings. We have lost most of the younger hunters to exposure and malnourishment."

"I didn't see any children, other than Freda's daughter."

"Jasmine," Nahini smiles. "Yes, currently she is the youngest of our band."

"How young can they joint the Hunt?"

"Traditionally seven winters are required unless a parent is an officer, like in Freda's case. Her daughter has been with us since the night she came into the world."

Immortal children, starving to death. The thought knots my insides. It had been my job to protect the hunters, both the living and those who the Hunt ensnared. Without me, they had no one looking out for their wellbeing. "Well, think of this as your home base now, summer and winter and I'll do my best to get whatever you need."

I only hope it will be enough.

With the soup finished, Nahini tells me to dress in comfortable clothes and meet her in the great hall, which I assume means the living room. I change into Pilates pants and a baggy t-shirt, as well as a thick pair of socks.

In the living room, I see Nahini has discarded her multi-hued armor. It shimmers in the firelight like dragon scales, crimson one moment and sapphire the next with all the hues in between. She wears a skintight black jumpsuit that shows off her remarkable figure. Without the weight of it, she looks delicate, smaller than I had thought, but with long lean muscles like a dancer. She has also pushed the couch back away from the fireplace so there is enough room for the two of us to sit before it.

"Come, mimic my pose." She sinks gracefully down until she is in a seated position with her bare feet and palms pressed together.

With a reluctant sigh, I remove the socks and copy her, though much less artfully. "It's hard to believe I was a fairy queen. I have zero inborn grace."

"That is because your mind is cluttered, churning and churning like one of the great mechanical beasts modern humans rely so heavily upon. Only when your mind is unburdened can you attain a true state of grace."

I make an unintentional noise that comes out sounding like, "Ma huh." It sounds like new age B.S. to me, but her fluidity of movement and her speed are undeniable.

"Close your eyes and take three deep breaths. Inhale slowly through your nose, exhale just as slowly through your mouth. Do not rush through them. With each inhale, you are giving your body fortification. Every exhale expelling all the unwanted bits that clutter your body and disturb your soul."

I do as she instructs, a slow deep breath then an exhale. Another. A third. "I don't feel any different."

"Don't be impatient," she says in her musical lilt.

I open my mouth to argue that I'm not, but then close it again. Instead, I crack an eyelid and peek at her. She sits like a statue carved from onyx, serene and completely composed.

"Now, I want you to picture the last thing you recalled about your previous life. The last vivid image."

The mental image from the night before. I recall the sweaty lather of my mount, the tinge of dust from the approaching sandstorm, the crackle of the campfire. The fever radiating off the doomed man's skin. "It was the night I met you. You were ferocious, guarding your brother."

"I remember it well." There is a smile in her voice. "The Hunt rode up and encircled our camp. Never have I felt so afraid."

"You hid it well."

"Fear can be a strength if you know how to channel it."

A log shifts in our own fire, sending sparks up the chimney, jarring me back into my body. "Weird, for a minute there it felt as if I were actually there again."

Nahini's eyes open and she fixes her level gaze on me. "That's the regression of the soul. We are all connected to our past and future selves through strands of fate. If you know how to grasp it, you can follow it back into a past life or follow it forward and see the next incarnation of yourself."

I stare at her in disbelief. "You're telling me you can see not just who you were but who you will be?"

"Not simply see experience. Did you not smell the desert air, taste it on your tongue?"

"I did."

She nods. "It's not without risk though, what we are doing. You should be aware of that before we continue. An untrained mind can get swept up in the moment, forget to come back to where her body and soul naturally resides."

Chills shoot through me. "You mean, I could get stuck in one of these scenes?"

A slow nod. "Your flashes of memory mean your thread is tangled, knotted between your past self and your present. All of us who have lived before are twisted to some extent, but the memories usually manifest as nighttime dreams that are forgotten when we wake. Yours are different, triggered by those you encountered in your past life and stealing you out of your body to relive them as they strike. If that happens in battle or in the gauntlet in the middle of a challenge, it could prove fatal."

"Hel said she was sending me the memories," I whisper.

Nahini's lips part. "The goddess of the underworld? You spoke with her?"

When I nod, she exhales. "If your memories are being forced on you by someone else, you will continue to experience them whether or not you are trained. Hel has her own agenda, one we know nothing about. The training at least provides you with some element of control and the knowledge to disentangle yourself. Do you wish to proceed?"

I swallow. I'd never thought of the memories as dangerous. "Yes."

She offers a reassuring smile and closes her eyes. After a moment, I do the same.

"Go back to the last nocturnal memory."

My last dream. I shut my eyes again. "Got it."

"Describe it to me."

Heat burns up my cheeks and it has nothing to do with the fire. "Aiden. He is touching me. Intimately."

"And how does his touch affect you?"

Is she serious? "It...well, it excites me. Sexually."

"You sound surprised by this."

"I am. Sexual attraction isn't natural for me." Even now, I feel the rasp of calloused hands on my skin, his breath on my neck, the ready state of his body as it presses into mine.

"It was before though, correct?"

"Yes." We'd just been fighting. My blood is hot and quick in my veins, release moments away. Every sensation is familiar, the longing, the need. A sweet ache and gentle pressure building, spiraling ever upward.

"Have you ever experienced those feelings with anyone else?"

Her voice jars me out of the memory and I blink. "What?"

She remains there with her eyes closed. I have a disturbing feeling she can see it, too. This is more than hypnotherapy. Nahini is sharing these moments with me.

"Nic?" Her brows draw together as though searching her mind for something. For me?

"Are you watching us?" I ask. The first time was understandable, it was a shared memory between the two of us. But if I knew she was going to see that private moment between me and Aiden….

Her eyes blink open. "Is something amiss?"

"You're experiencing it, too?"

"Not in the same way. I'm observing, not experiencing. It's like the difference between watching a performance vs. living. Just a show, not real."

I shift my gaze back toward the fire. "I'm not sure how I feel about you witnessing it. That was a private moment."

"It's not intended to be a violation of your privacy. You need me with you, so I can pull you out if you get tangled up in the threads of the past."

I nod. Still, it doesn't change the fact that something I couldn't understand is being viewed by an outside party. I remember trusting Nahini with my life. But like the passion I feel for Aiden, I'm not so sure that the feelings are part of me now or an echo from the past.

"Perhaps we should move on for today," her tone is light and without censure.

I swallow and nod. "What's next?"

Her smile is a little sad. "As much as we can manage."

CHAPTER 23

GARDEN OF EDEN

As the days grow longer, my training intensifies. The mornings are for physical combat. I improve vastly with the dull-edged blade, even managing to knock *Seelenverkäufer* out of Freda's hands once. After that, she shifts her focus to the crossbow, throwing knives and the bow staff.

"Why aren't we training with firearms?" I ask at one point.

"Guns," her lip curls up in revulsion. "A clumsy modern weapon that requires little skill and goes astray as often as not. The destruction from a firearm like that is great, but can be turned upon you in a heartbeat."

She has a point.

Her daughter, Jasmine, is with us, as she often is. Her training is about on par with my own, though her skill is much better, especially with throwing knives and stars. She is a shy girl, never saying much but watching everything with hawk-like intensity. Freda's parenting style is worlds away from Chloe and Addy's hands-off approach. An ache forms in my chest whenever I see Freda rest a hand on Jasmine's shoulder or pull her in for a quick hug, her face beaming with pride in the girl's blossoming abilities.

After lunch, I am turned over to Nahini's care for more mental and mystical training, as well as a crash course on fey politics. In these, I am much better, now able to draw up memories from my past life at will. I see the glittering fairy lights decorating the great palace of Underhill, a castle situated beside an underground lake, carved from what appears to be pearl. I recognize the symphony of spices from perfume and from food, the richness and decadence of a royal banquet, held every year to celebrate the transition of power between myself and Brigit. She is there, my sister-queen, though I never get a clear look at her face. I feel the silks and satins, the coldness of precious stones, all tributes from my subjects. I now know they filched the items from rich mortals either through fairy duplicity or outright theft. I breathe in the sharp night air of midwinter in Underhill from a balcony outside my room, feel the wind tugging play-fully with my braid, teasing it loose from the elaborate moorings as I ride with the Hunt. I experience as much as possible without getting pulled too far out of myself, though I am careful to avoid any intimate scenes, at least when Nahini is present.

I save those for late in the night, when I am alone in a house which once contained family. The memories of Aiden, both my own and those of Queen Nicneven, help distract me from the deep searing ache that I am beginning to associate with the sensation of loneliness.

I wonder how Laufey's recovery is going, and if Fern has been watching the kits or focusing all her fluttery energy on healing her lover. I wonder if Aiden truly does miss me if he is looking up at the night sky and picturing my face on the full moon even as I envision his.

Will he be proud of how much I've remembered, of how

well my training is progressing? Maybe it will please him to know I recall much of our past, especially how I came to trust him.

Even alone though, there are memories I avoid. What occurs behind the closed door of the Eternity room, where I meet with the fey chancellors and overlords during my fertile time. And our final fight, the one proceeding my death. My instincts of self-preservation scream at me anytime my thoughts try to drag those memories to the fore.

I sigh, leaning back in my window seat and let my mind wander. One memory pulls itself apart from the others and floats in the forefront of my mind like a soap bubble. *Winter has a firm hold on the land, her icy chill spreading out like a great white cloak that covers all in sight. It is late at night, the hall is empty, but I am restless, unable to sleep. My chambers have grown smaller until I leave them, needing to do something.*

The Hunt left without me, on my orders. My fertile time approaches, and there is no guarantee that they will be back in time for the moon of conception. I long for Freda's freedom to choose any bed partner she wishes to spend a night with or Nahini's to decline all offers that come her way. If I had just one child, a son or daughter of royal blood to ensure the line of succession, everything would be different. I could refuse the suitors that gather around me like dogs around a dinner table, hoping crumbs of my power will fall so they can gobble it up.

The iridescent pearl floor is cold beneath my bare feet, but I am unwilling to return to my room for shoes. Most of my kind do without shoes or clothing, or if they do happen upon them, they use the items until they are threadbare and full of holes. It bothers me immensely, that the fey possess such great powers but most are forced to do without, relying on tokens from humans or outright thievery. But what can be done?

I pause by one of the windows and stare at a shaft of moonlight playing on the endless lake. The light is bright tonight, the moon full so that even here we can feel the pull of the great celestial rhythms that are a part of us all. Though the palace itself is situated well below ground, the light from the moon and the sun is reflected down to us by tightly woven iridescent webbing, a gift from the great spiders long before my birth. Their gift of peace outlasted them. I hope the same won't be said of the Unseelie fey.

It is the loneliness I feel, the frustration and yearning that has attached this moment to my present self. Nahini says that just as familiar faces can act as a trigger, so too can my own emotions create tethers to a time from before when I felt the same.

Connection, yes and a healthy dose of frustration. Mostly at my past self for being so damn helpless. The poor wittle queen who accepted starvation and exposure of her subjects as part of life's unfairness. Who hated sex yet submitted to it, so she could turn around and pass the buck to her innocent offspring. Where is my will to fight? To kill or die in the attempt to make the world a better place? Is that so unique to me, to Nic Rutherford, the child that was abandoned and almost molested in her first decade of life?

Apparently, a life of entitlement and privilege has its downside. I wouldn't change places with that milquetoast version of myself for the world. I'm tempted to crimp the thread, to go to bed and seethe over my past impotence but I sense I am on the verge of some new revelation. I grit my teeth and stay with the memory. Curiosity will be my undoing.

It is as I stare out at the still lake the color of pitch that I first see the figure. At the distance, I can make out nothing more than the fur-lined cloak, dusted with snow and pulled up to conceal his or her face. The boots are coated with snow and ice. The traveler seems to be alone and judging from the quality and newness of the garments, is a fey of means newly arrived from the world above.

My fingers grip the windowsill until my knuckles turn as white as bone. An inward shudder racks me from head to foot. All the signs point to the same—another lordling with royal ambitions. That makes five for this month.

Fury bubbles up in me, and I want to lash out at him, with my words, with my powers. I should freeze him where he stands, send ice to encase him as a warning to the rest of them. Or maybe go greet him with a deadly kiss, catch him off guard, and then press my poisonous lips against his chill ones until they grow even colder.

Such thoughts are treasonous. This traveler has done nothing wrong. And deep down I know it's not him or any of the others I hate. It is myself and my crown. My duty.

He pauses in a shaft of that reflected moonlight and looks up. Directly at me.

My breath catches. Only once before had I seen eyes so green, as vivid as the first shoots of spring. That night, that oddly bizarre night with the young man who'd craved death, the fire, and the wolf with eyes the exact same hue. His face has changed much over the years, but I would recognize those eyes anywhere.

We stare at each other for an endless time. I drink him in, this strange man yet not a man. Power eddies around him in invisible waves. What is he? Who is he? How did he find me here? What does he want?

You. I hear his voice in my mind. I only want you. You told me to find something worth dying for and to live for it. I live because of you. I will die only for you.

A knock on the front door pulls me from the scene. I blink, my hand going automatically to my chest, feeling my heart pounding beneath trembling fingers. The intensity of the emotions rock me to my core. While many of my memories about Aiden are more vivid than the others, this is the first time since training began that I had been so caught up in the memory and lost track of who I really was, where I need to be.

Shaking the last of the past from my head, I hop off the

window seat and make my way to the door. After lifting the latch, I pull it open to see Jasmine and Freda on the other side.

"My queen." Freda is in her full armor with her winged helmet tucked in the crook of her elbow. She bows her head respectfully, as she always does when operating in the official capacity as leader of the Wild Hunt. "We have been called into service."

"When do you need to leave?"

She gestures to the open field in the distance, where the Hunt is mounted, the ghosts in line behind the living. "Immediately."

I nod and wrap my arms around myself. "Okay."

Freda shifts, appearing uncomfortable. "Might I beg a favor?"

"Of course."

"Would it be possible for Jasmine to stay here? I do not know how long we will be gone and the regular food and rest have been beneficial to her. She will not be a burden. She will go about her training and stay out from underfoot."

My gaze falls on the red-haired girl. She does look much improved. Her cheeks have lost the hollowness and her skin glows with health from regular meals. "Of course. Though I would like her to stay in the house, so I can keep an eye on her better."

After the protests Freda and Nahini had put up the first night, I expect some hesitation, but Freda surprises me. "We would both be honored, your highness."

She turns to her daughter. "You know the rule."

"If anything tries to kill me, I should kill it first," Jasmine's lyrical voice is definite.

A laugh bubbles up, my very first. "We'll get along just fine."

Freda grins. "So long as you don't try to kiss her goodnight."

IN A STRANGE WAY, having Jasmine in the house makes it feel like a home again. She's not little and impish like the fawn kits, which I doubt I could handle. She possesses her mother's adventurous spirit and appears to love all things modern.

"Show me how it works again," quickly becomes her constant refrain. She uses it for the television, the washing machine, the dryer, the toaster. Each time a machine performs its function her face lights up.

"I thought the fey couldn't touch iron," I say one day as we are preparing dinner. She picks up a cast-iron skillet, which prompts the question.

"That's only full-blooded fey, and there aren't many of them left, at least not on this side of the Veil." She sets the pan on the stovetop, turns the burner on and grins at me.

Questioning Jasmine is much more straightforward than with any of the adult immortals I've encountered. She is completely guileless and often volunteers information I would have to pry out of anyone else. "What about the lying thing. Can fey lie?"

"They can't speak an untruth, that's different." I watch as she mixes eggs and green onion with quinoa to form patties the way I showed her. "Neither can I or anyone else I know, including the turned humans."

"So, your mom can't lie? Or Nahini?"

She shakes her head and drops a fully formed patty into the pan with a plop. "No one that survives the gauntlet can lie. It's the curse of the gods."

"You forgot to grease the pan," I add some avocado oil and then turn the patty before it sticks. "Which gods? Last time I checked there were about a dozen different polytheistic religions."

"*The* gods." Another irregular shaped blob hits the pan.

At my blank look, she blows a strand of hair out of her face since her hands are still covered with goop. "Long ago there was only darkness. Then fire clashed with ice and formed the first giant. From his body, Odin and his brothers built the nine worlds."

I recognized the tale. It is in the book, the origin story of Norse mythos. "If there was only fire and ice, where did Odin and his brothers come from?"

"From the giants of course." Jasmine scrunches her forehead at me as though I'm a bit simple.

"Okay, so you're saying the Norse gods are *the* gods? What about the Greek and Roman gods?"

"They were the descendants of the Vanir, who warred with the Aesir until a truce was called and Freya agreed to join the Aesir."

Which explained why there were so many intersections between the Greek and Norse stories, like the Norns/ Fates. "So, tell me about this curse."

"I'm getting to it. I need to wash my hands, first."

I man the pan as Jasmine rinses the goop from her fingers.

"The fair folk are descendants of Freya before she joined the Aesir. She made them perfect, in her image from the light of a newborn star and her brother, Frigg, watched over them in the lands of Vanaheim, where the tribes of the Vanir dwelled. The fair folk possessed magic and glamour and were content. But the Aesir gods grew jealous of a race at peace that had no cause for war. They banished them to Alfheim and Svartalfheim, the land of light elves and the dark elves or dwarfs. The two worlds together make up Underhill."

"Let me guess." I remove the patties from the pan, add more oil and start forming the rest of the mixture for a second batch. "The Seelie Court went with the light elves, and the Unseelie Court with the dwarves?"

"Right, though those two races have blended with the fair folk almost entirely over the millennia. And many of the Seelie Court have bred with humans as well."

"Whereas the Unseelie just want to eat them. Yeah, saw that one for myself."

But Jasmine shakes her head. "Only when they cross the boundaries. It's more that the Unseelie want to be left alone. How would you like it if some man came to your home, ate all your food, polluted your water supply, burned down your house and put one up for himself in its place?"

No question about it. "I'd kill him."

She points the spatula at me. "Right. The Unseelie Court of Alba values survival above all things, their own survival and that of their offspring."

"Where does the lying thing fit in?"

"It's part of the banishment curse. That any with the gift of regenerating youth to speak no word that is untrue until the day when they're permitted to return to Vanaheim. This doesn't apply to the gods themselves."

"Our own personal Garden of Eden." Except the fey hadn't been booted because of anything they'd done. Just like Aiden's curse hadn't been because of his actions, but the sins of his father.

I was developing a major dislike for these so-called gods.

We sit down with the plate of quinoa patties and dig in. Jasmine eats three helpings with none of the cautious reserve I'd seen with other adolescents. Probably because she knows what it feels like to go hungry.

"I wish I could live in a place like this all the time,"

Jasmine says on a sigh. "To go to school the way you did and come back to the same place every day."

"You've never been to school?"

She shakes her head. "Just training."

"Some mortal children think of school as a special hell."

"Oh, but why? Imagine a place where anyone can learn anything they wish." A dreamy look passes over her face.

"And what is it you would like to learn?"

She scrapes some loose bits of quinoa into a pile. Mumbles something unintelligible.

"Say that again."

"To read."

I blink at her. "Your mother never taught you how to read?"

"It's not her fault," Jasmine is quick to defend Freda. "I'm sure she would have if she knew how. But reading wasn't something women were taught in her time."

My throat is dry. I reach for my water glass, trying to reconcile myself with the idea that Freda couldn't read, couldn't teach her daughter one of the most basic forms of communication. And Jasmine. Such simple things she desires, to go to school, to read to be normal. What did I want when I was her age?

Probably my next victim.

"Jasmine, if you want to go to school, I'll figure out a way to get you there."

"Really?"

I nod. If Aiden could saunter in like he always belonged in school, Jasmine can as well. "When Aiden comes back. We'll figure out what we need to do. You can be miserable right along with the normals."

She jumps up and rushes around the table, wrapping her arms around me. "Oh, thank you. Thank you so much!" The gesture is pure affection, with no motive other than the obvious.

I stand there frozen, unsure of what to do with my arms. Eventually, I hug her back and it's an awkward thing. "Have you had enough?" I clear my throat and start collecting dirty silverware onto my plate.

"Yes, thank you, my queen."

I fight the flinch. "When it's just the two of us, please call me Nic."

"Okay, Nic." She yawns so large her jaw cracks.

"Why don't you head up to bed? I'll do the clearing up."

"Thank you again." She pushes back out of her chair, gives me a final sunny smile and then retreats up the stairs to the loft.

Slowly, I set the dishes down and then stumble toward the fireplace, and lower myself onto the couch. My thoughts are in turmoil. Losing Sarah almost destroyed me. I hadn't recognized how important she was to me until it was too late.

Now I have feelings for more people, have more friends. Jasmine, Nahini, Freda. Aiden. More who can be taken from me. More to be used to cripple me.

More who can betray me.

I shift, uneasy as though bugs are crawling over my skin and glance about for something to take my mind off my troubles. The house is a mess, my mind has been on my training and not on tidying up. Organizing my environment always helps bring order to chaotic thoughts. It's as though by physically removing clutter I can mentally do the same.

Mind made up, I tackle the dishes then move on to wiping down the counters and table, then sweeping the floor. The last weeks' worth of newspapers, still wrapped in their protective plastic coating sit in a basket by the front door. I drag the basket over to the hearth. It's chilly out, much colder than it's been all summer. A fire would be perfect.

I stack the kindling and then slide the papers out and begin crumpling them up. The long-handled matches are in the lipstick tube tin Chole bought Addy as a gag gift last Christmas. Her grin had been infectious as she crowed, "I'll finally get to see her use lipstick!"

I strike the match and am about to light the fire when a headline catches my eye.

Grave robber strikes in high country.

Curious, I remove the paper from the grate and begin reading.

In what appears to be a pattern of grave-robbing incidents in North Carolina, the body of a local teen has been removed from her burial plot. Sarah Ann Larkin, age sixteen, died less than a month ago in a car accident and was buried in a local cemetery. The family cannot be reached for comment. This is the fourth incident of this kind to happen this year. So far, the police have made little progress.

The match falls from nerveless fingers. Why would anyone steal Sarah's body?

Cold to the bone, I crumple the paper, stuff it into the fire and then light a new match before heading into my bedroom to retrieve my laptop. The internet doesn't provide any more insight into the disappearance of Sarah's body than the article, but I do find more in-depth mentions about the other grave robberies.

One a month, since the end of January. An elderly woman in Gastonia, a middle-aged bank executive in Charlotte, a young boy in Wilmington. A range of ages, genders from diverse backgrounds with different causes of death. The body-snatching is the only common thread. No suspects yet in any of the cases.

I'm not aware of falling asleep, but the next thing I know I'm being pulled from its warm embrace.

"Nic," the voice calls my name urgently. "Nic, wake up."

Fatigue holds me down hard and my lids are heavy. "Who are you?"

"Come on. We don't have much time." It's a female voice, a familiar one.

"Huh?" Forcing my lids up, I stare at the smoldering embers that remains from the fire. At the hand protruding from it, with the little snake encircling a pale wrist.

"Come with me," Hel says. "Quickly, I can't hold this open forever."

"Why do you want me to come with you?"

"There are things you don't know yet, Nic. Important things that they won't tell you."

"And why should I trust you?" I ask the fire with a frown. "You tricked me and admitted that you'd been sending me nightmares. I'd be a freaking idiot to trust you."

Her next words change everything. "There's a way to get Sarah back. A way no one else will tell you. But I will."

I swallow hard. "What do you know about Sarah?"

"She was your friend. You feel responsible for her death and you crossed the Veil to retrieve her."

"Laufey told me there isn't a way," I say. "That Sarah can't be brought back."

"Laufey lied. She doesn't want you to know the truth."

"And you do?" I sense the trap, but can't seem to stop from taking another step toward it. "Why would you care?"

"Because, I want you, Queen of the Unseelie Court and the leader of the Wild Hunt for my ally. I do you a favor and you do one for me."

I shake my head. "I hate to break it to you, but I'm neither of those things."

"Maybe not now, but you were once and I'm confident

you will be again." Her hand extends. "I'm the only chance you have to retrieve Sarah. Come with me now or lose her forever."

I swallow, glance toward the stairs, to where Jasmine sleeps. The house is protected. She'll be fine on her own for a while.

I reach for the hand.

The cabin door bursts open.

"Nic, no!" Aiden's voice.

I whirl, my lips parting as I catch sight of him. Still wearing those damnable sweatpants, still the epitome of male perfection despite his shit wardrobe.

His eyes are wild as he looks from me to the hand stretching from the dying fire. "Don't trust her!"

But it's too late, the minute my skin connects with Hel's she pulls me through. The sickening swirling sensation as the world around me spins like a kaleidoscope and fades away.

The ground rushes up to greet me, the scent of decay and rotting things fills my nose. I look at the colorless great throne room of Hel's domain. The sovereign of the underworld again stares down at me, that eerie half alive half dead face visible from beneath her dark hood.

"Send me back," I gasp.

"But you just got here." Hel pouts. "And we haven't had our talk yet."

"What do you know about Sarah?" I don't waste any time, the haunted look on Aiden's face seared in my mind. "Do you know who took her body?"

"I know her soul is here, for a start. In the land of the dishonorable dead."

"She's here?" I glance around, hoping to catch sight of my friend.

Hel nods once. "In this realm. As one of the living, I'm

afraid I can't let you beyond this antechamber though. Only the dead and my sworn servants can walk my halls."

"How do I get her back?" I ask. "What do I have to do?"

"You need to do the same as was done for you." Hel smiles and it's an eerie sight, one half of her face turns up, the other frozen in death. "You need to sacrifice the heart of the one who loves you most."

CHAPTER 24

A HEART FOR A HEART

"What do you mean it was done for me?" I shake my head. "Whose heart could have been sacrificed for my life?"

"I think you know." Hel circles me, her long cloak making a wispy, slithering sound as it drags along the stone floor.

"Nari," I whisper, my throat gone dry. It's not memory fragment, but putting the pieces together so that all the bits of information I've collected over the past days form a cohesive picture. Laufey said Aiden had brought me back. He was the only one who cared. And Aiden—or rather Váli— had raised Nari in his father's place. Nari had loved him best and Nari had died. My stomach twists and I feel dizzy. "They used Nari's heart as a sacrifice."

"My youngest brother was already dead. He didn't need his heart any longer. So, your consort returned to the cave where our father is trapped and retrieved it." Hel says, her voice cold as midwinter's night. "My grandmother and Aiden hid the truth from you."

Because they knew bringing back Sarah would mean taking a life. And not just any life. Because there is no doubt in their minds that out of all the hearts in the world, Aiden's is the one that loves me best.

I shake my head slowly back and forth. "I can't."

"You can," Hel murmurs, her tone cajoling. "What is Aiden to you now? Not your lover, not your friend. You just met him a few days ago. He is nothing important."

I glare up into her hideously deformed face. "He's your brother, how can you encourage this?"

She waves my protest away. "He's my brother by mere happenstance. We've never met in the flesh."

"But you're family." That must mean something to her.

She rounds on me, one eye flashing fire, the other an empty socket containing the darkness of eternity. "The only family I've ever known was taken from me when I was barely an adult. One brother tossed into the sea the other bound for eternity. Aiden is nothing to me, except a means to an end."

"And people say I'm cold," I mutter.

Hel extends her dead hand, and something appears in it, pulsing with a golden glow. She holds it out to me. "Don't worry, it won't burn you."

Carefully, I reach out and take the thing. It's about the size and hardness of an apple. There's something familiar about it, though I know I've never seen it before. "What is it?"

"Sarah's soul."

My lips part and I stare down at it. "It's really her?"

"Yes." Hel's one eye narrows on me. "Has he told you yet how he's become Brigit's consort? Why he abandoned you in your hour of need?"

When I shake my head, she smiles that terrible half-smile that turns my insides watery. "Ask him. Before you do something foolish and throw away Sarah's life and your own mortal existence, command him to tell you how he spent every night of the last sixteen years in her bed. How he swore to her the same binding oath that he swore to you."

My stomach is in knots. Can I do it? Can I trade Aiden's life to bring back Sarah?

"One more thing." Hel continues her pacing around me, her cloak making that sound like a snake through a pile of bones. "The moment you remove the soul from my hall you have one day and one night to make the trade before Sarah's soul will be consumed by the Veil."

"What?" I stare down at the throbbing apple glowing in my hand. "I thought the Veil was made from other things, not people."

"All of us who broker in souls must contribute to the Veil's upkeep. For the good of all. Sarah has no family here, no friends. She's the perfect choice to fill in the gaps."

Bullshit. Sarah's leverage, to make me fall in line, pure and simple.

My throat feels as though it's closing but somehow, I force the questions out. "How do I make the trade? I don't have to actually cut his heart out, do I?"

Her smile reflects the heart of evil. "So squeamish? No, that would be unnecessarily messy. Just place this stone over his beating heart and give him your Goodnight Kiss. His heart will free Sarah's soul and Aiden will take her place in the Veil."

I stare from the pulsing stone to her ghastly features. "And what about the souls of the Wild Hunt. You asked me about them the last time you brought me here."

She sits on her throne of bones, steepling her hands together. It's a gruesome sight, naked bone pressing against tender pink flesh. "Yes, I want the souls of the Wild Hunt. The dishonorable dead are mine by right, and you've been poaching. They mean nothing to you. Turn them over to me and restore the balance to what it was before you died. Aiden for Sarah, half the Hunt for my help. Agreed?"

I stare down at the pulsing thing in my hand. She could

be lying. Hadn't Jasmine told me that gods were exempt from the speaking untruth curse? But I can feel Sarah in a way I hadn't since the day she died. It's nothing tangible but deep down I feel the truth of it. It's her, in this glowing ball. The girl who'd been my first friend. The girl I'd been trying so hard to save. Nahini's brother and the other ghosts were murderers, rapists, child abusers. They belong in this dreary realm or being absorbed into the Veil. Sarah doesn't.

"Sarah's soul in exchange for the dead of the Hunt. Her life in exchange for the heart of the one who loves me most?"

"It's a bargain well struck." The grin that splits her face is ghastly.

She rises and saunters toward me. Once again, she extends her hand, the living one with the serpent bracelet slithering around the wrist. I reach for it. In the moment we connect, the snake strikes, sinking its fangs into my wrist. Red hot fire shoots through my veins, pain sears like lightning throughout my body. I'm dizzy, staggering, but clutch Sarah's soul to me, afraid I'll drop it and lose her forever. The world tilts, my vision blurs and there is a great roaring in my ears. I am falling....

Falling....

I thump down onto the floor before the hearth, my entire left side bruising on impact.

"Nic!" Aiden is by my side in an instant those green eyes searching me for damage. "What happened?"

I scramble up and fling myself at him, wrapping my arms around his neck. He starts but then hugs me back, his arms tight and reassuring. His scent of cedar and sage, of wildness, barely tethered, fills me, makes me feel safe.

Loved.

The heart of the one who loves you most for Sarah.

The object throbs within my left hand, the venomous bite

singeing my right wrist where my bargain with the ruler of the dishonorable dead has been struck.

"What's going on down there?" Jasmine calls from the top of the stairs, her voice trailing off in a yawn.

I release Aiden and call up to her. "Nothing. I just fell off the couch. Go back to bed."

There's a pause and then she shuffles back into the bedroom. I hear the creak of bedsprings as she lies down.

"Come on, we can talk in my room." Not waiting for a reply, I take hold of his bare arm and drag him out of the main part of the house.

"What happened?" he asks the moment I close the door. "That was Hel, wasn't it?"

I nod. "She's a piece of work, your sister."

He winces. "Half-sister, and probably not the only one. My dad would stick his prick in anything."

"Like father like son?" I raise an eyebrow.

He flinches. "Nic—,"

"Tell me about Brigit," I command.

He shakes his head. "I don't know what Hel's been filling your head with—"

"This has nothing to do with Hel. Tell me about the Unseelie Queen and why Freda—who cannot lie—is under the impression you swore the same oath to her that you did to me. That you were her consort after I was brought back. Tell me why you abandoned me."

More trouble than you're worth.

"It wasn't like that." Leaf green eyes beg for understanding.

"Did you or did you not swear the same oath in front of her that you did to me? The one that gives her power to command you."

"I ...did." He holds my gaze, green eyes bright.

My heart pounds against my rib cage. "Why would you do that?"

"To keep you safe. Hidden. She needed to trust me completely. She didn't know Laufey had brought you back as a mortal woman and I made sure she had no reason to doubt me. Or to look for you."

"You've been with her. For my entire life, you've been by her side. In her bed."

He shifts to the left, not looking at anything, just away so he doesn't have to meet my gaze. A muscle jumps in his jaw.

"Aiden," I whisper. "Please, look at me."

He turns, his expression is anguished.

"Tell me why," I say. "Why didn't you just leave the court instead of…?"

"Whoring myself out?" he asks, the tone bitter.

"I'm trying to understand." I take his hand in my free one, Sarah's captured soul throbbing like a heartbeat on my other side. "Help me understand. Does it have anything to do with your father? Or Ragnorok?"

Those green eyes remain averted. "The Queen of the Elphame is a powerful ally."

Hurt spreads from the center of my chest like blood from a stab wound. "So, you just traded one queen for the other? Traded yourself for what? An Army? Or did you just enjoy her so much more than me?"

His laughter is bitter. "You don't understand."

"I'm trying to," I say, disturbed by his unwillingness to explain. "If you were so content with her, why not keep your bargain with my aunts? Why did you come to look for me at all?"

He says nothing.

"Aiden."

He turns away. "I'll be nearby if you need me."

The window is propped up, to allow the cool summer

night air to seep into the room. Aiden uses it as his escape, changing to sparks and floating through the screen.

I shut the window firmly behind him.

I LAY on my back in the dark and stare at the throbbing apple that contains Sarah's soul. If I strain my eyes enough I can see her dark hair spilling across the pillow, hear her voice. *God Nic, can we just leave this freaking place already?*

"Where should we go?" I ask the question aloud as I had many times before.

She doesn't answer, the glow in the hard object containing her soul flickering.

I made a deal with the devil to get her soul back. Traded Nahini's beloved brother and all the dead souls from the Wild Hunt just to have her here this way. Did they already get sucked into that dark realm? Is Nahini wondering even now why her brother vanished without a trace?

I'd promised her she could stay with him forever. But that was before I could lie.

All the pain I've inflicted, just to get Sarah back. And if I don't go through with the plan, it'll be for nothing. She'll be gobbled up by the Veil the same way Aiden downed that bag of M&M's.

Those souls I've damned not once but twice. Am I any better than they are, really? Chloe and Addy had always reassured me that I was doing a good deed, making the world a better place. That I was killing with a purpose and using my unusual gift in the right way.

What is Aiden to you now? Hel's question rings in my ears along with the answer she provided. *He is nothing important.*

If I truly believed that, I would have made the trade already. Because Sarah had been important, at least to me.

I remember telling Laufey, *I had a friend who deserved better.*

You still do. She must have been talking about Aiden. What had she meant? I still didn't know the reason we'd fought prior to my death, didn't understand what had enraged him to the point he left me pregnant and unguarded.

Still didn't know how I died.

But I know how to find out.

I close my eyes and search through the tangle of memories in my mind until I find the silver strand that connects me with The Queen of the Unseelie Court. With the Nicneven of two decades ago and follow it to just before the thread is cut.

"Someone here to see you, your highness," a sprite announces.

I'd been sitting before the open window of the topside palace, the green fields beyond rolling like waves of the ocean, cut with twisting waterways and a one-lane road that leads to the Glittering Woods. My hands clasped over my belly. It hasn't started to swell with the child yet, but I've felt the quickening, the life force of my babe.

Mine and Aiden's.

"Tell whoever it is that I am not receiving today." I rise to stretch. Aiden is just in the bathing chamber and will be out shortly. I am looking forward to the way his hands make my overly sensitive flesh come alive. All has worked out for the best, the way it was supposed to.

"Oh, you'll receive me, you bitch."

I whirl to see a hob forcing his way past the sprite into my chambers.

My hands clench into fists. "I am your queen. How dare you—?"

"How dare you! I know of your pact with my brother." His lip curls up in a snarl, revulsion twisting the light green skin on his

face until it forms something truly hideous. His whip-like tail with the sharp arrowhead barb rising above his shoulder.

"I don't know your brother," I raise my hands, trying to call on the powers from my court. A shield of water from the tribe of shellycoats that dwell in the nearby river should keep the mad creature at bay.

But nothing happens, the powers slip through my grasp like grains of sand.

"My brother was the fey creature your pet dog shredded." The hob advances. His tail looms like a scorpion's stinger over his shoulder.

Oh no. How much does he know? Again, I grasp for power, this time from the air sprites perched in the nearby trees. But those fail as well, the panic making my nimble mind fumble. I must get him out of here before—

"Your brother was an abusive rapist," Aiden says from the doorway. "He beat her bloody. I suggest you leave before the same is done to you."

The hob rounds on him, its red eyes narrowing to slits of fire. "And how exactly did my brother, who barely possessed enough magic to boil a kettle of water, manage to overpower the great and terrible Ice Bitch? She could have pinned him to the wall with air, burned him with fire, frozen him with ice. No, stupid dog, she asked him to beat her bloody. Promised him riches for his aid. He told other courtiers about it, about how he would reap the benefits in assisting the Queen of the Shadow Throne."

Aiden's gaze flicks to mine, his brows drawn together.

"What a wild story!" I exclaim. "Why would I want someone to beat me?"

The hob glares daggers at me. "Then deny it. Speak plainly so we know you aren't twisting the truth. Deny that you promised my brother a stewardship over the coastal province in exchange for that beating."

My lips part but not even a puff of air emerges, the curse of the fair folk preventing even a sound.

The hob lunges for me, stinger poised, but Aiden is faster. Coils of fire wrap around my attacker like chains at his ankles, his middle, his throat, pinning him in place. He yelps and the smell of burning flesh fills the room.

"Aiden," I breathe, unsettled by the wild look in his eyes. They glow with the wolf's inner light, that demonic fire that lurks in his soul. The son of a god whose terrible power is about to be unleashed.

Aiden ignores me, but the swirl of flames dies down. The hob smokes and smolders on the floor, blisters already bubbling up where the fire touched his green skin.

Uncaring of the damage, Aiden lifts the creature from the floor and marches him to the open door, where two Spriggin guards have appeared. "Lock him up for attacking the queen. She'll deal with him later."

The door slams shut with a crash so violent I can feel the stones rattle. Aiden faces away from me, his thick shoulders bunched with tension.

"Aiden," I move closer, my hand outstretched to touch him.

He dodges my touch and rounds on me, green eyes ablaze. "You tricked me."

I reach out again, this time to put my hand over his heart. "Aiden, we were trapped. It was the only way."

"You played on my instincts to protect you to get what you wanted from me. Congratulations. The trickster's son has been duped by the fairy queen." Waves of hurt roll from him, so thick and agonizing that I stagger.

I feel the gorge rising in my throat even as he drives the point home. "You used me, Nicneven. I trusted you, cared for you and you deceived me."

His use of the past tense has panic welling up inside me. "Aiden, please."

"I can't even look at you now." He turns away, heading for the door.

"But our babe," I implore him, my hand going to cover my midsection. *"You can't leave."*

He casts me a look over his shoulder and it isn't anger I see, but weary wretchedness that is even more heartbreaking. "I wish you had killed me the first night we met. It would have been kinder than this end."

He flings the door open and it is the wolf who surges down the corridors, out to the road and disappears into the forest beyond.

I fall to my knees, my hands covering my face, my whole body shaking. I am so caught up in my grief that I don't hear the thunder of hooves. With my face hidden I don't see the great army that swamps over the rolling hill like a plague of death.

My army, the army of the Unseelie Court, sacking my lands.

Don't hear the footsteps coming up behind me until it is too late.

But I feel the blade, the cold iron that impales me from the back, feel the burn of it with the last beat of my heart. I open my eyes and through my tears, I witness the face of my murderer, smell her citrus scent....

I jerk upright in my darkened bedroom, my hand going to my chest, half expecting to find a sword sticking out from between my ribs. There is nothing there, of course. Nothing but the thrumming glow that is Sarah's soul.

I pick it up, cradle it against my chest and whisper.

"I know what I have to do."

CHAPTER 25

KILL OR BE KILLED

The ritual is the same as always. One hundred strokes with my hairbrush and then a tight braid which I turn into a golden coil and pin-up into an elaborate bun. Less likely to lose a hair, leave a piece of myself behind as evidence. Choosing the right bait ensemble, a flashy purple dress which is both tight and short, topped with a matching jacket of the same color. It has hidden pockets for money, keys, and cell phone. Though this time I won't bring the phone since I have no backup, no one that will condone what I am about to do. Sarah's stone takes its place in the liner of my jacket.

Sleek black boots that are both sexy, stretching up to mid-thigh, but also practical. No high heels, I need to be able to run, to move quickly as my prey is unlike any I have stalked to date. No jewelry, minimal makeup, just a slick of blood-red lip gloss to enhance my mouth to make myself irresistible. I look at myself in the full-length mirror.

I look like what I am, a sixteen-year-old dressed for a night out. And it conceals my true nature perfectly. No one would believe I am the reincarnated Unseelie Queen, commander of the Wild Hunt, that I have killed more than a dozen people over the last ten years. Vaguely, I recall reading that purple is the color of royalty, at least in the human world.

Image is everything.

I am at the door, truck keys in my hand, when I remember Jasmine, asleep and defenseless upstairs. I could wake her, but Jasmine is her mother's daughter, she'd want to come with me and that I can't allow. Nor can I abandon her here. If my plan goes awry, no telling what will show up at the farm, looking for answers.

"We'll watch out for her," Addy says from behind me.

I turn to face her and Chloe both. They look the same as always, beautiful, strong and as immovable as stone.

"I guess that whole security alarm thing was a big joke to you," I say.

"Not a joke," Chloe steps forward. Her scent is like freshly washed cotton hanging on a clothesline. "We were always concerned with your safety, afraid of who or what might come after you."

"I guess since you're here, you know what I'm planning."

"We've always known this day would come." Addy's voice is rough like she's been gargling with sand. "You have a destiny, one we tried to prepare you for without tipping our hand."

I still don't understand. "Why not tell me? Why send Aiden away all those years ago?"

"If you had known what you were, why you have the Goodnight Kiss, you might have made different choices," Chloe explains. "Maybe even the same choices that hurt you and all those around you before. We kept Aiden away, kept the truth hidden to let you develop into your own person. You are stronger now than you've ever been."

"Stronger?" My laugh is hollow. "I feel as though I'm coming apart at the seams."

"Because you have empathy. You're not a serial killer, Nic. You never were. You were just a scared little girl that grew up to be a vigilante, to prevent others from suffering the way you almost did."

The way Sarah had. The way Aiden had.

"Some would call you a hero," Chloe adds with a smile. "Maybe not many, but they're out there."

I put my hand over the bulge in my jacket. "Will it work?"

Addy's eyes start that eerie swirling thing again, but after a moment she blinks, and her eyes go back to a more standard chestnut brown. "I can't see the outcome, there are too many variables. Your destiny is linked with others in an intricate web and the possibilities are too numerous to see."

"If you need to cut my thread tonight," I say to her, "Promise me you'll put it in the book with your sister's."

"I hope it doesn't come to that." The lines around Addy's eyes are taut with worry.

Chloe doesn't say anything, just pulls me into a tight embrace. I inhale her clean linen scent, feel the tickle of her red-gold hair.

"We're so proud of you," she murmurs before releasing me.

I feel as if I owe them something, some sort of thanks. But what comes out is, "I'm sorry I was so much trouble."

Then it's Addy's turn. She's never been overly affectionate, but puts her hands on my shoulders and holds my gaze. "You've always been worth the trouble."

"Really?"

Chloe nods in agreement. "Totally worth it. Forgive us?"

"Forgiveness is for quitters," I remind her, and she laughs.

"That's our girl."

I step back to take them both in, glad that they are back

where they belong. "One more thing. I promised Freda that the Hunt could stay here."

"Then they shall stay." Addy nods. "You're house, your rules now."

I raise an eyebrow. "That's a lot of responsibility for a normal sixteen-year-old."

"Good thing you're not a normal anything." Chloe winks.

Good thing indeed. I take a deep breath and head out to the truck, ready to do what I do best.

Ready to hunt.

HE APPEARS NOT HALF a mile from the house, the same way I saw him the first time, just a massive shape in the dark with glittering green orbs reflected by the headlights.

I reach across the seat and pop open the door. "I want to talk to you."

He moves to the open door and transforms as I watch, his body morphing into his human shape, complete with ratty sweats.

"Why do you keep wearing those things?" I ask.

His stare is unblinking as he surveys my dress. "They're the only thing you ever gave me, other than my life."

Ouch.

"You planning to just stand there all night?" I ask him.

He tilts his head to the side. "Where are we going?"

"You'll see." I don't say it playfully. I'm in no mood for games.

Aiden surveys me another moment and then climbs onto the bench seat beside me.

I wait until he's shut the door to ask, "How's your grandmother?"

He blinks, as though I've surprised him. "Irritable, but on

the mend. Fern wanted me to thank you for interfering on her behalf. And she wanted me to give you this along with a message."

He extends a vile of sparkling blue liquid it looks like window cleaner with champagne bubbles.

I take it from him with a frown. "What's the message?"

"That the conditions are still the same, no matter how grateful she is." He tilts his head to the side. "What is it?"

I put it in my pocket, the one opposite Sarah's Soul. "Something that will break your oath to me."

He goes still. "Nic, no."

"What are you so afraid of?" I ask him as I put the truck into gear. "How is ordering you about any better than willfully deceiving you?"

His whole body tenses. "You remember that?"

My gaze flits to the dashboard, 11:46. "Just tonight. And for whatever it's worth, I'm sorry. That was a terrible thing to do, to manipulate you like that."

"Isn't that what you do with your victims?" His gesture encompasses my ensemble. "Set them up to do what you know they want to do anyway?"

"That's different. Those people are looking for prey. You trusted me, and I betrayed that trust."

"*You* didn't. *She* did."

"I'm still the same person, Aiden. I finally realized what Nicneven and I have in common. Innate selfishness. The drive to get whatever I want no matter the fallout. Given the same pressures and set of circumstances, I'd make the exact same choices. You can't let me off the hook while condemning her. You know that. Isn't that why you never told me you knew what it would take to resurrect Sarah?"

He inhales sharply. "Hel told you about that?"

"That you used your little brother's heart to resurrect me? Yes. What I want to know is why I didn't hear that from you. Just like you didn't tell me about sleeping with Brigit."

"I didn't sleep with Brigit!" The words burst out of him like water from a geyser, a mammoth fountain of emotion that had been seething beneath the surface for far too long. "Gods damn it Nic, I have *always* been loyal to you! From the first moment, I laid eyes on you. Did I keep things hidden? Yes. Did I keep my distance? Yes. Can you fucking blame me? I thought I knew you before, but I never imagined you would play me for a fool. And yet you did."

He hadn't been Brigit's consort? "But the oath—?"

"I worded that oath *very* carefully. I vowed to protect and obey the one true Queen of the Unseelie Court and leader of the Wild Hunt. The original oath didn't hold me past your death, I felt it dissipate the instant you died. It knocked me to my knees when I realized what I'd done, how my rash reaction had cost you your life. So, I went back, took your body and brought you to Laufey. Begged her to bring you back. But she couldn't put you back as you were.

"The soul needed a new host. So, I found a pregnant human woman, one who planned to give up her child anyway. It took me months of hunting for just the right one and when we found her, Laufey put her in a trance and I retrieved Nari's heart. We merged your soul with the life she had already conceived."

"You know who my birth mother is?" I whisper.

He nods. "You really aren't the same person, part of you is a new soul. I wanted to stay with you, begged the Fates but they said the only way they would raise you is if all ties from your former life had been cut. And that included me. They sent me away before you were even born. Their protection in exchange for my absence.

"It drove me mad, knowing you were out there, more vulnerable than you had ever been because you wouldn't know about the Veil and what lurks beyond it. No way to know if any of your powers had manifested, or if you were as helpless as a mortal. I went back to the Unseelie Court because I knew that was the hub of information and where the Wild Hunt would report. If your powers manifested, they would know first, and I could get to you before anyone else. And yes, I swore a new oath. To you. I obeyed Brigit for years, doing everything she asked. She demanded I transform into the wolf, locked me in a cage beside the Fire Throne. Treated me as her pet. I could have left at any time, but I stayed and endured it all, so she wouldn't suspect that you were alive. Or that one day you would return.

"And then the reports started coming in, the new arrivals of the dead to the Wild Hunt. Scattered for a few years then more concentrated, like a ring around a bull's eye. No one could explain it, but I knew. I knew it was you, doing what you had been created to do, not once but twice. So, I ran, and Brigit, in her fury, set the Wild Hunt on me. I don't know if she suspects that I deceived her, suspects that you are alive. I don't much care. She never mattered to me at all. Since the day we met everything I have ever done, every breath I've taken, has been for you."

I can't seem to catch my own breath, my blood roaring in my ears like the ocean in the middle of a storm. Slowly, I depress the brake pedal, pulling the truck over to the side of the road.

"I craved death and you gave me a reason to live. The Fates do so love their irony."

After unfastening my seat belt, I turn to face him. Shadows stalk across the angles of his face, though his green eyes drink in the moonlight and reflect it out like beams in the night. "What do you mean?"

The back of his knuckles brushes down my cheek. "Now

that I so badly want to live, to be with you, I suspect it's time I must die for you."

My lips part.

His eyes are sad, so resigned to heartache. Millennia of disappointment weighs him down, yet here he sits, tall, proud, willing to accept whatever fate I deal him. "You can't have us both. It's me or Sarah. I knew that all along. I have lived much longer than I ever wanted, and she barely had the chance. I know how important she was to you and you should have her back. My heart is already yours." He spreads his arms wide. "Do with it what you will."

I am on him in a second, my knees on either side of his, my hands in his hair, my lips devouring his. He jolts, and a sound rumbles in his chest, agony, and despair, love and loss and anguish. But he kisses me back. His arms band around me, pressing my body flush against him. Holding me close one last time.

My skirt rides up my thighs. His hands slide up and down my back, beneath the short jacket, as though he's trying to imprint the feel of me on his hands. His heart pounds against my breastbone, and his mouth tastes of desperation. The scents of cedar and sage and his own unique traces of wildness fill my senses, making me forget everything.

The kiss to end all kisses.

And like all good things, it too must end. I pull back, gasping for breath. His eyes widen, and he touches his lips as if waking from a dream.

"I'm still alive."

"Always with the surprise," I say in a long-suffering tone.

A startled laugh erupts from him. It's a delightful sound, one I hope to hear again in the future. But then his countenance darkens. "But you need me, for Sarah."

I withdraw the stone from my pocket, holding it up so he can see the pulsing light. "You made one mistake. In bringing me back, you gave up the heart of the person who loved you best. Nari's heart. Do you really think that heart would ever willingly hurt you?"

His eyes go wide. "Then…?"

"Besides, as strongly as you might feel for me, I know for a fact there's a heart that loves me even more."

Dawning realization creeps across his face and for the first time he takes in the environment outside the truck. The flat land, the darkened farmhouse. His gaze slides to the dashboard, to the time. 11:58

"You can't—"

"Stay here for ten minutes. Do not step outside the truck unless you feel your own life is in danger." It's not a request. "If you feel the bond break, you're to take the truck and leave. Never return to the Unseelie Court."

"Nic—"

I cut him off with a final kiss, then pull away, open the driver's side door. "I'm sorry to do it this way, that I have to order you but you're so stubbornly loyal and as much as I want to, I still don't trust anyone at my back."

In the dashboard light, his hands clench and unclench, every muscle bulging with strain as he fights my order. "Don't do this."

"No matter what you believe, I did love you while I was a queen. I didn't really know how until you came into my life. But I do now." I shut the door on his roar of fury and stride across the street, up the rickety steps and through the hanging screen door at the stroke of midnight.

There is no living room, no ratty couch or pictures on the wall. The house is an In-Between, a large one at that and midnight made it accessible. Before me lies a stone bridge all one solid piece, no railing just a hand-hewn arch. Above me, the souls of the worlds shoot across the sky, ever in limbo between Midgard and Underhill, between life and death.

Laufey claimed many of the souls were from trees and animals, but according to Hel, there are people up there, too. Knowing what they are makes them no less beautiful. Can they sense my presence?

The snakebite on my arm throbs painfully, the sensation spreading up to my elbow. Time's running out.

"Is it done?"

I turn and see her, the familiar figure swathed in a robe to conceal her face.

A small smile curves my lips. "Hello, Brigit."

Showdown

"I wondered if you were on to me." Her hands, both normal now that she's let her glamour fade, reach up and push back the cowl of the cloak to reveal her perfect face. "How did you figure it out?"

"I always suspected there was something off about you," I admit. "You look nothing like Aiden, no family resemblance and Laufey's genes are strong. I imagine even his monstrous half-siblings have similar eye color. But I wasn't sure who you were until I remembered my death. When I saw your face."

She smirks. "Arrogant, I know. I should have donned a glamour. But I wanted you to see me."

"Why kill me though? We ruled the Unseelie Court well together. What made you turn on me?"

Her lip curls in revulsion. "Is that what you think? That we ruled well together? You, who could leave the court and ride with the Wild Hunt, cross the Veil and kill at random. You received all the glory, all the fear struck into the hearts of men and fairy alike. Do you hear how mortals talk about me? Mistress of the Mantel, patroness of healing, of smithcraft and poetry. Someone even turned me into a saint! Meanwhile, I was the one keeping up the traditions of our court while you were off gallivanting with your wolf. Like the rules never applied to you."

I shake my head in disgust. "That's the reason you sacked the palace and killed all the fey there? Petty fucking jealousy?"

"Where's the wolf's heart?" she snaps. "If you want to bring your precious Sarah back, you need the sacrifice to take her place."

"I have what I need. But you don't need the heart to bring her back." My voice is quiet. "You can do it with a kiss, the Kiss of Awakening. In fact, you already did, didn't you?"

"You are smarter this time, I'll give you that." Brigit snaps her fingers and then Sarah is there, standing before me. Only it's not Sarah. Her eyes are vacant, unseeing. The stone in my palm throbs with life.

Brigit walks in a deliberate circle around Sarah's body. "It took a few attempts to perfect the technique, separating the soul from the body once life was restored. How much of who we are burns within our souls? And what is left after that fire dies? Still, considering the barbaric way mortals treat their dead, I think I restored her rather well."

A chill goes through me. "The graves that were defiled. That was you practicing, to create this…?" I wave at the empty shell that had been my best friend.

Brigit smirks. "Sarah was such a good little spy for me. She brought me so much information about your activities. I had to make sure I did everything I could to restore her properly."

There is a roaring in my ears. "Sarah wouldn't spy on me."

"Have you forgotten what it's like to be one of us? To know that everyone has their price? Sarah would have agreed to anything to get away from her stepfather. Even befriending the strange girl in school. The one that I suspected was my dearly departed sister queen, brought back to life. Find out her secrets."

I stare at Brigit and the stone seems to pulse faster in my white-knuckled grip. That day in the cafeteria, when Sarah plopped down next to me. I'd thought it had been random, that she just wanted to get a reaction out of me.

"It was a simple bargain. Sarah would watch you and let me know if anything unusual happened. And in return, I would get her away from her stepfather for good. Mortals never see the variety of possibilities." Her smile is pure evil. "Death is the ultimate escape."

I'm barely listening to Brigit, my mind in the past, down by the lake.

You're different than I thought you'd be.

It's an effort to remain standing. She'd been onto me the entire time. Sarah had played me, and I hadn't seen it coming.

Just like I'd done to Aiden.

"How does it feel?" Brigit asks, victory coating her voice. "Knowing you sacrificed your loyal wolf for a traitor? How does it feel to know none of it was real?"

My gaze falls to the stone and then back to Sarah's expressionless face. It had been real. Riding in the car, music blaring with the wind in our hair. Dancing at the clubs while I eyeballed my prey, and she flirted. Those moments were pure, honest.

God Nic. Can we just leave this freaking place already?

Maybe she'd regretted her deal with Brigit once she'd gotten to know me. Maybe she'd been searching for a way out.

I look up and my gaze lands on the streaks of color there, the souls of the Veil. "How did you separate her soul?"

"With *Seelenverkäufer.* It's a complicated spell to remove a soul from the blade once it's been absorbed, but I was determined. As much as I'm enjoying our pleasant little chat, Nicneven, time is almost up. Either make the trade or go back to the mortal world. Forever. Now that I see you I know you're no queen."

I step closer to her, the woman who'd hunted me without my knowledge. Who now possessed control over the dead of the Wild Hunt. She'd set my best friend up for a zombielike purgatory. "You made one mistake, Brigit. Aiden's isn't the heart that loves me most. Mine is."

Her perfect eyebrows go up in delighted surprise. "So, it's you for Sarah, is it? Oh, I'm dying to see how this turns out. Will the selfish Ice Bitch sacrifice herself for the traitor she once called friend?"

"No." One more step and I'm there, within striking distance. "But I will sacrifice you."

I lunge, grabbing her by the shoulders so she can't pull away and seal my mouth over hers. She struggles but even with a few inches and several pounds on me, she doesn't have my strength or my experience in hunting.

Sparks arc out from between our lips as her Kiss of Awakening meets the Goodnight Kiss. Miniature bolts of energy zigzag every which way. A whiff of ozone surrounds us. She beats on me with closed fists. The arm where the snake bit me is on fire—literally. Her fire magic is nothing compared to Aiden's though, a mosquito bite next to one from a Pit Bull.

I feel her weakening and bring the stone, Sarah's stone, up to the place over her chest where her heart—shriveled blackened husk that it is—resides. There is a thin line between love and hate. I just hope it's thin enough.

The crackling energy forks through the sky, disrupting the shooting starlight, making the colors fade next to its blinding intensity. The lightning reflects in Brigit's eyes, a desperate light, the final rally. She is a cornered animal, responding to the instinct of self-preservation.

I feel the knife go in, just below my rib cage. She twists the dagger and her lips in a vicious sneer. No idea whether she conjured the weapon or had it on her. She pulls the dagger out and then strikes again, two inches below the first. And though I want to hold on, my strength oozes out with my lifeblood.

I let her go and fall backward onto the bridge. Though I still clutch the stone. Pressing one arm over the blood, I bring the stone to my own chest. If I'm destined to die anyway, at least it won't be in vain.

"No, you don't." Brigit's foot lashes out and kicks the hand holding the stone just above my elbow. The blow strikes my funny bone, causing my hand to go numb. The stone falls, strikes the bridge then bounces off into the ether.

Sarah's body crumples to the ground.

"No," I wheeze. Reaching for it though I know it's too late. That it's gone, and Sarah has been lost forever this time.

"Don't worry, Nic. You won't be parted for long," Brigit's eyes are wild. She raises the dagger up, my blood still slicking its black blade, poised for the killing blow. Her face is streaked with lines of black and red bulges from protruding veins as my poison races through her system. She's dying, more slowly than a mortal but she will die.

Just not before she kills me, too.

Roaring fills my ears, unearthly wind tugs at my hair. The galloping of hooves and great thunderous war cries accompany the howling of hounds and the screeching of falcons. In the air above our heads, the Wild Hunt forms, a tempest of unearthly power swirling like a vortex around us.

"What are you doing?" Brigit gasps. "You can't turn on me! I'm your queen."

The eerie melee continues to circle, though they come no closer. I fear she is correct. She turns back to me and bares her teeth in a self-righteous smirk. The Wild Hunt can't harm her, even if she is seconds away from murdering me.

Again.

A loud growl comes from behind me. I try to turn, but the wounds in my midsection prevent the motion. I see Brigit's eyes go wide, see the protest forming on her lips a second before the body of a huge black wolf crashes into her. Sending both tumbling off the side.

"Aiden," I reach out a hand, gasping. He can't be gone. He can't. I can't lose him and Sarah in one night.

Above me, I hear voices calling my name and then the clip-clopping of hooves as the mounts alight onto the stone.

"Nic," Nahini reaches me first, with Freda a heartbeat behind.

I can only stare over the side, to where he disappeared. A tear slips down my cheek as blood pools around me, warming my body from the outside. "Come back. Please. Come back."

A moment later sparks drift upwards from the dark, collecting into a familiar shape. His hand forms in mine and the last thing I see is the green fire of his eyes before the world goes dark.

THE NOISE PULLS me back to consciousness. Familiar voices arguing over who knows what this time. Addy and Chloe. At least they haven't started throwing things yet.

I shift, and pain burns through my midsection. A gasp escapes and my eyes fly open as I recall all that happened. "Aiden."

A moment later he's there, green eyes intent. "Nic? Are you in pain?"

"Yeah." I frown and glance around the unfamiliar surroundings. "Where am I?"

"The mortal hospital." Days' worth of stubble coats his chin and shadows haunt his face. "I wanted to bring you to Laufey for healing, but your aunts insisted you remain on this side of the Veil. They had to operate on you."

That explains the padding around my midsection. I feel it beneath the coarse fabric of my hospital Johnny.

Aiden is practically quivering by my bedside. "What can I get you?"

"Water." My lips are cracked, my throat parched. I struggle to sit up and reach for a glass of water. He leaps to my side, to assist in raising the bed and plumping the pillows before pouring me a cupful of water and aiming a straw at my lips.

I suck gratefully until the cup is empty and then request more. He pours another cup. I note that he is wearing the same clothing I spied on him the first day he appeared at school. T-shirt jeans, work boots. "You lose your sweats?"

"Your aunts insisted I change into something more appropriate for the sake of the hospital patrons and staff. I'm fairly certain Addy burned them while I was in the shower."

"Thank the gods for that." I study his face. "How did you break free?"

"The Hunt found me. You said I could leave the truck if I perceived a threat and there is no greater threat than the Wild Hunt."

"Tricksy wolf," I smile.

He doesn't return it. "Were you really going to sacrifice yourself for Sarah?"

I nod, then wince. "If I had to, though I wasn't going to let Brigit live either. I figured if her feelings were so intense, it might be enough to bring Sarah back. That was plan A, anyway."

"Why?" There's a plea in his voice. I'm not sure what he's asking for. An explanation?

"I felt like I owed it to her."

"Your *life*?"

"I'm a teenage serial killer, Aiden. What sort of a future does that have?"

His lips part but the door to the room bursts open.

"I told you I heard her voice," Chloe snaps. She shoves Aiden aside and takes my hand. Cinnamon and cloves waft from her and my stomach growls. "Nic, how are you feeling?"

"Like death warmed over," I say, though my eyes are still on Aiden. "Like I've been stabbed repeatedly."

Addy moves to the other side of the bed and takes my other hand. "I'm glad I didn't have to cut your thread."

"That makes two of us."

Other people are filing through the door. Freda, Nahini and Jasmine, all wearing normal clothes instead of armor, along with a few people in scrubs who I assume are the medical professionals.

"You're one lucky young lady." An older woman with salt and pepper hair cut to her chin says. Her name badge reads Dr. Tyson. "How are you feeling?"

Other than getting sick of that question? "Okay, I guess."

"Did you see the face of your attacker?" This comes from a man over by the door who I hadn't noticed. He's wearing a sheriff's uniform.

"My attacker?" I glance at Chloe with a scowl.

"You were mugged. Outside *Club Yours*," she supplies, her bright blue eyes sending me a *just go with it* look.

Message received. I put on a vapid helpless expression that I normally reserve for prey. "It's all so fuzzy."

"Were any of you with her?"

"I was." Aiden steps forward and hands the man a piece of paper. "I did a sketch of his face, so I wouldn't forget."

"Hmm, I know this guy. Joe Larkin."

I cough to cover my surprised gasp. Aiden's setting Sarah's stepfather up for my fictional mugging?

The sheriff's eyes narrow. "You know him?"

I nod. "I was friends with his daughter. She died a few months ago." The pang goes through me, the loss still fresh.

"I'll check it out." The cop folds the sketch and puts it in his pocket.

"Yes, and I need everyone else out of the room now, too." Doctor Tyson announces. "She needs her vitals checked, her bandages changed and most of all, peace and quiet."

"Five more minutes." I still have questions and don't want to wait to have them answered. I paste my best innocent lamb smile and look at the doctor, big doe eyes pleading.

She caves, as I knew she would. "Not a second longer."

Once the room is emptied of mortals, other than myself, Nahini and Freda kneel. "My queen."

"Get up, fools," I hiss, sounding and feeling a bit like Laufey. "Before someone sees."

They do, though I can tell it's with the utmost reluctance.

"What happened to Sarah's body?"

It's Aiden who answers. "It's at the farm, awaiting your instructions. We would have returned her to her original plot, but it would arouse suspicion."

I swallow and nod. "Thank you. We'll bury her by the lake after I get out."

My next question is for Nahini. "The dead of the Hunt?" Including her brother.

Her expression is regretful. "Gone."

"Gone where?"

She shakes her head, shoulders slumping inwards. "I can't say for certain."

I suck in a deep breath. "It's my fault. Brigit had Sarah's soul and she offered me a trade. I should have realized who she was then. She was trying to strip the Hunt all along, strip power from me. Taking the souls tethered to the Hunt was just another way to slice into me."

Nahini's eyes are round and filled with fear. "What would she do with them?"

"My best guess is that she traded them, for power. Brigit could lie, she had to in order to carry out her deception. The dead tied to the Hunt were probably a bargaining chip with some powerful entity." I look to Freda. "Do you know where *Seelenverkäufer* is?"

She appears puzzled. "I left her in my tent as I always do when she is not at my side. Why do you ask?"

"Because Brigit said she was using *Seelenverkäufer* to separate the souls from her revenants. She must have had some way to get her hands on it."

"There's a traitor in our midst." Freda's jaw clenches. "Fear not, my queen, I will flush the snake out of the weeds."

And it wouldn't be an easy or a painless process either. *Damn you, Brigit.* "Is everyone else all right?"

Freda puts a hand on Nahini's shoulder, a show of sisterly support. "Yes. But the Court is in shambles. War is brewing over the succession of the Fire and Shadow Thrones, as well as control of the Hunt."

My stomach aches and my temples throb. "What can I do about it?"

"As you are? Nothing. You'll have to run the gauntlet as we first planned to reclaim the Shadow Throne."

Something I'm still not sure I want. "Okay."

Freda offers a small smile. "It can wait until you heal. You fought well."

"Almost too well." This from Addy. "What were you thinking, merging your power with Brigit's like that?"

"She told me that only the heart of the one who loved me most could be used to resurrect the dead. And I was thinking how love and hate are two sides of the same coin. Brigit hated me, passionately. I was hoping I could kill two birds with one stone, take her out and get Sarah back."

Chloe shifts, looking uncomfortable. "You did a lot more than that, Nic. You tore a giant hole in the Veil."

"What? How?"

"By combining life with death." Addy's eyes start that eerie swirling again and for a moment I fear they're about to call upon their power and smite me as they had done with Laufey. "The fabric between worlds is in tatters. Any number of creatures can cross into this realm and start picking off mortals."

That doesn't sound good. "How do we fix it?"

She blinks, and her eyes go back to normal. "I don't know."

"All right, I think we've heaped enough on her shoulders for now." Chloe makes shooing gestures. "Let's leave her to rest."

One by one they exit and when I am alone I sag back against the pillows, tears slipping down my cheeks.

"Are you in pain?" I start at the sound of his voice.

"I thought you'd left."

"I have nowhere to go." Aiden brushes the wetness away from my lash line. "No place I'd rather be than here with you."

I put my hand over his and hold it against my cheek. "I've made a mess of everything, haven't I?"

"What do you mean?"

"The Unseelie Court is on the brink of war. There are giant rips in the Veil that protects the mortal world from the creatures of Underhill and the dead bound to the Wild Hunt are MIA. And I didn't even get Sarah back." More tears slide down my cheeks. "Am I forgetting anything?"

He brushes them away, his hands steady, gentle. "You're still here. I'm still here. The living members of the Hunt are at your command and you have two of the Norns on your side. All is not lost."

"Are you telling me to count my blessings? Because I don't really subscribe to that kind of feel-good crap."

Out in the hall, a baby cries. One of the disadvantages of a small hospital, pediatrics on the other side of the wall from the recovery suits. The nurse pushing the bassinet pauses outside my door. "Ssshhh, it's okay, Sarah."

My head whips to the doorway. Is it possible?

Aiden takes my hands and brings it to his lips. "That baby was born at the same time you collapsed on the bridge. You gave her a second chance, Nic."

I'd done it. Somehow the love and hate and all the wild energy had released Sarah's trapped soul. Tears sting my eyes and I glance out the window, toward the leafy maples in the parking lot. Four crows crouch there, looking like two couples out on a date.

"What's the family like?" I turn back to Aiden and squeeze his hand hard. "The one she was born into? Are they good people? Kind?"

His free hand brushes a strand of hair from my face. "They are. They raise horses. She already has two older sisters."

"Sarah sharing the spotlight. She'll hate that." I smile though.

"Maybe. But you gave her the chance to love or hate anything again. The chance to make different choices. You're a good and loyal friend."

My smile falters. "Stop trying to make me out to be some sort of hero. I'm still a killer, not a witless do-gooder."

He grins. "Then I'll just have to find another way to make you feel good."

I shiver. "Is that a threat?"

His grin turns wicked. "It's a promise."

~End of Book 1~

AFTERWORD

Read on for a preview from
The Immortal Queen Book 2 of The Unseelie Court Series

ONE

The worst three words in the English language are without a doubt, the ones spoken by the handsome prowler in my bedroom. "Time for school."

"How did you get past my aunts?" I mumble and burrow deeper under the covers, doing my level best to ignore the half-wolf, half-god that equaled one giant pain-in-the-ass alarm clock.

"You left the window open." Aiden gestures to the slit in the windowsill where sure enough, there is a one-inch crack. "I took it as an invitation."

Aiden's abilities include turning himself into nothing more than a collection of sparks. If he ever decides on a life of crime, he'll be the world's best cat burglar. "I'd tell you to go to hell but then you'd literally have to do it."

"Someone's in a mood. Training go that well last night?" Aiden, fresh from the shower and smelling of cedar, sage and his own unique wild scent, plops himself down on my bed. His weight makes the entire mattress quake and my sore muscles scream in protest. He tosses back the covers, exposing me to the late summer morning breeze that hints at cooler weather. The boxer shorts and tank top I sleep in provide no real barrier from the chilly air.

Or from Aiden.

I hiss and swat at him. Regret accompanies the groan that bubbles up as the aches and pains in my muscles intensify. "Freda's a sadist."

A chuckle from the werewolf. "Probably why the two of you get along so well. Turn over."

I glare up into his leaf green eyes. "Why?"

He's all normal innocence, eyes wide, dark hair neatly combed. The picture-perfect all-American teenage boy, and about as trustworthy. "I'm going to give you a massage."

Yeah, right. "You've gotten way too handsy with me since you figured out I'm not

going to kill you." It isn't an idle remark. I have killed people, several of them in fact, most recently a jealous fey queen who wanted my head on a plate.

In my defense, she started it.

"Who says I have to use my hands?" He makes a grab but I dodge him and sprint for the bathroom. The lock clicks. A rumble of masculine laughter emanates from the other side of the door. "Next time then, my little queen."

"In your dreams," I call through the oak.

"Every night," he murmurs, totally unashamed to admit such a weakness.

I rest my forehead against the door and press my palm to the scarred wood. That was close, too close. I *want* Aiden's hands all over me almost as much as he wants to put them there. But a physical connection will complicate an already overly thorny relationship.

No time to dwell on that now. Instead, I turn to the shower and set the water to tepid. Even though I crave lingering beneath a scalding spray, something needs to cool my blood, so I can face the world calm and collected. As the Ice Bitch.

A pang goes through me. It was a nickname that my best friend, Sarah Larkin had given me what felt like a lifetime ago. Sarah died last spring, in a head-on collision with a downed tree. It wasn't until Sarah was gone that I realized how much she meant to me and how much I regretted not sharing my darkest secret with her.

Namely, that I am a sixteen-year-old serial killer. A punisher of evil incarnate. A hunter of men.

And that's not even the half of it.

Clean and shivering, I step from the shower and wrap one towel around my hair, another around my body before tip-toeing to the bedroom door and opening it a crack. Not that I suspect Aiden is lying in wait for me. Better safe than sorry.

No sign of him. The window is still open, the sheer curtains dancing in the morning breeze. I shut it and turn back to make the bed. It's then I see it, a lone pink rose on my pillow. My heart kicks up as I retrieve the flower. It's perfect, the petals still tightly closed but soft as a newborn's cheek. There's a note, too, four words written in spidery scrawl on a page torn out of one of my notebooks.

It's not all bad.

I blow out a sigh and plunk the rose in the glass of water on my nightstand. Aiden's right, it's not all bad. He's the most understanding potential boyfriend an asexual sixteen-year-old girl could ever hope to have. He doesn't try to pressure me or convert me. He's willing to wait until I am ready, even if that means we never have sex. He just wants to be with me, whatever that entails.

I'm not sure what that says about his sense of self-preservation since I can kill a full-grown man with a kiss. And since my adoptive parents are two of the Fates who give him the hairy eyeball at every opportunity.

Fully dressed in cut off denim shorts and a black tank top, I stare at my reflection in the mirror. "This is stupid," I tell the petite blonde with narrowed blue eyes. "I have better things to do than repeat the tenth grade."

A knock sounds on the bedroom door. "Nic? Are you ready?"

I open the door to Jasmine, the elfin twelve-year-old strawberry blonde cherub whose mother gets off on subjecting me to some of the most gruesome physical challenges known to the forever young. Jasmine grins up at me, practically vibrating with excitement. Today is her first day of school. Ever. And she couldn't be more thrilled with the prospect. Picking out school supplies with her took a ridiculous amount of time. She lingered over every notebook, tested every pen.

I wonder how long her enthusiasm will last. In my experience, public education has a way of dulling the edges of the sharpest minds.

"There you are." This from Chloe, the gorgeous redhaired Fate who today smells like cupcakes. "Breakfast just hit the table and coffee will be ready in five."

"I'm the Queen of the Unseelie Court," I point out. "It's undignified that I have to repeat a grade."

Chloe, usually the more understanding of my aunts, shrugs me off. "You should have thought of that before you dropped out of school halfway through last semester."

"And you're not the queen yet." This comes from Addy, the fatalist of our little trio. She peers at me over the top of her glasses, her brown braid bristling like a cat's tail. "It's a title you have to earn back."

"All the more reason I should stay here and train with Freda," I say but no one is listening, instead, gathering

around the table for pancakes topped with late-season strawberries and fresh whipped cream.

Frustration makes me grind my molars. How am I
supposed to rule the Unseelie Court when I can't even get
my family to hear me out?

Someone raps on the front door.

"Don't open it," Addy grumbles from behind her laptop
screen.

Chloe sets down her fork. "We have half an army camped
in the field, we can't

ignore the door all day." She pushes back from the table
and rises.

The hinges groan as the farmhouse door swings inward.
Chloe casts the newcomer a black look and her cupcake
smell shifts to one of burnt toast. "Oh, it's you."

"Told you so." Addy doesn't bother to look up.

Aiden stands there, wearing the same blue jeans and black
t-shirt, military-style combat boots he'd been wearing the
first day I'd seen him at school. As a part-time wolf, Aiden's
need for clothing is limited and so is his wardrobe. While I
appreciate his minimalistic style, I've been ordering a few
more pieces suitable for high country fall and winter. I am, in
many ways responsible for his basic needs, the same way I'm
responsible for Jasmine's education and the aforementioned
army's support.

Aiden bows formally to my aunts. "Ladies. I've come to
escort the queen and Lady Jazz to school."

His speech is unnecessary, we agreed on the details weeks
ago, but Jasmine grins in delight, loving the nickname.
Aiden's courtly manners enchant her, unlike her mother who
still harbors ill will against him for things that happened in
my past life.

"We know that," Chloe snaps.

"Come in," I call. "Have some breakfast."

There's a spark in Aiden's leaf green eyes as he crosses the threshold. The way I phrased the invitation had been worded as a command. And when I issue him a command, he is unable to refuse.

He chooses a seat beside me, takes the plate Jasmine passes to him and loads it with seven pancakes. Under his breath, he mutters so only I can hear, "I know what you're doing and it won't work."

"I assume you brought your own syrup." I grin at him, safe in the knowledge that he won't try any of his shadier tricks with my aunts and Jasmine present.

Aiden might not be willing to break bread with two of the women who had ruined his life on more than one occasion, but his oath to me leaves him with no choice but to obey. It's a power I hate having over him. Our relationship is made up of a series of whacked-out power struggles. I've been needling him lately to encourage him to drink the magic syrup that will break the connection between us once and for all.

"I'd rather have the strawberries. One last taste of summer." There's a wicked gleam in his eye as he says the words.

I jolt in my chair as a memory surfaces, not one from my current lifetime.

I am lying on my back in a meadow, long dark hair falling over my shoulders to cover my naked breasts. Aiden, also naked, is kissing his way down my body. The last rays of sunlight bathes our bare skin in an amber hue.

"I wish we didn't have to leave," I murmur, my hands fisted in his rumpled hair. It's clear from the state of dishevelment that it isn't the first time I've done so.

"It's not over yet," he kisses the inside of my thigh, his eyes molten with lust. "One last taste of summer."

"Nic?" Jasmine's voice breaks me from the reverie.

I turn to her and realize I've completely zoned out, the effects of my cold shower long gone. "Sorry, what was that?"

"Mom said you should stop by the base of operations before we go. Nahini wants to talk to you first thing."

I turn to Aiden. "Did she say anything to you?"

He shakes his head. "I would have told you if she did."

Excitement builds in my belly. "Maybe she's found them."

Nahini is third in command of the Wild Hunt. A tribal wise woman with the inborn grace of a dancer and the heart of a warrior. Until recently, she controlled the souls of wicked men who were sentenced to the Hunt as punishment. Unfortunately, those souls have been MIA for several weeks, including Nahini's brother.

"Don't get your hopes up." Chloe cautions me. "The souls might have moved on, or been consumed by the Veil."

I spear a few strawberries viscously. "I know. But their disappearance is my fault." In one of my impulsive decisions, I'd traded their afterlives for the soul of my former best friend.

"Nahini doesn't blame you, Nic." Aiden puts a hand over mine. The gesture doesn't go unnoticed by the rest of the table.

Uncomfortable with the gentle affection and their scrutiny, I pull away from his comforting touch. "I should probably go if I'm going to speak with her before we leave."

"Should we come with you?" Jasmine jumps up, nervous energy effervescing from her like bubbles in a champagne glass.

I glance to her half-filled plate. "No, you two should stay and finish eating. Meet me down at HQ when you're finished and we'll drive into town together."

Aiden's lips twitch as he picks up on the ring of command in my voice. His lids lower, a dark promise of retribution for abandoning him with the Fates and his twelve-year-old fangirl.

My backpack waits on the bench seat by the door. I pick it up on my way out. The thing is worn but sturdy. It holds some sentimental attachment for me as well as books. I carried it into Underhill, the mystical fairy realm on the other side of the Veil, on my quest to save Sarah. Slinging it over my shoulder feels like the beginning of a new journey, its weight a subtle reminder that I have all the tools I need at hand.

It might be a lie, but at least it's a comforting one.

ALSO BY GWEN RIVERS

ABOUT THE AUTHOR

Gwen Rivers is the changeling of a *USA Today* bestselling mystery author. When not writing urban and rural fantasy with kickass heroines, you can find her poring over Norse mythology, dicing with the Fates, cavorting with werewolves or hunting for fairy wine in the deep, dark woods.

Sign up for Gwen's author newsletter Beyond the Veil

Made in the USA
Monee, IL
02 August 2020

37455299R00215